THE GIRL AT THE RENAISSANCE FAIR

A MAGICAL LOVE STORY

TIMOTHY BEST

Copyright © Timothy Best 2024

All rights reserved.

No part of this book may be reproduced in any form or by any electronic or mechanical means, including information storage and retrieval systems, without written permission from the author and publisher, except for the use of brief quotations embodied in critical articles and book reviews.

This is a work of fiction.

ISBN: 978-1-963705-81-2

Published in the United States of America by Harbor Lane Books, LLC.

www.harborlanebooks.com

To those who are open to the possibilities.

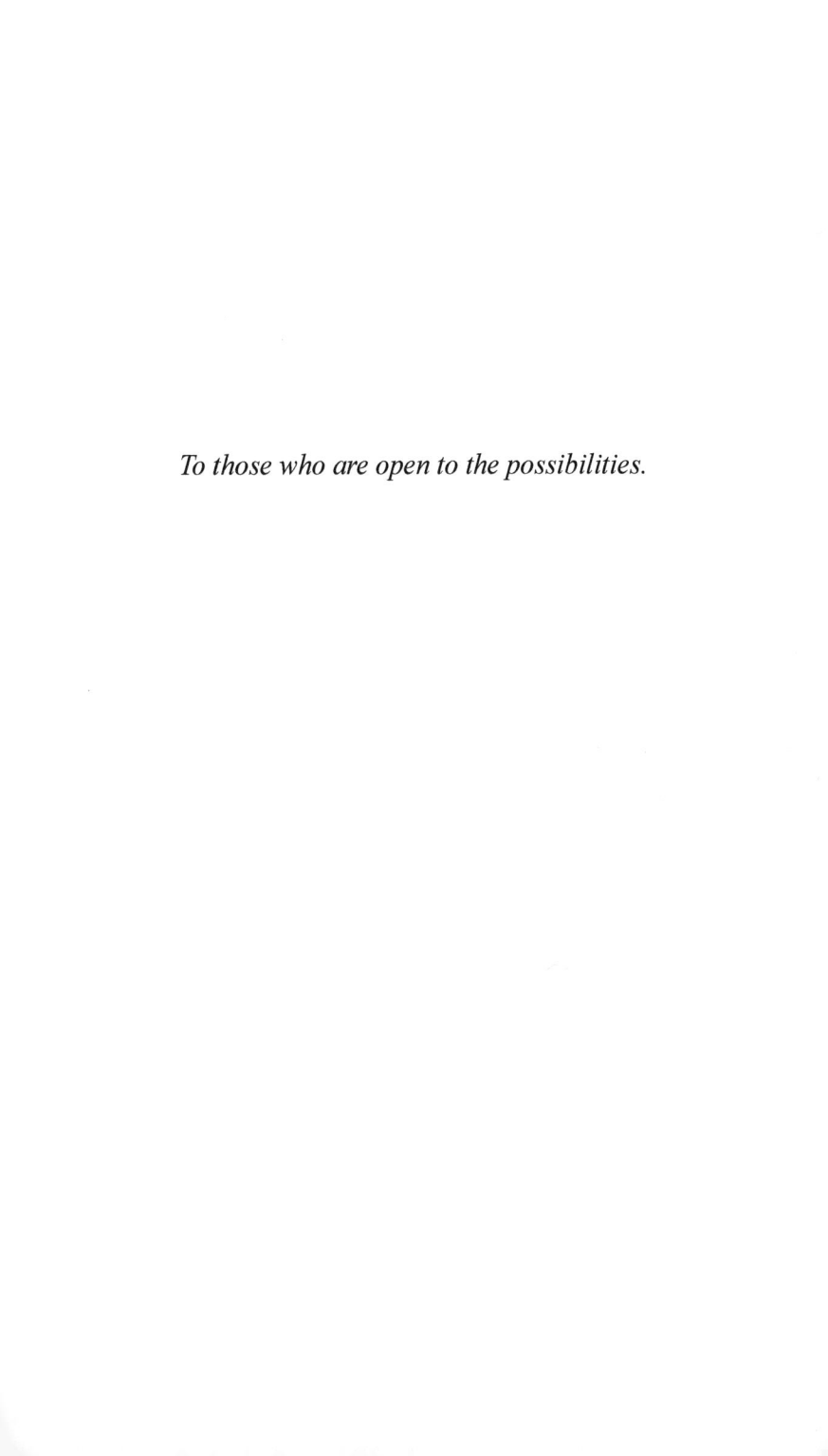

"The world is full of magic things, patiently waiting for our senses to grow sharper."

— WILLIAM BUTLER YEATS

1

APRIL 5, 1497

The twilight attack caught the villagers by surprise. There had been stories of other villages being reduced to ashes, but they were all closer to Clan Fergus's borders. This attack was happening a good three-day ride beyond those borders. Warriors wearing chain mail shirts and silver helmets with face-concealing nose guards rode on snorting horses and swung broadswords as villagers fled. If their steel connected with a victim's flesh, there was an agonizing scream and a spray of blood. Some of the attackers had swords. Others used bows and arrows. A few even carried what looked like black, flat frying pans and swung them around in the air, occasionally connecting with what looked like small birds buzzing around their heads. In the melee, details were hard to discern. Some villagers tried to defend themselves with pitchforks, axes, and shovels. But these were no match for the well-equipped, well-trained invaders of Clan

Fergus, whose very culture was battle. Smoke was thick as several thatched roofs were set ablaze with torches. Dust swirled from running feet and galloping horses. Arrows flew, and bodies fell. Goats, chickens, geese, and pigs ran wildly in every direction. Animals and humans alike zigzagged and cried across what had been a peaceful farming community for generations. Now, it was being consumed by flame, greed, and hate.

Overlooking the village were three gently rolling hills to the south. Each one was progressively higher the further they got from the village. They were known as the Three Sisters. While an early evening moon was rising, a young woman in her early twenties, barefoot, wearing a kerchief on her red hair and a plain cloth chemise, ran for her life in these hills. In the frenzy, she'd somehow been separated from her parents and two brothers, but she wasn't sure how. When the attack first happened, she'd looked away while standing next to her younger brother, and a moment later, he was gone in the noise and confusion. She had no idea what had become of him, but it didn't matter now. She had to save herself and pray that her family would somehow survive.

She had already chugged up and down the first two hills of the Three Sisters before a warrior on a black stallion spotted her from the village. Deciding to pursue, he turned and kicked his horse in her direction. At the top of the third and highest hill were the ruins of an abandoned Catholic church. All that was left was a stone archway where the faithful used to enter and some crumbling rock walls no more than two or three feet high. Most of the stones from the centuries-old structure had been taken and repurposed by farmers for homes, barns, and walls to contain animals. Hearing the gallop of a horse heading in her direction, the running woman looked over her shoulder as the warrior drew his sword, then momentarily disappeared into the depression of the first hill. She knew when he reappeared a few seconds later, he'd be closer.

She turned and ran toward the church as fast as her already tired legs could carry her. She realized if the warrior caught up to her, she'd die. Maybe not right away. Maybe he'd do things to her first, but she would certainly be killed. Perhaps there would be a place she could hide amongst the ruins, she thought. Or maybe she could grab a loose stone from one of the church walls and try to defend herself. It was odd, she realized. She'd seen this old building on the top of the hill overlooking her village every day but had only been to it less than a dozen times. It held no special significance for her or those in her village.

The warrior reappeared from the first hill's depression as he moved up the second hill. He had already covered half the distance between them. Still running for the church, the woman's eyes darted around quickly at the sinking daylight, rising moon, and the fresh spring grass she was running through. *Are these the last things I'll see?* She wondered. The muscles in her legs were aching. Her breathing was rapid, and her heart felt as if it would burst. Just as she approached the arch of the church, she quickly looked behind her and saw that the warrior had temporarily disappeared again from view down the second hill's valley. Suddenly stopping, she realized these might be the last few seconds she'd ever have to herself.

Just as the warrior was about to reacquire line of sight with his prey, there was a sudden flash of light. He didn't see the source of it, only a bright-white burst like an explosion but without sound near the church. Galloping out of the depression from the second hill and racing up the third, the warrior discovered the young woman was nowhere to be seen. Within another eight seconds, he was at the church and brought his horse to a halt just outside the archway.

Climbing down from his saddle and still clutching his sword, he carefully looked through the arch at what was left of the ancient structure but didn't pass through it, being cautious about the strange light. Perhaps the entrance was enchanted. He knew this was a land of unexplained things. Instead, he walked around the arch and stepped over some rocks into what would've been the church. He paused and looked carefully around, eyeing every patch of taller grass and the shadows cast by what was left of the walls to see where a body might hide. Then, he looked up at the sky around him. There was nothing. As he turned his head one way, then another, his horse wandered through the arch to be closer to its master. Seeing that his animal entered the ruins through its formal entrance without incident, the warrior relaxed a little, deciding the arch wasn't bewitched. But he still had no idea what had become of the woman or what had caused the flash of light. After a few more moments of searching, he figured one scared young girl wasn't worth any more of his time. He sheathed his sword, remounted his stallion, then rode through the arch and back down the hills toward the village, where the increasing flames threw an ominous orange aura into the growing darkness.

2

MAY, PRESENT DAY, HOLLYWOOD

Diary Entry, Wednesday:

Does magic really exist?
I'm not talking about a magician doing an illusion or sleight of hand.
But real, true, honest-to-God, magic.
Something no one can explain.
Something you never saw coming.
But something so special—it changes your life.
Magic!

"Noah? Where are my panties?"

"You weren't wearing any last night," a man's voice replied.

"Oh, yeah. Panty lines."

A naked twenty-six-year-old woman stopped rummaging around the rumpled sheets and hastily discarded clothing from the night before that sat on the king-size bed in her suite at the Four Seasons Beverly Wilshire. Her name was Z-Rae, and she was a pop star on the rise. She was born Zeana Ray Colton in Oakland, California, but had been using her stage name since she was eighteen and legally changed it to Z-Rae five years earlier. She was five-foot-five and lean, had three tattoos, and had short brown hair cut closely to her head so she could wear different colored wigs to suit her changeable tastes. Today, she wore a realistic-looking wig of golden hair that spilled over her shoulders. But tomorrow, she could have brunette hair, red hair, or even white. Her looks were as unpredictable as the weather. She was also a woman of contradictions. She worked with a trainer and dietician during the day to keep fit but then loved to party and ignore them at night. Case in point was the empty bottle of Lamborghini Spumante and empty Pringles can on the floor. But she had the youth and body chemistry to get away with it. Although sometimes contradictory in actions and chameleon-like in looks, she was always laser-focused when it came to her career.

"What're you doing?" she called, grabbing her black bra that had been thrown over the arm of a chair the night before.

"Just finishing up something," the man's voice replied. "You want breakfast?"

"Yes. But I've got to do a wardrobe thing, so no. I don't want my stomach sticking out."

She found some small white spandex pants and stepped into them. It was cute how she pulled and wiggled into them, causing her bangs to dangle over her brown eyes in a sexy manner. As she did, Noah Galloway entered the bedroom through a doorway connected to the suite's living room and front foyer. He was thirty years old and had longish brown hair hanging down around the edges of his face in a cool, don't-give-a-damn kind of way. He had green eyes, a two-day growth of stubble on his handsome face, and wore a tight-fitting gray t-shirt that showed off well-defined abs and a tattoo that encircled his upper left arm. The tattoo was two inches wide and contained thin, wavy lines intermixed with diamond patterns and dots, reminiscent of tattoos from the South Pacific nation of Togo. He was six feet tall, one hundred seventy-five pounds, and liked to go camping and rock climbing. He was a gifted photographer by profession, and like Z-Rae, or Z for short, he had worked hard on his career. He was gaining a reputation with celebrities, movie studios, and record companies. He'd worked with Snoop Dogg, Coldplay, Chris Stapleton, Marvel Studios, and others. Besides his t-shirt, he wore jeans, carried a little leather notebook with a pen, and was shoeless. He and Z-Rae had hooked up before. The first time was nearly a year earlier, right after he shot the cover of her debut album. Since then, they'd gotten back together for a one-night stand on three other occasions. Their attraction was instant and intense, but they were two ships passing in the night, and the winds that powered those sails were ambition, career, and self-absorption.

"What wardrobe thing?" he asked.

"Where's my phone?" she said, looking around. "Shit. I don't think I plugged it in last night." She spotted her iPhone and stuck it into the waistband of her tight-fitting spandex pants. Then, she looked around for her shoes.

"Some guy wants to design clothes for me," she replied. "He's good. I've seen his sketches, and he's paid attention to my X and Instagram pages. He works over at Paramount in their wardrobe department but wants to do his own thing eventually."

"And you want to have your own clothing line," he remembered from previous bedroom conversations, looking around and spotting his shoes and socks. "Grammys. Your own fashion line by the third album. Then become a film producer if I remember correctly."

"Well, I've got the Grammy already."

"Wasn't it your engineer who got the Grammy? he asked, setting his notebook and pen down, then grabbing his shoes and socks and sitting in a chair.

"It doesn't matter. It was *my* album. This is my time, baby. My LP went platinum, and my brand is molten hot."

"Well, since it's 'your time,' don't you want to shower?"

"Do I smell bad?" she asked, suddenly concerned, raising a slender arm and smelling one of her armpits.

"Never to me. But I was talking about the smell of sex. Especially if you're meeting with a blossoming clothing designer."

"I'll shower after the meeting," she waved off. "He won't care."

"As you wish," he said, sitting in the chair and pulling on his socks.

"Those Grammy voters, though," she sighed, shaking her head. "They cheated me out of Best New Artist and Song. You *know* "Rave Baby" shoulda won Best Pop Song. I mean, it was a Billboard Top 10 for seven weeks."

"Yes," he agreed, going along. Then, he quoted some of the lyrics. "'Arms in the air. I ain't gonna behave. Just give a DJ and rave, baby rave.' Rivals "Hotel Californía" and "Eleanor Rigby" for storytelling."

She rolled her eyes. From anyone else, she would've taken offense. But she actually liked that Noah didn't blatantly cater to her ego. It was just one of her contradictions.

"Don't be harshin' my vibe," she scolded. "And that sleazy ho, Carrie Hooligun. She dissed me on X after the nominations came out."

"First it was Twitter, now it's X. But it ought to be called Ass," he suggested, "'cause when celebrities are angry—that's what they make of themselves."

"It's all about who takes charge," she defended.

"Maybe... but it's also all about numbers," he reminded. "Carrie's got thirteen million followers. You have a little less than a million."

"The bitch called me stupid!" Z-Rae angrily recalled.

"Well, you're not that, but perhaps you shouldn't have called her a 'peckulent child' when you meant to tweet 'petulant.' Social media's a slippery soapbox. You've got to be careful. Tend to your knitting, and don't get sucked into a war of words. Always take the high road, and I have no doubt you'll get those Grammys, a fashion line, and a producing deal."

She nodded reluctantly while he finished tying his shoes. Then she picked up and slipped on a white blazer that matched her pants. Not wearing a blouse with a blazer was one of her current clothing statements.

"Hey, this was fun," she said, changing subjects.

"Yeah, it was," he agreed with a smile. "But I have to admit, the first time we got together, I was a little nervous."

"Why?" she asked, stepping into some alligator platform wedges.

"Well, I don't exactly fit the profile of your pop culture posse. Plus, the scenario's a little scary."

"That's because I'm a driven, independent woman," she assumed.

"Because you're a client, and I've pole-vaulted over a bar of professionalism," he corrected.

"Uh, let's not flog each other over that," she reasoned. "We're not the first people who've worked together and become intimate."

He nodded, getting her point. "True. And for the record, I did like 'Rave Baby.'"

"Really?"

"It's actually on one of my playlists." He rose, took

his notebook and pen, and headed for the bathroom. "You keep doing what you do and I'm positive, sooner than later, I'll be saying I knew you when."

"Then you'll post naked pictures of me online," she half-joked. She turned and looked at herself in the mirrored wall behind the head of the bed and checked the makeup she hadn't taken off the night before.

"I've never removed the lens cap when you've removed your clothes," he reminded from the bathroom.

"Too bad," she replied, playing with a false eyelash and still looking at herself. "I've got a great body, and you've got an amazing eye for composition. That's why I hired you."

He reentered the bedroom carrying a toiletry bag in one hand, his notebook and pencil in the other, then turned into the living room. He walked over to a knapsack, lightweight leather jacket, and camera bag in the foyer. He put the toiletry bag, notebook, and pencil into his knapsack, then zipped it up and looked at his wristwatch.

"I've got to go. Got to be at the airport by 2:00 p.m. You want to split the cost of the suite?"

"Fuck off," she said dismissively, coming into the living room.

"Well, I slept here, ate food, and drank wine. Let me pay my share."

"I make, like, ten times more money than you," she replied.

"And if you want to keep it, you've got to watch your expenses," he answered. "Don't forget to take your

Adderall, by the way. It's in the bathroom on the counter."

She walked over to him, a little sad.

"Why do you have to go back to Atlanta?"

"'Cause that's where I live."

"You'd make more money if you lived here."

"I don't know about that," he pondered. "Atlanta's got a lot going on. It's a huge production hub now, with lots of TV shows, films, and recording studios. It's like here, only without the mudslides, wildfires, and valet parking at IHOP."

She slipped her arms around his neck. "If you were here, we could see each other more often."

"You're the one who set the ground rules," he reminded. "No strings. No attachments. We see each other when we see each other, remember?"

"Yeah, but that was at first. Stay another couple days."

"I can't. I've got another shoot this weekend."

"With who?" she said, removing her arms and showing a flicker of jealousy.

"Not with *who,* with *what,*" he said. "I'm shooting the Georgia Renaissance Festival."

"The what?"

"It's a festival. You know—a Renaissance fair?"

"You mean, with knights and people dressed up like Frodo and shit?"

"Exactly. It's a client of my studio partner. He recently had a procedure done on his foot, and he's still wearing a surgical boot. So I said I'd shoot it for him."

"That's sweet… but can't you get somebody else? An assistant or someone?"

"It's one of my studio partner's bigger clients. The only reason why they're keeping their contract is because I've got some notoriety. But I'll be in Santa Monica in three weeks. I'm doing production stills for Lionsgate. We can get together then if you want. I'll text you when I'm back."

He slipped on his leather jacket, did the same with his backpack, and grabbed his camera bag. As he did, Z-Rae watched him analytically.

"You've got my back, don't you, Noah," she realized.

"What?" he asked.

"You tell me not to get into fights on X. You don't take compromising photos. You offer to help pay for the suite. You remind me to take my focus medicine. You've got my back."

"It's totally mercenary," he smiled, only half kidding. "Say something nice about my work on Facebook."

He stepped over to her, kissed her, and, after a few more pleasantries, was out the door.

After he left, Z-Rae turned and headed toward the bathroom, deciding to shower after all. She got undressed again, took an Adderall, and started to consider her growing feelings for Noah Galloway.

3

LILBURN

Old Town Lilburn was a part of the larger community of Lilburn, Georgia, one of Atlanta's bedroom communities some twenty miles away from the heart of downtown Atlanta. In the 1890s, as little communities sprang up around Georgia's capital city, the Seaboard Airline Railway helped to establish the town with a railroad line, and trains still rumbled through Old Town hourly. Though Lilburn was outside of what locals called "the perimeter"—a circle of highways that defined most of Atlanta's city boundaries—plenty of Lilburn residents still commuted daily to and from the city. It was a town of approximately twelve thousand six hundred. Old Town, in particular, was being touted as a hip place for the big city commuter who wanted to retreat to a small-city lifestyle.

Behind an antique store off Main Street was an anonymous brown metal building that looked like it belonged in an industrial park. Years earlier, it had been a paint warehouse for Sherwin-Williams. Now, it was the photography studio of Noah Galloway and Cole Huggins, who ran separate photography businesses but shared certain things like an answering service, studio space, and an office manager named Annie. Noah was more of a glamor and celebrity photographer and was great at portraits that appeared to be candid, even though they were carefully orchestrated. He adapted well on location and was gaining a national reputation in the entertainment world. Cole was more of an in-studio commercial photographer and a good journeyman shooter for tabletop items, e-commerce, and catalogs. He also did the occasional location work, and the Georgia Renaissance Festival was one of those clients. It took place in Fairburn, Georgia, twenty-four miles from Atlanta, and was one of the biggest Renaissance fairs in the country. It happened over eight weekends, Saturdays and Sundays, every spring from April through May and had been around for nearly forty years. Each year, it attracted over two hundred fifty thousand visitors. Cole recently had a cyst removed from his foot and was still under orders to wear a surgical boot. So, walking the extensive festival grounds for eight hours a day for two days was still premature. He was twenty-nine, had ginger hair, and slightly resembled Ed Sheeran. He had also been mostly deaf since childhood, so he read lips to help him overcome the challenge.

He and Noah stood at a worktable in their studio, where several eight-by-twelve-inch colorful photos from previous Renaissance festivals were spread out. Both men were casually dressed but wore hoodies to compensate for the studio's cooler open spaces. When clients or models weren't there, the large space heaters they used were usually turned off.

"The festival splits up the weekends between a couple of photographers," Cole explained. "On my weekends, I take maybe a couple hundred pictures. But they only use a fraction of them."

"What do they use 'em for?" Noah asked.

"Their website, banner ads, sponsorship emails, Facebook, Instagram—they've got over seventy thousand followers on Facebook alone. Plus, some of the onsite vendors have offsite stores and use them there for posters."

Noah scanned the photos. "Anything in particular I should pay attention to?"

"Yeah. There are certain cast members you should pay special attention to. There are the joust riders, an acrobatic troupe, a guy that's got this really cool bird show. They have several stages on the grounds, and the daily performances attract hundreds of people, so they're kind of the stars of the festival. I'll give you a list of names. Some costumed ambassadors wander around. There is a gargoyle, stilt walkers, jugglers—you'll know them when you see them. Visitors like to take selfies with them."

Noah eyed the collection of people dressed up as elves, court jesters, noblemen, queens, Druids, and wizards then started to chuckle.

"Crazy," he muttered.

"What?" Cole asked.

He turned his face to his studio partner so Cole could read his lips.

"Crazy," he repeated, shaking his head. "There are just as many tourists who dress up for this thing as the people who work there. I had no idea."

"It's no different than adults who dress up for Halloween, or people painting their faces for their favorite sports teams, or people wearing antlers or Santa hats at Christmas."

"I guess not," Noah conceded.

"This fantasy stuff is a huge business," Cole reminded. "A quarter of a million visitors at twenty-seven dollars per ticket. Then, there are the games, food, and merchandise they buy once inside the grounds. Think about it, man. *Game of Thrones, Harry Potter, Lord of the Rings, The Witcher, Skyrim;* everybody wants a little magic in their life."

"A sunrise at Long's Peak in the Rocky Mountains is all the magic I need," Noah answered. "But I get your point. I'm going to stay on the grounds in my RV and take some extra equipment. A tripod, lights, battery packs, fog machine… maybe I can get some moody stuff above and beyond the usual ye ol' merriment."

"Hey, don't be showing me up now," Cole said seriously. "I don't want to lose this gig."

"No worries," Noah assured, "I'll tell the festival manager," he paused, "what was her name?"

"Wanda Harrington."

"I'll tell ol' Wanda anything extra I do was entirely your idea. *If* I even do anything extra. But if I do, I'd rather be looking at the right equipment than looking for it."

Cole smiled. "I appreciate this, man. You're really helping me out, though I know this type of tourism thing is beneath your skills."

"Hey, we're partners, right?" Noah replied, smiling.

He never would have admitted it to Cole, but he agreed with him. He did think this assignment was a little beneath him.

4

PERFECT BLUE

After researching online, Noah discovered that Renaissance fairs and festivals happened all over the United States, including Alaska. After just a few minutes of investigating, he found no less than sixty-two different festivals in twenty-seven states and another half dozen in Canada.

"Geez! They're definitely a *thing,*" he admitted to himself, although he'd never been to one. Several of these events celebrated the medieval times of the British Elizabethan Age, from 1558 to 1603. But going back to King Henry VIII's reign from 1509 to 1547 was also very popular. Because of its length, the Georgia Renaissance Festival had themed weekends like "Pirate Weekend," "Pet Weekend," "Scottish Highlands Weekend," or the very convenient "Time Traveler Weekend" with no theme, where anything from Harry Potter costumes to Star Wars Stormtrooper suits was acceptable.

Georgia's festival was one of the better events in the

country. The thirty-two-acre wooded area dedicated to the fair featured a sixteenth-century Tudor-style village called New Castle with dozens of permanent open-air stores as opposed to the mere tents, display tables, and temporary shelving of other festivals. During operating weekends, New Castle was a bustling community of period clothing and jewelry stores, food courts, alehouses, sword and knife stores, pottery stores, and candle shops to name some. The activities included ax throwing, a hay maze, camel rides, a haunted house, swinging gondola rides, numerous stage shows, and a large circular tournament field where knights in shining armor fought jousts and had sword fights. In the interim, jugglers, musicians, fire eaters, stilt walkers, and numerous other performers in costumes wandered the grounds to entertain and pose with guests. The grounds had a fenced perimeter, but there were wooded access roads behind the fences of New Castle where vendors and artisans could camp very close to the back ends of their stores. Many of them traveled to several Renaissance fairs a year, like some sort of magical circus.

The festival opened promptly at 10:30 a.m. on Saturday and closed at 6:00 p.m. Being a contractor, Noah had a vendor's pass and, following Cole's instructions, arrived early because the traffic would start to get horrendous shortly after 10:00. He arrived at the festival grounds in his RV at 9:37 and was directed to an employee's area very close to but outside of the village's wooden fence. Not far from where he parked, and hidden from the public, were the campers, vans, and

RVs of those who camped behind the fences of New Castle for the eight-week duration. Not everyone who worked at the festival stayed on the grounds throughout its season. Several went home on Sundays and returned the following Saturday.

After prepping his stroll-around camera, a Nikon D850 with a 24-70 mm lens, Noah packed up a knapsack with some lens wipes, bottled water, sunscreen, notebook, pencil, and a few other essentials, then hitched a golf cart ride to just inside the main gate where he introduced himself to Wanda Harrington, the general manager. She was sixty-two, carried a walkie-talkie, and reminded him of actress Blythe Danner, Gwyneth Paltrow's mom. She was slender, had a thin face, and frizzy blondish-white hair that bounced around her shoulders. In her youth, she might've been labeled a "hippie chick," except she was born at a time when the hippies were already fading into history. Still, she seemed to have that "Ladies of the Canyon" vibe and frequently preferred peasant blouses, jeans, and wearing patchouli oil as she tooled around the city of Fairburn in an old Honda Civic that had "Coexist" and faded "Bernie Sanders for President" bumper stickers. She adored Cole Huggins and was sorry he couldn't shoot for her, but after visiting Noah's website and seeing pictures that featured the likes of Z-Rae, Chris Martin, Jeff Daniels, and others, she felt lucky to have him working for her.

When the front gates opened, traffic was already backed up for miles, with costumed fans waiting to get in. May in Georgia could be tricky. It could be rainy and sticky, with humidity so thick you could cut it with a broadsword, or it could be beautiful, warm, and not humid. This particular day happened to be the latter. Noah wandered through the ever-increasing crowd wearing jeans, Nikes, and a simple snug-fitting blue t-shirt with a staff lanyard around his neck. The day was gorgeous. There was no wind, the dogwood and crabapple blossoms were in full bloom, the temperature was seventy-four, and the cloudless sky was a perfect blue. Blue as a field of Forget-Me-Nots. Blue as a swimming pool at a five-star resort. The kind of southern, blue-sky day the Allman Brothers sang about on their album "Eat a Peach."

Taking the lens cap off his Nikon, Noah's first shot was that of a young boy with his parents pointing happily at a festival ambassador dressed up as a gargoyle with gray body paint, horns, a gray tunic, gray wings, pointed teeth, and gray hoof-like feet. He looked like he belonged in a horror movie until he smiled and waved impishly at the kids. Next, he snapped a photo of a visitor who looked remarkably like Queen Elizabeth I, complete with a high lace collar gown, painted white face and hands, red hair, and no eyebrows. After that, a vendor motioned him over to his small tent. He was selling sets of horns that people could wear on their heads. The horns came in different lengths and colors. They were secured by a tie on the back of the head just above the neck. The vendor was in his late fifties and was dressed like a village shopkeeper, complete with a puffy-sleeved linen top, knee britches, and a leather apron.

"You remember the movie *Labyrinth*?" he began.

"Uh, must've missed that one," Noah admitted.

"It's a 1986 film directed by Jim Henson, who created the Muppets, and was produced by George Lucas. It starred David Bowie."

"Oh. Okay," Noah nodded.

"When I was younger, I worked on the creature horns for that movie. Same horns you can buy here, only they're made better now. That's worth a photo for the festival website, eh?"

"Uh, sure," Noah agreed. "But I just take pictures. I don't have any say about what goes onto the website. I'm Noah Galloway, by the way," he said, extending a hand.

"Harry Toadel," the vendor replied, shaking his hand. "But everyone just calls me Horny Toad."

Noah looked at the display of horns hanging inside the small tent and nodded. "Horny Toad. Yeah, I get it."

"I've got the best selection of horns you'll find at the festival," Harry said proudly. "Six inchers, four inchers, two… I can even custom make, say, some twelve or fourteen inchers if you want to go to a Halloween party as Loki. They filmed some of that TV series right here in New Castle, you know."

"Actually, I did know that," Noah remembered. "Somebody mentioned that to me when I did some shooting for Marvel in California."

"Cool. These horns are lightweight ceramic," Harry

continued. "Every set hand-formed, baked, and painted. No mass production here."

"That so?"

"Yep. Horns are a lost art. Plastic doesn't hold paint well or stand up to multiple uses, and dried clay gets too heavy for the head and can cause headaches. Lightweight ceramics are the way to go. But you've got to be careful when you mix your ingredients. It's all in the mix."

"Really?" Noah asked, not caring but trying to be polite.

"Absolutely. People have actually offered me money to know my exact mixture. Students from art schools have even asked to intern with me."

"'Hornaculture' students, eh?" Noah cracked.

"For sure," Harry agreed, not getting the joke. "On a good day, I'll sell a hundred sets. At an average price of twelve dollars per set, that's $1,200.00. Times two days per weekend, that's $2,400.00."

Noah smiled faintly, not quite believing he was engaged in a serious discussion about horns with a guy wearing knee britches who went by the name of Horny Toad. Still, he went along.

"So, this is what you do? You're a horn aficionado?"

"I'm a circuit traveler," Harry replied. "I'll do maybe four of these festivals this year, then head home to my mom's."

"You live with your mom?" Noah asked, amused.

"It's not like she's supporting me or anything. We work on the business together. She helps me when I run out of stock. I use her garage for a studio." He dipped a hand into his leather apron, produced a business card, then handed it to Noah.

"'The Horny Toad,'" Noah read. "'Mystical appendages that amaze.'"

"Yeah. Check out our website," Harry invited. "It's righteous."

Noah opened his mouth to ask another question but was interrupted by a mother and daughter who wanted to know about horn prices. Turning to them, Harry went straight into his sales routine.

"You remember the movie *Labyrinth*?" he began.

The daughter, about thirteen, shook her head. The mother searched her memory with vague recognition.

"It's a 1986 film directed by Jim Henson, who created the Muppets and was produced by George Lucas," Harry said. "It starred David Bowie."

The mother nodded, now remembering and seemingly impressed with Harry's affiliation. The teenager didn't care and just liked the horns. While Harry went on with his sales pitch, Noah stepped away, then turned and took a few shots of Harry interacting with his customers. He even took a shot of the daughter sitting on the stool outside of Harry's tent while he tied some four-inch horns on her. Hearing Noah's Nikon clicking away, Harry smiled, appreciating the attention.

As Noah started to wander around again, he did some calculating. If Harry's numbers were correct and he made $2,400.00 per weekend, and there were eight weekends to the Georgia Renaissance Festival, that was a total of $19,200.00. Many other festivals weren't as long as the one in Georgia, but if Harry did three other festivals a year and they were all two weekends apiece, Harry could gross over $33,600.00 from making horns. True, traveling expenses and vendor fees would eat into that, but the notion that one could make a modest living as a costume horn maker blew Noah's mind.

The next thing that caught his attention was also a potential mindblower, literally. Fifty yards away from Harry's tent was a swinging gondola ride called the Dragon Sea Slide. The swing was suspended in a large wooden frame where as many as six people would climb into a wooden gondola that had a green sea monster's head and tail. Then, the swing would be pushed higher and higher by a wiry young man about twenty-five years old named Orrie. He was shirtless, had glitter on his chest, and wore bright-green tights with pirate boots that featured big brass buckles. He also had long, thick cornrow braids that went well beyond his shoulders. At a certain point, the pendulum-like swinging of the gondola became self-sustaining, and instead of pushing anymore, Orrie would stand mere inches from the gondola's swinging path. He'd extend his arms sideways and bend backward just before the huge wooden structure would've otherwise struck him. He did this time and time again with a defiant smile on his face, literally daring the moving swing to strike and decapitate him. And while it could be argued this was an acrobatic talent that required exact foot placement and timing as Orrie weaved backward, it also seemed incredibly stupid. But it gave onlookers a thrill, and Noah got a great shot of the swinging gondola just missing Orrie's face by no more than four inches.

This is definitely a different kind of mentality and lifestyle, Noah thought. *The people who work here are like the carnies at a county fair. Only with swords and tights.*

As the day went on and more and more people strolled up and down the thoroughfares of New Castle, it became apparent to Noah that his street attire was in the minority. Only about one in five people weren't dressed up in some sort of costume. When he saw someone dressed in street clothes, like a Georgia Power lineman working on a transformer atop a power pole outside the perimeter of the village fence, it stood out. He even heard costumed visitors refer to passing visitors not in costume as the "Boring Tribe." Everyone else was a colorful current of strolling musketeers, knights, scullery maids, archers from Sherwood Forest, and storybook characters that ranged from Rapunzel to Simple Simon. The fact that the crowd was mashing together the attire of different centuries didn't seem to matter, and walking in and out of the overhanging trees with wisps of lute and harp music drifting here and there, it didn't.

Around noon, the festival grounds were packed, and people were pulling out their sunscreen and standing in long lines at the food court. By this time, Noah had explored most of the grounds and had taken about fifty pictures, half a dozen of which he thought were exceptional. He'd gotten used to seeing people in elaborate costumes and had lost any condescending attitude he might've previously had. He was genuinely getting into the spirit of things and enjoying himself.

Over in an area called the Royal Highlands, not far from an attraction where visitors could try their luck at ax throwing, one particular woman caught his eye. She was in her early twenties and dressed like a fairy. She wore a green short-sleeved dress that came down to her upper thigh with uneven edges and a fitted waist. It also had two ten-inch slits in the back to accommodate her wings. The dress was short but not in bad taste. Likewise, the front had a V-neck but wasn't too revealing. Overall, the garment had a distinct homespun look to it. She had bare, pale legs, fur skin slippers, and two very realistic large wings coming out of the slits in her back. Noah guessed her total wingspan from tip to tip to be about six feet. They were mostly transparent but featured a visually attractive arrangement of veins, or "venation," as an entomologist would say. She was five-foot-three, slender, had fair skin, and long, thick, fiery-red hair that was slightly curly and spilled some seven inches over her shoulders. She also had a woven wreath of flowers on her head, a sprinkling of glitter on her neck and chest, and a slightly triangular face. She was, quite frankly, the ideal vision of what one might think of when imagining a life-size fairy. When Noah first saw her, she was standing but bent over with her hands on her knees and her wings standing nearly straight up off her back while she spoke to a family with a little girl who was dressed up as a princess. The way she was bent over and talking to the child reminded him of the 1922 painting *Daybreak* by Maxfield Parrish. The famous painting featured two young girls—one lying down and the other bent over her—between two marble columns with a beautiful mountain landscape in the background. As she spoke to the little girl, the fairy's wings slowly opened and closed like a butterfly sitting on a flower absorbing the sun. This motion fascinated the little girl, and the fairy was clearly an ambassador for the festival, like the gray gargoyle he'd seen earlier.

Noah snapped a picture of the fairy speaking to the little girl, then headed in her direction after the family moved on. As he did however, two other visitors, both dressed as sword-carrying lords and about twenty years old, approached the fairy first. With other crowd noises around him, Noah couldn't hear what the two young lords were saying, but the ambassador didn't seem amused by their comments. As he came over, one of the young men reached out with two fingers and pinched one of her wings.

"Ouch! Don't be touchin' me wings!" the fairy scolded loudly with an Irish brogue.

"Just tell me how you make them move," one of the young men persisted. "'Cause you're certainly making some of *my* parts move," he winked.

"I think I made it with your sister once," the other snickered. "She goes into bedrooms at night and has a thing for teeth, right?"

"Hey guys," Noah interrupted, smiling. "Outstanding costumes!" He looked through the eyepiece of his Nikon. "Mind if I take a picture for the festival email?" He looked at the young woman and gestured her aside. "Eh, you mind, Tinker Bell? I just want these guys. Wanda wants to see you in the office anyway."

The young redhead looked at him for a moment, saw his staff lanyard, then realized what he was doing.

"Aye," she nodded, with her Irish accent. "Off I go."

Before she left, Noah noticed her bright-blue eyes. Blue like the sky, he observed, a perfect blue, but this was only for a moment as he kept his attention on the two lords.

"Could you stand over there by that tree?" he asked. "The framing's really nice."

The two youths forgot about hassling the fairy, felt complimented by Noah's attention, and the photographer kept them occupied by having them strike a couple of lordly poses. This lasted about forty-five seconds, and by the time Noah was finished and thanked them, the fairy had long disappeared into the crowd.

"Mission accomplished," he muttered to himself as the two lords continued on their way. "I prevented a couple of hormonal guests from bugging a staff member and did it without ruffling any feathers. Or wings for that matter."

5

CLOVER RESCUE

It wasn't until nearly an hour later that Noah saw the beautiful redheaded fairy again. She was now over by the corkscrew tower slide and was holding the hand of a little boy dressed as Spiderman. He was crying because he'd been separated from his parents. Seeing a relieved mom and dad hurrying over to the child from a distance, Noah watched as the fairy reassuringly reunited Spiderman with his family. The mother was dressed as a Scottish lass, and the father was a Highlander, with a sword, kilt, and beret. After the parents had given their sincere thanks and moved on, the fairy walked over to a sitting area by a magnolia tree to take a break. She didn't sit but stood in the tree's shade as Noah approached.

"No, really, that's okay," he began, slipping his camera into his knapsack. "You don't have to thank me for getting those two idiots off your back earlier."

"I wasn't going to," she replied with her Irish

accent. "Do ya know how many times a day I have ta deal with lads who toss an eye me way and think they're the biggest bull in the pasture?"

"Well, if you're going to wear your wings like *that*..." he joked.

"I can look after meself," she assured.

"Fair enough," he granted. "Or fairy enough as the case may be. Are you really from Ireland? Or is that accent a leftover from your part in Kenneth Branagh's *Belfast?*"

"I don't know what that means," she replied. "But yes. I'm from Ireland."

"Miss?" a passing woman said, dressed in a flowing medieval gown with a tall, cone-like hat, "that is, bar none, the *best* fairy costume I've ever seen! And your wings! *Amazing!*"

"Tis very grand of ya ta say," the fairy smiled. It was a smile Noah liked immediately. "Enjoy the rest of yer day."

After the woman had moved on, Noah continued.

"So, I wasn't wrong about you working here, was I?"

"No, ya weren't wrong. I'm one of the character ambassadors that roam about. Me name's Fayetta. But everyone calls me Fay."

"Hi," he said, extending his hand, "Noah Galloway."

"Galloway," she acknowledged, reciprocating with hers. "A fine Irish name. Where are yer people from?"

"Franklin, Tennessee," he replied. "But my family moved to Atlanta when I was eight."

"I don't remember seein' ya here before," she said.

"No, I haven't been. I'm filling in for a friend who usually shoots the festival. Cole Huggins. Do you know him? He's our age with ginger-colored hair."

She thought. "Aye. I think I know who ya mean."

"Shooting this kind of event isn't usually my thing," he offered.

"Oh? And what is?"

"Album covers, celebrity portraits, promo stills on movie sets or music videos—stuff like that," he said, hoping to impress her. "You know Z-Rae?"

"No," she admitted.

"Chris Martin?"

She shook her head again.

"Uh… okay," he shrugged. "So, what exactly does a character ambassador do?"

"Pose fer picture makin' with guests, give directions, answer questions about performance times fer the shows and jousts, point folks in the direction of the privies, keep lost children calm, and overall, try ta bring a sense of magic ta things." She reached behind Noah's ear and presented him with a four-leaf clover. "I bring people luck. See?"

"Nice," he smiled, taking the clover. "Uh, look—I'm thinking of putting together a photo shoot with a few central characters early this evening after the festival closes. Portraits with mood light, fog, that kind of thing. Would you be interested in posing?"

She looked at him suspiciously. "And exactly how

many others have ya asked ta take part in this photo shoot?"

"Well, actually, you're the first."

She arched a dark-red eyebrow. "So, at the end of it, you're just another bull in the pasture too, I see."

He cracked a small smile. "No. You don't... but it was nice to meet you."

He started to turn and walk away, but something caught his eye. He saw a spider web in one of the branches of the magnolia tree near where they were standing. Caught in the web was an injured, struggling moth. Taking the four-leaf clover in his left hand, he stepped over and used it to free the moth, then gently scooped it up with his right hand. He turned back to Fay, took her right hand, and placed the moth in her palm.

"Here. You winged creatures need to stick together."

He turned and walked away, dropping the clover as he did. She opened her mouth to say something but turned her attention to the moth instead. Raising it to her eyes for examination, she took her left hand, cupped it over her right, closed her eyes, and murmured something. After a moment, she opened her blue eyes and hands, and a rejuvenated moth flew away.

6

FOR TWO

New Castle had an area called the Royal Joust Tournament Field, where there were jousts, sword fights, and marvelous feats of horsemanship three times a day. This was all done in the presence of a festival king, queen, and their royal court. A castle façade with a sitting area overlooked the field to accommodate the royal thrones and people who wanted to pay for premium joust seating. There were also arched doorways and balconies to the right and left of this seating where other members of the court could appear and make a speech, blow a horn, read a proclamation, and then disappear. It was all part of a scripted show to showcase the action on the dirt tournament field. On either side of the castle façade was a tall wooden fence painted to look like the stone walls of a fortress, complete with crenels that left regular gaps at the top of the fence every six feet for imaginary sentries to peer through and keep watch. The castle façade and wall wrapped around 50 percent of the oval-shaped tournament field, while the other 50 percent—or the front of the field—had a split rail fence. On the other side of the fence was bench-style seating for festival guests, and after five or six rows of benches, the ground went up onto a slight hillside where additional onlookers could stand among the trees and watch the action on the field. The benches and hillside could accommodate a few hundred guests, and performances in front of the royal court happened at 11:30 a.m., 2:30 p.m., and 5:30 p.m. So, if visitors wanted to see tournament derring-do from days of old, they had multiple opportunities.

But now, it was nearing 7:00 p.m., the festival had closed an hour earlier, and Noah had transformed the woods on the hillside overlooking the tournament field into a setting for a series of portraits he was taking. He was at a lower angle down the hill and was shooting a knight on his horse up the hill amongst the trees, so his subject looked quite heroic. He had five-hundred-watt studio lights on stands just out of the camera frame connected to battery packs on either side of the armor and chain-mail-wearing knight, while a fog machine that slightly resembled a leaf blower provided just the right amount of drifting white ambiance. Noah shouted out various poses for the knight to strike while clicking away with his Nikon and even got a great shot of the horse rearing up on its hind legs while the knight raised his sword above his head. After that, he shot a juggling jester, then the gray gargoyle he'd shot earlier in the day, then the king and queen from the royal court. As this happened, a few other employees and the festival manager, Wanda, lingered around. She watched from the tournament field, holding her walkie-talkie with her arms perched on the split rail fence just before the benches. Fay stood next to her.

"I didn't quite know what he had in mind when he approached me with this idea," Wanda quietly told Fay. "But I have to admit, these photos are going to be amazing."

"He asked me about posin'," Fay admitted. "But I thought he was goin' somewhere else with the suggestion."

"Understandable," Wanda nodded, still watching Noah. "A pretty young girl has got to be careful. I, uh, I know you're leaving later, but if you've got the time, you ought to pose. He's better than our usual garden variety photographers. Not that they're bad, but this guy's exceptional."

Fay nodded a little, waited until Noah had finished shooting the king and queen, then climbed over the split rail fence and approached him from behind.

"Do ya still want me ta pose fer yer pictures?"

He turned to her, pleased that she'd shown up.

"Sure." He turned back to the wooded hillside, gauged the sinking sun, and looked for a flatter piece of ground to shoot. Spotting an area over by the Fool's Knoll Stage, he gestured her that way.

"C'mon," he said. "Earlier today, you were fluttering those wings. What've you got? Some sort of wiring mechanism connected inside your costume?"

"Something like that," she replied.

He looked around, then picked up a sitting bench from the audience area of the stage and took it over to the flattest area he could find.

"Here's what I'd like you to do," Noah said. "Hop up on this bench and get on your knees. Then, spread your wings straight out, facing me. I mean, if you can. I don't know how flexible they are."

"They're flexible enough," Fay acknowledged. "But me kneelin' on a bench is going to look a little odd."

"Not by the time I'm done," Noah said confidently. "You'll be kneeling on a boulder. Maybe a large fern leaf or a tree stump. I'll photoshop it."

She got onto the bench while he set his Nikon down, then went to reposition the lights and battery packs for the new location. "I'll take out any booths, signs, or stores that I catch in the background," he said as he worked. "By the time I finish, it'll just be you in a lush, green, beautiful forest."

She smiled and shook her head.

"People change the pictures they take with their cameras so much; ya might as well just do a paintin'."

"It *is* painting," he agreed. "You just do it with software instead of oils and canvas."

"I like oils and canvas," she said. "Sometimes, the old ways are the best."

"No argument there," he said, moving the lights.

"So, what's Wanda going ta do with these pictures?"

"Anything she wants. It just gives the festival an elevated visual tool to market itself. It was actually my friend Cole's idea," he lied. "He talked to me about doing a shoot like this for quite some time but had to go in for foot surgery. So, I'm just bringing his vision to life."

They were quiet while he repositioned the lights and connected them to the battery packs. When everything was where he wanted, he pulled a light meter out of his pocket and took a reading. Satisfied, he slipped the meter back into his jeans and approached her. She had gotten into her kneeling position with her wings open wide.

"Wow," he admired, "those wings are, like, really big. Don't they get heavy?"

"No. They're quite light."

He looked at her clothing. "That's not store-bought, is it?"

"No. It was handmade," Fay admitted. "Special materials."

"Very Stanislavski method," he quipped. "Okay to touch your hair?"

"I 'spose."

He gently took the left side of her thick red hair and tucked it behind her ear to see how it would look; when he did, he discovered her ears were pointed.

"Whoa! I didn't notice those before," he announced. Then he leaned in closer. "Jesus—those are the most realistic fake ears I've ever seen. Straight out of the Spock School of Pointyism."

"Uh… it's been a long day, so I'd appreciate it if ya wouldn't—"

"Sure. No worries," he interrupted, understanding. He put her hair back over her ear and fluffed it a little. "Actually, your hair looks better covering them anyway. But those ears are outstanding! Really!"

"Thanks," she smiled subtly. "Grew 'em meself."

"I want to remove the wreath, though. Your hair's so pretty, it doesn't need anything else. Is that all right?"

She nodded, a little self-conscious. He gently removed her wreath, then flattened a few wild red strands with his hand. As he did, she realized she liked his soft touch and how he asked permission before doing things with her. Stepping back, Noah looked her over. Satisfied, he grabbed his Nikon and walked several feet away. Turning back to her, he moved around, looking for the right angle. Deciding he needed more height, he went over and got another bench to stand on.

"Aren't you going ta make smoke with yer machine like ya did fer the others?" Fay asked.

"Don't need it," he replied. He stepped onto the bench, took a few moments to adjust the focus on his lens, and then brought the camera up to his eye.

"Okay… straighten your back and casually fold your hands in your lap."

She did as he asked.

"Great. Look at me, but don't smile."

Fay complied.

Click, went the Nikon.

"Now, smile a little. But *just* a little."

She did.

Click, went the Nikon.

"Now smile a little wider," he instructed, "like you're looking at your boyfriend."

"Don't have one," she replied.

"Girlfriend, then."

"Don't have one."

"No one special? I find that *very* hard to believe," he said.

"Right now, 'tis better I'm alone," she replied, offering no further explanation.

He clicked the Nikon again. "Okay. Use your imagination. "Look at the lens like it's your lover. Look at it like you see your future in there. Your children."

This instruction visibly saddened her. Her wings, with their beautifully patterned venation, drooped, and she cast her eyes down at the bench.

"Hey," he said, concerned, his face popping up from behind the camera. "I'm sorry, Fay. I-I surely didn't mean to say something to upset you. I was just going for a warm expression."

"No," she said. "It's not yer fault." She tried to recover from the exposed nerve he had obviously stepped on and looked up at him with a fragile smile.

Click, went the Nikon.

Noah looked at her for a couple of moments and came up with an idea.

"Okay. New direction... bring your palms together and open them like you're holding a handful of delicate feathers. Hold the pretend feathers up just below your chin."

She did, and her wings perked up again.

"Now, keep your back straight and slowly blow the feathers toward me."

She puckered her lips and blew, her bright-blue eyes looking straight into the lens.

Click, went the Nikon.

Noah lowered his camera and smiled knowingly. "Perfect. That's the money shot."

He hopped off the bench.

"We're done?" she asked. "You made a lot more photos with the other folks."

He checked his viewfinder and recalled the photo. "I got what I wanted," he assured. "Thank you."

He walked back over to her, set the camera on the ground, then walked over and turned off one set of lights. "Busy day, huh?" he said, disconnecting the lights from the battery pack. "I need a dark beer."

"I wouldn't mind one meself," she agreed, leaning back on her heels. "That, and a shower. The glitter on me skin gets ta itchin' fearful after so many hours."

He stepped over to the other set of lights and turned them off. "Well, would you like to, I mean, I-I've got Sam Adams in my fridge and a shower in my RV. You're welcome to shower while I break down the gear outside. You can even lock the RV door to ensure your privacy. And after you get cleaned up, maybe you'd like to have some dinner. I've got homemade chili. Do you like chili?"

She looked at him suspiciously again, as she had done earlier in the day.

"And I 'spose this invitation has no ulterior motive?" she asked.

"Oh, it absolutely does," he confessed. "You'll have to help me carry the equipment back to my RV. It's a schlep."

She smiled a little, then pursed her lips, thinking.

"Chili… that's kind of like a stew, isn't it? Only reddish."

"Yes," Noah said dryly while disconnecting the other battery pack. "I'm offering brown beer and red stew."

"What time is it?" she asked.

He looked at his wristwatch. "7:17."

She thought for a few moments, then decided.

"Alright. I'll accept yer invitation on two conditions: First, I don't like talkin' about meself. So, don't be askin' me about me family, how I came here from Ireland, or what I do outside of these grounds. I'm a very private person."

"Illegal immigrant," he assumed. "Got it. What's the second condition?"

"I didn't say that, did I?" she corrected. "Don't be makin' assumptions. That's how people get into trouble."

"You're right," he agreed. "Sorry. What's the second condition?"

"I expect you ta be a gentleman. Fair warnin', Noah Galloway, I have the power to turn ya into a frog if yer not."

He looked around at the woods. "That would explain all the croaking I hear in the trees."

Her smile widened. He smiled back, a little surprised but pleased he would be cooking for two.

7

DINNER

Noah had a Dutchmen Aspen Trail RV. Its brochure said it could sleep four, but comfortably accommodating two adults was more realistic. It had a kitchen, a U-shaped dinette area that extended outward when parked, and across from the dinette area was a wall-mounted TV with a heater underneath it that gave the illusion of flames in a fireplace. It also had a bathroom with a shower and a separate master bedroom with another TV. He towed it on the back of his Ram 3500 pickup truck and used it more for camping and climbing than shooting on location. But when he did use it for work, it was very convenient and held a lot of equipment.

After they had stored the lights, battery packs, and fog machine, Fay allowed Noah to be in the kitchen while she used the shower. Although he didn't realize it, this was a big leap of trust for her. While he warmed up some chili he'd made the night before and prepared fresh salads, he sipped on his Sam Adams, not quite sure what was going to happen. Fay was certainly a beautiful woman and the fact that she was naked and using his shower just eight feet away was certainly enticing and full of innuendos. But then again, he considered, maybe she was just tired, hot, dirty, and liked the idea of washing off the day while someone prepared a meal for her. *I'm sure she gets hit on all the time,* he thought. *Better not be my usual pretentious self.*

She emerged from the bathroom after about a half hour. Her hair was tied back, her wings were gone, but she still wore her pointed ears. She was also wearing the same homemade short green dress and fur-covered slippers she'd worn earlier, but over her dress was one of Noah's red plaid long-sleeved shirts.

"I found this on the back hook of yer bathroom door. I hope ya don't mind," she said. "Me arms are a little chilled."

"Not at all."

"I, uh, I hung me wreath on the hook."

"Feel better?"

"Much, thanks," she smiled.

"Here," he said, stepping over to her with a pilsner glass of dark Sam Adams already poured. "I didn't know how long you would be in there. Sorry if it's too warm. I can get you another."

"Actually, I like me beer on the warm side."

"Right," he realized. "They *would* serve it warm in Ireland."

She smiled and took a sip. "Mmm… bit of heaven, that is."

"Glad you approve. Why don't you sit down at the dining table and relax? Dinner will be ready in just a second."

She looked at the flames dancing in the fake fireplace, smiled a little, and then went over to the dinette area. Sitting down, she noticed his MacBook on it.

"I see you took off your wings but not your ears," he observed.

"They're the only ones I have, and there's a bit of a process to it," she explained.

"But they're apparently waterproof," he noted.

"Of course. It's spring in Georgia. We get our fair share of rainy days at the festival."

"Yeah," he realized. "I guess you would."

He brought silverware and placemats to the table while she eyed his computer.

"Do you have a website?" she asked.

"Yeah. Gallowayshoots.com."

"Might I peek?"

"Go ahead," he said. He opened the computer and used a finger to unlock it for her. She typed in the web address while he returned to the kitchen.

"So, how long have you been working at the festival?" he asked.

"This is me third season."

"Got it. I know your name's Fayetta, but what's your last name?"

"Smith."

"Smith?" he chuckled. "That's not very Irish."

"Says the man with the very Irish name who's really from Franklin, Tennessee," she responded, glancing at his homepage. "Are you famous for what you do?" she asked, looking at his landing page. "I don't keep up with society much, but I think I've seen some of these people before."

He walked over to the table carrying the salads, set them down, then moved around and looked over her shoulder at the pictures of the celebrities that were appearing, then dissolving into another celebrity, then dissolving into another on his homepage.

"I'm gaining a reputation for shooting famous people, yes. But no, *I'm* not famous."

"Do ya want ta be?" she asked.

"A famous photographer? Yeah," he replied honestly. "That wouldn't suck."

"Did you always want ta make pictures?"

"Actually, yeah. Ever since I was a yearbook photographer in high school. How about you? Did you always want to be a fairy?"

"Well, if you study paintings or drawings of what fairies are supposed ta look like, I *do* seem ta fit the mold."

He walked back over to the kitchen. "You do, indeed. Have you ever done any modeling?"

"That's outside of what I do here and now," she reminded.

He returned with two bowls of chili and set them down.

"I remember. But it *does* make it hard for me to get to know you."

"And why would ya want ta?" she asked.

"First off, you're very pretty. And while I realize pretty girls get tired of being flirted with and being told they're pretty, the fact remains you are. I'm not going to apologize for noticing God's handiwork. Second, you're very kind. I saw you interfacing with kids today, and the attention you gave them was something more than just a smile and a selfie. You were truly connecting with them. You like what you do."

"Children are innocent," she explained. "They're not tainted and still believe in the magic of things."

"Third, I like the fact that you're a private person. I work in a world where my clients want to be anything *but* private. They've got brands, social dialogues, and agendas. They never stop talking about themselves. Somebody who consciously chooses *not* to is unique."

He turned and returned to the kitchen to get a bowl of grated cheese and some salad dressing.

"Fourth, you do magic tricks," he continued. "I've never known a woman who does magic." He returned to the table with the items and set them down. "Fifth, you say things with unusual phrasing. 'Did you always want to make pictures?' 'I have to deal with lads who toss an eye me way and think they're the biggest bull in the pasture.' I've been to Ireland, and I've never heard anyone talk like that."

"My goodness," she said, "I guess ya *do* have yer reasons for curiosity."

He set the items down, then returned to the kitchen to get his beer.

"On the other hand," he considered, getting his beer then returning to the table, "oftentimes, the desire to know someone is actually *more* enticing than gaining the knowledge. If you got to know me, I suspect I'd disappoint you in a dozen ways. So, in hindsight, you're probably right. I *shouldn't* get to know you. So, let's eat our dinner with limited knowledge. 'Cause we're never going to be this interesting again."

He held out his glass for her to clink it.

"Well reasoned," she smiled, clinking his glass.

He returned the smile and sat down across from her.

Noah asked Fay if she wanted Alexa to play some music, and, not surprisingly, she requested instrumental Celtic harp. Even though they didn't talk much about themselves while they ate, they still found plenty to discuss. He talked about the interesting characters he had photographed during the day, from Orrie, the young bare-chested daredevil at the Dragon Slide Swing, to Horny Toad and his passion for horns. Fay told him such passion was common among the artisans, and she had gotten into deep discussions with some of them about everything from jewelry to cutlery to stitching leather dresses. "I'm comfortable with these people," she admitted. "Even foolhardy Orrie. They want ta connect with nature and simpler times through the festival. Oh, I understand sure enough they want ta make money, but they can do that anywhere without the bother of heat, costumes, and horseflies. Here, they're a community. If only for a bit."

After dinner, Fay offered to help with the dishes, but Noah said he'd clear the table and take care of things. So, she asked him to unlock his computer again, noted the time of 8:41 p.m., and looked at his website one more time while he used the bathroom. A folder on his desktop behind the site caught her eye. It was titled "Landscapes." Intrigued, she clicked on the file, opened it, and started to click on pictures. She discovered one beautiful nature scene after another, a shoreline of emerald-green land and turquoise sea with a ribbon of white sand in between. A dirt road at sunrise, going off in an endless straight line toward the horizon. A field of yellow-and-red spring wildflowers. Another field of slightly tilted golden wheat shot low and set against a blue sky of puffy white clouds. The more she looked, the more her emotions were stirred to the point of her eyes becoming slightly moist.

Coming out of the bathroom, Noah noticed she seemed emotional.

"Hey—you okay?" he asked, stepping over to her.

"Yer landscapes," she said softly. "They steal me breath… they remind me of—well—simpler times. Ya ought ta be sellin' these at the festival."

He stepped around, looked over her shoulder, and saw the folder she had opened.

"Oh… thanks. But any Photography 101 student has a collection of landscapes."

"No," she said. "These are special. But they're lonely. No people. No life."

"Scoot over," he said.

She did, and he sat down next to her.

"There may not be people, but they're not empty. On the contrary, they're full of life and movement."

He clicked on the photo of a leafless tree. Between the bare branches was a big yellow moon sitting low in a November sky. "See this tree?" he said. "I shot it in Yellowstone. You can sit and watch the moon and, in less than an hour, watch it rise higher and higher between the branches. You can use 'em as markings, like a mother might make on a doorway for a growing child. You can watch the moon get smaller as it rises higher and changes color from yellow to spotted white. All while hearing elk calling to one another in the distance. That's not empty."

He clicked on another photo. It was of a pink sky, and the lens was pointing straight up, but it was taken from the middle of a cornfield with green stalks of corn about three feet high peeking around the edges of the frame. "I took this one in Indiana, in Amish country, lying on my back in the middle of a cornfield just before sunset. Have you ever laid so still, Fay, you thought you could hear the earth move? You thought you could hear —I don't know—voices from the past buried deep in the ground? Or maybe it was just someone playing a radio the next farm over. Anyway, it's not empty. It's movement. Life."

She stared at the picture knowingly.

"Guthanna beaga," she said. "It's Gaeilge fer 'little voices'. The voices some say they can hear deep in the earth. Although I've never heard one of yer kind speak of 'em."

He looked at her.

"My kind?"

"Eh, American," she clarified.

They were quiet for a moment, then she said, "See? They *are* special."

"That's only because of my narrative."

She looked at him.

"Why did you free that moth today from the spider's web? They don't live that long, you know."

"I freed it because I could," he replied. "Sometimes, little creatures just need a break."

She looked into his green eyes for a moment, then leaned over and kissed him. Her lips were warm and soft on his, and he was momentarily surprised but quickly reciprocated. After five or six lingering seconds, she opened her eyes, looked into his, and softly said, "I have to be somewhere."

Disappointed but understanding, he paused, nodded a little, then slid out of the dinette. "That was very nice," he said. He picked up their empty chili bowls, turned, and took them to the kitchen sink. "If you promise to tip like that again," he said over his shoulder, "I'll make you dinner tomorrow night, too."

He set the dishes down and then turned on the faucet. "Do you like steaks? I only know how to make a few things, but I'm not half bad at grilling. My dad taught me how to make this great homemade seasoning. Lawry's ain't got nothin' on me. Bring the salad bowls over if you don't mind, would you?"

It was another twenty seconds of him washing the dishes with his back to her before he realized the salad bowls weren't arriving. Looking around, he saw that the dinette area was empty, and the salad bowls still sat there.

"Fay?" he called, turning off the water. He ordered Alexa to stop playing the Celtic music and looked toward the bathroom.

"Fay?"

Drying his hands with a dish towel, he realized the bathroom was unoccupied, so he turned and looked toward the bedroom. Setting the towel down on the counter, he went over to the doorway. Much to his surprise, he saw Fay's slippers, green dress, and his red plaid shirt on the floor. Fay was in his bed under the covers, her hair now loose. She was sitting with her knees drawn close to her chest while she held a sheet against her with an earnest expression.

"I want ya ta come lay with me, Noah," she said softly. "I'm tossin' some rather fixed principals ta the wind I set for meself while in Georgia—but I don't care. I'm askin' ya ta be with me."

He looked at her with a half-smile, perplexed.

"I'm sorry… I'm a little confused here… First, you kiss me. Then, you tell me you have to be somewhere. Now you're in my bed?"

"I'm lonely, Noah," she confessed. "I told ya earlier

I didn't have anyone. Don't ya ever just want ta *be* with someone? No history. No promises. Just feel a warm body next to yers for a little while to make everythin' go away."

"Yeah. Every night," he quipped. "I'm a guy."

She smiled a little.

"Well, then?"

He took a willing step into the bedroom but then stopped.

"Um—look—I don't mean to ruin a truly fortunate moment, but I have to ask, are you in good health? I mean—"

"I know what you mean," she interrupted, taking a little umbrage. "What do ya think? That I just turn me wings toward any handsome human in the forest? What kind of girl do ya take me for?"

"Don't be upset," he urged. "I mean, I-I *want* to be with you. It's just, in the times we live in, you have to be careful."

"The times we live in," she repeated with melancholy. "That's exactly what I need ta escape from."

He looked at her for another moment, then made a decision. He turned to a wall switch, clicked on the lights above his bed, then adjusted them to low via a rheostat.

"No. Leave the lights off," she requested.

He turned off the lights, disappeared out of the bedroom momentarily to turn off the lights in the kitchen and dinette area, then returned to the bedroom with only the flames from the fake fireplace dancing off the walls in the next room and silhouetting his frame. He slipped off his shirt. There was no hair on his chest, but because of his rock climbing, he was in excellent shape, not overly muscular, but taut like a competitive swimmer. He sat on the edge of the bed, untied his Nikes and took them off, then slipped off his socks. Standing again, he unbuttoned and unzipped his jeans, then took them off. Finally, he slid off his black Fruit of the Loom briefs.

As her eyes adjusted to the darkness, Fay couldn't see a lot of detail on Noah's body, but she could make out that he was clearly aroused and that she'd soon be satisfied. Similarly, as he climbed into bed and saw Fay's curved, pale, naked form, he couldn't see a lot of detail, either. He saw her round breasts, flat stomach, milky skin, and briefly wondered how a young woman could spend eight hours a day working outside at the festival but not have any trace of a tan or a sunburn. After he lay down next to her, they drew each other close and shared a long, sweet kiss. Noah didn't traditionally put a lot of stock in first kisses. There was always the mixture of nerves, potential bad breath, and the question of how much one should use one's tongue. But kissing Fay felt right. Immediately comfortable. She wasn't afraid to use her tongue and sighed ever so slightly at the embrace, which made him feel more confident. After their lips parted, he buried his face into her clean-smelling Aveda-shampooed hair whispering, "What do you like? What would make you happy?"

She gently pushed him onto his back, then climbed

on top of him with a knee straddling either side of his hips. Already damp with expectation, she slid his manhood into her and, after she gasped a little, slowly started to move up and down as her red hair fell forward. She knew what she was doing, he thought, but he certainly wasn't judging. If anything, right at this moment, he was grateful for her experience. Her breathing intensified, and her breasts hung over his face as if taunting him to kiss them, which he tenderly did. This went on for what seemed like a long time but was really only a few suspended perfect minutes. Then, they climaxed at the same time, their breathing becoming even heavier; he filled her longing as she sat perfectly still atop him with her mouth open and her eyes closed. After about thirty seconds, she slowly relaxed, leaned her warm body onto his chest, and hugged him tightly. He ran his fingers down her back, trying to memorize the curves of her body. In the darkness, just below her shoulders, he felt two long parallel lines of unusually thick skin about ten inches long to the right and left of her spine. The skin felt like two long lines of calluses because they were slightly elevated and rough. They sat where her wings would be if she had them on, and he figured wearing the wings for hours and hours had caused the lines. He was going to ask her about them, but having just made love to her, it didn't seem to be the right time.

The last thing Noah Galloway remembered before he fell asleep was Fay whispering sweetly to him in a foreign language. He assumed it was Gaeilge, but he didn't know for sure. Fay, however, did say one word he recognized.

The word was, "Magic."

8

MYSTERY WRAPPED IN AN ENIGMA

Noah awoke a few minutes after midnight to find himself alone. He climbed out of his queen-size bed and went into the dinette area and the kitchen to find the dishes cleaned and put away. The flames in the fake fireplace were still dancing, but there was no evidence of Fay. No note, no heart-shaped smiley face, nothing. He stood there naked and ran his fingers through his tousled, long brown hair, not sure what to make of things. He'd had a few other brief encounters with women before, but he was usually the one who left in the early hours. He remembered Fay said she had to be somewhere, but she didn't elaborate. He remembered that she emerged from the shower without her wings, but he didn't recall seeing them when he used the bathroom. He remembered she spoke softly in a foreign language and assumed it was Gaeilge, but he didn't know for sure. He knew that he'd seen her naked but couldn't recall any of her physical details because it was dark. And yet, despite all the things he didn't know, he knew her mouth was the most perfect he'd ever kissed, the fit of their bodies was warmer and tighter than any other lover he'd been with, and the lilt in her Irish voice was sweet and soothing. He also recalled she used the word "magic" to describe their encounter, and this lingered in his mind like a pleasant dream. The bottom line was he couldn't wait to see her again.

The following day was just as gorgeous as the previous one. Noah went about his duties as an official festival photographer and kept an eye open for Fay but didn't see her anywhere. Once again, the village of New Castle was filled with a new collection of guests dressed up as knights, druids, noble ladies, and stately lords, and he even saw excellent versions of William Shakespeare and Nimueh, the Lady of the Lake from the King Arthur legend. He wandered around clicking off shots and genuinely enjoying himself.

He caught up with Wanda, the festival manager, about 4:30 p.m. near the Drunk Monk Pub. Her blondish-white hair bounced freely over her shoulders, and she wore a cotton blouse and a multi-colored cotton skirt. But he honestly couldn't tell if she was going for a costumed look or simply wearing pseudo-hippie apparel.

"Hey, Wanda."

"Noah. How ya doin'? I can't wait to see your photos. That was quite a shoot you had going last night."

"Thanks. But it was all Cole's idea. I was just bringing his vision to life. Hey, I've been kind of keeping an eye out for Fay today. I wanted to thank her again for participating in the shoot, but I haven't seen her."

"Oh, she's gone," Wanda replied casually. "She won't be back until next year. I mean, y'know, *if* she comes back. We have a pretty loyal cast of characters, but people do come and go."

"Wait," Noah said, concerned. "She won't be back at all?"

"Well, there's only one more weekend this season, and she told me she might not be able to work all of the dates."

"Uh, um, I don't suppose you'd care to share her contact info with me, would you? A phone number? Email?"

Wanda shook her head. "Employee information is confidential." She started to continue on her way. "But I can't wait to see your pictures."

"No. Wanda. Hold up," he insisted. "I'd *really* like to get a hold of her. I made her dinner last night and we had a nice—er—talk."

"Employee information is confidential," Wanda repeated. "But I've got your card. I could pass your info along to her and say you want her to call you."

"Yes, that'd be great," he said. "Thank you!"

"If she calls me, I'll do it," Wanda promised.

"Well, can't you call her? I mean, would you mind?"

"What are we? In high school?" Wanda replied,

becoming annoyed. "Look, if she calls, I'll tell her you want her to reach out. But she never calls in between seasons."

Noah thought momentarily. "She said she was from Ireland. She didn't—like—go *back* to Ireland, did she?"

Wanda pointed to his Nikon.

"Speaking of going back, why don't you go back to work," she said. It wasn't a suggestion so much as an end to their conversation.

She turned and walked away, leaving a frowning Noah behind.

Realizing that Fay was attractive and certainly must've captured the attention of other men who worked at the festival, he decided to make some inquiries.

Dale, a blacksmith in his late fifties, said:

"Fay? Sure. I know her. But she kind of keeps to herself. Great wings, though."

On the other hand, Brandon, a wandering lute player about thirty, wearing puffy sleeves and a velvet vest, commented:

"Yeah. I know her. Even asked her out a couple of times. But I think she's gay."

Meanwhile, two elf ear salesmen in their twenties, Theo and George, reported:

"Fay? Sure. We know her," George verified. "Wicked ears! They're Moon Elf Ears."

"No. High Elf Ears," Theo corrected.

"No. Moon Elf," George insisted. "Check the lower angle and points."

"No," Theo said. "You're confusing Moon Elf with Wood Elf Ears."

"No. *You're* confusing your Wood Elf Ears with *Wild* Elf Ears," George clarified.

"You tellin' me I don't know my ears?" Theo countered, insulted. "How 'bout you? How many cartilage points to a Sea Elf's Ear?"

"Well, if you wanna be tricky," George challenged, "tell me about the contours of Space Elf Ears?"

Still later, Orrie, the bare-chested daredevil at the Sea Dragon Swing, revealed:

"Fay? Yeah, I know her. Man, I hit on her so many times, she said if I didn't stop bugging her, she'd put a spell on me, and I'd break out in a rash."

"So, what happened?" Noah queried.

"I got bit by some wonky ass type of spider and had all these bumps on my arm. It was just a coincidence, but she made a big 'Told-ya-so' thing out of it."

It was a lot of rejection and testosterone to wade through.

By the end of the day, Noah had taken another forty or so photos but had gained no further insight into Fay. He didn't know where she lived, what she did outside of the festival, or how he might get ahold of her. He'd heard of the phrase, "A mystery wrapped in an enigma" before, but now, he was truly experiencing it. All he knew for sure was that there were apparently a hell of a lot of different types of pointed ears.

9

REUNIONS

Diary Entry, Saturday:

Why do we still scan the skies on Christmas Eve?
Even though we know there's no Santa.
No sleigh full of presents.
No reindeer.
It's because we still want to believe.
We need to believe.
Magic is essential.

A Year Later

The memories of Fay alternately intensified at night and became vaguer during the day. Especially if Noah was busy with work. He'd made all of the reasonable efforts a person could make to try and find her. He searched for Fayetta Smith on Google, Facebook, X, and LinkedIn. He researched how many Fayetta Smiths were listed in the Greater Metro Atlanta Phone Directory. He even asked his friend, Cole, to intercede with Wanda about releasing Fay's personal information. Since Cole had shot the Renaissance festival several times, he knew Fay by her first name, but he was uncomfortable pushing Wanda for contact information he wasn't entitled to, and Noah reluctantly understood. He briefly thought about purchasing one of those online services that help to locate people. But he stopped short of using his credit card because he decided he was slipping into creepy stalker territory. He ultimately decided he had to live with the mystery of who she was. Still, he found himself looking at the picture he'd taken of her near the Fool's Knoll Stage quite a bit. As he had promised, the finished photoshopped portrait looked very different than the original. It featured Fay blowing a kiss with her wings spread and kneeling on a flat boulder in the middle of a forest stream while animated water moved along both sides of the boulder. Noah even animated a few whisps of her long red hair to blow in the breeze. He used a software called Plotagraph, and the effect was something straight out of *The Daily Prophet* from the Harry Potter films. Considering the last word she said to him was "Magic," pining over this manufactured piece of photo magic seemed oddly appropriate.

On the first weekend of the Georgia Renaissance Festival in April, Noah paid his twenty-seven-dollar admission and went into the village of New Castle as a guest. He was dressed similar to the year before: jeans, a red Orvis golf shirt, and even though he wasn't working the event, he carried a small shoulder bag with an Olympus Mark IV Mirrorless Camera, a 14-42 mm lens, and his notebook and pencil. The day was warm, and no rain was predicted, but it was overcast with only a few stretches of blue sky showing here and there. The trees were also barer than his visit the previous year because he was attending the festival seven weekends earlier. Amongst the usual fare of tourists, costumes, and the smells of vanilla cones and grilled sausages, he spotted Fay within ten minutes of walking through the front gate. She was standing near a fortune teller's shop, and when he saw her, a rush of adrenalin raced through him like a kid seeing his first crush in junior high school. She wore the same green short-sleeved dress as the year before, had bare legs, and wore fur skin slippers on her feet and a floral wreath in her hair. She also wore the same mostly transparent wings with the attractive venation and was doing pretty much the same thing she was doing when he first set eyes on her: talking to guests and posing for a picture. But one thing was very different than the previous year. She had a green pouch-like garment on the front of her chest, and peeking out of the pouch was an infant dressed like Fay but without wings. The child was about two months old.

Still at a distance and stopping to take this in, a thunderstruck Noah immediately wondered if the child was his. He hadn't used any protection the night they spent together, nor did he ask if Fay was on the pill. All he had asked about was if she was in good health, which was a polite way of inquiring about a sexually transmitted disease. While he stood there stunned, she spotted him. The hesitancy on his face could have meant any number of things, but she took it as disappointment and rejection. Becoming immediately angry, she turned and walked away.

Recovering from his surprise, he started to jog after her and called out her name.

"Fay! Hello! How are you?"

"Don't worry, Noah," she said, continuing to walk. "She's not yours."

Catching up to her, he nodded with a half-smile for her and the baby.

"Uh—so—so I guess there have been a couple of new developments in your life since last year. Did, did you get married?"

"Do ya suppose every woman with a child needs ta be married?" she asked. "That's not very modern thinkin'."

"It was just a question," he clarified. "So, who've you got there? A little boy? Girl?"

"Her name is Erin," she answered, matter-of-factly.

"Oh. A little girl. Th-that's great."

He leaned forward to look at the infant as they walked.

"Aye, I could tell by yer expression when ya first laid eyes on her," she muttered sarcastically.

"How old is she?"

Fay stopped and turned to him, her wings standing upright in the middle of her back like a butterfly at rest.

"What're ya doin' here, Noah?" she demanded. She eyed his camera bag. "Are ya workin' the festival again?"

"Uh, no. My friend Cole is back this year and, I'm sure, somewhere around."

"Then why are ya here? Did ya have a wild cravin' fer a turkey leg?"

"You disappeared on me last year after what I thought was a pretty incredible night."

"I told ya, I had to be somewhere," she reminded.

"Yeah, I know, but—"

She turned and walked away, her fiery red hair bouncing. He followed after her.

"Could you stop walking for a moment, please?"

"I'm workin'."

"C'mon, Fay. Please?"

She stopped in front of a clothing store and turned to him unemotionally.

He looked at the baby, still at a loss, but offered a compliment. "She's very pretty."

"Why are ya back, Noah? You're not supposed ta be here."

"Look, we spent a wonderful evening together, but you left in the middle of the night. I-I haven't forgotten about you, and I wanted to see you again," he confessed. "Didn't Wanda tell you I wanted you to call me? I told her to give you my contact info?"

"I already had it, gallowayshoots.com, remember?"

"Well—why didn't... I mean, I thought maybe... maybe we'd—"

"Maybe we'd what?" she interrupted. "Ya invited me ta supper, I told ya I was lonely, we shared a moment, then I had ta leave, which I told ya. I also recall sayin' I was a private person and didn't want ta discuss me life outside of the festival. So, what more is there?"

Thoughts of Z-Rae flashed in his head. Was this the same type of hit-and-run arrangement, he wondered. With Z, it had been discussed and mutually agreed upon. But with Fay, it hadn't. It was more like an unexpected bolt of lightning that struck his heart.

"How about some common courtesy?" he suggested, becoming agitated. "I mean, Jesus, were you already married when we met? Already pregnant? If not, you *had* to have gotten lonely with somebody else not long after me. Guess you're really not that lonely after all, huh?"

She started to raise a hand as if she might slap his face but then stopped, remembering her role as an ambassador.

"Don't impugn me morals, lad. Ya know nothin' about nothin'."

He looked her over and realized the potential he saw in their one-night stand was one-sided.

"No… no, I guess I don't."

He held up his hands, conceding defeat. "Okay, Fay." He glanced beyond her at something, then scoffed at himself as his eyes shifted back to hers. "You, you and Erin have a nice life."

He turned and walked away toward the front gate.

The Girl at the Renaissance Fair

She watched him go for a few moments, then turned behind her to see what had caught his eye.

There was a t-shirt hanging on a display at the clothing store's entrance. It was blue and had a message in old-world script on the chest that read: "Don't let anyone steal your magic."

During the fifty-minute ride back to his condo, Noah had plenty of time to mentally kick himself over the entire year he'd wasted thinking about Fay.

"I've been played," he said, driving down I-85. "What an idiot!"

Noah had a townhouse in Old Town Lilburn on Lula Street, about a five-minute walk from the studio he shared with Cole. It was in a building that was one of a dozen newly constructed buildings that contained two-story townhouses designed to attract Atlanta commuters. Each building contained two or three units and sat just a block away from Old Town's downtown on one side and an inviting city park on the other. The townhouses were all "shotgun style" in design, meaning they were long and narrow. Some units had garages, while others, like Noah's, had carports.

On the ground level of Noah's residence was a kitchen with a spacious island, dining area, a half bath, laundry room, and a living room. Upstairs, there was a master bedroom and bath, then two smaller bedrooms that were connected by a full bathroom. The layout never quite made sense to him. The stairs were narrow for moving furniture, and why couldn't there be a laundry room on the second floor where all the clothes were? But what the place lacked in functionality, it made up for in newness and presentation. It was designed with crisp, modern lines that suited his Scandinavian Ludwik Styl furniture from Ikea nicely.

Arriving home, he parked his truck in his carport, entered his townhouse through the back kitchen door, and just as he did, his cell phone rang. The caller ID was "Yo Momma," which was code for Z-Rae. He felt a pleasant rush of adrenalin. Maybe it was because he was starting to like Z more than he was supposed to, given the terms of their get-togethers, or maybe it was because another woman had just wounded him. Either way, he took a moment to breathe, then answered.

"Hey, stranger," he began. "Haven't seen you in a couple of months."

"I've been busy with this upcoming tour," she replied. "You know how it is."

"Sure," he agreed. "So, where are you?"

"Look out your front window."

Moving past his kitchen island, then going into his living room and looking out the front window, he saw a long black limo parked on Lula Street in front of his place. Standing outside of it and leaning against its back door was Z-Rae. She wore red stiletto heels, fashionably ripped jeans, and a red military-style Drummer's Parade jacket. It had brass buttons running up and down its middle with gold braiding, called soutache, running horizontally across the chest. The jacket also featured a stand-up collar and epilates with brass buttons. Today, Z-Rae was a brunette with long hair hanging over her shoulders and yellow eyeshadow. To say she looked hot was an understatement. She also had a large Kate Spade shoulder bag sitting on the ground by her feet.

Smiling and hanging up his phone, Noah opened the front door.

"Hey, Sergeant Pepper," he called, referring to her jacket, "better come in before the neighbors recognize you."

She turned off her phone, dropped it into her bag, then picked up the bag and strolled down his short sidewalk. "I want people to recognize me," she said. "I want them to know you're important. Rented the biggest limo I could find."

"How did you know where I lived?" he asked.

"You once told me you lived in Old Town Lilburn in a new townhouse complex just a couple blocks from your studio. I already had the studio's address, so I started there. This is the only new construction around, and some kids were skateboardin' on the sidewalk. So, I asked 'em if they knew where a man lived who was always walking to your studio, and, voila."

He smiled. "That's pretty good detective work."

"Pretty smart kids," she replied. "Plus, I saw you through the front window coming in your back door."

She kissed him as she entered, then glanced around.

"Yeah. This place looks like you. Uncluttered. Modern. But bohemian touches here and there," she noted, spotting a Ghanaian Kpanlogo drum sitting decoratively in a corner.

"Would you like something?" he offered. "Soda? Beer?"

"Got any San Pellegrino?"

"Uh, no. Sorry."

"That's okay. Nothin' then." She stepped over and looked at one of his landscape photos. It was matted, framed, and hanging on a wall. "Where was this taken?"

"The big island in Hawaii. Eh, Z, I'm delighted to see you, but what're you doing here?"

"I came in from LA yesterday for a wedding."

"Oh? Friend of yours?

"No. Never met the couple. The bride's mother invited me."

"Excellent PR," Noah nodded. "You're following in the great tradition of other celebrities: Taylor Swift, Katy Perry—even Tom Hanks have shown up at fan's weddings. Where was it held?"

"City of Hope."

Noah furrowed his brow. "City of Hope? The only place I know around here by that name is a cancer hospital in Newnan."

"Newnan, yeah," she confirmed. "That's where it was, and I'm not turning it into a PR thing."

He was genuinely surprised and curious by this gesture and wanted to ask her more about it but got the vibe she didn't want to discuss it further.

"I don't know the details," he offered, impressed, "but what you did sounds incredibly selfless, Z."

She glanced at some of the books on his bookshelf. "I had a cousin who died of bronchial cancer when she was nineteen. She never got to have a life. It's the same type of cancer the bride has. So…" her voice trailed off.

"That's too bad," he sighed sadly.

"Besides," she said, changing subjects, "it wasn't entirely selfless. As long as I was in town, Leah arranged for me to have an evening drink with Tyler Perry so I could pick his brain about producing."

She was referring to Leah Shively, her manager.

"Okay," he said, forming no opinion one way or another.

"And coming here also gave me the chance to track you down," she said, turning to him and lightening her mood. "I've got a gig for you."

"Yeah? What's that?"

She arched an eyebrow. "Tour photographer. Four months in Europe, baby."

"I asked you about doing your tour months ago, and you said it was out of your hands. You said the label was going to handle the photography, and they already had someone booked."

"Yeah, but that was before my latest single went to number one and my *Saturday Night Live* appearance. I'm an A-playa now with more clout. I can choose more of my own posse, and I choose you."

He smiled at the news but then realized something.

"Don't you start, like, really soon?"

"Kickin' it off in London in five days."

"I've got a shoot this week for Harley Davidson," he said. "Matter of fact, I've got shoots lined up for two months."

"Yeah, well, tell *The Wild Angels* you're gonna be wild with me over in Europe. This is huge exposure for you, Noah. You're gonna be global."

"I can't cancel booked jobs, Z. It'll damage my reputation."

She walked over to him and put her arms around his neck.

"This is major ex-pos-sure. London, Edinburgh, Paris, Athens, Rome, Madrid. Everywhere I go, I'll be giving interviews, and every interview, I'll be talking about the album and my amazing team. I'll be droppin' names, and yours will be one of 'em. Film companies, studios, other music acts—this puts you in the path of all of it."

She let go of him, turned, and started to pace around his living room like a general giving orders, her stilettos click-clacking on and off his bare wood floors and area rugs. "Call your clients and tell them you have to cancel, but say the next time they book you, you'll give them a 30 percent discount for the inconvenience. Tell 'em your assistant will also contact them with alternative photographers you recommend. That way, it'll save them from scrambling to replace you. Then send them all a nice gift basket. Fruit, candy, flowers, and the like. That should minimize the damage. You can even toss in VIP seating at my next Atlanta appearance."

She set her shoulder bag down and pulled out a large manila envelope.

"Everything's here: itinerary, hotels, plane tickets… We have to fly over commercially, but once we're in

Europe, we've got a private plane. By the next tour—we'll be takin' my own jet."

Noah shook his head, absorbing the news.

"Man, I—I didn't expect the day to go *this* way."

"You're good with your passport, right?" she asked.

"Uh, yeah."

"And you *are* going to clear your schedule and do this for me, right?"

"I need to take a look at my calendar, talk to Cole, I know I've got a dentist appointment…"

Z-Rae tossed the envelope on a nearby sofa and then started to unbutton the brass buttons on her jacket.

"You're going to clear your schedule and do this for me, right?" she repeated.

He watched as she undid button after button. As the military-style jacket opened, he could see that she was braless. She slipped the jacket off, and her breasts hung firmly and freely as she stepped over to the sofa, sat down, then began to unbuckle her stilettos.

Noah's green eyes shot toward the open living room window as she did.

"Jesus, Z, the curtains are open. Your limo driver's probably loving this."

"Close the curtains then," she said calmly, slipping off her shoes.

She stood up and began to undo her snug-fitting jeans, so he hurried over and closed the curtains. Then he turned and pointed a finger at her.

"You can't use sex as a tool to get your way. My whole life doesn't revolve around you, y'know."

She sexily wiggled out of her jeans, slid them down her attractive legs, then stepped out of them. The only thing she had left on was a white lace thong. Smiling confidently, she slid it off.

"You're *going* to clear your schedule and do this for me," she repeated a third time.

He gazed at her attractive body, Brazilian wax, and natural-looking wig. It was too much to resist, and after being so disillusioned with Fay, he didn't want to.

"Oh, hell yes!" he agreed.

She giggled with delight, ran over to him, jumped into his arms, and wrapped her legs around him. Anticipating the move, he caught her by the bottom, and they embraced in a deep kiss.

10

THE DAMNEDEST THING

Four days later, Noah was in his studio late in the afternoon, packing up a half dozen photography boxes. They were made of heavy gray plastic and had egg-crate foam linings to keep cameras, lenses, battery packs, lights, reflectors, cords, and stands safe. All the boxes had "Noah Galloway Photography" stenciled in white on their exteriors.

While he was checking the contents of his final box on a worktable, the studio doorbell rang. Continuing to check the box, he called out for the studio manager he and Cole shared.

"Annie? You still here?"

When no reply came, he walked through the studio, into the lobby area, and opened the front door. Fay stood on the other side. She wasn't wearing her usual green dress and wings. Instead, she was casually dressed, with a bandana in her red hair and it actually took him a couple of seconds to recognize her.

"I just came here by Uber and gave the driver a handful of dollar bills for a tip and one of Erin's pacifiers by mistake," she announced with her Irish accent. She held up a hand holding the pacifier. "He kept the bills but returned the paci."

Noah shrugged. "It's always nice to get an Uber driver who doesn't suck," he quipped.

He stepped aside and gestured for her to enter.

She came inside, waited until he closed the door, and let him lead the way into the studio.

"So, this is the place ya share with Cole?" she asked.

"Yes."

"Is he about?"

"No. Both he and our studio manager are gone for the day. Did you come to see him?"

"No. But I'd say hello if he were here."

Now in the studio proper, she stopped and looked around. It was a large open space with a fifteen-foot-high ceiling. Besides the worktable with the camera box in front of her, there was a second worktable on the other side of the studio to the right with an overhead camera brace attached to it. This second table was where Cole did close-up tabletop shots of products for clients. There was also a wall where different types of ten-foot-wide photo backdrops were rolled, hung, and waiting for use. The backdrops varied: from a blue sky to a field of sunflowers to the dusty red rocks of Monument Valley on the Arizona/Utah border. A collection of c-stands, lights, and apple boxes was in another corner. Directly across from her were two dressing rooms with lighted makeup mirrors, chairs, and empty clothing racks on rollers. She took it all in, then focused on the five packed hard plastic boxes sitting on the floor next to the still open and unpacked box sitting atop the worktable nearest her.

"Are ya goin' somewhere?"

"Europe. Tomorrow for sixteen weeks. I'm the official photographer for Z-Rae's No Holds Barred Tour."

"Aye, I remember ya mentionin' her before," Fay acknowledged. "I looked her up. She's a singer."

"Right."

"Groans a lot in her songs."

"Yes."

"Changes her hair color a lot. Her head is like a box of Skittles."

Noah smiled but wanted to get to the heart of the matter. "What can I do for you, Fay?" he asked. "Where's Erin? Why have you come?"

She set the pacifier on the worktable next to the box he was packing. "Erin's bein' watched by a friend of mine who works at the Renaissance festival. Wanda Harrington. I think ya know her, right?"

"The festival manager, sure," he remembered.

"She and Erin have become great pals," Fay smiled. "Anyway, I wanted ta personally apologize for me foul temper this past weekend at the festival. Ya would have, of course, been very surprised ta see me with a child, but I took yer reaction as: 'Oh-I-don't-want-this-kind-of-trouble.' Me red hair is no lie. I spark ta anger quickly and now realize I was wrong. So, I just wanted ta say—I'm sorry."

"And you got the studio address from the website," he concluded.

"Aye."

"Well, you didn't have to come all this way to apologize."

"Yes, Noah. I did. I don't want ya walkin' around in this world thinkin' ill of me. And after me bad treatment of ya, it's not likely yer ever comin' back ta Fairburn or New Castle."

He nodded and smiled a little, not sure what to say. She smiled faintly, too, also at a loss.

After a few awkward moments, she said, "When ya go to Europe, will ya be visitin' Ireland?"

"No, England and Scotland are as close as we're getting."

"Oh, 'tis a pity. It's very beautiful. But ya said ya were there once."

"Yeah," he recalled, impressed that she'd remembered. "It was only for a couple of days, but yeah."

There was another uncomfortable silence, then Fay decided, "Right. I'm off." She started heading toward the lobby and front door.

"Would you like to call for another car and hang out here until it arrives?" he offered.

"No thanks. I actually thought I'd explore some of the shops I saw comin' in. There's a nice village feel to this place."

He looked at his wristwatch. "I'm not sure if much

is still open now except a couple of restaurants, but okay."

She walked to the door and put a hand on the doorknob but then paused and turned back to him.

"It *was* special. That evening we spent together. I don't blame ya if ya don't believe me. But… it's just… me life's very complicated, Noah. *Very* complicated."

"You don't have to explain, Fay," he said graciously, although he didn't mean what he was saying. He did want an explanation. He wanted to know more about her. But he suspected if he did, it would only lead to trouble, and at the moment, he had to focus on Z-Rae's tour.

"It was kind of ya ta seek me out again," she said. She nodded slightly, repeated the word "kind," then opened the door and left.

He stood in the entranceway between the lobby and the studio and looked at the closed door for a moment. He felt the weight of many things unsaid. With an expression of uncertainty, he turned and went back into the studio and his worktable. When he got there, he immediately saw the pacifier she'd forgotten.

Grabbing it, he turned, hurried out of the studio, passed through the lobby, and went outside. But when he did, Fay was nowhere to be seen. She'd been outside maybe thirty seconds, and if she were going toward downtown Old Town, she'd just be crossing the studio's parking lot.

"Fay?" he called, looking around.

Only two vehicles were in the twelve-space parking

lot: his detached and locked RV and his pickup truck. He didn't see Fay anywhere.

"What the hell?" he muttered.

He walked around to the back of the building, where there was a brush-filled empty lot and some old, thick oak trees.

"Fay?"

He hurried back around to the front of the building, jogged across the parking lot, and went another hundred feet down the sidewalk toward downtown Old Town Lilburn. If she were heading for the stores, or the city park across the street, he would've absolutely seen her, but he didn't.

"That's the damnedest thing," he said to himself. "What'd she do? Fly away?"

He looked at the pacifier, then returned to the studio.

11

ROME

"Z-Rae, you and BD were spotted having an intimate dinner together in Covent Garden. Then, BD joined you on stage in both London and Paris, where you two sang your new duet, "Temperature Rising." Now, here he is again in Rome. Are temperatures rising for real between you two?"

Z-Rae sat in a folding director's chair on the Sala Santa Cecilia Auditorium stage in Rome while a few of her tour crew members worked in the distance. She wore a lavalier microphone on the lapel of her blue jean jacket decorated with dime-sized silver studs and wore a bright-pink wig with a short bob cut. She was in the middle of an interview for *Entertainment Tonight*. Sitting next to her in another director's chair was a handsome dark-skinned man named Bobby Dragon, but everyone called him BD. He wore a long-sleeved salmon-colored shirt that was half unbuttoned, had tattoos encircling his neck and stopping just below his chin, and wore sunglasses with light-yellow lenses so the female interviewer, sitting across from them, could still see his eyes.

"We're just collaborators who are really proud of the new single," she replied.

"But we're tight," BD offered. "And, y'know, gettin' tighter all the time."

"That so, Z?" the interviewer asked.

Z-Rae flashed a coy smile. "Maybe."

"So, is this going to become a regular feature of your tour?" the interviewer asked. "You two on stage together?"

"Naw, it's just, y'know, a happy coincidence," BD responded. "Z's on tour in Europe, and I'm in Rome too, workin' on an album that I guarantee people will be talkin' 'bout for years. It'll be the crown jewel of my career, and "Temperature Rising" is just the first single from that crown. But since we're both on the same continent, it's like, 'Well, I gotta hang with my girl a few times', y'know?"

"Well, there certainly is chemistry between you two," the interviewer noted. "Both on the single and on stage."

"He wrote a beautiful song," Z-Rae said. "I'm really grateful BD asked me to do it."

"Hey, I been lookin' for an excuse to get next to this woman forever," BD admitted. "And now, here we are."

"Do you see more collaborations in the future?" the interviewer asked.

"You never know," BD smiled.

"You never do," Z-Rae teased.

While the interviewer thanked the stars for their time, Z's manager, Leah Shively, watched from the wings. She looked like a younger version of Gale King and was thrilled with the interview. In her universe, the stars were aligning for her client. Just before Z-Rae's tour kicked off, Bobby Dragon released his single, "Temperature Rising," a duet with Z, and the song quickly became an international smash. Its race up the charts surprised even BD's record company and the management teams of both artists. Bobby was hurrying to finalize a couple more tracks for his album that featured the single and was working at a studio in Rome. But he had also hopped on a couple of planes to perform the new single with Z in London and Paris. This was partly because he wanted to promote the single and partly because he wanted to add Z-Rae to a long list of conquests and muses. Leah watched her client carefully, then turned to the back of the twenty-eight-hundred-seat auditorium where Noah had some umbrella lights set up and was taking photos of Z's backup singers. She was one of the few people in the forty-two-person touring company who knew about their intimate relationship.

Taking his last shot of the backup singers, Noah turned off his lights, then saw Z-Rae and Bobby handing over their microphones and talking pleasantly in their director chairs while the *ET* crew broke down their equipment. Seeing a photo op, he dipped a hand into his camera bag, quickly changed lenses, and slowly walked down an aisle of the theater, clicking off shots as he approached with his camera bag slung over his shoulder.

Seeing him come, BD leaned over toward Z-Rae and slid his right arm around her shoulder.

"Hey, Camera Boy," he called, "grab this action." Then, he kissed Z on her cheek.

Noah captured the moment just as Z's eyes shot to BD with a little open-mouthed surprise. From a purely photogenic standpoint, it looked like blossoming love.

"You get it?" BD asked, hopping out of his chair and coming over to the stage's apron. "Lemme see."

Noah called up the shot in his viewfinder without saying anything, then handed his Nikon to the celebrity.

"Hey—that ain't bad!" BD nodded. "Not bad at all. What's your name, man?"

"That's Noah Galloway, and he's my official tour photographer," Z-Rae replied, sliding out of her chair with a hint of possessiveness.

"Official photographer, huh?" BD said, sliding his glasses down his nose to look Noah over. "I'm gonna remember you," he promised. "Got a card?"

"Sorry," Noah shrugged.

"I'll get you his contact info, BD," Z promised. "But first, I need a word with Noah about tonight's show. One of the nice things about playing multiple nights in the same venue is you get time to figure out the best camera angles."

"Well, I'm all about angles, baby," BD agreed. "Carry on. Catch ya later, Camera Boy."

Noah smiled faintly as Z-Rae walked off the stage in her usual stiletto heels. Then, she motioned for Noah to accompany her as she walked toward the back of the auditorium.

"Are you out of your mind?" she asked quietly, smiling to mask her concern for Noah. "You do *not* turn down an opportunity when Bobby Dragon expresses an interest in you!"

"I don't like Bobby Dragon," he said just as quietly while they walked. "He's a narcissist and about as deep as a birdbath."

"So are half the people in this industry," she reminded. "Including you and me at times."

"I don't care. I don't like him," Noah decided.

She stopped and looked around the auditorium to make sure no one was in earshot.

"This has kind of turned into a shitty deal for you, hasn't it? I wanted you to do the tour so we could spend time together. But then the single dropped, Bobby's publicist and my publicist concocted this stupid romance thing, and even if they hadn't, you and I could've never been too obvious because I'm the boss, and you're an employee."

"I never expected this to be *The Bachelorette,*" he said. "This is business, and you're paying me a lot of money to enhance your image. I understand the advantage of Bobby Dragon. Your first two albums sold five million copies combined. His last album sold nine million copies alone. I get it. I just don't like the dude."

She looked at him with a twinkle in her eye. "You're jealous. That's so cute!"

"I'm not jealous."

"Yeah, you are," she smiled.

"No. I'm not," he insisted.

"Hey, Z!" BD called from the stage. "Let's do lunch. "I got a Ferrari Pista out front. That sucker will hit a hundred miles per hour in under four seconds. My security will follow in their kiss-ass little Fiat."

She looked toward the stage, nodded, then turned back to Noah. "This will all be over tomorrow. He's going back into the studio, and we're moving on to Greece."

"You'd better get going," Noah advised, eying the stage. "Don't wanna keep the Fast and Frivolous waiting."

"You're so jealous," she whispered, walking away. "I love it!"

"No, I'm not," he reiterated.

"You *are*," she said over her shoulder.

He watched her go, and after she climbed the six steps that led her back onto the stage, BD locked an arm around her waist, and they strolled away. Noah turned toward the back of the auditorium and took the lens off his Nikon, then slipped it, and his camera, into his shoulder bag. After he had broken down the umbrella lights, he unclipped the iPhone from his belt and checked his recent messages. Then he looked at a particular message he'd already read a dozen times. It was the results of a DNA test matching his blood with the saliva from Erin's pacifier. The test revealed a 98.3 percent chance that he was Erin's father.

"You know it's all just a show, right?" Leah asked.

She'd come up behind him from the stage. He turned back to the stage again and glanced toward where BD and Z had left.

"Sure," he nodded, forcing a smile. "Just a show."

12

TIME DIFFERENCE

The offices of the Georgia Renaissance Festival were separate from the thirty-two-acre festival village of New Castle. The property was originally a four-bedroom ranch home built in the 1970s, but now, half a dozen full-time employees used it. Festival Manager Wanda Harrington's office was in what had once been a formal dining room. Her desk and chair sat facing away from a big bay window. Once upon a time, there were landscaped shrubs under the bay window and a manicured lawn. Now, the shrubs were gone, and the yard was a mostly dirt and gravel parking lot. Wanda had a small farmhouse and six acres of wooded land about a half mile away. Her morning exercise was usually to walk to and from the office every day, and quite often, a black Labrador Retriever named Lancelot accompanied her. However, this July morning her dog was at home, her employees were out doing one thing or another, and she was sitting behind her desk with her bifocals on. Her frizzy blondish-white hair hung down around her shoulders, and her nose was buried in a copy of Noah's DNA test. Cole Huggins, Noah's studio partner, sat in one of the two chairs in front of her desk that faced the bay window.

"Why are *you* showing me this?" she finally asked, slipping off her bifocals. "Why not Noah?"

"He's in Europe shooting Z-Rae's tour," Cole answered, "and frankly, since we've known each other longer, he was hoping you'd be more predisposed to share Fay's contact information if I made the request personally. Normally, Wanda, I wouldn't get involved. Except Noah's under the impression that when Fay isn't working at the festival, she goes to Ireland. If that's the case, and since he's currently on the same continent, he'd like to go to Ireland and assure her he wants to play an active role in raising their daughter, regardless of their status as a couple. Frankly, I think it's a fair request."

Wanda thought for a moment, then responded.

"So do I. She's always brushed men away like so many flies. Your friend Noah must have something special. Yes, I can confirm she *does* return to her homeland of Ireland. At least, that's what she tells me. But that's all I know. I have no way of contacting her when she's gone, and she doesn't contact me."

"What do you mean?" Cole asked. "You've got to have a job application, emergency contact info, an address to send tax forms to."

"Normally, yes," she agreed. "But some of the

people who work at Renaissance festivals are like those who work at traveling carnivals or county fairs," Wanda replied. "They fly under the radar. They're modern gypsies. If they wanna disappear, the Renaissance fair circuit is a place where they can do that."

Wanda leaned forward in her chair and showed Cole her left wrist. He looked at the scars from a very different and desperate time in her earlier life.

"I understand better than most the need to run away and reinvent yourself," she confessed. "Four seasons ago, Fay just showed up on the festival grounds during our opening weekend dressed as a fairy, the same outfit she wears every year. I don't know if she bought a ticket or snuck in. But I *do* know that with her looks and those wings, kids and parents gravitated to her like bees to honey. You've seen her. She's exceptional with kids. She does these little magic tricks, and although I didn't know it at first, I also think she's got some healing gifts."

"Healing gifts?" Cole asked.

"One weekend, there was a kid with a sprained ankle. According to the EMT on duty, it was a bad sprain. But after Fay laid a hand on the kid's leg, he was up and running around. Another time, a woman was carried to the First Aid Station, suffering from sunstroke. But after Fay held her hand for a few moments, she seemed fine. Other employees have told me similar stories about her."

"That's crazy," Cole said.

"Is it? Haven't we all heard stories or seen documentaries about people with healing powers? Anyway, her first day here, other ambassadors were coming up to me and asking who this new girl was who never attended any auditions or cast meetings. And, of course, *I* didn't know, either. But I *do* know fear, and underneath all her gentleness and beauty, that girl was afraid. I thought: If she's *this* good as an ambassador when she's scared, what could she do if she felt safe? Far as I could see, she had no phone, money, or ID, so I didn't ask a lot of questions. I just asked if she wanted a job and had a place to stay. She answered yes and no. So, I paid her under the table and set up a cot with a sleeping bag in an old tool shed my late husband built."

"That was pretty nice of you," Cole noted.

"No, it wasn't," Wanda waved off. "The shed was hot, and the sleeping bag was old. But since that first year, our relationship has grown. When she showed up the second year, I invited her to stay in my guest room. When she wasn't working the festival during the week, she helped me out with chores at home all season, and we bonded. Now, when she's here, it's kinda like I have a daughter for eight weeks. I got her a fake ID, she works the festival, and is invaluable around my place. She cleans, sews, paints, does *amazing* things with a vegetable garden and flower beds, and I swear to God, when she sings to the birds, they answer back."

"Wait. You got her a fake ID?" Cole asked.

"You don't know about my younger life. I know people who know people, including people who can make all types of documents. She didn't have any ID when she first showed up. And you're right; there has to be some kind of paper trail for employees. So, we created one. Her formal address is my place. But don't ask me how she goes back and forth to Ireland. She's *got* to have a real passport and ID stashed somewhere, but, for whatever reason, she doesn't show up with 'em here, and when she leaves, I never take her to the airport. She just sort of disappears. It's this big secret."

"Have you asked her about it?"

"Of course I have. More than once. But then she does something sweet, like painting the tool shed or the window trim, and asks me to please respect her privacy."

"And you're okay with that?" he wondered. "I mean, she lives under your roof."

"I think I have a pretty good nose for reading people," Wanda replied. "Little by little, year after year, I've come to know a few things about Fay. Yeah, she's private. But she's genuinely kind, eager to help, hungry to learn… there is this 'innocence' about her. She spends hours and hours online reading about all sorts of things like she's never had any formal education. I take her to places like grocery stores or the car wash, and she looks at them with this quiet amazement. But I've also heard her converse with guests at the festival in a half dozen languages. There are mysteries to her for sure, but I don't believe they're hiding bad intentions."

"I don't think I could live with that kind of mystery," Cole observed. "I mean, this *has* to be hard for you."

Wanda chuckled slightly. "You have no idea. If she *does* go back to Ireland, what kind of life does she have there? If she doesn't go to Ireland, why lie about it? Is she a spy of some kind? My heart says no. When she's gone, how can I contact her? I never know whether or not she's coming back from year to year. She just shows up. She claims she doesn't know if she can come back, either. So, it's very tough when we say goodbye. Whatever her other life is, Cole, I think it's something unusual. Is she escaping from an abusive husband when she's here? Why are her visits always during the festival? Is she some rich eccentric who likes to play dress-up? Maybe she is. She showed up with a little sack of antique gold coins the second year. Does she have multiple personalities?"

"And still—you've opened your home to her."

"Yeah…" Wanda admitted. "I've always had a soft spot for strays. Even as a kid. I can't explain it… I just understand the need to escape and find myself wanting to look out for her."

Just then, a dark four-door Chevrolet with US Government plates pulled into the parking lot and parked next to Cole's Toyota, sitting right outside the bay window behind Wanda. Swiveling in her office chair and looking outside, she grimaced.

"Government plates… I see ibuprofen in my future."

She turned back to her visitor.

"I'm sorry, Cole. I *would* help if I could. I was stunned when Fay showed up this past season with Erin. But she never said anything to me about the father other than it was a brief encounter. I'm glad Noah wants to take responsibility, but I've got nothin' to give you."

"Okay," Cole said, rising out of his chair as Wanda handed over the copy of the DNA report.

"Alright if I sit in my car and make a couple of calls outside?"

"Grab an office if you want. I'm the only one here right now."

"Outside will be fine," he replied.

He smiled and left Wanda's office as two men came into the building. Seeing Cole heading out, one of them asked, "Wanda around?"

"In her office. The, uh, dining room," Cole gestured.

The men nodded as he left. Both were casually dressed and had short hair. Both were fit and looked businesslike. One of the men had blond hair, and the other had brown hair with a receding hairline.

"Ms. Harrington?" the blond one asked.

"Call me Wanda," she replied, rising from her chair in her jeans and peasant blouse.

Both men reached into their pockets and produced ID.

"I'm Special Agent Jacobs, and this is Special Agent Grimble from the Federal Bureau of Investigation," the blond one introduced. "Do you have a couple of minutes?"

"Sure," Wanda smiled casually, sitting back down. "What can I do for the FBI?"

She gestured for the men to sit in the chairs in front of her, but they both remained standing.

"Well, first off, we're both big fans," Agent Grimble admitted, putting his ID away. "We were talking on our way out here about how we've brought our families to the festival. It's quite an operation you run."

"Thanks. Much appreciated. Is there a particular weekend you like more than another?"

"Pet Weekend is real big with my kids," Jacobs replied.

"Personally, I'm more of a Viking Weekend guy," Grimble admitted.

"Very cool. Thanks for your patronage. So, what can I do for you?"

"We understand you have a vendor who works the festival named Dale Taylor?"

"Dale? Sure. He's a blacksmith and weapons vendor. He's worked the festival for years."

Agent Jacobs pulled a business card out of his pocket and handed it to Wanda. "This is his business card. You recognize his logo?"

Wanda looked at the business card that read: Dale Taylor, Blacksmith & Fine Weapons. The "T" in Dale's last name was an illustration of a broadsword, purposely larger and longer than the other letters.

"Yes," Wanda said.

"He stamps that DT logo on everything he makes," the blond-haired agent noted. "The T's very distinctive because it's a sword."

"Yes, I've seen it before," she verified. "He owns an insurance agency. He learned blacksmithing from his father and, I think, even his grandfather. When he's not working the festival, he sometimes works weekends doing blacksmithing at the Atlanta Historical Museum."

"Yeah, we know," Grimble revealed. "We spoke to him there."

"Oh?" she asked, putting the card on her desk. "He's not in any kind of trouble, is he?"

"Does he work other Renaissance fairs? Travel the circuit, as they say?" Jacobs inquired.

"I'm not sure, but I don't think so. Like I say, he has an insurance business."

"Has he ever mentioned anything to you about having customers abroad?" Jacobs asked.

"Particularly in Ireland," Grimble added.

The mention of Ireland made the hairs on the back of Wanda's neck stand up straight, and her face turned ashen. But she cleared her throat and quickly recovered.

"No, he's never mentioned anything about overseas customers. Then again, people from all over the world attend the Georgia Renaissance Festival. Why?"

"Do you have any employees at your festival who have work visas from Ireland?" Grimble queried.

"No. Everyone who works at the festival is a United States citizen," she lied. She looked at one of the standing men, then the other, becoming impatient.

"Guys, what's goin' on? Was one of Dale's weapons used in a crime in Ireland or something?"

Agents Jacobs and Grimble looked at each other, and then agent Grimble took out his cell phone and called up some notes he had.

"A few months ago, a farmer named O'Connell was

plowing his land in County Sligo, Ireland. He dug up some human remains, a couple of buttons from clothing, and several very old weapons: daggers, swords, that kind of thing. Archeologists were called in from the National University of Ireland, and they think this farmer's land was once the location of an ancient battle. They're not sure who was fighting who, but from radiocarbon dating, the bones and artifacts indicate the battle took place in the late 1400s or early 1500s. This is consistent with many clan wars that were happening in the Benbulben region of County Sligo at the time. Or, if it wasn't one clan fighting another, it could've been a battle against Nordic invaders. There are parts of Irish history that are, frankly, very vague."

"Okay," Wanda said, wondering what this had to do with the festival and Dale Taylor.

"There were some weapons—swords and ax heads in particular—that were confusing to the archeologists," Jacobs added.

"I don't understand," Wanda said.

"Ancient swords and weapons found in locations that we know today as England, Ireland, and Scotland were made in bloomeries," Grimble continued, referring to the notes on his phone. "These were metallurgical furnaces that generally used a particular type of iron with varying amounts of steel alloy. Based upon these mixtures and how the weapons were made, scientists can tell the area where the steel came from."

"For example," Jacobs added, "swords were often made from steel bars, also referred to as 'currency bars.'

From these bars, archeologists can tell if a sword was made from a bar that came from Rome in 700 BC or Denmark in, say, 400 AD."

"And there are all sorts of other ways to pinpoint the origin of where a metal weapon came from," Grimble shared. "There's diagnostic machinery, from optical emission spectroscopy to metalwork wear analysis, or MWA, that can get pretty specific about age and origin."

"This is all fascinating," Wanda said. "But I don't see what this has to do with—"

Jacobs interrupted her with a pronouncement.

"Weapons made by Dale Taylor, from iron that came from Pittsburgh less than ten years ago, were found in farmer O'Connell's field among other artifacts where everything had been buried for over five hundred years."

Wanda paused, not understanding.

"You recognize his smithy logo, right?" Grimble said, gesturing to the business card on her desk. He closed his notes and called up a picture on his phone. Using his fingers, he enlarged the photo, and then turned the screen toward Wanda. It was a partially rusted broadsword, but the part that wasn't rusted had a faint logo stamped onto the steel with a D and a broadsword next to it for a T.

"How did weapons made of iron from a foundry in Pittsburgh less than ten years ago wind up being buried in an Irish field for over five hundred years?" Jacobs asked. "And not just one, but a half dozen."

Wanda paused for a moment, open-mouthed and perplexed, then smiled slightly and shrugged.

"Th-that's insane. It's a coincidence. Dale probably saw that same stamp on an ancient sword in a book and decided to use it as his own."

"Yeah," Grimble agreed, clicking off the picture. "The head of the archeology department at the National University of Ireland thought the same thing. Except, Mr. Taylor said the logo was his own design. And that still doesn't explain the age of the iron that came from a town in a country that didn't even exist five hundred years ago."

"Well—obviously, the analysis of the metal's age is wrong," Wanda concluded. "It couldn't have come from Pittsburgh."

"If we had done radiocarbon dating on one weapon from one source, I'd agree," Jacobs replied. "But testing was done on numerous weapons with the DT stamp at the National University of Ireland, then again at Oxford, then again at Yale University right here in the good ol' USA. It was the opinion of all three institutions that you can fake the metal aging, but only to a certain extent, and these artifacts weren't faked. They've been lying in the ground for centuries."

"The Irish government thought this might be of interest to *our* government. So, the FBI ran its own tests, and guess what? We concluded the same thing. So, here we are," Grimble smiled, putting his phone away. "Quite a mystery. Wouldn't you agree?"

With her mouth open and at a loss for words, Wanda

finally found some. "I-I would indeed. You've obviously had a prior conversation with Dale about this. What does *he* say?"

"We asked if he'd volunteer to share his sales receipts with us, and he said he didn't want to talk to us any further until he conferred with his attorney," Jacobs revealed. "We asked if he sold a quantity of weapons to someone that he knew was from Ireland and, again, Mr. Taylor refused to answer our questions. Now, why do you suppose he'd take an attitude like that? There isn't any crime here, Wanda. But there *is* a type of time travel conundrum."

"Except for Mr. Taylor's mail-order business, which is very minimal, ninety-nine percent of the weapons he makes are sold during the eight weekends of your festival," Grimble shared. "So, you can understand our interest in seeing his receipts and having a chat with you."

Wanda paused, looking at the agents, then shook her head.

"No, guys, I don't. Why would *I* know anything about Dale's receipts? Or maybe you think the Georgia Renaissance Festival has a time machine on its grounds?"

Grimble smiled at the notion.

"Do you?" Jacobs asked.

"Look—" she rationalized, trying to keep their conversation grounded in reality, "I'm sure Dale was intimidated by you two guys showing up with this *X-Files* story. If I were him, I wouldn't want to talk to you without first conferring with my attorney, either. And if you're asking, could someone have bought weapons from Dale during the festival and shipped them to Ireland—yeah. That's entirely possible. Like I say, we get visitors from all over the world."

"Would you mind sharing your employee records with us?" Grimble asked.

"Why?"

Jacobs shrugged. "We're just looking for any possible connection between someone who might work here, Ireland, and our unsolved mystery."

Making a decision, Wanda rose from her chair. "You said it yourself, Agent Jacobs, there isn't a crime. So, if you don't have a warrant, no, I'm not going to share employee records."

"Why not? We're not after anyone," Jacobs justified.

"Because they're private," Wanda reminded.

"We *can* get a warrant, you know," Grimble said threateningly.

"Then get it. Meantime, guys, I'm pretty busy. So, if you'll excuse me."

Deciding they weren't going to learn anything further, Jacobs and Grimble thanked her for her time, left their business cards, and departed. As they went outside and shut the front door, Jacobs noticed Cole was sitting in his car and talking on the phone.

"What do you think? the blond one asked his coworker.

"She's lying," Grimble decided. "She knows something about Ireland. Did you see her face when I first mentioned it?"

"Yeah, I did," Jacobs verified. "What do you want to do?"

"I think we *will* come back with that warrant if we can find a sympathetic judge. But we'll time it during the festival. She'll be more inclined to cooperate if it's right in the middle of her busy season."

As the two men returned to their car, they were unaware that Cole hadn't really been making calls. He had just been pretending to and was actually reading the lips of the agents through the bay window while they stood in front of Wanda's desk. Although Wanda had her back to Cole so he didn't get her part of the conversation, he learned enough from Jacobs and Grimble to conclude Fay was buying and sending historic-looking weapons made by Dale Taylor back to Ireland. But how they had wound up in an ancient battlefield, he couldn't figure.

Once he finally drove out of the parking lot, he made a real call, but all he got on his phone with an app for the hearing impaired was a notification that he'd reach voicemail.

"Noah—hey, it's Cole. I don't know what the time difference is or where you are, but, dude, call me as soon as you get this message. It's important!"

13

AWESOME

Diary Entry, Saturday:

Some say magic is everywhere.
Who can doubt it when there are rainbows?
Or fields of wildflowers?
Or an endless sky of stars?
Who can doubt it when deeply moved by music?
Or after seeing the birth of a child?
But I say—I want more.
Amaze me!

Cole Huggins sat at his kitchen table in his townhouse in Lilburn. He was exhausted and hadn't bothered to change out of his navy-blue terry cloth robe or comb his ginger hair. He'd been awakened at 2 a.m. by Noah returning his call from Athens, where it was 9 a.m. Noah had responded to his studio partner's voicemail at his first opportunity.

He was calling from a small but nicely appointed room at the Four Seasons Astir Palace Hotel. His room had a balcony that overlooked the turquoise Aegean Sea. Both men were using earbuds as they spoke, but Cole's phone had a transcriber app so he could read what Noah was saying. Although the app occasionally misunderstood a word, they had been speaking for a while and had ironed out any words that had been lost in translation.

"So, what do you think?" Cole asked, reaching for a cup of coffee he'd made from his Keurig Coffee Maker.

"There are more questions here than answers," Noah summarized. "Wanda has no way of reaching Fay, no way of knowing if she'll ever return, and I have no way of knowing if I'll ever see my daughter again."

"True," Cole agreed, taking a sip of coffee.

"And we have no way of knowing what her other life in Ireland is. Only that she apparently bought some weaponry from Dale Taylor and sent it to her homeland."

"So it would seem," Cole verified.

"And this whole FBI thing," Noah continued, "they showed up because some weapons made by a blacksmith in America were found deteriorating in a farmer's field from a battle that took place five centuries ago. Before America even existed."

"It doesn't make any sense," Cole noted.

"None of it does," Noah agreed. "But out of everything you've told me, what the FBI said to Wanda about Dale's weapons rusting in a field for over five hundred years is bullshit. Either the FBI is wrong, or they're lying."

My transcriber spelled out "renting," but I assume you said "rusting."

"Yeah, r-u-s-t-i-n-g," Noah spelled.

"Why would the FBI lie?" Cole asked.

"I-I don't know."

"Three different universities and the FBI's own lab reached the same conclusions," Cole reminded. "They can't all be wrong?"

"But it can't be true, either, Cole! Unless you wanna entertain the notion of time travel."

Both men were quiet for a moment, thinking. Cole took another sip of coffee while Noah stepped onto his balcony to look at the water.

"Look, maybe this is all an elaborate con," Cole suggested. "I know from working the Renaissance festival and talking to people that there is big money in collecting ancient weapons. Huge money! Maybe Fay is working with this farmer, O'Connell. Maybe she's a girlfriend or sister. Maybe O'Connell's a genius at aging things with chemistry or something and found a way to treat modern weapons so they appear as antiquities to fool radiocarbon dating. Maybe he's planting the weapons himself at night and, as long as he keeps plowing them up by day, he's got a huge source of income."

There was silence on the other end of the line.

"I really, really hate that explanation," Noah said.

"But you're right. It *could* be something like that. I mean, what else could it be?"

"The FBI is looking for a connection to O'Connell, and *that* could be why they asked to see Wanda's staff employment files," Cole concluded.

"Yeah," Noah admitted regretfully.

"Of course, I'm just spitballin' here," Cole reminded. "But I do think the FBI agents left cards with her. Maybe she could call them and see if she can find out more about O'Connell. Ask if he's married or—"

"If she does that," Noah interrupted, "she's all but admitting a connection between someone who works at the festival, O'Connell, and Ireland. If Fay has become Wanda's pseudo-daughter like you said, she won't give her up. Especially after providing her with a fake ID."

"Well, she had to have a *real* ID to get to Georgia from Ireland in the first place," Cole reminded. "And why Georgia, anyway? Maybe, maybe she's lying to Wanda about returning to Ireland. Maybe she never leaves the country."

"Maybe," Noah agreed.

"It's complicated," Cole said, stating the obvious.

"Very," Noah confirmed.

Just then, there was a knock on Noah's hotel room door.

"I gotta go," he said. "My workday is getting started here. I'm really sorry I cost you a night's sleep and dragged you into this."

"It's actually kind of fun," Cole said. "Playin' detective and all that. I'm sure everything will be explained in time."

"Yeah. Well, thanks again, Cole. Go back to bed. And I'll get Z to sign that CD for your sister."

"Thanks. Talk to you later."

"Later," Noah said, disconnecting the call.

He removed his earbuds, then walked over to the door and opened it. Z-Rae stood in the hotel hallway, wearing a red wig and dressed down in a mid-cut t-shirt, shorts, and sandals. She also had a duffle bag slung over her shoulder.

"Good morning, she said from behind some sunglasses. You ready to cruise to the cruise?"

"Hi. Did my equipment—" he began.

"It's all on the boat," she finished. "The roadies took care of it first thing this morning."

He looked around, grabbed a pencil and notebook, and put them in his backpack.

"Why do you always carry that notebook?" she asked.

"So I can remember all the colorful things you say when I write that tell-all book."

"Okay," she shrugged, knowing he was kidding.

"Hey," he cautioned, "are you sure I'm the right guy for this job? There are plenty of talented photographers who specialize in fashion, and I don't want to give you anything subpar."

She looked up and down the hall to make sure no one was around, then stepped into his room and gave him a morning kiss.

"No. You're the shooter I want. Toned bodies, blue water, next-to-nothing product—what's to screw up?"

They spent the next four hours aboard a gleaming white rented Princess Yacht under clear blue skies. The eighty-five-foot craft rounded the picturesque Astir Peninsula, cruised about a mile out into the calm Aegean Sea, then dropped anchor. Thirteen people were on board the 110-ton craft, including the yacht's crew, Z-Rae, Noah, Leah Shively, and others from the pop star's entourage. The purpose of the journey was a still photo fashion shoot for a swimsuit manufacturer that had struck an endorsement deal with Z. It was a prelude to launching her own fashion line someday. The yacht had several great places to shoot: the lounge area on the long bow, the teakwood aft swimming deck, and both the front and back of the flying bridge.

First, Z donned a long blonde wig and posed in a bright-yellow micro bikini that barely covered her nipples. The next suit was a white splicing one-piece with tan mesh that wrapped around Z's left shoulder and then went around her body like a piece of white ribbon. That called for a blue wig. After that, she wore a huge black curly wig with a red two-piece halter top and a thong that, from the back, left little to the imagination. Noah used two other female models in some shots, but not at the same time. Noah used them as background. For example, when Z was stretched out in the foreground on the teakwood swimming deck, another model was in the background and slightly out of focus as she climbed up a ladder having just come out of the water. Since Noah wasn't a fashion photographer per se, he worked with a photography assistant and took his time figuring out and carefully lining up the shots. But the marketing director from the LA-based manufacturer, who had flown in especially for the shoot, loved every minute of it. They snapped behind-the-scenes pictures on their phone in between sips of champagne.

At about 2:30 p.m., the yacht returned to its berth in the marina, and the marketing director, support models, photography crew, hair and makeup artist, Z's social media manager, and the yacht's captain and first mate all departed shortly thereafter, leaving only a hospitality steward, Z-Rae, her manager Leah, Noah, and a bodyguard named Billy on board. Z had a soundcheck at the concert venue at 6:00, but the boat had been rented until 4:00. So, still having the craft for ninety minutes, Z asked Leah to leave her and Noah on the boat while the hospitality steward remained in their cabin unless needed. Meantime, she ordered her bodyguard, Billy, off the boat but suggested he hang around the dock entrance to make sure they weren't disturbed. She wanted some private time with Noah. Leah didn't like the idea. She had noticed a boat with a photographer that followed them out to sea. It was all but a certainty that other paparazzi were watching the yacht, and Noah and Z would be photographed leaving together.

"So what?" Z rationalized. "We'll say I continued the photo shoot in the master stateroom and shower area, and we were featuring supporting creams, lotions, and shower gels. The roadies aren't arriving until 3:45 to pick up Noah's photo gear, so it'll look totally legit."

Leah grimaced at the idea but did as her client asked. She had nothing against Noah and actually liked him. But she also knew that if they were found out as a couple, there could be problems.

After nearly an hour of passionate, sweaty lovemaking in the master stateroom, Noah slowly rolled off of Z, who, in a rare instance, wasn't wearing any makeup or a wig. She looked younger and more vulnerable without her false eyelashes, foundation, eye shadow, and lipstick. Her short, natural brown hair gave her a cute tomboy look. She was definitely hot when she was made up, but there was also an understated beauty when all of her warpaint was off. It was a beauty she had always felt insecure about.

"Oh, my God," he sighed breathlessly. "You're exhausting, girl."

She looked at him, smiled, and pointed to the space between her legs. "Heaven's in there… I'm paraphrasing David Bowie."

"I didn't know you liked Bowie," he said, impressed.

"There are a lot of things you don't know about me," she said. "I guess there's a lot we don't know about each other. Like, do you ever stop and sometimes think about how incredibly lucky we are? I mean—we just made love on a multimillion-dollar yacht. Not bad for a girl from Oakland whose dad owns a UPS store.

The Girl at the Renaissance Fair

Sure, there was talent and hard work involved—but also a huge element of luck."

"Sure, I think about that," he agreed.

She turned onto her side, looking at him, and after a moment, asked: "Do you ever think about where this is going?"

"You mean us?"

She nodded.

"Well, I'm not supposed to, right? I mean, you set the ground rules when we first got together. No strings, remember?"

"One night is a hookup. A few hookups and we're fuck buddies. But this has become more than a few times."

He likewise turned on his side to face her. "Well, you're pretty hard to resist… but if you really wanted to examine it—I think there are complications."

"Like?"

"Like, we have two very different schedules and live on opposite sides of the country. The press thinks there's a blossoming relationship between you and BD, and journalists have a funny way of turning on you if they feel manipulated. And even if you weren't spinning that story, we're both A personalities, competitive and impatient. I've worked hard to build my reputation, and if people knew about us, they could say I just slept with you to further my career."

"But you did sleep with me, and it *has* furthered your career," she noted.

"Do you think that's why I slept with you?" he asked.

"Was it?" she countered.

He paused. "I, I hope it had more to do with other attributes: your smile, your eyes, your determination… But—maybe… that's a part of who you are. The point is, careers are delicate things. They're built on a house of cards. This is your time, Z. I wouldn't want to cause any of your cards to tumble."

She looked into his green eyes, wanting to know more. Was he saying what he was saying because he really cared for her? Or did he just want to keep things casual? Was she too aggressive for him? Too "A" personality?

Just then, the intercom buzzed on a nightstand next to the bed.

"Yes?" Z replied, answering it.

"Miss Rae, it's Marci," the hospitality steward answered. "Bobby Dragon is here to see you. He's in the main salon."

She looked at Noah wide-eyed, then shook her head and shrugged.

"Uh, j-just tell him to give me a few minutes, and I'll be there."

She clicked off the intercom button and hopped out of bed. "What the hell is *he* doin' here?" she asked. "He's supposed to be in Rome recordin'."

"Like I said," he reminded, also getting out of bed, "you're pretty hard to resist."

"Noah—he can't see you and me like—I mean—it wouldn't be cool if—"

"Don't worry about it," he interrupted, slipping on his gray Hanes briefs. "Put yourself together, and I'll go buy you some time."

Within another two minutes, now dressed and carrying his camera bag to give the impression he was still working, Noah came up the stairs from below deck and went into the main salon where BD was wearing a hoodie with the hood over his head, drooping jeans, brightly colored Hermes sneakers that went for about $1,200 a pair, and sunglasses. Considering it was eighty degrees outside, Noah had to resist smiling when he saw the pulled-up hoodie.

"Hey, BD," he greeted, "this is a surprise."

"S'up, Camera Boy," the star said. "Where's your boss?"

"Downstairs changing. We just finished a swimsuit shoot for Saint Bart's Swimwear, one of her sponsors. Thought you were in Rome still recording."

"Yeah, well, my engineer came down with Covid, so we're pausin' for a few days, meanin', I can hang with my girl."

"How'd you know where we were?" Noah asked.

"Your security man, Billy. We're tight, so I rang him up. He's also done some security for me." He looked down the stairs toward the master stateroom. "She downstairs?"

He started to move in that direction until Noah realized BD had been exposed to Covid.

"Hey—wait a minute—if you were exposed to Covid, you can't see her. There's an entire touring company that's depending on her good health."

BD shrugged. "It's cool, don't worry 'bout it."

"Did you get tested?"

"Eh, yeah." The visitor lied.

"Well, first of all, you didn't say that very convincingly. And second, even if you did but were infected, it wouldn't show up right away. It'd be more like one to three days."

BD took off his sunglasses and looked at Noah unamused. "Hey, Doctor Oz, shut the fuck up. I didn't come all this way to see the Parthenon. Where the ho?"

Bobby turned and started to go down the stairs. Noah slid off his camera bag and hurriedly followed after him. "Hey, BD, don't call her that!"

Once they were both down the stairs, Noah grabbed him by the arm as he headed toward the closed master stateroom door.

"Hey, Bobby, stop. You might be infected."

"GET OFF ME, MAN!" an enraged Bobby Dragon yelled. He dropped his glasses on the carpeted floor, quickly spun around, and forcefully pushed Noah away. They were in a narrow hallway, and Noah slammed into another stateroom door. Stepping toward him, Bobby swung at Noah, who quickly veered backward to avoid the punch. Thinking fast, Noah took his right hand and slapped Bobby's swinging arm, which caused the singer to spin around with his back to Noah. When this happened, Noah locked Bobby in a half nelson, slipping his right arm under the star's right arm. Placing his hand on the back of the star's neck, Noah plowed him into another stateroom door on the opposite side of the hall, just as Z-Rae, now dressed and wearing a wig, opened the master stateroom door at the end of the hall.

"GET OFF ME!" BD yelled.

"Noah! What the hell—" Z started to say.

"He was exposed to Covid. Shut the door!" Noah ordered.

She took three steps back into the stateroom, left the door open, dipped a hand into her tote bag, and pulled out a portable container of mace.

"HEY!" she yelled at the two struggling men. This thing sprays twenty feet!"

Seeing the mace, both men froze and looked at her.

"You!" she said, aiming the container at Noah. "Back away from Bobby and pick up the man's glasses!"

Surprised, Noah relaxed his grip, and Bobby quickly shoved him away.

"And *you!*" Z continued, now turning the spray toward him. "Don't you lay a hand on my photographer or take one more step closer to me with your germ-exposed ass!"

Both men continued to stare at Z until BD finally spoke:

"Bitch—you're awesome!"

14

NO GOOD DEED

At 12:10 a.m. Sunday, Noah sat on a stool in the Four Seasons Astir Palace Hotel bar sipping a Mythos, a popular Grecian beer. He wore a plaid shirt and jeans; the same plaid shirt Fay had once borrowed. Leah Shively, Z's manager, came into the bar wearing a lightweight jacket and a large purse slung over her shoulder. She looked tired and had just returned from an outdoor concert at the Faliro Olympic Complex, a concert that Noah was not allowed to attend. She quietly walked up to the bar and sat down two empty bar stools away from him.

"So—how was the show?" he asked.

"Packed… fabulous. She killed 'em."

"Did 'he' show up?"

"Yep. Wearing a mask, carrying two dozen roses for an apology, and keeping a good six feet away from her. But he didn't go on stage. They didn't perform together."

The bartender came up to Leah and asked her what she wanted. She also ordered a Mythos.

"I don't care how pissed she is," Noah said. "I did the right thing. If Bobby has Covid and passed it on to Z, the whole tour could shut down for a week, maybe longer. It would've cost hundreds of thousands of dollars."

"Which we would've made up eventually," Leah said matter-of-factly. "The virus isn't the threat it once was, and you can't grab one of the biggest music stars on the planet, Noah."

"He called her a ho."

"So do haters on social media ten times a day," she brushed off.

"He threw the first punch," he reminded.

"Yeah, but you grabbed his arm first. That's assault." She eyed his fit physical form. "And you with your chest and arms looking like you bench press Volvos and shit. I don't disagree with your intentions, but your methodology sucked."

The bartender delivered Leah's beer while Noah took a sip of his, then grumbled, "He gets exposed to sickness, shows up uninvited, speaks degradingly of Z, thinks nothing about putting her health at risk, and throws a punch. But *I'm* the one who was banned from tonight's show. Man—talk about no good deed going unpunished."

Leah took a swallow of her beer before responding.

"Z didn't want you around so she could smooth things over with BD. She knew he'd show up tonight, and she was successful. He's *not* going to press charges against you, and they're going to continue their…" she paused, not wanting to say "relationship," and said, "collaboration" instead.

"Well, that's somethin', I guess," Noah conceded.

"Believe me, you do *not* want to wind up in a Greek jail," Leah assured. "But we can't control what he'll say on social media. You *know* he's gonna slam you or say you attacked him or some damn thing."

"Yeah," Noah figured, taking another sip of beer. "I've been thinking about that. It'll be a hit to my career. Probably cost me some work."

Leah also took another drink of beer before continuing.

"Yeah—well—speaking of hits."

"What?" he asked.

Leah paused and breathed out a heavy breath. "BD won't press charges, but he has a price. He wants you off the tour beginning now."

Noah started to chuckle at the absurdity of the notion until he saw Leah's face.

"And Z agreed?"

"You pack tonight," she confirmed. "When the company wakes up in the morning, you need to be gone. Your equipment will be shipped out tomorrow and a plane ticket on American Airlines will be sent to your phone within the next hour."

"No-no-no-no," he said, hopping off his barstool and reaching into his back pocket for his wallet to pay his tab. "This is bullshit. I'll go talk to Z."

"No, Noah. You won't. Security will stop you. Z agreed to this. She doesn't want to see you."

"I was trying to *help* her," he argued.

"If BD starts tweeting tonight," she continued, "tomorrow morning there will be paparazzi all over this hotel looking for a juicy controversy. That's not helpful. You can't be here."

He paused and looked at her with disbelief while she slid off her stool, then pushed some tired strands of hair off her face. "Look, I'm sorry. I know this is shitty, but this is a negative story that's got to be contained. I like you, Noah, but the reputation of my artist and solving her problems will *always* come first, and your presence just became a problem. But there is a silver lining. Z will pay your full contract price for shooting the tour."

Noah closed his eyes and shook his head, feeling very much like the victim. After a moment, he made a decision and put his wallet back into his jeans pocket.

"Pay my bar tab, and we'll call it even," he said, walking away.

15

COFFEE AT JUDY'S

Fairburn, Georgia, home to the Georgia Renaissance Festival, was a small, sleepy southern town of seventeen thousand. It was bigger than Lilburn and not as charming. It was more utilitarian in looks, with railroad tracks that paralleled a good part of the downtown area that went by several empty storefronts. In a small strip mall on Smith Street was Judy's Restaurant, a good local place for breakfast. The food was solid, hearty, and made up for the terribly corny and sexist signs that adorned the walls. Signs like: "If a man says he'll fix it, he will! There's no need to remind him every six months about it." Or "The Six Deadly Terms Used by Women: Fine. Go ahead. Nothing. That's okay. Whatever. And, Wow."

Dale Taylor, the insurance man and sometimes blacksmith, sat at a table in Judy's with an empty plate before him holding the remnants of scrambled eggs and sausage and a nearly empty cup of coffee. He was forty-seven, had a combination of blond and gray hair, and a round face with a ruddy complexion. He was a hefty man and had strong arms—especially his forearms—from pounding and shaping lengths of red-hot iron into swords, ax heads, knives, and other tools from days of old. He wore a golf shirt, blazer, and slacks, and as the waitress topped off his coffee, he spotted Wanda Harrington coming through the front door. She had her hair hanging loose around her shoulders, a nice blouse with honeybees on it, jeans, sandals, and said hello to a couple of patrons before going over to Dale's table and sitting down.

"You told me to go ahead and order if you were late, so I did," he began, explaining the empty plate before him. He looked at the wall clock. "But I didn't think you'd be thirty minutes late."

"I'm not late," she said. "I've just been sitting outside in my car and watching the restaurant to make sure you weren't followed."

"What?" Dale said, surprised. "Followed by who?"

"The F-B-I," Wanda spelled out quietly.

His expression revealed that she knew the FBI had talked to him at the Atlanta Historical Museum. He sat back in his chair, self-conscious.

"Oh... you know about that, eh? You said on the phone it was important. I thought you wanted some life insurance or something."

The waitress came over and gave Wanda a menu, but she said all she wanted was coffee. After the waitress poured her a cup and left, Wanda spoke in quiet tones. "You've worked the festival for eight years, Dale. So, I think I'm entitled to some straight answers. I promise, what you tell me will stay between us, but I *have* to know. Have you been making weapons for Fayetta Smith, and has she been sending them to Ireland?"

Dale folded his arms and nodded. "Yeah."

"How many?"

"It's been more and more every year."

"How many?" Wanda repeated.

"Hundreds of pieces," he admitted. "Swords, axes, daggers, knives, shields. I couldn't make everything she wanted and had to use outside sources to help supply her."

"A-and you didn't tell the FBI?"

"No. They don't know anything about Fay. There's a couple of good reasons for that. First, Fay paid for the weapons with gold coins. Very old, very valuable gold coins."

"Yes," Wanda acknowledged. "I know something about that. She didn't have a penny when she first showed up at the festival four seasons ago. But ever since that first year, she shows up with this little bag of gold coins like some Irish leprechaun."

"Then you know how much they're worth," Dale assumed.

"No, I don't," she admitted.

"The second year she worked the festival, she wanted my entire stock. Wanted to pay me with one of her coins. Before I agreed, I had it appraised it at an antique coin dealer, and he offered me eighty grand on the spot."

"What?" she asked, astonished.

"He said he'd never seen a coin that old in such good shape. Then I heard he turned around and sold it for over a hundred grand."

"I-I had no idea," Wanda gawked. "I only know she had 'em."

"I had to buy a competitor's weapons just to have something to sell in my store that year," he explained. "Which brings me to my second reason for not sharing with the FBI. I-I haven't exactly declared the transactions I've had with Fay, my subcontractors, or the coin dealer to the IRS."

Wanda rolled her eyes in exasperation. "Oh, Christ, Dale."

"Hey, I've got an ex-wife, one kid in college, and another one starting college next year. If it ever became public that I've defrauded the government with undeclared revenue, it'd be the end of my insurance business."

"Then why the hell did you *do* it?" she asked quietly but angrily between gritted teeth.

"It's not like we're hurting anybody," Dale justified. "The stuff I sold her is for decorations. They hang on the walls of Irish pubs, hunting clubs, estates—that kind of thing."

"That's what Fay told you?"

"Yeah. She said there's a big market for 'em over there."

Wanda thought for a moment, and they both took sips of their coffee.

"What about the FBI saying some of your weapons were found in an ancient battlefield, and they've been buried for—like—five hundred years?"

"Now *that* I don't know anything about it," he admitted. "I thought they were jerking my chain just to rattle me."

"Do you know of any aging or oxidation process that would make something made out of today's iron look older than it is?"

"Sure. You can cover it with antiquing paint, tarnish it with corrosive materials like acid cleaner and salt, elevate the temperature of the solution of heat-treated metal alloy to a point below its recrystallization temperature, but high enough to speed up precipitate formation."

"In English, Dale," she deadpanned. "Would any of these ways fool someone about how long weapons have been sitting in the ground?"

"I'm no geologist, but I doubt it. I volunteer at the Historical Museum and have heard radiocarbon dating is pretty accurate."

She took another sip of her coffee. "Well, if that's the case, aren't you curious how your swords could be buried in an Irish field for centuries?"

"No," he replied with certainty. "Because it's impossible. I'm more concerned about the FBI talking to Fay and showing up with a warrant to review my banking statements."

"Okay," she nodded.

They took a sip of their coffees.

"So—what now?" he asked.

Wanda thought for a moment.

"I said I'd keep your secrets, and I will. But I absolutely don't want you selling any more weapons to Fay. I mean, if she even shows up and wants to work the festival next year. And Dale, if the FBI recontacts you, let me know immediately, will ya?"

16

STORMY RETURN

The opening weekend of the Georgia Renaissance Festival promised to be a wet one. The days leading up to the grand opening were overcast and drizzly as landscapers planted flowers in New Castle, vendors unpacked merchandise, and horses and riders practiced in the jousting tournament field. Despite the blustery weather, the show was going on. Wanda Harrington had been directing the food and beverage trucks and the dozens of artisans arriving in vans and campers like a medieval ringmaster. Now, it was the Friday night before the opening, 9:03 p.m., and the weather was the worst it had been all week. It wasn't raining yet, but it seemed inevitable. The cloudy sky boomed with thunder and crackled with lightning as if there was a series of short circuits in heaven. The festival would open Saturday on schedule at 10:30 a.m., rain or shine, but the first weekend's attendance was going to be off predictions.

A mile away from the festival village of New Castle, at the corner of Wanda's six acres of wooded land, stood an odd-looking oak tree. It had been struck by lightning three times over the decades, which had caused the top half of it to crack and eventually be blown off in a storm. It looked deformed, but it was still alive, with a trunk that measured forty-two inches around, and it was still sprouting new branches. Wanda had owned the property for eleven years and had inherited it from her late husband, Gunnar. Nearly an acre of her land was dedicated to her house, lawn, garden, and tool shed, while the remaining five acres had been left alone except for a few walking paths. Just ten feet or so from the oak tree and Wanda's property line was a dirt service road for utility trucks to have access to the large silver electrical towers that were just a couple hundred yards beyond her property and provided electricity to most of the people and businesses in Fairburn.

While the treetops swayed and the thunder rolled, there was another flash of light. But this time, it didn't come from the clouds. Amazingly, it came from inside Wanda's oak tree. Specifically, from a rounded hole in the trunk twelve feet off the ground. It was a hole large enough for an owl to nest in. The flash only lasted a second or two. But if someone had been standing in the woods and seen this phenomenon, the burst of light from the hole would've been bright enough to prevent them from seeing the shadows and shapes of anything else. After their eyes readjusted, however, they would've observed Fay standing in front of the tree in her green fairy outfit with her wings slowly fluttering on her back. In one hand, she carried a gunnysack. In the other, she held the small hand of fourteen-month-old Erin also dressed in a green fairy outfit like her mother.

"Oh my," Fay said, looking around at the sky and setting down her sack. "There's a storm brewin', eh, darlin'?"

The child looked around at her dark and thundering surroundings, a little fearful and anxious. Seeing this, Fay bent down and scooped up some dirt and leaves. She pressed and rolled the leaves and dirt together in her hand until it was a small circular sphere about the size of a golf ball.

"Solas," Fay ordered in Gaeilge.

Immediately, the sphere illuminated. Then, Fay tossed it underhand out in front of her, and it remained a sphere as if the leaves and soil had been magically glued together. The sphere suddenly stopped in midair about six feet away, then hovered, awaiting further instruction.

Fay turned to Erin. "Better?" she asked, now that her daughter had a night light and things didn't look so scary.

The baby nodded.

"Good," her mother smiled.

She picked Erin up, then retrieved her gunnysack.

"C'mon. We'd better get to Grandma Wanda's before we get drenched." She looked at the illuminated sphere. "Air adhart," she said, which was Gaeilge for "Forward."

The sphere started to move slowly and steadily

ahead into the woods, following a path and floating by itself through some mystical force and guiding the way for the two travelers.

As Wanda's house came into view through the branches, Fay saw that Wanda and Lancelot, her black Labrador, were in the backyard. Wanda held a flashlight and was starting her portable generator just outside the screened-in back porch. Her house was dark; the storm had knocked out the electricity. But after a few pulls on the starting cord, the generator hummed to life, and a string of bulbs hanging from the ceiling inside the porch flickered on. Seeing this, Fay looked at the suspended illuminated sphere and muttered, "Ar ais an domhain." As soon as she said this, the light inside the sphere quickly faded, and it fell to the ground, becoming leaves and dirt again.

Hearing movement in the woods, Lancelot perked up his ears and started to bark. But the tone of his warning barks suddenly turned into happy whines when he recognized the familiar figure of Fay stepping out of the woods. As the dog ran over to greet her, Erin, still anxious and tired, moaned, "Nil!" Responding, Fay outstretched her hand a little, and Lancelot stopped, sat down, and didn't whine or bark anymore, although he wagged his tail happily. Going over to him, Fay gave him an affectionate pat and smiled.

"Dia duit Lancelot croga," she said tenderly, which meant "Hello brave Lancelot," in Gaeilge. Then she turned to her daughter. "We'd better stick ta English in this world, darlin'. I know it's confusin', but it's important."

Turning her flashlight to the backyard, Wanda spotted Fay and Erin.

"Do ya have room for a couple of weary travelers?" Fay asked.

Wanda smiled and nodded. "For you two? Always."

An hour later, Erin had been fed, put to bed in the guest bedroom, and was surrounded by a nest of pillows so she couldn't roll off the bed. She was wearing a fresh cloth diaper and was using one of Wanda's t-shirts for a nightgown. Fay had taken a shower in a candlelit bathroom and was now dressed in jeans, a blouse, and bedroom slippers from a closet full of clothing purchased for her over the years. She came into the living room with her red hair tied back, exposing her pointed ears and feeling at ease in the familiar surroundings. Wanda was an avid antique shopper, so the room featured a mahogany book cabinet from 1910, a spinning wheel from the 1860s, and a pink velvet Victorian loveseat from 1893. With only a small desk lamp on and several candles placed here and there because the power was still off, the room looked like something from another time.

"I can't believe how she's grown," Wanda said, turning off the kitchen's generator-powered lights as she entered the room carrying a mug of tea.

"She's speaking nearly in full sentences," Fay said proudly.

"Really? Fourteen months is early for that."

"She's an exceptional lass," Fay smiled, sitting on the loveseat. As soon as she did, Lancelot hopped up on the loveseat to lie beside her. "She understands more than she speaks, so full sentences can't be far off."

Wanda sat down in a leather reading chair near the fireplace. "You want some tea?"

"No, thanks," Fay smiled. "I'm good."

Fay looked around the place admiringly as Wanda blew and sipped her tea. "So," she finally said, "openin' day tomorrow, huh? With the weather, it's probably not goin' ta be the corker ya were hopin' for."

"We need to talk," Wanda announced, switching topics. "As always, you know I'm glad to see you. But I need to ask you some questions, and for both of our sakes, you need to give me straight answers."

"What's wrong?" Fay asked.

"This will be the fifth festival season you've stayed with me. In the past, I've always respected your privacy —you're 'other life' in Ireland—because there are things in my past that I frankly don't want to talk about, either. So, on a certain level, I get it."

"I've always admired yer curtailin' of curiosity," Fay said. "And I know that's been difficult ta do."

Wanda took another sip of her tea, then continued.

"But things have changed, Fay. You've got a child now. What kind of mother comes walking out of the woods at night with a baby wearing costumes? What's in the bag you brought? And what about those costumes? I know they're old, like they've been hand-woven on a loom or something."

Fay opened her mouth to speak but Wanda cut her off and continued, "I've seen enough antique clothing to know what I'm talking about, Fay. And why do you always show up with no cell phone? No other clothing unless you brought some in the bag this time? Don't tell me it's because you don't have money because you *do*. You're loaded. You've got a pouch filled with valuable gold coins. You started showing up with that in your second year."

"There *are* explanations for all this," Fay offered.

"Are you a criminal?" Wanda asked bluntly.

"What? No!" Fay replied.

"Are you selling those coins on the black market or something? Were they stolen?"

"No! 'Tis nothin' like that!"

"Have you been buying swords, axes, and other weapons from Dale Taylor?"

Fay looked at Wanda nervously.

"And, and how might ya be knowin' about that?" she inquired.

"Is it true?"

Fay hesitated for a moment, then answered. "Aye, that's true enough. There's a large demand for them where I come from."

"Is it *where* you come from, Fay? Or *when* you come from?"

Wanda set her tea on the small table beside the chair and leaned forward, eying her guest's ears. "You once told me you were born with those ears, that they were a one-in-a-million birth defect, and your parents were too poor to get them surgically fixed."

"That's true," Fay affirmed. "They *are* poor."

"Then how can you afford to fly back and forth to Ireland every year? How can you even *do* that without identification? Without a passport? And what are you doing with gold coins worth hundreds of thousands of dollars? Where are your wings, Fay? You arrived with them, but where are they now? In your bedroom? In the closet? I've never seen them stored anywhere." She leaned back in her chair while a peel of thunder rolled in the distance.

"Why does the whole area lose power shortly before you show up and then lose it again after you leave?"

"Look outside yer window, woman." Fay defended. "There's a bad storm outside."

"That's just tonight," Wanda countered. "We *always* lose power shortly after you arrive and leave."

Fay's shoulders slumped, and her eyes looked at the floor. She looked at Lancelot and silently stroked his head for a few moments.

"These are too many questions to ignore, Fay," Wanda said. "I can't ignore 'em any longer."

The young redhead paused for a few more moments, then rallied her courage.

"Wanda, you've become a very dear friend, and you'll never know what that means to me. You're entitled to some answers, so I'm goin' to tell ya about me 'other life.' But I fear you're not goin' ta believe me."

"You're special," Wanda acknowledged. "You've

got unique abilities. I already know this. But I need to know the whole story. And whatever you tell me, you've got to tell Noah Galloway, too. He knows Erin is his daughter."

Fay's blue eyes widened in the candlelight, then she recalled something and slowly nodded.

"The pacifier I left at his studio last year... I wondered if he'd be curious enough to do some testin'."

Wanda cocked her head a little.

"You left it on purpose?"

Fay didn't answer. Instead, she petted a dozing Lancelot again and returned to an earlier question.

"Why did you ask, 'when' I came from?"

"Was I wrong to use that particular word?" Wanda asked. "Tell me quick, what year were you born?"

Fay's eyes darted slightly, trying to do some calculating. The seconds of silence spoke loudly.

Wanda cracked a faint smile, picked up her tea, then settled back in her chair.

"In the absence of logic, only the illogical is left. Tell me your story, Fay. The truth... I've got all night."

17

THE HORZIKAAN

Clan Fergus Castle was formidable. It had two huge thirty-foot round stone turrets that were fifty feet high and had a forty-five-foot stone wall connecting them. The rectangle of stone walls behind these turrets could comfortably house four hundred men, and behind the castle and outside of its walls was a second clan encampment of another three hundred men behind fifteen-foot-high stone walls. The clan had built the second encampment recently, but the original turret castle with its towering walls had been standing since the 1200s. The original builders were unknown, but it was widely believed that Anglo-Norman knights had built it.

On Tuesday evening, March 19, 1501, a single rider slowly approached the large castle gate on a brown mare. There were lit fire cauldrons sitting on neatly stacked stone piles with a flat metal top on either side of the road for a good sixty yards leading up to the two-foot-thick wooden and rounded arched gate. The guards on the wall walkway above had plenty of time to see the rider coming. He was an elderly man with a three-inch white beard and a weathered, leathery, wrinkled face. He wore a dark robe with oversized sleeves and had a hood over his head. He carried a staff with a jewel in its top tied to the side of his saddle. As he drew nearer, the guards realized he wasn't alone. There was a shadow in the night air flying around him. When his horse stopped in front of the gate, the shadow perched on the man's left shoulder; it was a black raven.

"Who are ya?" a helmeted guard called from atop the wall in Gaeilge.

"I've come ta see yer master, Ardal Fergus," the stranger answered in the same tongue. He reached under his robe and produced a piece of parchment with a red wax stamp and the seal of a ring on it. "You recognize his seal?" he said, holding it up. "He sent fer me."

"Did he now?" the guard answered impudently, trying to act important in front of his fellow clansmen on the wall. "And who might ya be? What's yer name?"

The stranger leaned forward a little in his saddle.

"Me name is impatience," he said in Gaeilge. "Me horse is thirsty, and me arse is stiff from ridin' all day. Go tell yer master the one he sent fer has arrived and expects a good meal."

The guard looked to the right and left at his companions on the wall, then made a decision.

"Well, I'll tell ya, old man," he replied in his native tongue. "I can't see what yer're holdin' from up here, and the master's gone ta bed fer the night. Best ya return in the morn."

While the rider still held the parchment in one hand, he untied his staff with the other. When it was free of its binds, he pointed it up at the guard, revealing his inch-long pointed fingernails, and muttered something. Suddenly, a beam of white light shot out from the jewel at the end of his staff and enveloped the entire body of the guard. The man was conscious but helpless in the light. As the stranger raised his staff slightly, the guard felt his feet leaving the walkway of the castle wall, and while the stranger slowly pointed the staff upward, the terrified guard found his body slowly floating forward, over the wall and moving downward through the air and toward the rider as if he were nothing more than a life-size marionette. As this was happening, the other men on the wall quickly started to murmur a word amongst themselves that evoked fear and awe at the same time. The word was: "Horzikaan!"

When the wide-eyed, fearful guard was about seven feet off the ground and four feet in front of the rider's horse, the old man held up the parchment again.

"Can ya see the seal better now, lad?" he asked.

The guard wanted to nod but found he was powerless to do so.

"A-a-aye, sir," he cried instead. "I-I see it clearly! Forgive me, sir!"

"Run along and deliver me message, then. Meantime, open the gates."

"Yes, sir," the guard promised in Gaeilge.

The horzikaan carefully moved his staff forward, and the guard began to rise and move backward toward the top of the castle wall. The stranger knew this demonstration would command the respect of everyone inside the castle. Horzikaans were the most powerful of wizards in ancient Ireland and among the most feared beings on the continent. Many believed they didn't even exist and were simply the stuff of stories shared in taverns or told to children. But those who knew better also knew that trying to strike a bargain with a horzikaan was a dangerous endeavor. They were so powerful that there was a fifty-fifty chance the king, lord, or clan leader who wished for their services would be killed, and the horzikaan would just take whatever riches had been promised him without actually doing anything.

Within another six minutes, the horzikaan stood with his staff in the great hall of Clan Fergus Castle. It was a huge dining and meeting place with a twenty-foot-high wooden beamed ceiling and no less than four five-foot high fieldstone fireplaces, all burning and being tended to by a young girl about fifteen years old. The room was outlined with a series of feasting tables that, from an overhead view, made up a square horseshoe. While the wizard's raven perched on a five-foot-tall unlit candelabra, Ardal Fergus, wearing boots and pants but no shirt, appeared at the top of a stone stairway with no handrail. He was fifty years old and fit for his age but bore the scars of several battles. He had wild, long blond hair, eyes as piercing as his guest's, and a blond beard tinged with gray. He also had an elk-skin blanket wrapped around his muscular shoulders. He descended the stairs with an equal mixture of pleasure and caution, for he was very aware the horzikaan could kill him just as soon as look at him.

"Ya came," he began in Gaeilge. "I wasn't even sure if you'd receive me letter. There were only rumors that ya sometimes went ta the tavern where I sent it."

The wizard slowly lowered the hood from his head, revealing mostly white shoulder-length hair. "It would've been more respectful ta send a personal envoy," he replied in their native language.

"Aye. But if ya were in a foul mood when ya received him, you could kill the envoy. Ya can't kill a letter. Isn't that admission of yer great power respectful enough?"

The horzikaan smiled slightly at Ardal's logic as his host stepped off the final stone stair.

"Ardal Fergus," the visitor said as if pronouncing a sentence of judgment and slowly walking toward him. "Invader. Killer. Pillager. Rapist. Enslaver… what be it ya want from me?"

"More," Fergus answered. Then, he turned to the girl tending to the fires. "Clodagh," he barked. "Wake up the cook. Tell him to prepare food fer our guest. Be quick about it!" Then, he noticed the wizard's raven. "And a plate of bread and fruit fer our honored feathered guest as well."

The girl hurried away while the horzikaan sized Fergus up, stroked one side of his mustache with one of his long, pointed fingernails, then decided to hear him out.

"Yer letter promised a chest of gold just fer hearin' what ya had ta say," he reminded.

"And so ya shall have it. And twenty more like it if ya accept my proposition."

"The Tuatha Dé Dannan," the horzikaan said knowingly, turning and walking with his staff toward the nearest fireplace. "Ya want more, but the fairies haven't turned out ta be the easy conquest ya were hopin' for."

"It was supposed ta be a quick campaign, and it's dragged on fer nearly five years. Not continuous fightin'. Strike and ride. But these days, I'm wonderin' if they have a horzikaan of their own."

"And why would ya be saying that?" the visitor asked, leaning his staff against the hearth and warming his hands.

"They've now got more weapons than farmers and creatures of the wood should be holdin'. They've also got powerful magic. More than mere fairies can do. I've seen things. I've seen 'em use fire that shoots across the night sky, lights up the dark, and prevents a surprise attack. They can call up a fog and lose themselves in it. Not long ago, we learned of a secret encampment. Me men attacked it, but it was empty. While they were there, rings of fire suddenly sprung up around me men and trapped them. If they got through one ring, there was another behind it. Some got out, but all were burned, and I lost nearly fifty good men and horses that day. There have been similar embarrassments all over the country. Surprise attacks on the road, wells poisoned —the fairies have gotten very smart."

The horzikaan continued to warm his hands, thinking, then turned to his host.

"They've not enlisted one of me kind, or else I'd know about it. But I agree, this is magic beyond what they can do. There is opportunity here, I think."

"As close as I can figure," Fergus said, "the center of the resistance is a village at the base of some hills called the Three Sisters. Some years ago, we attacked it, burned it, and killed hundreds. We lost no men, thought nothin' of it, and moved on. Our campaign headed west. Over the weeks and months, the fairies took ta hidin', and it took some time ta weed out several nests. A little after a year, we circled back ta the Three Sisters ta finish the job in that village. But the fairies had rebuilt and knew we were comin'. They flew out of the trees in their wee form, then suddenly transformed ta human size on the back of me men's horses with daggers and slit their throats. Then, they'd transform and fly off again. I lost over three dozen men. They didn't have those daggers before."

"They've learned tactics. They've been fortified," the wizard concluded.

Two servers appeared from the kitchen, walking toward the table at the head of the great hall. One carried a platter of fruit and bread; the other carried a pitcher of ale and two mugs. One of them announced that food for the guest would be coming shortly. After they departed, Ardal Fergus continued with his story:

"We've returned ta this village again and again. Every time we attack, it's empty. Every time we burn it, the fairies rebuild. They've even surprised attacked *us* in route ta them. So, instead of attackin', now, we observe."

"And?" the wizard asked.

"And there's one young girl the elders are clearly heedin'. She disappears in the spring, and when she returns, the fairies seem ta be newly supplied. Me archers have asked more than once ta kill the bitch, but she's just the conveyor of these supplies and new magic, not the source. I need ta find the source of this magic. For that, I need magic meself. I need a horzikaan."

The elderly guest turned and looked at the bird. Then the raven squawked and flew over to the head table, where it landed and began to pick at the fruit.

"Ya say she disappears," he noted, retrieving his staff, then heading toward the pitcher of ale. "Be it only in the spring?"

"Aye," Fergus replied, likewise walking toward the head table.

The host filled a mug for his visitor, then filled one for himself. The horzikaan took a long drink, then wiped one of his large sleeves across his bearded mouth. "I wonder if she's found a corridor," he pondered.

"Ya mean, fer the heathen gods? Those are just stories the Tuatha Dé Dannan like ta tell their children."

The guest took the pitcher again and refilled his mug. "Perhaps. In any event, yer fairy conveyor knows *somethin'* about magic that's more powerful than what her kind can do, and that interests me."

Fergus looked at his guest hopefully as the servers returned with platters of cheese, ham, chicken, red meat, and a type of custard. They set the food down and were followed by the young girl named Clodagh, who'd been tending the fires. She carried two plates for the men and also had three fat candles in her apron. After she set the plates and candles down, she quietly hurried over to one of the fires and set a long, thin stick ablaze. Then she carefully walked back to the table and used the stick's flame to light the candles. The horzikaan watched this simple domestic chore with appreciation. When she was finished, Clodagh disappeared into the kitchen again.

"Will ya strike an accord with me then?" Fergus asked.

"Thirty chests of gold. Not twenty," the older being declared. "And mark you, they be large chests."

"Agreed," Fergus nodded, toasting him and taking a drink.

"And women," the wizard continued, anyone I want whenever I'm here. Beginnin' with Clodagh."

"Done," Fergus agreed.

The horzikaan took his staff and began making his way around the table so he could sit and eat. "One more thing," he added. "There may come a time when I require the men of yer clan ta fight fer me. I'll only use 'em once, but if I ask, you'll immediately come ta where I direct."

The clan leader thought for a moment, then nodded. "Yer enemies will be mine."

"Then, congratulations, Ardal Fergus," the horzikaan announced, sitting down, "yer borders will soon be expanding yet again." He took a piece of grilled meat and put it on his plate.

"Tomorrow, direct me to this village near the Three Sisters."

"What're ya gonna do?" Fergus asked.

"Horzikaans have many talents," the wizard replied, taking a bite of meat, "but one of our greatest is patience. Simply watching and waiting. That's where I'll begin, lad. Watching and waiting."

Fergus nodded and smiled, then rounded the table to likewise sit down with his guest. As he did, he called toward the kitchen.

"Clodagh!" he called in Gaeilge.

A moment later, the young girl came into the hall.

"Prepare a comfortable room and bed fer our guest," Fergus smiled.

18

EVIL ARRIVES

At 9:06 p.m., a mere three minutes after Fay and Erin appeared in the woods near the edge of Wanda's property, another bright flash of light emanated from the oak tree with the broken off top. When the light disappeared, a small vertical shadow appeared in front of the tree, no more than six inches high and two inches wide. But after a few moments, this shadow grew taller and wider. As it did, it morphed into a full-grown man. He was elderly, with a three-inch white beard and a weathered, leathery, wrinkled face mostly hidden by a hood attached to a long dark robe. Sitting upon his shoulder was a large black raven. Its menacing black eyes and beak darted here and there, taking in its surroundings. The robed figure clutched a six-foot-high wooden staff with a crystal in its top. He opened his other palm upward to determine if it was raining. When he did, he exposed inch-long pointed fingernails. Slowly looking around, then turning, he saw the silhouettes of a line of tall silver power poles a couple hundred yards away. Intrigued and having never seen anything like them before, he slowly started to walk toward them and off Wanda's property but then paused and remembered something.

The horzikaan turned back to the oak tree and looked up at the hole in the trunk about twelve feet off the ground. Then, he spoke to the raven.

"Fan. Faire," he ordered. Which was Gaeilge for "Stay. Watch."

The bird cawed, then hopped off its master's shoulder, took to the air momentarily, and perched itself in a maple tree just twenty yards away from the oak. Turning back to the power poles again, the mystical stranger continued on his way.

As he neared the metallic towers and wondered what they were, he heard the distant barking of a dog. This was Lancelot spotting Fay and Erin coming out of the woods. But between the thick woods and lightning, he couldn't see anything even though Wanda's back porch lights were now on. Looking down a slight hill at the clearing made for the power poles, he saw the generator-powered lights of another house. This was Wanda's neighbor, Darius Larkin, a semi-truck driver who lived with his wife, Piper. Knowing he could get answers there, he started down the hill toward the Larkin residence about a quarter mile away.

The Larkins lived in a small two-bedroom brick ranch that was, like Wanda's, in a rural setting with no other houses nearby. Hearing a knock at the door, Piper, a hefty woman in her late thirties, lumbered to the front door wearing stretch pants and a Georgia Bulldogs t-shirt. Opening it, she saw the hooded, bearded stranger standing in the stormy night with his dark robe and crystal-topped staff.

She looked the horzikaan over and chuckled. "You're a day early and about a mile from where you need to be," she declared.

"Who is it?" her husband's voice called over the episode of *MythBusters,* the TV show they were watching.

"I'm not sure," Piper called back, bemused. "It's either Gandalf from *Lord of the Rings* or Emperor Palpatine from *Star Wars*," she leaned toward the visitor. "Which one were you going for, hon?"

With a sudden move, the wizard thrust out his arm and put his staff in front of Piper's face as if throwing a punch. Although he never touched her, the jewel on the staff shot out a beam of white light, and she flew backward with her arms and legs sprawled like she'd been hit by a hundred mile an hour gust of wind. She flew back through the foyer, sailed across the living room, and slammed into the wall next to the back door as if she were no more than a small tree branch. She hit the wall so hard that her spine put a considerable dent in the drywall and fractured two vertebrae. Sitting on the other side of the living room in his La-Z-Boy recliner, a stunned Darius, also in his late thirties and overweight, watched as his wife fell to the simulated wood laminate floor. He sprung up and raced over to her to discover she was either stunned or unconscious. Next, he looked toward the front door to see what could cause such a thing. The robed figure stepped inside the house, and as soon as he did, the front door behind him slammed shut under its own power. During these few seconds, Darius determined there was nothing he could do for Piper unless he first dealt with her attacker. Spotting the fireplace poker just a few feet away, standing on the brick hearth in a stand with the other fireplace utensils, he rushed over to it.

The horzikaan calmly walked down the short hallway and entered the living room. Seeing Darius come toward him, he thrust out his staff, which lit up again, and ordered, "Stop!" He was speaking Gaeilge, but the word was the same in English. Darius suddenly found himself frozen in place. As the magical intruder slowly walked over to him, his piercing, narrow gray eyes put Darius into some kind of hypnotic state. He was awake—but under the will of the visitor.

As the beam of light faded from the jewel in the staff, the intruder noticed the television and the episode of *MythBusters*. He turned toward it suddenly, pointing his staff at the screen.

"Stop!" he commanded.

His staff lit up for a third time and a beam of light shot across the room at the flat screen, but the TV continued to play unaffected.

Not understanding, the assaulter stepped over to Darius as the light from the crystal faded again.

"What be that?" he asked, switching to English in a

low voice thick with an Irish brogue. "Is it another corridor?"

"It's *MythBusters*," Darius answered in a monotone voice, compelled to respond.

"What's *MythBusters?*" the robed figure suspiciously inquired.

"It's a TV show. Entertainment," Darius explained.

The attacker looked at the television again, then back at Darius.

"Make it cease."

Darius lowered the fireplace poker, turned, and walked over to the side table beside his recliner. He picked up the remote control and obediently turned the device off. Then he returned to the robed figure and stood in front of him like some sort of strange slave. About this same time, Piper began to come around, moaning painfully.

"What's your name, lad?" the intruder asked, slowly taking the remote from Darius' hand and examining it.

"Darius," the homeowner replied blankly.

"Well, Darius—have ya got somethin' ta drink around here? Ale? Whiskey? I've come a long way, and me pallet is dry."

The semi driver immediately turned and went into his kitchen, ignoring a plea from Piper for help. During the next half minute, the visitor set the remote down, removed his hood, revealing long mostly white hair, and then looked around, taking stock of his surroundings. Piper cried half painfully, half angrily, "Darius, *help!* I can't get up!" And "Who the fuck are you, asshole? Get out of my house!"

Darius returned to the robed visitor holding a shot glass of whiskey. By now, Piper's rising temper was becoming agitating.

"Y-y-you're giving him *Canadian Club?*" she asked, astonished. *"Darius!* Get your gun and kill that son of bitch!"

The attacker took the glass, smelled it, then downed its contents in a single gulp.

"Aah!" he said agreeably. "Not bad, lad. Not bad."

"DARIUS!" Piper screamed, *"WHAT THE HELL ARE YOU DOING? HELP ME!"*

The bearded attacker looked at Piper, annoyed, looked at the fireplace poker her husband still held, and decided.

"Four good whacks to the top of the head ought to do it," he commanded, pointing a long fingernail at Piper.

Darius turned toward his open-mouthed wife, raised the fireplace poker and, despite the tears welling in his eyes, couldn't control himself.

As Piper screamed and Darius struck her over the head again and again, the ominous robed figure calmly walked into the kitchen, lit only by a light above the stove, and saw the open bottle of Canadian Club sitting on the counter. He poured himself another drink, and by the time he'd finished it, the screams and thudding sounds coming from the living room had stopped.

Noting the silence, the horzikaan then poured himself a third drink.

"Darius, come here."

The spellbound and now blood-streaked truck driver came into the kitchen, still holding the dark-red and dripping fireplace poker at his side. His controller took another large gulp of whiskey, then turned to him.

"I require information about where I am. The time I'm in. The devices and tools you use. Let's begin with somethin' the wench first said to me when she opened the door. What did she mean by, 'You're a day early and a mile away from where you need to be?'"

19

STUDIO FLIGHT

Two days later, Sunday at 7:17 p.m., Noah was in his studio in Old Town Lilburn, sitting on a stool at one of the large worktables. He was, as usual, in jeans, but his customary solid color t-shirt had been replaced with a black Hawaiian-style button-up with green palm fronds. He was writing something down in the little leather notebook he frequently carried, then turned his attention to his MacBook on the table and its calendar. Several entries had "Canceled" typed into their blocks by Annie, the studio's office manager. There was a shoot in Miami with Bad Bunny, canceled. Another for Warner Brothers in California, canceled. Still another, a cover shoot for *Cowboys & Indians Magazine* with actor Kurt Russell, canceled. This was some of the fallout from a series of highly uncomplimentary tweets by Bobby Dragon, who repeatedly tweeted about Noah's "amateur abilities" and his "utter lack of creative vision unless he's stealing ideas from somebody else." His business was down nearly 40 percent from a year earlier. And he hadn't heard a word from Z-Rae since she had brandished mace at him on the yacht in Greece. In fact, she and BD had teamed up on another song that would drop shortly before Memorial Day weekend. He didn't necessarily feel that his career was over, but it had certainly taken a serious stumble.

He closed his calendar, which returned him to his home page. It featured the photoshopped portrait of Fay kneeling on a boulder and gently blowing at the camera he'd taken a couple of seasons ago. He heard a knock on the studio door. Checking his wristwatch, he hopped off his stool, walked through the lobby, and opened the front door to find Fay standing outside. She wore a long-sleeved blue button-up top, faded jeans with one of the knees purposely ripped, and some Kizik step-in shoes. Her thick red hair was loose and looking a little wild. Her hands were stuck in the back pockets of her jeans.

"Hi," she said shyly.

"Hi," he said, pleased but trying not to let it show.

"It's been a while," she offered.

"It has indeed."

"I, uh, introduced meself to yer friend Cole at the festival today, and he mentioned ya were goin' ta be cleanin' and organizin' yer equipment here tonight. So, I thought I'd grab an Uber and take a chance."

"Uh, sure... c'mon in," he invited. "Cleaning and reorganizing equipment," he repeated with a self-deprecating tone. "I've got the time to do that these days. Anyway—it's good to see you."

"Is it? I'm heartened ta hear ya say that."

She came into the lobby and then stepped into the studio.

"It's much warmer in here than I remember."

"Well, I've been here for a while, so I turned the space heaters on. Would you like something to drink? Soda or a glass of white wine, maybe?"

"Wine would be grand," she said, looking around and familiarizing herself with the place. Noah headed for a large closet with swinging doors that had been transformed into a kitchenette, complete with a sink, refrigerator, and cabinets for glasses, dishes, and snacks. "We keep some food and drinks here for clients and models, working late—that kind of thing."

"If yer workin' late on a Sunday, ya must be busy then?" she assumed.

"Not really," he admitted, getting the wine out, then some glasses. "So, you're obviously back and working at the festival, huh? I knew this was opening weekend."

"It doesn't always work out where I can be here openin' weekend or stay until the final weekend, but the moon and stars aligned this time. At least for the opening. As for me actually workin' the festival this year, that's another story."

"Oh?" he asked, pouring the wine. "And what about Erin? Is she here in the States with you?"

"Yes. When I'm here, I stay with Wanda Harrington, and she's watchin' her for me."

"Right," he said. "Wanda told Cole that you stay with her when you're in town."

She nodded. "It's very unusual Wanda would speak to Cole about that. She's usually very mum about me whereabouts when I'm here. As I've said before, I like to keep me private life private. But me sharin' some information is what brought me here tonight."

"I see," he said.

He brought the wine glasses over to her and handed her one. After she took it, he said, "to sharing," and they clinked glasses.

After they both took a drink, she looked at her glass for a moment, then raised her blue eyes to his.

"Noah, I know that ya know Erin is yours. I know ya had some tests done on the pacifier I left behind, and I know that Cole knows. And because *he* knows, I know that Wanda knows."

"Yeah, we're very knowing people," he joked, taking another sip of wine. "But just about *that*. Just about me being Erin's father."

"I'm so sorry I lied at the start of it. I never dreamt I'd become pregnant because of the timin' of me monthly cycle. And then, when I saw your initial reaction of Erin, I just… I just—well—it was a mistake. So, when I came here to apologize last year, I left the pacifier as a way of givin' you a forewarnin' in case we ever saw each other again. I mean, if you were even curious enough to find out. Which, obviously, you were."

"You left the pacifier on purpose?" he asked.

She nodded again.

"You figured I'd do a DNA test?"

"I've seen 'em advertised on Google," she admitted.

"Or you just could've told me about Erin the old-fashioned way and used your words," he suggested. "Christ, Fay. I've already missed a year of her life."

"So, am I understandin' ya right? Ya want to be a part of her life?"

Noah set his glass down on the worktable.

"Yes. No matter what your deal is, or no matter whether or not there is an 'us'—yes. I've had time to think about it, and I'd like to be a part of Erin's life. But you've got to want this, too. And if you do, I've got to know some things about you."

Just then, his cell phone rang. Noah took the cell out of his back pocket, looked at it, and sighed.

"Uh—it's my mom. I missed one of her calls earlier today. Do you mind? This will just take a minute."

"No. Not at all," she said.

"Excuse me a moment."

"Hi, Mom," Noah said into the phone, heading for the lobby and a little privacy. She heard him ask something about his father's fishing trip in the mountains, then she turned her mind elsewhere, thinking it rude to eavesdrop. She carried her glass, took another sip of wine, and wandered around the worktable, going nowhere in particular but wanting to absorb more of her baby daddy's world. She thought it was nice that he would interrupt a conversation—even an important one—to take a call from his mother. While thinking this, she strolled by his computer and saw the photo of her with her wings spread and kneeling on the boulder in the middle of the stream. Wanda had shown it to her the previous year, but she was clearly moved by the fact that out of all the photographs Noah had to choose from, this was the one on his homepage. She couldn't help but wonder if it signaled that he still kindled a flame for her.

After another minute, he returned and picked up his wine again.

"Sorry," he offered.

"No. Children should give their parents priority," she agreed.

They both were quiet for a moment and took another drink of their wine. Just when the silence began to get awkward, Fay set her glass down.

"Okay, here's the bottom of the mug as me da says. I've got to tell ya somethin'. But after I do, yer never goin' ta glance at me the same way again. It's gonna freak ya out a little. Well, actually—a lot."

"I work with some pretty eccentric people," he reassured. "It'll be fine."

"I very much hope so," she replied. And with that, she started to unbutton her blouse. By the time she reached the third button, Noah asked: "Eh, Fay? What're you doing?"

"A certain amount of disrobin' is required," she replied, unbuttoning then taking off her top.

Noah looked at her pale skin and the freckles on her neck and chest. Then she reached behind her and unfastened her lavender-colored bra. As it slid down her arms, she quickly covered her bare breasts by crossing her arms.

Confused, Noah asked: "Is this the freaking out part?"

"No," she answered. She turned around, and a second later, two parallel seams, each eleven inches long, opened on her back on either side of her spine, and a pair of transparent wings with beautiful venation unfolded then opened. Within five seconds, they were fully spread to six feet in length and fluttered fast enough to lift her off the ground.

"Holy fucking shit!" Noah cried.

"This is the freakin' out part," she said, turning back to him as her wings fluttered faster and faster until there was a subtle but distinctly audible whir.

The studio had a fifteen-foot steel sheet and iron girder ceiling, and Fay began to glide around in the air effortlessly with her arms still crossed. Goosebumps covered Noah's body as he watched in open-mouthed amazement. After nearly thirty seconds of Fay flying around the studio, her wings slowed down, and, with the grace of a ballerina, she gently landed by the worktable where she had begun.

"A-a-are you an angel?" Noah asked with childlike earnestness.

"No, Noah. I'm exactly what I was the first time ya saw me: an Irish fairy of the wood. My people are called the Tuatha Dé Dannan."

"The what?"

"Two-ah-dee-danon," she pronounced phonetically.

"We're a highly developed race of magical fairies who usually appear to be the same size as humans."

"Th-that's impossible," he said breathlessly. "F-fairies aren't real. They don't exist."

"Aye. Sadly, that's true," she agreed. "Not in this time, anyway. Believe me, I've looked."

She turned her back to him and grabbed her bra while her wings folded up then retracted into the parallel seams of her back. When they were tucked away, skin slid over the seams like two sliding doors, leaving only a pair of long, thin lines to the right and left of her backbone that were thick as calluses. He remembered feeling them from when they made love but assumed they were caused by her wearing artificial wings for hours on end. Then, he recalled how he hadn't seen her wings sitting anywhere in his RV after she used his shower.

"Does that hurt?" he asked, referring to what looked like two long scars.

"No," she smiled, connecting her bra then turning back to him. "It's perfectly natural fer me, but it's sweet that ya asked."

He stood there speechless and processing while she calmly retrieved her blouse and slipped it back on. "I *am* from Ireland, although I fear a very different Ireland than the one you visited," she clarified, rebuttoning her top. "In the Ireland I hail from, fairies are real. But that was a long time ago."

His eyes looked around a little and spotted his wine glass on the table, still about half full. He stepped over, picked it up, and downed his remaining Riesling in one gulp.

"Holy fucking shit," he repeated, setting his glass down. "I'm sorry, Fay. I-I don't understand."

She took his hand and led him to the stool at the worktable he'd been sitting on.

"Sit down, allow me ta bend yer ear a little. The first thing I should tell ya is don't think about it logically. Scientifically. Who and what I am doesn't fit into yer conventional explanations."

She walked over to the kitchenette, retrieved the wine bottle, and then came back.

"In the time and part of Ireland I'm from, fairies are as commonplace as robotics are in yer factories today."

"What do you mean—'In the time and part of Ireland that you're from?'" he asked.

She refilled his glass as she answered. "I'm from an area known on yer modern maps as County Sligo. I was born in a farmhouse at the foot of some hills known as the Three Sisters in 1473."

"What?" Noah gasped, newly amazed. He thought for a moment, calculating in his head. "That was 550 years ago."

"551, to be precise," she corrected. "I traveled ta this time by a fluke. Me village was under attack, and I was runnin' away from a warrior who surely would've killed me. Our elders used ta tell stories about corridors our gods used ta travel ta the Otherworld. I never really thought much about those stories other than they were entertainin' ta hear around a campfire. But the night of this horrible attack, I ran ta the top of a hill, went through an old archway that used ta be the entrance of a Catholic church, and wound up here. Since then, I've learned how ta use this corridor, determine when it's open, and use it as a portal ta go back and forth in time ta help me people."

Noah put his elbows on the worktable and sunk his forehead into his hands, overwhelmed.

"I'm sorry, Fay," he repeated. "I, uh, I-I wish I was handling this more suavely. But in five minutes time, you've confirmed that I'm a father, announced that you're a fairy *and* a time traveler, and that you came to this century because someone was trying to kill you."

"It's not exactly first date conversin', is it?" she admitted.

"No," he agreed, "not even close."

She stepped over to him, put a hand on either side of his head, and gently rubbed his temples. Within seconds, his racing heart slowed down, and the mounting tightness of stress he felt in his chest evaporated.

"Better?" she asked empathetically.

"Yeah," he said, surprised. "Don't tell me—you've got healing powers, too?"

"Within reason," she smiled. "C'mon, have some more wine, and then let's stroll a bit. There's a lot more ta the story."

20

A WALK IN THE PARK

The Southern air was warm on this Sunday April evening, although the leaves and edges of the sidewalks were still damp from the rain. A quarter-mile walking path encircled the Lilburn City Park, and Noah and Fay strolled around it with him listening intently to her every word. Occasionally, they were passed by a jogger or someone walking their dog.

"If I've learned anythin' about humans," she said, "I've learned that man's science and technology has changed, but not yer greed ta possess what's not yours, nor yer fear to destroy what ya don't understand."

She looked at him and felt she had to qualify such a harsh statement. "Not all humans, of course. But many."

She waited until a lady walked by with her dog. Then continued.

"I've been on your internet, Noah, and read about the genocides: in Darfur, Rwanda, Bosnia, Cambodia,

Germany, right here in yer own country with the Native Americans—the list seems endless."

"Yes," he agreed. "Sadly, that's a tragic part of the human condition. There are good people and greedy people, Fay. That's a gross oversimplification for what you just listed, but greed's a large part of it."

"Where I come from, there's a powerful clan of humans named Fergus," she said.

"Fer decades, they've expanded their territory by warring with other clans. It began with the elder, Fionn Fergus, and now continues with his son, Ardal. Fer many who've grown up in that clan, fightin', killin', and takin' what's not theirs is all they've ever known."

She stopped talking while a jogger passed by, then continued again.

"In recent years, Ardal has turned his eye to *my* people and their lands. But he doesn't want to rule the Tuatha Dé Dannan; he wants to extinguish them. I've heard there are many reasons fer this. Some say he was wronged by one of us. There could be some truth to that, fer fairies can be quite mischievous. I've also heard it's simply about our land. Others say it's because fairies have magic and humans don't, which frightens him. Still, others have said it's religious purification because we're not Christians. As ya might imagine, it's been talked about over many a pint."

"Maybe it's a combination of all those things?" Noah suggested.

"That's what I suspect," she agreed.

They were quiet for the moment while the tree frogs

sang their evening songs and another dog walker went by.

"Tell me about the attack that first brought you here," he asked.

"Aye, that was the first attack on me village. We'd heard about other fairy villages bein' destroyed, but they were all close to the borders of Clan Fergus. The Three Sisters are several days' ride away, so we were all taken by surprise. I lost a baby brother and an uncle that night."

"My God, I'm so sorry," he offered sincerely. "It must've been horrible."

"It was," she recalled, "it happened at twilight, just as the evenin' mist was settlin' in. Ya can't imagine the melee of it all: cottages ablaze, farm animals scatterin', people screamin', horses kickin' up dust… twas a nightmare fer sure. The village I live in had a little over three hundred occupants. After that night, a hundred or so were all that was left.

"I was runnin' up and down the Three Sisters headin' fer the ruins of the church I told ya about atop the highest one. A warrior was chasin' me on his horse and—"

"Wait," he cut in. "Why didn't you and your people just fly away?"

"Many tried. But there were archers with deadly accuracy. Some got away. But many didn't. Then there were the wee ones, the children, who couldn't fly yet. Naturally, parents stood their ground to protect them."

He nodded as she went on with her story.

"Just as I got ta the church, I changed ta bird size, which changed me clothin', and flew through the old archway. When I did—"

"W-wait a minute," he interrupted again. "You changed to *bird size?*' What does that mean?"

"That means fairies can become the size of a hummingbird and change their clothin' for freer movement ta fly in the blink of an eye. Surely, you've seen us depicted as tiny creatures."

"Well, yeah," he agreed. "But—but you mean you can *literally* change to the size of a small bird? And your clothing? You could do that, like, *now,* if you wanted?"

"I could, but I'd rather not. It takes a lot of magic, and I've only got so much in your time and place."

"Oh, sure. Understandable," he agreed, not understanding at all. "So, why didn't you transform to bird size and fly away the night of the attack? Surely, an archer can't hit a bird at twilight."

"Some of our people did change and get away. Some were swatted out of the air with pans like so many dragonflies. But who thinks straight, Noah, when you see your friends and family bein' slaughtered? *I* didn't anyway."

He nodded again, noticed they were halfway around the walking trail, and made a suggestion.

"C'mon. Let's go this way. I want to show you something."

They changed course and headed toward a parking lot while Fay went on with her tale.

"As I say, I changed just before goin' through the church's archway. I figured I could hide behind a rock amongst the ruins. But when I flew through the arch, I was struck by a fearful bright light. When it faded, I was flyin' out of the hole of an oak tree on Wanda Harrington's property. Here! In this time! *That's* how I discovered the corridor. Like I said, it was purely by chance."

He stopped walking, squinted, and tried to process all the supernatural information.

"Hold on… the corridor you came through goes from the doorway of a church—"

"Actually, it's just an arch," she corrected. "The door and walls of the church are long gone."

"Whatever… you flew *into* the archway of a Catholic church in the 1400s but flew *out* of a hole in an oak tree in the 2020s?"

"Aye."

He looked at her.

"You do realize what you're saying is absolutely batshit crazy, right?"

"It's not crazy. It's magic. Our elders used ta tell stories of corridors with portals that would open up at certain times that our gods could use. I heard these were usually in burial mounds, but there are powerful conduits in nature, too. I was always told these corridors were only accessible twice a year. During a certain alignment of the moon and stars called 'Shea Karna.' Now, of course, I *know* those two times a year are between the first and second weekend of April and the third and fourth weekend of May. Nearly the exact time of the Georgia Renaissance Festival. Finding out the precise day the portal ta a corridor opens is a matter of trial and error. But once ya know it's open, ya have about twenty-four hours to use it before it closes, and I haven't missed a window yet."

They started to walk again, reached the parking lot, walked across it, and then down a sidewalk on Lula Street.

"If this 'portal' opens twice a year," he wondered, "and you came here by mistake, why haven't others used the same corridor and shown up here?"

"Believe me, I've pondered that one over the years," Fay admitted. "The best I can figure is the gods were in a non-physical form, or at least very small. I was the size of a sparrow, remember? No man or beast could use the portal to the corridor at one end and then fit through the hole in Wanda's tree at the other. A need to *use* the corridor might have something to do with it, too. I'm not an expert at this. I can only tell ya what I've heard in stories and experienced firsthand over these past five seasons of the festival."

"And during all this time, Clan Fergus has been at war with the fairies?"

She nodded.

"Jesus," he said, shaking his head. "There's so much to unpack here; it could fill the Taj Mahal."

"That's in India," she recognized. "As you might imagine, I've studied a lot about yer world to fit in. Wanda has Xfinity."

"Does she know about all this?" he asked.

"She does now. She just learned the whole story two nights ago. But I think she's had suspicions fer a long time that I wasn't—well—normal."

They walked in silence for several seconds. Finally, Fay asked.

"Are ya okay, lad?"

"Not even a little bit," he replied. "But I can't deny the wings, you're flying around… I *did* wonder about your ears, too."

She nodded and smiled slightly. "I've had to tell Wanda some awful fibs to keep me identity secret so I can help those back in me own time."

"Help those back in your own time," he repeated. Then he realized something. "The weapons," he said. "Dale Taylor—you're helping to arm your people."

"You know about that?" she asked, surprised. "How?"

"How do you get weapons through the hole of an old tree?" he countered.

"Magic," she shrugged.

"Rrright… we clearly have a lot more to discuss," he concluded. "But not now. Now, I want to switch subjects and talk about our daughter. And part of that discussion is showing you where and how I live."

He stopped on the sidewalk and gestured to his townhouse.

"This is where ya live?" she asked.

"This is my home. Would you like to come in?"

21

POWER OF THE MOON

Fay stood in Noah's living room, looking the place over. She saw all the stainless steel in the kitchen, his contemporary furniture, his Ghanaian Kpanlogo drum, and the matted landscapes sitting on his wall, then she tilted her head and read some of the titles of the books sitting on the bookshelves. Not surprisingly, a lot were about photography, the national parks, and rock climbing. While she took in her surroundings, Noah eyed her from his kitchen island, putting some milk and sugar into a mug of coffee. The incredible things she had shared with him swirled around in his head like insects buzzing around a backyard light on a hot summer's night. It was so much to believe and take on faith that it gave him a headache. Yet he had to concede with her ears and wings that some of it must be true. But all of it? And if some parts weren't true, which parts? And if some parts were lies, why would she lie? He didn't have the answers, but he knew one thing for sure. What Fay had said earlier in his studio was right: he would never look at the mother of his child the same way again.

"What do you think?" he said, coming over to her with the coffee mug."

"It's very sparse," she observed. "Not a lot of what I'd call comfy touches. But I like yer landscape pictures."

He handed her the coffee. She smiled gratefully.

"Coffee is one of the best things about yer time."

"They don't have coffee in fifteenth-century Ireland?"

She shook her head, taking a sip.

"What do your people drink at breakfast?"

"Beer," she replied.

"I knew I liked the Irish," he quipped. Then he gestured toward the stairs. "I've got three bedrooms upstairs. A master bedroom, then two smaller ones with a Jack-and-Jill."

"A Jack and who?" she asked.

"A Jack-and-Jill. You know—a connecting bathroom?"

"Ya name yer bathrooms?" she wondered.

"No. It's from the nursery rhyme."

She looked at him with a blank expression.

"Y'know," he explained, "Jack and Jill went up the hill to fetch a pail of water?"

"What's that got to do with a privy? And what were

Jack and Jill doin' goin' up a hill? Wasn't there a stream closer to their house?"

"No. There was a well on the hill."

"Who'd be diggin' a well on a hill?" she questioned. "You want yer wells dug on flatter land closer to gardens and houses. Goin' up and down a hill is a lot of carryin'."

"It doesn't matter where the well was," he said. "At least, not in this context. The point is, Jack and Jill were connected. Just like the bathroom connects the two bedrooms. Understand?"

"So, they were married then?" she asked. "Why would they be needin' two bedrooms?"

"No," he replied, frustrated. "They were kids. A brother and sister."

"Well, I still don't understand what goin' up some hill to get water has ta do with bedrooms."

"It's not about the *bedrooms,*" he insisted. "It's about the *bathroom* that *connects* them."

"Namin' toilets after siblings doesn't make sense," she said dismissively, sipping her coffee. "But then, I've learned there are a lot of things in yer language that don't make sense. Why do 'fat chance' and 'slim chance' mean exactly the same thing?"

"What?"

"Why do they call it a 'pineapple' when it doesn't have any pine or apple?"

"Uh—"

"How can yer weather be both 'hot as hell' and 'cold as hell?'"

"Well…"

"Why do they call it 'quicksand' when it takes ya down slowly?"

He looked at her, giving up this line of thought. "Drink your coffee," he finalized.

She took another sip from her mug while he tried to get the conversation back on track.

"I only mentioned the other two bedrooms because if you and Erin wanted to spend time here, they could be fixed up. Right now, one is empty, and the other has some boxes and climbing gear, but I could get furniture, a rocking chair, a dresser, a crib, stuff like that."

She smiled warmly, appreciating the offer.

"Aye, I'd like ta talk ta you about that," she said, moving over to the sofa and sitting down. "I've found no evidence of fairies in this time. That can only mean one thing: the war with Clan Fergus may continue fer a while—perhaps even several more years—but ultimately, I fear they succeed, and me kind will be wiped out. We'll fall the way of your saber-toothed cats and so many different types of animals I've read about on yer internet. Our entire civilization will be lost like the Mayan Empire, or those on Easter Island, or the Sumerians. And because we live on farmlands or in forests, there's no great monuments or temples we're leavin' behind. We'll just be—gone. Like we never existed."

She took another drink of her coffee while he likewise walked over and joined her on the sofa.

"But, maybe, if yer willin', I—I could leave Erin with ya when I go back this time. She hasn't developed any magical powers yet, nor will she if she's away from her homeland because our magic literally comes from our ground. Ya have ta understand, Noah, it was a different Ireland back then. And if she's here, with her da, she'll be safe. And at least one of me kind will survive."

He sat back on the sofa, thinking about her proposal. Concerned that she had overwhelmed him with too much information in the past hour, Fay gave him an option.

"Wanda said that if me story was too much fer ya, she'd be willing to take Erin when it's time fer me ta return if I decided to ta do that."

"No," he found himself saying more quickly than he expected. "No. She should be with me. But, Fay, why even go back? You're safe here, too, y'know."

"It's not just about sendin' back weapons; I've been studyin' what you call guerilla warfare and small strike force tactics, and have ideas ta share. I can't leave me parents, other brother, cousins, and an entire species. I can't leave me homeland when my people need me most. Surely, ya understand that."

"You have another brother?"

She nodded.

"Okay, I understand you don't want to leave your family," he said empathetically, "but you said it yourself: there are no fairies today. So, you already know the outcome. Isn't going back futile?"

"Maybe it's not," she said hopefully, setting her mug down on the coffee table in front of her. "I mean, I'm helpin' ta extend the lifetime of an entire race. And who's ta say history can't be changed? Me first year here, I was just runnin' away. But in the subsequent years, by transportin' weapons back, studyin' guerilla warfare, and advisin' me people, I'm makin' a difference. We're slowin' the clan's advance. We've actually won battles. People are dependin' on me, Noah."

She looked at a clock he had on one of his bookshelves; it was almost 8:30 p.m.

"Speakin' of people dependin' on me, I'd better call an Uber and get back to Erin. I've already missed her bath and bein' tucked in, although Wanda knows some grand bedtime tales." She reached into her jeans pocket and produced a cell phone. "She lends me her cell with the app when I go out. She's still got a landline at her house so we can call each other."

"Don't go," he suggested. "I mean, not just yet."

She smiled faintly. "Haven't I twisted yer brain enough for one night?"

"Gee, let's see: You've told me I'm a father, that you're a fairy, and to prove it, you sprouted really big wings and flew around my studio. Then, you told me you're a time traveler who goes back and forth through a corridor between an old church doorway and a hole in an oak tree. And now, you'd like me to do single parenting for—what—about a year? Have I got everything? Why in the world would any of this twist my brain?"

Her smile broadened, but at the same time, it was etched in sadness. "Now ya understand why I didn't want ta talk about meself, and how, sometimes, it all closes in on ya. Ta the point of where all ya want ta do is, is—"

He leaned over and gently kissed her. This surprised her, but she didn't pull back.

"Lie down with someone," he concluded when their lips parted. "Make it go away for a while."

"Aye," she answered quietly.

They looked at one another longingly for a moment, then their mouths came together again in a more passionate embrace. They had kissed several times before, but never with her truth fully known and never with the mutual knowledge that they had created a child. Fay's lips were full, warm, and soft. Noah's were likewise soft but more forcefully pressed upon hers with equal amounts of desire and fear. Their tongues didn't express words, but each spoke to the other of their need. It wasn't their first kiss, but it was their most important. It was a reawakening. A reaffirming.

After the embrace, she looked at him with her blue eyes becoming moist.

"I dunna think this is a good idea," she whispered. "It has heartache written all over it."

He tenderly kissed her cheek, then her neck.

"You want me to stop?"

She closed her eyes and drew him close.

"Ya do, Noah Galloway, and I'll just die!"

A little over two hours later, Fay awoke naked and alone in Noah's queen-size bed. The scent of their lovemaking still hung in the air as she brushed her long, thick red hair off her face. Looking around, she climbed out of bed, looked toward the master bathroom momentarily, then walked down his upstairs hallway, past a small, empty bedroom, then the Jack-and-Jill bathroom, and spotted him in the second bedroom that had a few packed U-Haul boxes and two coils of ninety-six-foot climbing rope. He stood with his back to her in the dark, likewise naked, staring through some open simulated wood Venetian blinds at a slightly waning moon. She admired his firm butt and muscular legs, then stepped into the room, moved her shoulders slightly, and the fleshy parallel seams in her back opened as her wings came out and extended.

Hearing something behind him, Noah turned to see the incredible vision of a pale-skinned, naked fairy with extended wings walking toward him. He drank in the vision of her body and instinctively knew he'd never see anything more beautiful again.

"What're ya doin'?" she asked warmly. "I woke up alone."

"I understand now why you looked so sad that day when you were kneeling on the bench while I took your picture," he replied. "I told you to look at the lens like it was your lover, like you saw your future in there. Your children. You didn't believe you'd live long enough to have any, did you."

"Or, if I did, I was worried about the future they'd have."

He nodded, then eyed her wings. "What're you doin'? Gonna fly back to Fairburn?"

"I just wanted to free me wings. They're like any other muscles and need a good stretch."

He nodded again, then turned back to the moon.

"Y'know, I was just thinking, every person who's ever lived has seen the moon. Wondered about its power. Its effect on tides, the migration of birds, even our moods. You said the moon has something to do with 'Shea Karna,' as you call it?"

"I'm sure it does," she confirmed. "But it's more than just the moon's monthly phase. During Shea Karna, the opening and closing of the corridor happens every fifty to sixty days, around the first weekend in April and the last weekend in May. Then it's done fer the rest of the year. Each time the corridor opens, it only lasts about twenty-four hours."

"How do you check to see when Shea Karna is happening?"

She came up behind him and wrapped her arms around him while her wings slowly moved back and forth contentedly.

"I have ta go ta the oak tree I came through every day, reduce me size, and fly into its hole. If the other side of the tree is just 'tree,' then nothin's happenin'. But if it's more like water and I can stick a hand through the other side, then it's occurrin'. I've gotten better at the calculatin', but like I've said before, it's trial and error."

"Now that you know this corridor exists and the approximate times of Shea Karna, why not just bring your people here?"

"We'd lose our magic," she said plainly. "Not right away, but eventually. The magic comes from our homeland. That's a land worth fightin' for."

He turned around to face her and wrapped his arms around her waist.

"But, wouldn't the magic still be in the land today?" he asked.

"I've wondered about that," she said. "But I've seen no proof of it. I've not seen anythin' on the internet that would suggest unusual or unexplained occurrences in Ireland. The magic might've disappeared centuries ago because there were no souls left ta use it. Like ink in a bottle for a quill that dries up if not used. The only way ta know is fer me ta go ta Ireland now, spend I don't know how long there ta be sure me magic doesn't diminish, then return ta Georgia and the corridor. If I did, I'd miss Shea Karna and the Tuatha Dé Dannan wouldn't have additional weapons fer an entire year. Who knows what deadly consequences that would have?"

"But, if it's still there," he suggested, "your people could just come through the corridor, be saved, then return to Ireland."

"Think about what yer askin', Noah," she said. "We're thousands upon thousands. That's like askin' all humankind ta live under the sea or move ta the moon for a while. It's easier said than done. And up until two days ago, nobody here knew me true identity. So, everythin' I've been doin', I've been doin' entirely alone."

He nodded, realizing she was handling things the

best way she could. Seeing the worry on her face, he decided to change topics.

"That first night after we made love in my RV," he recalled, "you whispered a strange language in my ear but said the word 'Magic.' Why?"

"Most of what I whispered was Gaeilge, and I was thankin' you. I don't know how sexually experienced you are, Noah, but we fairies tend ta be less inhibited than many of the cultures in your time. Don't be thinkin' ill of me because of it. To us, it's just natural. But when we *do* find someone special, we know it's more than physical. We know it's magic."

"Yeah, but in my RV, you said that you didn't just turn your wings toward any handsome human in the forest."

"That's true. I'd never been with a human before. I didn't say anythin' about other fairies. Besides, didn't I move alright fer ya?"

She glanced down and could feel him becoming aroused again.

"I can see ya formulatin' yer answer," she grinned. "But I really do have ta go. Returnin' to Wanda's much later isn't fair to her, and Erin deserves ta have her mother there when she awakes."

He nodded, understanding.

"Okay. No need to call Uber. I'll drive you home. But let's agree on something. We need to be together now, Fay. You and me. We have to see each other every day. As a couple, as lovers, as parents—whatever label you want to put on it. I don't know what the future holds, but for however long it is, I know ours begins now. We *have* to be together."

She looked into his green eyes, briefly looked toward the window, then nodded.

"Aye, luv… by the light and power of this moon, I agree—we *have* ta be together."

22

IN PLAIN SIGHT

The following morning, Monday, the festival village of New Castle didn't have any visitors since the festival only occurred on Saturday and Sunday, but there was still activity on the grounds. The main gate was made up of three arches with the balcony above it, and on the balcony a couple of construction workers were replacing spindles. Wanda stood on the ground in front of the arches, watching what the workers were doing. She wore her usual peasant blouse, jeans with colorful patches on the butt and legs, and held a walkie-talkie in her hand. The cell phone Fay had with her the previous night was now on her belt.

"I've got green paint to match the other spindles," she called. "But it's about five years old. So, if it doesn't match, we'll have to repaint the entire front of the balcony."

"It should match," one of the workers called.

"I hope so," Wanda replied, "I've got a half-dozen other things I wanted you guys to work on today."

She heard someone approaching and turned to see Noah walking toward her from the parking lot. He wore boat shoes, jeans, a t-shirt, and a red zip-up hoodie since the mid-morning April air was still a little on the cool side.

"Noah Galloway," she said with a little acknowledging smile.

"Hi, Wanda," he replied, approaching. "Sorry if I disturbed your evening by getting Fay home a little late last night."

She casually put a finger to her lips because nobody who worked at the festival knew where Fay lived. He nodded as he came closer, but it didn't matter. The workers on the balcony hadn't heard him and were talking among themselves.

"So, what's new?" she asked, knowing his entire life and knowledge of reality had changed in the past twelve hours.

"Nothin'," he shrugged, underplaying it. "What's new with you?"

"Same ol', same ol'," she answered with the same enthusiasm.

They looked at one another for a moment, then their smiles widened for the incredible secret they shared.

"You alright?" she asked.

"No… you?"

"No," she agreed, but neither seemed unhappy with what they knew.

"What're you doing here?" she asked.

"I guess… I just wanted to drive out and get verification about Fay's story from you personally."

She nodded. "I understand. *Boy,* do I understand!"

He looked up at the workers, then leaned into her quietly. "She sprouted wings and flew around my studio to convince me she was who she was. What did she do to convince you?"

"Nothing so dramatic," she replied, just as hushed. "She just told me her story, and suddenly, things I've wondered about for years fell into place." After a moment, another thought struck her. "Does Cole Huggins know about her?"

"No. But he does know I'm Erin's father, and he also knows about weapons made by Dale Taylor, one of your artisans, being dug up on an Irish farm from a battle that happened centuries ago."

"How does Cole know about Dale?" she asked, surprised.

"Cole was at your office the same day the FBI paid you a visit. He reads lips and was sitting in his car right in front of your office window when the agents were talking to you. He didn't mean to eavesdrop, but he was making some calls, and it just sort of happened. Then, he told me."

"God, that's right," she remembered. "He reads lips."

Noah glanced up at the workers again, then back to her.

"Look, I don't want to interrupt your day. I guess I

just needed to see somebody who—well—knows what *I* know."

"C'mon," she said, taking him by the arm and walking under the balcony, through the center archway, and into the festival village. Just beyond the front gate was a little pond with lily pads, frog figurines, and water shooting from their mouths. The fountains helped to mask their voices.

"She, she did tell you everything, right?" he asked, returning to conversational volume.

"You mean that she's a Tuatha Dé Dannan?" Wanda replied. "That she recently arrived from the year 1501? That she travels back and forth through time using some sort of corridor that defies all science, and she first discovered this corridor by mistake when somebody was trying to kill her in 1497?"

"Yeah… I didn't know the exact years, though," he said.

"And that you're Erin's father?" she continued. "Yes. I know all this. And *she* now knows that the FBI has been made aware that weapons made by Dale Taylor were found on a battlefield with over five hundred years of rust on them. I'm not having her work the festival this year just in case they come back with a warrant to go through my employee records and start interviewing cast members."

"Do you think they will?" he asked.

"Absolutely. It's too big a mystery to leave alone. They'll lay the warrant on me during a busy weekend to get me all flustered and make me cooperate. At least, that's what *I'd* do."

He looked her over. "You don't like the government much, do you?"

"The way politicians serve their own agendas instead of people? Don't get me started," she replied. She looked around. "I've got to walk down by the Tourney Bridge. I've got another crew working there. C'mon."

As they walked, she used her walkie-talkie and called an associate named Brandon to say she was on her way.

"So—you *do* believe her story, then?" Noah asked, wanting verification again.

"I've known Fay longer than you," Wanda answered. "I figured out some time ago there was something special about her. And I never bought that story about her ears being a birth defect."

"Is that what she told you?" he asked, amused.

"Originally," she nodded.

He chuckled. "Well, that's at least more realistic than being a fairy… I mean, it's just *so incredible!*"

"Is it?" she wondered. "We've all heard that legends and myths are based upon some degree of fact. Legends are based on known history, while myths are based on religious or faith-based beliefs. For instance, witches flying on brooms. There was a time when witches were considered valuable members of a community. They studied herbology, delivered babies, and even helped crops to grow. They used to straddle brooms and leap through newly planted fields. The belief was the crops would grow to the highest leap of the witch. Today, of course, that's expanded into witches flying around the sky."

"Interesting," Noah mused.

They walked past a directional sign with a unicorn on it. Wanda gestured to it.

"Then, there's unicorns." She clipped the walkie-talkie to her jeans pocket, grabbed her cell phone, and began to look something up.

"While there's no record of a horse growing a single horn out of the middle of its head, there have been plenty of genetic misfires in nature that have produced a horn in the middle of an animal's skull: cows, goats, elk, and deer." She paused and showed Noah a photo of a deer she had called up on her phone with a horn in the middle of its head. "So, it's easy to see how the legend of the unicorn came about."

She clicked her phone off, and they started to walk again. "How about the Loch Ness monster?" she continued. "The modern legend began in 1933 when a local couple claimed to have seen an enormous animal rolling and plunging on the surface of Loch Ness. Several explorations of the loch have revealed no monster, although, in 2019, researchers did announce that the water contained large amounts of eel DNA. So, could Nessie have been a giant eel? Scientists say it's plausible."

"I understand what you're saying," Noah conceded. "Many things have a basis of truth, and maybe we should be open-minded enough to accept that some legends and myths could be real. But if there was an entire civilization of fairies that once existed and were wiped out, wouldn't we have found *something* to back it up? A skeleton with wings, a skull with pointed ears, or—"

"Maybe we will," Wanda cut in. "They just found an ancient battlefield on that farmer O'Connell's land in Ireland. And new civilizations are still being discovered, Noah. In December of 2022, an international team of researchers from the United States, France, and Guatemala found a very large two-thousand-year-old Mayan civilization in northern Guatemala, complete with some sort of sporting field, that nobody even knew existed."

"How the hell do you know all this?" he asked.

"I work at a place that sells fantasy. It's my job to know about myths and legends. Besides, I get *Nat Geo.*"

They were quiet for a few moments while she returned her cell phone to her belt and put the walkie-talkie back in her hand. Then she looked him over.

"Don't you *want* to believe Fay?" she asked.

"With all my heart," he replied. "There's just so much I don't get."

"Arthur C. Clark said: 'Magic is science we don't understand yet.' So, what does your heart tell you?"

"To stay close to her. I want to be with her, get to know her and Erin, and help them in any way I can."

"Do that then," she said simply.

They stopped talking for a few moments again, then Noah inquired where Fay was, and Wanda replied she was at her house with Erin. As they walked, they passed a few people on the grounds. Some were vendors unpacking boxes of merchandise for the shops. In the far distance, a Coca-Cola delivery man with a dolly full of canned soft drinks was heading for the food court. In between, closer to Noah and Wanda, was a worker in gray overalls picking up trash scattered around from the weekend crowd. He carried a trash picker and a thirteen-gallon plastic bag about half full. He wore a ballcap, gloves, and had his mostly gray hair tied back in a five-inch ponytail. He had a three-inch white beard, a leathery, wrinkled face, and piercing gray eyes. The clothes he was wearing weren't his. They belonged to Darius Larkin. He watched Noah and Wanda like he watched everything in this strange land called New Castle. He didn't know where Fay was or if she was affiliated with the two people he was observing, but he knew from Darius showing him the internet that this was a place where a fairy could hide in plain sight.

23

OAKLAND

Three days after Noah and Fay had decided to be together, Noah, Fay, and Erin, in a stroller, were walking through Oakland Cemetery in the heart of downtown Atlanta. Opened in 1850, it was the final resting place for over seventy thousand Georgians. But it was more than just a cemetery; it was also a lush city park featuring mature trees, manicured shrubs and hedges, and too many flower beds planted on the tops of old graves to count. Noah's mom had once said, "If you took a botanical garden and put it on top of a graveyard, you'd wind up with Oakland Cemetery." True, it was a place for the dead, but between immovable tombstones chiseled in rock and darkened by the decades, there was a swirling current of life. Young women jogged through the property, amateur photographers sharpened their skills there, catching the Atlanta skyline framed by white dogwood blossoms, and families had picnics there. More weddings took place on its forty-eight acres than many would imagine. It was on the National Registry of Historic Places. In April and May, there was nowhere more blooming and beautiful in Atlanta.

Erin was enjoying the outing in a brand-new stroller her father had bought. Noah had a camera bag tucked in the stroller's undercarriage, and Fay wore a breezy summer dress and a straw hat with a wide floppy brim to conceal her pointed ears. It was a beautiful sunny day with the temperature in the mid-seventies, and the three of them looked like any other young family out for an urban adventure.

"I have ta admit," Fay said, pushing the stroller, "when ya told me ya wanted to take us to a cemetery, I wasn't very keen on the notion, but I can see this is a pretty place."

"It's quite famous," Noah said. "Six Georgia governors and twenty-five Atlanta mayors are buried here. Then there are people like Margaret Mitchell, who wrote *Gone With The Wind,* golf legend Bobby Jones, Kenny Rogers—"

"I don't know those names," Fay admitted while they walked.

"Kenny Rogers? *The Gambler?* You gotta know when to fold 'em?"

"Fold what? Did he own a laundry?"

"No."

"Kenny Rogers—is that another name for a type of toilet, like a Jack-and-Jill?" she joked.

"He recorded a famous song called *The Gambler.* I'll sing it to Erin sometime."

"Oh, she'd like that." She looked down at her blue-eyed daughter. "You'd like Da ta sing ta ya, wouldn't ya, darlin?"

The baby looked at her mother, then at Noah, and smiled.

"I like that you want her to call me Da," he said.

"And why shouldn't she? She's your daughter," Fay said plainly.

"I know—but—it's just nice."

They walked past some people speaking French. Fay greeted them with a, "Bonjour." There were always a lot of different languages and cultures in Atlanta.

"A movie Tuesday night," she recalled, "the aquarium yesterday, and now a promenade through this place. Ya don't have to be entertainin' us every single day, y'know."

"Yesterday and today had ulterior motives," he admitted. "I'm shooting the mayor for *Atlanta Magazine* next week, and his PR person said he wanted to be shot in a few key landmark locations. So, I'm actually doing some scouting. After we leave here, I want to check out the Krog Street Tunnel. It's not very far."

"Aye, I've noticed you haven't spoken much about work. Is everythin' alright with yer picture makin'?"

"I'm not as busy as I used to be," he confessed. "A celebrity—a well-known singer named Bobby Dragon—has been slamming me on social media, and it's taken a toll on my business."

"Why is he 'slammin' you?"

"We had an altercation."

"What's that mean?"

"A fight. Well, kind of."

"Well, either ya did, or ya didn't," Fay reasoned.

"It was a little fight… he took a swing at me, and I pushed him into a door. Then, another singer I was working for at the time pointed a canister of mace at both of us and broke the thing up. Later that night, she fired me from her tour."

"Mace," she acknowledged. "I know what that is—a type of liquid weapon. Burns the eyes. What were ya and this Dragon fella fightin' about?"

"The other singer," he answered honestly.

She slowed down her pace, becoming concerned. "Is this someone ya have feelins for?"

"You know what Covid is?"

"Aye, 'twas a plague."

"A virus, right. Anyway, this Bobby Dragon was exposed to it and showed up one day during a photoshoot I was doing for the singer. He wanted to see her, and I wouldn't let him because I didn't want to put her health at risk. He didn't like that, and a scuffle occurred."

Fay thought for a moment as they continued.

"So, ya were really tryin' ta protect the singer ya were workin' for, then."

"Yes, but I overreacted. The virus isn't as dangerous as it once was. Still, I didn't want her to get sick."

Fay stopped the stroller as Erin became a little fussy.

She asked the baby if she wanted a drink. The child looked at her, not understanding. So, she repeated the question in Gaeilge. The child nodded, and Fay gave her a box of cherry-flavored water.

"Our daughter is learning two languages at the same time?" he asked.

"Me people are gentle but very intelligent and good at pickin' up languages," she replied.

Once Erin was happily sipping away, Fay continued with her questions.

"This singer ya were protectin'... is she the one ya once told me about, Z-Rae?"

"Yeah."

"The one who changes her hair color all the time?"

"Yeah."

Fay thought for another moment.

"Is there somethin' goin' on between you two?"

"Well, I don't like Bobby Dragon, I can tell you that," Noah answered, evading the question.

"That's not what I asked," Fay said, arching a jealous eyebrow.

Noah looked beyond her to see a large statue of an angel with a raised sword above its head. Beyond that were some blooming cherry blossoms and daffodils, and beyond that was the city's skyline.

"That's a cool perspective," he said, reaching for his camera bag under the stroller. "Would you mind being a model while I line up a shot?"

"Can I take Erin with me?" she asked.

"Absolutely."

She waited until Erin was done drinking, then put her water box away and picked her up from the stroller while Noah retrieved his camera bag and pulled out his Nikon. Fay asked where he wanted them positioned, and Noah instructed them to stand in front of some red tulips about nine feet away. As she moved in that direction, Erin became fascinated with her mother's big straw hat and started to pull it off her head, momentarily exposing Fay's pointed ears. Fay smiled, said, "No, honey, leave Ma's hat alone," then adjusted her hair and hat to hide her ears again.

"Will her ears become pointed?" Noah asked, noting that the top of Erin's ears were rounded like his.

"I honestly don't know," she replied. "Children of Tuatha Dé Dannan are born with rounded ears, but they start to grow points around twelve months. She's nearly fifteen months, and that hasn't happened yet. Seams on her back for wings usually start to appear around twenty months. That hasn't happened, either, but it's still early."

"If she stays here with me after Shea Karna, will anything with her ears and wings happen at all?" he wondered.

"Again, I don't know… she might physically develop as a fairy, but she wouldn't have any magical powers. She wouldn't be able to fly if her wings sprouted. So, I don't know how nature would reconcile that."

He nodded as he snapped a lens onto the Nikon, then took the cap off and lined up the shot.

"Move a little to your left until I tell you to stop," he requested.

She moved until she and Erin were in the foreground, the angel with the sword was in the mid-background to the right, and the city skyline was a half mile away in the far background.

"Perfect," he said.

Seeing Fay hold Erin through his viewfinder on this bright, beautiful day, it wasn't lost on Noah that he was taking the first portrait of his family, and a warm rush of affection washed over him. As for Fay, she smiled genuinely at first for the camera, but as Noah changed position and clicked off a second picture, then a third and a fourth, he noticed her eyes were darting around with an increasing sadness.

"What?" he asked, his head popping up from behind the camera. "What is it?"

"All these people," she said, looking around. "Ya can see their names, when they lived… husbands, wives, and children. But for the Tuatha Dé Dannan, there isn't a city, monument, or even a tree with a carvin' on it ta remember them by. They're just gone like a wisp of smoke, reduced to children's stories and garden figurines in someone's backyard."

She turned around and looked at the angel with the sword raised above her head.

"I've got to buy more weapons, Noah. If Wanda doesn't want me workin' the festival or dealin' with Dale Taylor, that's fine. But I've got to buy more weapons."

"How're you going to do that?" he asked, lowering his camera and indicating he was done.

"I've got some coins. Me people have taken up a collection," she said, carrying Erin back to him. "In my time, it's not a lot of money, but in your time, they're valuable antiques. I can buy the weapons online through other sources and have 'em delivered at Wanda's now that she knows the truth about me. Can ya help me with this?"

"You can have 'em delivered at my place, too," he said, smiling at Erin as she pointed to him. "But how do you get hundreds of weapons into the hole of an oak…" his voice trailed off, remembering what she had casually mentioned when they were walking in Lilburn City Park. "Your magic. You reduce their size. That's why you want to preserve it."

While Noah was with Fay and Erin in Oakland Cemetery, back in Fairburn Julie Downey, Piper Larkin's sister was pulling into the driveway of Darius and Piper's driveway deeply concerned. She and Piper worked at the same Walmart, but her sister hadn't been showing up for work or answering her cell. She was thirty-six, smaller than Piper, and hopped out of her Kia Soul with the determination of a woman on a mission. A determination that grew more intense as she eyed the cab of Darius' semi rig and her sister's Ford Fiesta as she approached the front door. After a few loud knocks, Darius opened the front door. His face was calm and mostly expressionless.

"Hi, Julie," he greeted.

"What the fuck's goin' on, Darius?" she demanded, getting straight to the point. "Piper quit her job at Walmart, and she's not even the one who quit? *You* called it in for her?"

"She asked me to," he explained. "She's been ill."

"Is that why she's not answering her cell?"

"Yes."

"What kind of illness? Has she been to a doctor? I wanna see her."

"I don't think that's a good idea," he warned.

Julie took a step forward and pushed him aside. "Get out of the way, Darius. I wanna see my sister!"

The visitor walked into the small house and paused when she stepped into the living room, startled by what she saw. The first thing she noticed was the indentation of the broken drywall. But there were other odd things as well. Several sheets of yellow paper from a legal pad were taped to the wall with lists on them that had been written with a Sharpie. One list had the names of Darius' family members. Another had a listing of his trucking contracts. Another had Piper's family members, including Julie's name. Another was a list of utilities that Darius and Piper would owe monthly payments to, like electric, garbage, phone, and gas. Still another was a list of the weekend events at the Georgia Renaissance Festival. Another was a list of general facts that read: "The 21st century," "The United States of America," "The state of Georgia," "The town of Fairburn," and so on. It seemed like these were lists of people, things, and places that someone would need to know about if they wanted to be familiar with their environment. Then she looked to her left and saw a large stack of dirty dishes in the sink. On the counter, separating the kitchen from the living room, were empty liquor bottles, Darius' credit cards, and a considerable stack of twenty and fifty dollar bills like he'd made several withdrawals from the bank.

Julie took all this in for a moment, slack-jawed while her mind raced with possibilities, none of which were good. She turned to her nearly expressionless brother-in-law.

"Where's my sister, Darius?" she asked seriously.

"You must be Julie," she heard a stranger's voice say.

She turned to the other side of the living room and a short hallway that led to the back of the house. Coming from the master bedroom was the horzikaan, who spoke English for her benefit. He was carrying his staff and wearing clothes that she recognized were Darius'.

"Who the hell are you?" she asked. Then, she reached for her cell phone.

"I'm callin' 911," she announced.

"Stop!" he commanded. "Julie, look at me."

The wizard pointed to his gray eyes, and she suddenly found herself frozen and compelled to look into the hypnotic gaze of the stranger standing in Piper and Darius' living room.

"Julie, I want ya ta listen ta me carefully," he instructed with his Irish brogue. "You'll be tellin' everyone who asks that you've seen Piper. You'll be tellin' everyone that you've seen her and that she's been ill, but she's on the mend. You'll also be tellin' 'em that she wants to take a break from work and travel more with Darius in his truckin' job. If anyone asks why they can't get ahold of her, you'll say her old communication device is broken, and she's gettin' a new one, but she can't keep the same number. You'll say she'll be sharin' her new number with everyone real soon. Have ya got all that, Julie?"

The young woman nodded.

"That's grand... now, ya gotta be convincin' when ya tell people this. If yer not, you'll find yerself breakin' into an awful fever, and ya don't want that now, do ya?"

"No," Julie said blankly.

"Good girl. Now, when ya leave here, everythin' will be fine. You'll feel fresh as a daisy. All the worry about your sister will be put ta rest. Ya understand?"

"I understand."

"Well, then, off ya go."

Julie turned and left the house. Darius watched her go but showed little visible interest one way or another.

"That's how we'll be handling things, lad," the magical visitor said. "One inquiry at a time. But let's hope there's not many."

The horzikaan turned, leaned his staff against Darius' La-Z-Boy recliner, then clasped his hands together with satisfaction hearing Juli's Kia start up outside.

"Now then," he said, changing subjects. "I think maybe a nice piece of beef for dinner. I'd like to learn about this thawin' of meat I saw online. Get somethin' from the freezer, will ya?"

Darius turned and went into the kitchen. He opened a door into the garage and turned on some lights. In the garage was an older Kenmore fourteen cubic-square-foot horizontal freezer. He opened it and retrieved an eye-of-round roast, but before closing it, he paused, clearly struggling with himself to fight the spell he was under as he eyed the grayish-white body of his wife in the freezer with half of her skull caved in.

24

THE SECOND SATURDAY

On the second of the nine Saturdays for this particular season of the Georgia Renaissance Festival, the theme for the weekend was Pet Weekend. And unlike the opening weekend, the weather was beautiful, mostly cloudless, and the temperature was in the low seventies. The front gates opened promptly at 10:30 a.m., but Wanda called as many wandering ambassadors, stage performers, and shop vendors as she could to the Halfwit Harbor Stage around 9:45 for an impromptu meeting. While trumpeters and drummers serenaded the growing crowd waiting outside the front arched gates for entrance, Wanda addressed her employees.

"I want to thank everybody for coming on very short notice," she said, standing on the stage in a flowery summer dress and speaking to about fifty people. The festival employed over two hundred, but so close to opening, not everyone could take the time for such a meeting unless it was an emergency.

"I'll keep this short," she began. "We're in the business of making sure our guests have a wonderful, entertaining time. That's our mission. But there's a difference between paying guests wanting an enchanting day and people who are on the grounds because they have some sort of hidden agenda. I'm talking about people who may want to ask you about certain cast members or seek out proprietary information. I know everyone here on a first-name basis. I've known most of you for several years. So, I don't think it's a stretch to say that we're a professional family, and, as a family, I'm asking you to be cautious. Look out for one another, and keep our family's privacy in mind."

"What are you talking about, Wanda?" an EMT asked. "Are you talking about the cops who might be looking for someone working here?"

"I didn't say anything about the authorities," Wanda responded in a cagey manner. "I'm just saying there's a difference between paying guests and people pokin' around trying to learn about the inner workings of this festival and the people who make it special. I *am* saying I want you to recognize the difference between a casual question and an interrogation. Don't lie, but be respectful when sharing information about your fellow cast members. We're entertainers and entrepreneurs, but that doesn't mean our lives are open books for just anyone to read."

"Sounds like the cops are lookin' for someone,"

Orrie, the gondola-pushing daredevil from the Sea Dragon Swing, concluded.

"Who are you worried about, Wanda?" Harry Toadel, the horn maker, asked.

"Let me just say: I respect the talents and integrity of every person here. Let me also say I don't know if people will be asking questions and trying to interrogate some of you this weekend, next weekend, or the next. All I have is a gut feeling. But I *can* tell you this: if people do come around asking questions, it has *nothing* to do with a crime or breaking the law. Nothing!"

"Oh, so it's a domestic thing?" Theo, the elf ear vendor, asked.

"Not necessarily," George, his store partner, chimed in, "could be an immigration thing."

"If it's an immigration thing, then it's a crime," Theo countered. "She just said there wasn't a crime involved."

"Okay, okay… don't speculate," Wanda said. "Just be aware. Thanks for your attention, and have a great day."

She walked off the stage while a few people stood there, more confused than informed.

"Well—*that* really helped to calm my nerves before we open," the gray gargoyle ambassador said sarcastically.

"If you read between the lines, I think what she said was pretty thoughtful," Dale Taylor, the weapon-making blacksmith, noted.

The gargoyle ignored him, dipped a gray hand into a

pocket on his costume, and pulled out two Delta-8 gummies. "This is definitely a two-gummy morning."

An hour later, Cole Huggins was over at Jacob's Ladder taking photos. The attraction was a pirate ship built to look like it had mostly sunken into the ground, with its bow poking up from the dirt and a ladder made out of rope that ran from the ground to a sailing mast at about a twenty-degree angle. The rope was about four feet off the ground at its highest, and the incline wasn't very steep, but it was, nevertheless, a challenge of agility. The rope ladder was anchored only to a single point at each end and could easily spin around if balance wasn't maintained. The idea was that a guest would pay for three attempts, climb up and down the ladder without losing their balance, and hop into the soft sand beneath it. It was a midway ride of the very best type, homemade and not mechanical. But year after year, it challenged both children and adults alike. Even the festival employee demonstrating how "easy" it was fell off the ladder in three out of ten demonstrations.

Cole's picture taking was interrupted when he spotted Noah coming toward him with Fay at his side and Erin in her stroller. He knew she was back in town and that his studio partner had been spending time with her and Erin, and although she'd officially introduced herself to him the previous weekend, he didn't recognize her today because she was incognito. As they came nearer, Noah quietly reminded Fay to keep her mouth visible to Cole's eyes so he could read her lips.

"Hey, man," Noah greeted. "Getting some good stuff?"

"It's the same ol' stuff year after year, but I never get tired of shooting it. Especially the kids."

Noah gestured to Fay. "You know Fay, of course."

"I do. But I wouldn't have known it's you if you hadn't been with Noah." He was referring to her jeans, yellow blouse, sandals, long black wig, sunglasses, and a hat to cover her ears. He smiled at the baby in the stroller approvingly. "And this must be Erin."

"It is," Fay said. "She's fourteen months. Almost fifteen."

"She looks like you," Cole acknowledged. "More you than Noah, which is very fortunate."

"I agree," Noah grinned.

"So, you're not working today?" Cole asked her.

"No. I'm not workin' the festival at all this year."

"Oh? I saw you in street clothes last weekend too, but just figured you hadn't changed into your costume yet."

"She's keeping a low profile," Noah confirmed. "We shouldn't be here at all, except Fay wanted to walk through the village one more time this season while it was active."

"Tis like a second home ta me," she confirmed.

"Yeah," Cole nodded. "Wanda made an interesting speech this morning before the festival opened about employees being discreet if they felt they were being questioned by someone about another employee. She didn't name names or give specifics, but I figured it had something to do with Fay."

"How did people react?" Fay asked.

"To tell you the truth, I think people were confused by it. But it was well intended."

"Speaking of which," she said, "I understand you played a role in helpin' Noah and meself find our way back to one another. I'm very grateful for that, Cole. For both meself and me daughter."

"Thanks… I really didn't do that much. But there *were* some very interesting side topics that arose out of me trying to reconnect you two."

"Yeah," Noah answered quickly, knowing he was referring to the artifacts found on farmer O'Connell's land in Ireland. "And it's all easily explained. But let's do it over drinks or something later this week. I don't want Fay to hang around here long, and you're working."

"Sure," Cole replied, understanding. "Sounds good. I look forward to those 'easy explanations.' We'll circle back at the studio or get together for drinks."

"Absolutely," Noah promised. "Catch ya later."

"Very nice ta see ya, Cole," Fay smiled. "And thank ya again!"

After they had moved on, Fay quietly asked. "What're ya gonna tell him about the weapons found on O'Connell's farm?"

"No fucking idea," he admitted.

Just as Noah, Fay, and Erin were moving on, back at the festival's main gate, Wanda, with Lancelot on a leash, had been called over to the ticket booth on her walkie-talkie, where two men were waiting for her. She recognized them instantly. They weren't wearing costumes and were casually dressed.

"Hello, Wanda," the blond-haired one greeted. "Do you remember us?"

"Of course," she replied. "You're Special Agent Jacobs, and your friend is Special Agent Grimble. This is Pet Weekend, your favorite themed weekend, Special Agent Jacobs. And yours, Special Agent Grimble, is Viking Weekend."

"Good memory," Grimble nodded.

"Yeah, well, the FBI doesn't come and talk to me every day," she admitted.

"And who's this?" Jacobs asked, petting her dog.

"Lancelot," she replied. "But since neither of you have your dogs or are wearing costumes, I'm guessing this is official business."

"It is," Jacobs verified. He reached into his back pocket and produced a folded piece of paper. "I have a warrant to seize all of your employee records. Based on what we find, we may want to interview some of your employees. If you have any questions, you're certainly welcome to call your attorney and have him review it. In the meantime, we have the right to retrieve those records, and we want to go to your office right now and get them."

The blond agent handed the warrant over to Wanda, who examined it.

"Wouldn't you two do better concentrating on Dale Taylor?" she suggested.

"Don't you worry about Mr. Taylor," Grimble grinned. "We have another warrant for his sales receipts and financial information."

She looked at the two men. "You want me to leave the festival grounds *now*? At our busiest time of day?"

"Please," Jacobs smiled.

She looked at both men exasperated, rolled her eyes, then grabbed the walkie-talkie off her belt.

At the same time this happened, the horzikaan wandered around another part of the grounds, unconcerned. He wore his dark hooded robe with the hood down, ancient sturdy boots, and carried his bejeweled staff. His mostly white hair was loose, and his gray eyes moved back and forth, scanning the grounds and people like some medieval Terminator looking for his target. Seeing two young female guests dressed in long period skirts and corsets approach, he raised a long, pointed fingernail indicating he wanted them to stop.

"Tell me, beautiful ladies," he said, speaking English in a low, growling voice that was trying to be friendly. "Have ya seen any fairies strollin' about? Especially one that might be wearin' a very realistic costume?"

They both shook their heads.

"Maybe one that was carryin' a wee lass?"

They both said "No" and shook their heads again.

Without saying another word, he moved on.

He walked for another couple of minutes, then paused at a kiosk selling sunglasses.

"What be these?" he asked a costumed salesman.

"Sunglasses," the young salesman said.

The horzikaan lifted a pair of John Lennon-style wire-rimmed glasses with blue lenses off a rack and examined them.

"And what do they do?" he asked.

"Uh, block the sun," the salesman responded, not sure if the wizard was trying to be funny. The horzikaan looked around and noticed many people had sunglasses on, so he opened them and slipped them on his head. Suddenly, everything he saw had a distinct blue tint. Surprised, he quickly removed them from his head, looked at them for a moment, then nodded.

"Amusing toy," he concluded.

He turned and began to walk away carrying the sunglasses.

"Uh—they're $19.95," the salesman said, stepping quickly over. "And I don't take cash. Only credit or debit."

"What be yer name, lad?"

"Peter."

"Peter, look at me," the horzikaan said, pointing to his gray eyes. "Yer makin' a gift ta me."

The salesman stared blankly at the old man, then said: "Oh. Okay."

The horzikaan smiled a little, slipped the glasses on again, then walked away.

A couple of minutes later, he approached a store that featured nothing but dragons. Inside were paintings of dragons, statues of dragons, warrior shields with dragons, dragon windchimes, and more. He paused for a moment to watch two women in their twenties standing outside of the store and looking at a wall display of dragon stepping stones. Each twelve-by-twelve square stone had a different type of dragon embossed on it and a salesman was explaining the thinking behind each image.

"There's a different dragon for every lawn and garden setting. For example, if you've got bamboo on your property, you might consider an Asian Dragon stepping stone. If you get a lot of nightcrawlers after it rains, a Wyrm Dragon stepping stone. If you've got poison ivy on your land, a Wyvern Dragon. They've got a deadly, venomous tail."

One of the women who had short, spiky hair, put her arm around her partner's waist, intrigued. "Got anything for a disapproving mother-in-law?" she asked.

"Hydra Dragon," the salesman replied without missing a beat. "It's got three heads."

Both women grinned while the other one pointed to a stepping stone featuring a dragon with the head of a rooster. "And what's this one for?"

"Cockatrice," the salesman replied. "For properties facing east."

Both women reviewed all of the choices, then the one with the spiky hair observed: "This is a lot of thought for something that never existed."

"Don't be ta sure!" the horzikaan announced. Then, he turned and continued on his way.

"About what?" the other woman asked.

"That dragons weren't real," he called back.

Within another couple of minutes, the horzikaan came to some kids with their dogs being entertained by a juggler wearing a court jester costume complete with a multi-pointed hood with bells. After his routine was done and the children had moved on, the robed figure approached.

"Fool, I'm searchin' for a fairy. A very realistic lookin' one."

The jester cocked his belled head, noticing the older man's Irish brogue.

"She's Irish, like you, right?"

The horzikaan's eyebrows raised with surprise because this was the first time anyone had acknowledged that Fay might be on the grounds.

"Aye, lad," he nodded. "Irish."

The jester looked around. "I don't remember her name. I haven't seen her this year, but I know who you mean. Red hair, real pretty."

"That's the one."

"I'm not sure she's working this year, but you might ask Orrie. He had the hots for her once upon a time."

"The hots?"

"He liked her," the jester clarified. "I heard he asked her out several times."

"And where might this Orrie be?" the horzikaan asked.

The jester pointed to the Sea Dragon Swing. "That's him over there. The one with the braids and no shirt."

Without saying anything further, the wizard walked toward the Sea Dragon Swing, where Orrie was assisting a group of costumed visitors out of the gondola. As in previous years, he had glitter on his bare chest and wore bright-green tights with pirate boots featuring big brass buckles. He also still had his long braids that hung over his shoulders.

"I'll be havin' words with ya, lad," the visitor announced as he approached.

"Whoa," Orrie greeted, eyeing the horzikaan's clothing. "Kinda doin' a Dumbledore thing today, huh? I dig your staff with the jewel."

"I believe you know a particular fairy who wanders about these grounds. She speaks with the same kind of tongue as meself."

"Do you work here?" Orrie asked.

"I need ta know if you know where this fairy is," the older one insisted. "Red hair. Very pretty."

The bare-chested man paused for a moment, remembering Wanda's speech earlier that morning, then responded.

"No, man. I don't know of any one particular fairy. But there's plenty wandering around."

"This one would look especially authentic," the wizard continued.

"Yeah? Well, a lot of people have authentic-looking costumes around here," Orrie replied.

"This is a lass I believe you were interested in seein' socially."

"No, man," Orrie repeated, wondering if this person might be Fay's father or another relation. Either way, he decided he didn't feel the need to cooperate.

Still insistent, the stranger put a firm hand on Orrie's bare arm. The younger man looked down at the long, pointed fingernails and didn't like being grabbed.

"Orrie, look at me. Tell me where she is."

Unfazed, Orrie removed the intrusive hand. "Look—you want a ride? It's five bucks. If not, I'm workin'."

The horzikaan looked at the festival employee sternly. "It's not wise ta refuse me, boy."

"It's not wise to call me 'boy' old man," Orrie shot back. "Run along and toddle on back to Hogwarts."

The younger one turned away and attended to a family of four that wanted a ride on the swing. The wizard meanwhile pulled up his hood and walked away, heading for an area not far from where Noah had taken his after-hour portraits of key cast members two years earlier. The horzikaan was confused; Orrie should have succumbed to his hypnotic powers. But then, he realized he was wearing sunglasses. Taking them off and looking at them, he concluded the lenses must've shielded his magic. He wouldn't make that mistake again and tossed them to the ground.

When the family of four had been seated in the Sea Dragon Slide, Orrie went to the front of the gondola where the dragon head was and began to push. He was wiry but strong and in great physical shape from the considerable energy it took to start and stop the momentum of the large gondola. Within a minute, he had it soaring back and forth like a giant green pendulum while the passengers smiled with delight. Within another minute, he began his daredevil maneuver of extending his arms and suddenly bending backward as the oncoming head of the swinging dragon missed his body by mere inches. It was dangerous for sure, but a very practiced routine. He did it once, twice, then a third time as the passengers screamed with each near miss, which Orrie loved.

As the gondola receded and Orrie prepared to do his move a fourth time, he suddenly found his legs frozen and his feet slowly skidding forward as if a gust of wind had struck him from behind on an icy lake. Not understanding, he quickly turned his head to see the robed figure in the distance extending his staff toward him. Its jewel was illuminated, and a beam of light emanated from it. Orrie tried to move his legs and step back from the weird force field that held him. While he struggled, the beam from the jewel suddenly flickered, and he could finally take a half step back. But not before the nose of the dragon came swinging at him and grazed his arms and chest. Even though it wasn't a full body blow, the force of the wooden gondola, weighing hundreds of pounds, sent Orrie flying backward in the air nearly twelve feet. He landed hard on his back and lay motionless as the screams of delight from the passengers suddenly turned into shrieks of horror. As this happened, the horzikaan, still with an extended arm, looked at his staff, not understanding its malfunction. Then, he quickly turned and walked away.

25

PATIENCE

At 6:30 that evening, the horzikaan stepped out of Darius and Piper Larkin's front door and looked around at his isolated and rural surroundings, which were full of golden light. He was wearing one of Darius' sweatsuits and a pair of his sneakers, had his hair tied back and a Georgia Bulldogs ballcap on his head. He looked up at the few clouds in the sky, then walked around to the side of the house and stared at the cab of Darius' large diesel truck, which hadn't been used in over a week. Darius owned his own rig but had quit his trucking job, compelled by the time traveler who held him in a continual trance.

As the mystical man looked at a vehicle so large there was an attached two-step ladder used to climb into it, the visitor's companion raven landed on the hood of the cab and squawked at its master.

"Has the fairy returned ta the tree?" he asked the bird in Gaeilge.

The bird made a short cluck, meaning no.

"I think this land, this time, is drainin' me magic," the old man concluded in his native tongue. "Someone almost got away from me today. Me constant hold on Darius and the spell on his sister are takin' their toll. We'll have ta do somethin' about that. But first, Darius will be teachin' me about taxi cabs. It's time ta change locations. We've been here too long. We need to be closer ta food and drink."

The bird squawked a few times.

"No," the old man answered. "I don't have ta keep goin' to the weekend festival. I know she either works there or used to. This is a time for patience. Conservin' strength. I may go again, but for now, we need new quarters. Keep watchin' the tree but also start patrollin' in larger circles: a half-mile radius, then a mile—she can't be far away, and sooner or later—she will return ta the tree. She *has* ta."

26

EVENING VILLAGE

At a little after 8:00 p.m. that same evening, Erin sat in an antique highchair in Wanda's kitchen, using her fingers to eat some Gerber Spaghetti Rings. Noah sat in a kitchen chair in front of her, encouraging her self-feeding skills and occasionally wiping red tomato sauce off her chubby cheeks. Fay stood in the doorway between the kitchen and living room and watched the interplay between father and daughter warmly while Lancelot slept nearby in his favorite living room chair. Even though the sun had set, there was still some light in the April sky that promised longer summer days ahead. It was a simple and almost serene family scene until the headlights of Wanda's Honda Civic pulled into the gravel driveway. Then, the more disturbing events of the day came to their minds.

A weary Wanda came into the house a couple of minutes later. She patted Lancelot, who got up to greet her, waved and blew a kiss to Erin, who flashed a red saucy smile and said, "Hi." Then, she went into the living room and plopped onto her pink velvet Victorian loveseat. As Noah continued to attend to Erin, Fay followed her into the living room.

"How's Orrie?" she asked, concerned.

"He's in the ICU," Wanda answered. "Two broken arms, a cracked sternum, the back of his skull is fractured… they've put him in an induced coma until the swelling in his brain is reduced."

"Is he goin' ta live?" Fay asked, not completely understanding everything Wanda had just said about Orrie's injuries.

"I don't know," she replied. "Right now, it's wait and see."

"Does anyone know what exactly happened?" Fay asked.

Wanda opened her empty hands slightly. "He misjudged the distance and got distracted. As far as I know, nobody actually saw the accident. Thousands of people wandering around with cell phones, and nobody saw or recorded a thing. Not even those on the ride."

"How'd it go with the FBI?" Noah called. They had spoken on the phone since the accident, so he and Fay knew about this development, too.

"They're not going to find anything," Wanda replied. "Yes, I created an employment file for a Fayetta Smith if we ever needed it for anything, but since the FBI kindly told me in their initial visit they'd be back with a warrant, it's off premises and locked in a safety deposit box at Chase Bank. Anyway, Fay's file lists her as a volunteer, and any money I gave her was in cash and under the table. So, they got nothin'."

"Until they start wandering around the grounds and talking to your people," Noah reminded. "You've got two hundred employees, and Fay's worked there for years. *Somebody's* going to spill the beans about a fairy with an Irish accent."

"I know," Wanda sighed, "I know." She shook her head. "Why's the FBI even *doing* this? There's no freakin' crime!"

"There's a mystery that can't be explained," Noah reminded. "Our government doesn't like mysteries."

"If it's any consolation, governments aren't much different where I come from," Fay offered.

"I've had four life-changing things happen to me in the past few days," Wanda said. "I've learned that fairies are real, time travel is real, the FBI is investigating my employees, and for the first time ever, we've had a near-fatal accident at the Georgia Renaissance Festival. Three of these four things are connected. I can't help but wonder if the fourth thing is, too."

"What, Orrie?" Noah asked, now clearing away Erin's empty dinner dish. "How do you figure that?"

"I don't know," Wanda answered, rising from the sofa. "But I don't believe in coincidences, and we don't know what the fallout will be from the warrant laid on Dale Taylor today, either."

"Do ya think yer position at the festival is in trouble?" Fay asked.

"Well, I don't think what happened today did me

any good," Wanda answered. Then she looked at her dress. "I'm going to go change, wash off my makeup, then get myself a stiff drink."

She went into the bathroom while Noah went to the sink and washed Erin's plate. Fay went into the kitchen, got a sponge, went over to Erin's highchair, and began to wipe down the eating tray in front of the baby.

"I think I better stay close to Wanda tonight," she suggested. "She seems pretty upset."

"Yeah," he agreed. "I'd rather have you and Erin at my place, but I get it."

"Besides," Fay continued, going to the sink, putting the sponge down, then opening the top of a box of baby wipes and pulling one out. "I know a little girl who's pretty tired." She returned to Erin and wiped off her hands and face. "No bath for you tonight, darlin'. We'll do it in the mornin'."

"You don't think Wanda's right, do you?" Noah asked. "That what happened to Orrie is somehow connected to you?"

"The festival has jugglers that balance on a stack of chairs, people that walk on stilts, riders who do tricks on horseback in the tournament field, ax throwers, spear throwers, sword fighters—there *are* risky activities about. That's part of the fun of it, I 'spose."

He nodded as Fay lifted Erin out of her chair.

Within another seven minutes, Erin's diaper had been changed, and she'd been put into new pajamas that, ironically, featured a visual of the Fairy Godmother from *Cinderella*. There was a rocking chair in the guestroom, and Fay held and rocked her with only a nightlight on while Noah quietly stood near the door and watched. But Fay had been right when she said Erin was tired. She was not only tired, she was overtired and whined, fussed, and refused to settle down. Finally, Fay laid her down in the middle of the queen-size bed surrounded by a circle of pillows, stepped over to the bedroom window, opened the curtains, then raised the window.

"What're you doing?" Noah asked quietly.

"Callin' for reinforcements," she replied.

Fay leaned out of the window and began to sing, although it was no melody that Noah recognized. It was more like a few sustained notes, a kind of siren call. The notes were sweet and perfect in pitch, and Noah had no idea Fay could vocalize like that. Her song lasted about twenty seconds, and shortly after she had finished and stepped away from the window, a cabbage butterfly flew into the room, then another one, then a monarch butterfly, followed by a promethea silk moth. After that came a large imperial moth, followed by another monarch butterfly, then a rose hooktip moth. Fay pointed to Erin and made a circular motion with her finger, and the seven winged insects—some from the night, some from the day—fluttered over to the baby. They hovered three feet above her head and began dancing around like some kind of magical child's mobile. Erin's wide blue eyes watched the creatures with delight. She outstretched her arms to touch them, but after a minute or so, her eyelids became heavy, and she fell asleep. As Noah watched, open-mouthed and in awe, Fay then slightly bowed to the insects and said, "Go raibh maith agat," which was Gaeilge for "Thank you." The insects then fluttered away from Erin, went to the window, and flew off into the night. A couple of seconds later, a female deer approached the window, stuck her nose into the room, and snorted.

"Tá sí go breá. Go raibh maith agat as iarraidh," Fay said.

The doe looked at Fay, then turned and disappeared into the night.

Fay went over to the window, shut it, then drew the curtains.

"What did you say?" Noah asked.

"I said, 'She's fine. Thank ya for askin'," she replied.

"That is the coolest thing I have ever seen!" he quietly gawked.

"What do yer people like ta say? It takes a village," Fay smiled.

27

MEETING WITH MEADOWS

The following Monday, Special Agents Jacobs and Grimble walked into the director's office of the FBI on Century City Parkway NE in Atlanta. The director's name was Thomas Meadows. He was a dark complected no-nonsense twenty-three-year veteran of the Bureau with a passion for historical documents. On the walls of his tidy office, he had a framed and matted letter from William H. Seward, Abraham Lincoln's secretary of state, another from James Madison, America's fourth president, and still another from Thomas McKean, one of the signers of the Declaration of Independence. There were also pictures of him with President Joe Biden and former Congressman John Lewis. Meadows was forty-eight, stayed fit, and wore his hair a little longer than might be expected for an FBI field office director. It was reminiscent of Samuel L. Jackson's character of Jules Winnfield in *Pulp Fiction*.

"Gentlemen," he greeted as the agents came in. He

gestured for them to take a seat. "The Mystery of the Irish Time Traveling Weapons," he announced, as if it were a novel. "What have we got?" He looked at Special Agent Jacobs. "Speak," he invited.

"We reviewed all of the employment records for the Renaissance festival employees going back three years," the blond-haired agent reported, knowing his boss wasn't one for small talk. "There are several employees with Irish surnames that we could speak to. People with last names like Kelly, Sullivan, and Doyle. Anyone, or all, might have active ties to parties in Ireland."

Meadows turned to the brown-haired Grimble with the receding hairline. "What about our blacksmith?"

"His financial records turned up something interesting," Grimble informed. "During the past three years, he's been making yearly bank deposits to a bank in Switzerland."

"How much?" the Director asked.

"Unknown. We're still trying to access the information. But why would Dale Taylor, an insurance agent, need a Swiss bank account unless he wanted to hide money?"

"He could be hiding money for any number of reasons," Meadows replied. "To keep an ex-wife from accessing funds, for example. That doesn't necessarily mean the account has anything to do with the sale of recently made weapons found in a five-hundred-year-old battlefield."

"True," Grimble agreed. "But consider this: yesterday, there was an accident at the Renaissance festival.

An acrobatic artist who works there misjudged the movement of one of the festival's rides, and it slammed into him. He's in the ICU of Piedmont Fayette Hospital and, from what I understand, in pretty bad shape."

"That's unfortunate, but I don't see what—" Meadows started to say.

"Since we were there yesterday, I tracked down the paramedics who took the employee to the hospital," Grimble continued. "I spoke to an EMT named Chris Kramer. He couldn't tell me much about the accident, but he did volunteer there was a strange last-minute staff meeting that Wanda Harrington called before the festival opened."

"Why was it strange?" Meadows asked.

"Because its only purpose was to tell employees not to volunteer any information about other employees or festival operations to visitors if the employee felt they were being interrogated. Now, why would Wanda Harrington have such a meeting unless she was trying to hide something or someone? Why would Dale Taylor initially refuse to talk to us and be hiding money in Switzerland?"

"Okay. Fair points," Meadows agreed. "What do we know about Wanda Harrington?"

Special Agent Jacobs called up some notes on his phone. "Sixty-two years old. Widowed. Originally from Yoakum, Texas. She's lived in Fairburn for eighteen years. She started working at the festival as a seasonal employee and has been the full-time manager for the past ten. The festival's done well under her management but she did have some trouble in her past. Shoplifting, using fake IDs, minor stuff. She was raised in a series of foster homes back in Texas. Ran away a lot. Stabbed her last foster father four times with a steak knife. Claimed he was sexually abusing her."

"Was he?" Meadows asked.

"Inconclusive," Jacobs replied, clicking off his phone. "The foster father survived, didn't press charges, and she was put on probation. A probation, incidentally, that she didn't honor. She broke probation by leaving the state and wound up in Georgia years later. But by then, she was an adult. Since no formal charges had ever been made about the stabbing in Texas…" his voice trailed off to indicate no one ever pursued the broken probation.

"So," Meadows concluded, "we've got a festival manager who doesn't like authority and wants her employees to keep mum about what? We don't know. We've got a part-time blacksmith who denies selling weapons to anyone with a direct link to Ireland, but he's got a secret bank account. Why, or how much is in it? We don't know. We've got some festival employees with Irish last names that may or may not have connections to people in Ireland and the weapons." He sat back in his chair. "Pretty thin, gentlemen. Pretty thin. The Bureau is curious about this, but we've also got some real crimes to solve. I'm emailing you two a brief about new drug cartel activity in Johns Creek. I'm also preparing another brief about a serial killer of blonde females. He's connected to murders in Michigan and

Kentucky, and he might be connected to a murder last week downtown near the Fox Theater. I want you to focus your efforts on these new briefs."

"Sir, if I may," Jacobs interceded. "What we have with this ancient weapon mystery is something truly unique."

"When I began this meeting by saying: 'The Mystery of the Irish Time Traveling Weapons,' I was being facetious," Meadows clarified. "You're not really suggesting time travel here, are you?"

"No, sir," Grimble offered. "But three highly respected universities and our own forensics lab can't explain the aging process of these weapons. It's fooled radiocarbon dating, meaning something big is going on here. If someone has developed a new way to age weapons this convincingly, it could set the antiquities world on its ear. These weapons *had* to have been planted in that farmer's field to test this process. Dale Taylor made an egotistical mistake by stamping his logo on the swords, and he screwed up by using modern steel, but if this aging process is this good *now,* forgeries like this are only going to get better."

"Sir, the antiquities market in this country is 2.8 billion dollars," Jacobs offered. "Worldwide, it's twelve billion. Dale Taylor and Wanda Harington are both hiding something, and we believe they have direct knowledge about this aging process."

"Look at the documents on your wall," Grimble continued. "They're hanging there because of *their* historical importance. A drug cartel in Johns Creek and a serial killer are certainly important. But this—what we're working on—could be *historically* important."

"Not just to the antiquities market, but the whole field of archeology," Jacobs added.

The Director thought for a few moments before continuing.

"Alright... continue with your investigation. But only between these two new cases I'm sending. I admit, there's something strange and compelling here. But keep your efforts proportional to actual crimes, gentlemen. You understand? Proportional."

28

VEGAS

Diary Entry, Thursday:

Is magic just another name for miracle?
In their purest form, neither magic nor miracles can be explained:
The infant that survived buried in the rubble days after an earthquake. The cancer patient told she has less than a year to live but lives for another ten. The person who was underwater in a turtled kayak for twelve minutes but was resuscitated without damage.

Nineteen days after Orrie's injury at the Renaissance festival, there was a knock on Noah's hotel room door at the MGM Grand in Las Vegas just before noon. When he opened it, his client, a smiling Gino Girard, was on the other side. Gino was a Canadian crooner in the Tony Bennett/Frank Sinatra Great American Songbook tradition. He was forty-one years old, trim and handsome, with dark wavy hair, and had six multi-platinum albums and four Grammys. He was currently doing a six-week residency at MGM's Dolby Live Theater.

"Hey, good morning," the star greeted.

"Good morning, Gino. C'mon in," Noah invited.

Both men were dressed casually in jeans and t-shirts, but this was a business meeting. The souvenir program for Gino's residency needed updated photography. So, Noah had been hired by the singer's manager, Ted Albus, to shoot the first two performances, which Noah had already done. The programs used for the first two evenings had old photography, and new photography featuring Gino on stage at the Dolby Live Theater would be quickly switched out. Updated files would be sent to the printer, who promised a twelve-hour turnaround time. Noah was surprised but thrilled when the call came in. It was, without question, his highest-profile assignment since he'd been dismissed from Z-Rae's European tour over eight months earlier.

Noah had a long folding table open and spread out. On it were the separated pages of the program with his new selects photoshopped over the old photos. After offering the star a bottle of mango/strawberry juice, which he accepted, the singer stood over the table, carefully reviewing the pages. Noah also had the selects called up on his MacBook in case his client wanted a closer perspective.

"These are amazing!" the singer beamed approvingly. "I love the shadowing; it's very intimate."

"Thanks. I used a Hasselblad 2XD 100C. It does nice things with shadows and also close-up detail. You know cameras?"

"Not as well as I'd like, but I know enough to know you can have the world's best camera, and if you don't have the eye, it doesn't mean a thing. And you, my friend, definitely have the eye!"

"Thanks, man. That's very kind of you."

The star pointed to one photo in particular. "This is usually my bad side. But here—it looks good."

"I've got plenty of shots from your other side if you'd like to see 'em," Noah offered. "But I like the more full-dimensional perspectives where you see the subject as a whole person: Right side, left, eye level, three-quarter overhead; I especially like this one from the back of the stage and over the drummer's shoulder."

"I agree with you. Let's go with these selects."

"Wonderful. Thank you, Gino," Noah smiled. "Is there anyone else that needs to be brought in on the process? Ted? Your publicist? Someone from MGM?"

"No. Just send the selects to Ted with this layout, tell him I approved, and he'll get 'em to the printer for the update."

"Okay then. Excellent. You're an easy and decisive person to please."

"Hey—I'm workin' with talent," the singer smiled, taking a drink from his bottle of juice. "So, you gonna hang around for a day or two? Enjoy some of the delights of Vegas?"

"No. I've got a flight back to Atlanta at 6:30. Unless you need me to stay for something."

"No. I was just wondering. But I'm glad Ted took Leah Shively's suggestion and hooked us up. I've got a new CD coming out later this year, and we should kick around some ideas for the cover."

"I'd love to… Leah Shively recommended me?"

"Yeah, according to her girl, Z-Rae, you're the best photographer in the business. Based on what I see here, I don't disagree."

Noah paused and looked down at the floor, slightly embarrassed.

"That really means a lot to me, Gino. A lot! I've taken some hard knocks on social media this past year and was getting a little wobbly legged."

Gerard extended his free hand, and Noah shook it.

"I wouldn't worry about it," the singer smiled, heading for the door. "Everybody knows Bobby Dragon's a prick. We'll talk later about the CD cover. Safe travels home. Thanks for the drink."

As soon as his guest was out the door, Noah clenched his fist, pumped his arm, and quietly said, *"Yes!"* He felt like he had finally turned a corner, like his career might be on the upswing again. He hated that, in his opinion, he'd been wrongly fired by Z-Rae, but perhaps Leah's recent recommendation was an admission of that.

About ten minutes later, while sitting at a desk in his room and writing in the leather notebook he always carried, there was a knock on the door. Half expecting it to be Ted Albus, he was very surprised when he opened the door to see Z-Rae. She wore a black duster nearly to her ankles, a yellow low-cut bra underneath, black slacks, and yellow stiletto shoes that matched her bra. Today, her hair was long and pink with a couple of thin braids on either side of her face; she also wore Ray-Ban sunglasses. As usual, she looked super cool and alluring. She held a dozen wrapped roses in one hand.

"Hey, boo," she greeted with a wide smile. She didn't wait for an invitation but instead handed the roses over to Noah as she entered the room.

"Hey, boo?" he asked, surprised and displeased. "No. I'm not your boo. We're not booing here. What're you doing in Vegas?"

"Well, I haven't seen you in a while," she said, slipping off her sunglasses and looking around the room. "Thought we were overdue for a chat."

Noah shut the door, not appreciating the intrusion, and set the roses down on a nearby chair.

"The last time I saw you, you pointed a canister of mace at me. That was just before you fired me from your tour for trying to keep you healthy. And now, after what, eight months, without hearing a word from you, you show up with flowers and want to have a chat? Fuck off, Z."

"Okay," she nodded, going over to his mini fridge, opening it, looking inside, then closing it again without making a selection, "that's your reality. Here's mine: You assaulted one of the biggest celebrities in the world. A man who wanted to press charges. A man who had just sent my career into hyperdrive. A man who also wanted to follow up our first duet with another, which, in fact, happened. By firing you from the tour, I saved you from charges being filed, being arrested, going to court, a major paparazzi smear, and you *still* got paid for the entire tour. I've kept a distance because the buzz and press from the second duet had to run its course. But now that it has, here I am. With apologies and roses."

"Bobby Dragon bitch slapped me all over social media," Noah complained. "My business has dropped 40 percent from where it was a year ago!"

"But you followed your own advice and didn't get into a war of words with him, which eventually made his claims look baseless. You just finished an assignment with a major star. A star you'll work for again on your own merit. But—" she arched an eyebrow—"I opened the door."

She slipped her sunglasses into her duster pocket, then put her hands into her slack pockets, causing her duster to be pulled back and revealing her appealing bare chest except for the bra.

"C'mon, Noah," she said sincerely. "It's too bad what happened. But I wouldn't be here unless I still cared."

He spat out an exasperated breath while she noticed the leather notebook on the desk.

"You still taking this thing everywhere with you?" She walked over to it. "What is it, a diary?"

She picked it up, intending to look through it, but he moved over and quickly snatched it out of her hand.

"I don't know about where you come from, Z, but where *I* come from, people don't threaten people they supposedly care about with mace."

"Oh, for Christ's sake, I never would've used it," she defended.

"And that makes it alright in your world?" he retorted. "Well, not in mine. You need to go."

Her face softened as if lowering defenses. "Look, I cleared my weekend schedule, charted a private plane from LA, and brought an overnight bag full of nothing but t-shirts, sweatpants, and maybe a little sheer next-to-nothing nightie. I was hoping maybe we could hang inside, order room service, take long showers, and lose some of our hardened veneers. My legal name is Z-Rae, but I was born Zeana Ray Colton. You kinda know one, but I'd like you to know both. If we took some time where neither one of us didn't have to fly off to somewhere, we might actually—y'know—truly *like* one another."

She slipped off her duster, tossed it onto the bed, then reached up to take off her wig.

"I'm with someone else," he announced unemotionally.

She stopped mid-reach and looked at him.

"What?"

"I'm with someone else," he repeated. "It's pretty serious."

The pop star took a moment to let the news sink in, then she reached over and picked up her duster. She was quite hurt by Noah's announcement. She suddenly felt exposed and vulnerable. In the space of ten seconds, her defenses had gone up again.

"Really? So, who is she? No doubt, some recent photography grad who thinks your pictures are all full of sensitivity and vision."

"C'mon. It's been over eight months, and I haven't heard a word from you."

"Yeah? Well, that goes both ways."

"You threatened me with bodily injury, fired me, embarrassed me with coworkers and peers; my business took a nosedive—"

"I told you, there were reasons," she interrupted. "I had a strategy."

"I'm not a strategy! I'm a person! Look—spending time with you was really nice," he said, taking the high road. "I'm sure I'll look back someday and think more fondly of our times. But that's not today. Besides, I'm with this other woman now, Z, and that's not going to change."

She looked at him for a long moment and knew he was serious.

"Okay," she finally said, demonstrating remarkable restraint for someone used to getting her own way. She pulled her duster back on. "Okay," she repeated as if it were another nail that needed to be hammered into the coffin of their affair. She felt there was a lot more to say, like she'd already checked into a suite for the weekend. But, surprisingly, she felt her feet moving toward the door, where suddenly her hand was on the knob. Pausing and looking over her shoulder, she mustered a smile, said, "bye," and then slipped out.

Once in the hallway, Z-Rae walked down a long corridor toward the elevators and slid her sunglasses back on so one could see her eyes. But within seconds, tears started to run down her cheeks.

"Shit!" she uttered under her breath, picking up her pace. *"Shit!"*

29

BEDROOM TALK

Two days later, a little after 11:00 p.m. Sunday, Noah stood in the kitchen of his townhouse where he had just finished preparing a plate of sliced pear, cheese, and crackers. He stood shirtless, shoeless, and sockless but was wearing sweatpants. Just before he turned off the kitchen lights, he looked at the kitchen table. There was a box sitting on it that held twenty 20" old world style daggers. On the floor next to them were four boxes holding twenty 44" broadswords; each box held five swords complete with scabbards. They weren't the hand-crafted style of weapons that Dale Taylor made; they were mass-produced. And although they would never fool a historian or archeologist, they could still kill an enemy. At this point in the war between Clan Fergus and the fairies, that was all that mattered. Noah looked at the weapons that he and Fay had ordered online, then briefly thought about the nearly $5,000.00 he'd already put on his Capital One card to buy them. Fay had the money to repay him and much more in gold coins, but he wasn't concerned about that. He was concerned about all the additional weapons they'd need and all the magic it would take to shrink them down to a size small enough to fit into the hole of an oak tree. The broadswords would have to be the size of plastic cocktail swords, and he wondered how in the world Fay was going to do it. He was also concerned about whether or not she'd survive another year of the war she was fighting in another century so she could return to him and Erin. There was an entire other world of magic, lifestyle, and danger that he knew nothing about.

Once he was back upstairs with the plate, he checked in on Erin in one of his spare bedrooms. She was sleeping peacefully in a newly erected crib, and there was a moon-shaped nightlight for her as well. Satisfied that his daughter was okay, he took the snack down the hall to the master bedroom, where a naked Fay was sitting up in bed and waiting for him.

"This is so luxurious," she cooed. "Thank you! No one's ever brought me food in bed before."

"I was looking at the weapons you have to shrink," he noted. "You need to keep your strength up."

"It's not hard as long as I don't use too much magic between now and then," she replied. "It's like preservin' a battery ta keep it from runnin' down."

He brought the food over to the nightstand next to her, then rounded the bed and went to its other side. "I still think you should just take a crate of AR-15s and a few thousand rounds of ammo. That would pretty much do the trick," he said, lying down beside her but outside the covers. "Don't they have guns in your time?"

"Aye. Clan Fergus has some. But they aren't very good fer quick movement and surely no good on horseback. The long barrels need ta be propped up with a wooden brace. They often misfire, and the wicks don't stay lit."

"They've gotten a little better since then," he understated.

She smiled and helped herself to a slice of pear and cheese.

"I agree with the notion. Except buyin' guns would cause a bit of a red flag with yer authorities. I have a false ID, but I fear it wouldn't survive a background check. Plus, I don't know a thing about guns, how ta load 'em, clean 'em, change the casings…"

"You mean—the magazines?"

"Yes, 'magazines,' another word that makes no sense in yer time for the object in question. Swords, axes, and knives are things me people understand. They don't have enough of 'em, but they understand them. If I got into trouble with yer police for buyin' modern weapons, me mission could come to an end, and that would be the death knell of me kind, fer sure."

He thought for a moment.

"There's so much I don't know about your struggles. About your world."

"What do ya want to know?" she asked, taking

another slice of cheese and pear. She offered him some food, but he put up a hand of "no thanks."

"Tell me about your family," he asked instead.

"They're farmers," she said, sweeping some of her thick red hair off her face. "Me father's a farmer, as was his father, and his father before him."

"I don't think of fairies as farmers," he said, turning on his side and propping up his head with a fist and an elbow in the mattress.

"We don't fly around or sit on sunflowers and lily pads all day," she replied. "Although lyin' on a lily pad on a hot summer's day can be quite nice. We're farmers, healers, carpenters, a few are blacksmiths, we have some gold coins fer commerce with humans, but mostly we trade services with each other."

"Do you live mostly in small form or human size?" he wondered.

"We mostly stay the same size as humans. Where I come from, I might not shrink me size for days, and certainly rarely at night."

"Why?"

"Predators. Hawks, owls, foxes… we're fast but vulnerable when we're small."

He nodded. "And you *do* interact with humans?"

"Aye. Not often, but occasionally. There *are* some good ones out there."

"Are any humans helping you in your war?"

"And invite the wrath of Ardal Fergus?" she asked rhetorically. "Not likely."

"Tell me about your other brother, your parents,

your grandparents, the beliefs of the Tuatha Dé Dannan; I want to know everything."

She looked at him and smiled. She was sitting up with her pale legs crossed Indian style and didn't have any covers on her, so she knew he was drinking in various parts of her body while she nibbled on her pear and cheese, but she didn't mind. She felt comfortable and safe, and although they hadn't verbally expressed it yet, loved.

"You said you missed Erin's first year of life. That's true, but I made good use of the time. Every day while I was gone, I wrote a letter ta her, telling her about her grandparents, uncle, great-grandparents, our village, customs, abilities, history, and much more. I brought over three hundred letters back ta Georgia with me. They're sittin' in a gunnysack in me bedroom at Wanda's. I'll be leavin' 'em with ya when I go back. If I leave Erin, and should anythin' happen, it'll be a sort of documented history. Y'know—just in case."

He looked at her with an equal mixture of desire and admiration.

"What you've done. What you've been through… I'm gonna get you those AR-15s."

"Too risky ta purchase. But I'll take things that won't draw attention: flare guns, disposable lighters, smoke bombs…" her voice trailed off as he put a hand on the inside of her inner thigh, inches from the soft area between her legs.

"Ah," she said, smiling and noticing the increasing

stiffness in his sweatpants. "I see I'm done eatin', and we're done talkin'."

She reached over to the plate on the side of the bed, grabbed a napkin Noah had provided, and dabbed her lips with it. Next, she ran her fingers over the tattoo on his arm. "Were there any other questions ya wanted to be askin' at the moment?"

"Just one," he said, looking at her warmly. "Would you like a sibling for Erin?"

Her blue eyes sparkled.

"Aye. Yes, please," she whispered.

30

ORRIE

Fay and Wanda sat in the second floor waiting room of the intensive care unit of Piedmont Fayette Hospital. Fay held a vase with a dozen daisies in it that she'd gotten from the hospital gift shop. The hospital was a 310-bed facility, and its ICU had a particularly good reputation in the Atlanta area. It had now been twenty-three days since Orrie's accident at the Sea Dragon Swing, and he had been awakened a few days before from his induced coma. Orrie's parents had called Wanda with an unusual request. Their son wanted to talk to Fay, and his folks had contacted Wanda to see if she could reach out to her and arrange it. Wanda had originally advised against such a visit, but Fay wanted to go. So, Noah was watching Erin over at his place and Wanda drove Fay to the hospital. The two women had been informed that Orrie's doctor was cautiously optimistic about a full recovery, and while they were relieved by this, they couldn't imagine why Orrie wanted to see Fay.

After a few minutes of waiting, Orrie's mom, whose first name was Jenna, came out of the ICU to get Fay. She had met Wanda before at the hospital, and they had also met one other time when Orrie's parents had attended the Renaissance festival. She was a pleasant-looking woman in her late forties who was lean like her son. Fay and Wanda both rose to greet her as she came over.

"You must be Fay," she greeted. "I'm Jenna Sercombe, Orrie's mom."

"'Tis so nice ta meet ya," Fay said, smiling. "I'm very, *very* glad that Orrie's on the mend. We've been thinkin' about him and wishin' him well every day."

"It's going to be a long road, but we're hopeful," Jenna nodded. She said hello to Wanda, then turned back to the young redhead. "Those are nice," she said, referring to the flowers.

"I wanted to bring him something," Fay said, "but I don't know any of his favorite foods or drinks or even if he'd be allowed ta have 'em."

"The flowers are very thoughtful," Jenna acknowledged. "But, I-I have to ask. Are you and Orrie an item? He's been very insistent about seeing you."

"We're coworkers and friends," Fay replied. "We've been known ta tease each other a bit."

"I see… well… he's through the doors there," Jenna gestured toward the two doors that led into the ICU, "the second room to your right. He said he wanted to speak with you alone, so I'll wait here with Wanda."

"Sure. Right. Thanks," Fay replied tentatively.

Jenna put a gentle hand on Fay's arm as she turned to go. "He's fragile, Fay. Wanting to see you is very important to him. Even if you don't feel the same way—"

"I understand," Fay reassured. "Your son came back from the brink of darkness and asked ta see a woman ya never heard of. Naturally, you've got questions. Believe me, I'm just as surprised by his request as you. But we *are* friends. I totally understand sensitivity is the order of the day, and I'll not be sayin' anythin' to upset him."

"Good. Thank you for understanding."

Fay smiled and headed for the ICU doors. When she was gone, Jenna turned to Wanda.

"Do you know anything about her? What she means to him?"

Wanda just smiled politely.

Orrie sat in an electric bed propped up about twenty degrees. He wore a gray-and-white hospital gown, and his face was nearly as gray as the gown. He had dark circles under his eyes, and his braids were greasy and tied back with a hair scrunchy. Both of his arms were in white casts, and his fingers were bruised and swollen, but he could still move them. He was just taking a drink of fruit juice from a straw when Fay came into his room. She wore a yellow summer dress with a small white cardigan, and had a paisley headband under her hair to cover her ears. Between her yellow dress, white sweater, pale skin, and red hair, she looked every bit as pretty as the flowers she held.

"Hello, stranger," she greeted warmly. "'Tis grand to see yer smilin' face. That was quite a scare ya gave us."

He smiled faintly at her. "You came… I-I didn't know if Wanda could get ahold of you. Somebody said you weren't working the festival this year, and I hadn't seen you there, so…"

"I'm not workin' this year," she confirmed, stepping over to him. "But I heard about yer terrible accident, and when ya asked ta see me, came immediately." She set the flowers on the stand next to his bed. "I brought you these. I hope ya like daisies."

"What happened to me wasn't an accident," Orrie abruptly announced, ignoring the flowers and wanting to get right to the point.

"What? What're ya talkin' about?"

He looked her over. "I've never seen you in anything but your fairy dress. Never seen you without your wings. You look normal now. But you're not normal, are you, Fay?"

"Orrie, what happened?" she asked seriously.

"The way your wings move…" he continued, "the magic tricks you do… some at the festival say you've even got healing powers."

"What happened?" she repeated.

"A man came up to me when I was working. He was old and dressed like a wizard. Dark robe, long gray hair and beard, he carried a staff with a jewel in it. He had an Irish brogue and was asking about you. He knew that I'd asked you out a few times. He knew my name. Meaning, he'd been grilling people for information about you. He wanted to know where you were. But I knew he didn't work at the festival or was the usual guest. I basically told him to go fuck himself. He seemed…"

"What?" she asked.

"Otherworldly," he replied. "Evil. When I told him to move on, he said it wasn't smart to cross him. But he did move on, and I went back to work. I loaded the next group of guests onto the Dragon Swing, got it movin' back and forth, and started to do my thing. But, during my performance, my legs suddenly locked. I couldn't move 'em. Then, they started to…" his voice trailed off as he fought off the wave of a painful memory.

"They started to what?" she encouraged.

"Slide forward," he answered between gritted teeth. "I was sliding *over* the ground like being pulled by some huge magnet. I looked around and saw the old man in the distance, and for just a second, I thought I saw a beam of light shooting out from the jewel in his staff. I finally broke free from whatever force was holding me but still got grazed by the dragon. If I hadn't broken free—it would've hit me square on, and I'm sure I'd be dead."

He looked at her with dark, baggy eyes. "Does any of this make sense to you? Do you believe me?"

Her eyes searched for an answer for a couple of moments, trying to piece possibilities together. Finally, she responded. "Orrie, you've had a fearful accident. You've been on all sorts of medications. I wouldn't be tellin' stories like this ta people. They might think yer—"

"I haven't told anyone," he interrupted. "I've just told *you*. I think you're in danger. I had to see you. Warn you."

She stepped closer to him, nodded, and looked him over empathetically. "Where does it hurt the most?"

"The middle of my chest. It hurts when I move too much or take a deep breath."

She gently reached over and put a hand on his sternum, then closed her blue eyes and murmured something in Gaeilge. After twenty seconds or so, she removed her hand and opened her eyes.

"Better?" she asked. "I can only do so much, but—"

"No," he cut in. "It *is* better! Jesus, Fay. Who *are* you?"

"Not Jesus," she reassured. "Ya can't repeat this story, Orrie, or what I just did. Not to yer ma, yer da, no one. And ya can't go back to New Castle. Not this season, anyway."

"I don't think there's any chance of that," he said.

"Keepin' a confidence is hard. It's the hardest thing fer a person to do. But I'm goin' ta ask that you keep this confidence between us. I know yer a man of strong character. You're also a man who's goin' ta get better. *All* better. Ya understand me, lad?"

"No. I don't understand any of this," he replied. "But, I'll try."

"Thank ya for tellin' me this, Orrie. And I'll deal with the man who did this to ya. I promise. Rest now."

She leaned over and gently kissed him on the lips. When she did, Orrie fell into a peaceful sleep.

Ten minutes later, Fay and Wanda were driving back to Wanda's, and Noah was on speakerphone.

"Wait a minute," Noah said after hearing Fay's conclusion based on what Orrie had shared with her. "You think somebody *followed* you through the corridor?"

"Aye. I think Ardal Fergus sought out the services of a horzikaan."

"What's a 'horzikaan'?" Wanda asked while driving.

"A wizard. A very powerful and dangerous being. He can be multilingual like me and very temperamental. I've heard tales of people retainin' them, but then they turn on their masters and steal their wealth simply because they can. I've never heard stories about them bein' able ta change size, but bein' in wee form is the only way he could've gotten through the oak tree."

"If this clan leader hired such a wizard," Noah concluded, "then, he must be getting desperate. Your efforts must be making more of an impact than you thought."

"Perhaps," Fay agreed. "But it also means we're all in great danger."

"Do you think he knows where I live, that you've been staying with me?" Wanda asked.

"I don't know. But I suspect he *has* figured out a few things. He knows that me bein' part of the Renaissance festival community is the perfect cover fer a Tuatha Dé Dannan. He's probably figured out I'm transportin' weapons back to our own time. And I think he's *definitely* figured out that Shea Karna is going ta have another cycle, but he doesn't know when. So, I'll wager he's got a familiar watchin' the oak tree on yer property, Wanda."

"A what?" Noah asked.

"A familiar," Wanda knew from her position at the festival, "an animal that assists a wizard or witch with their magic. Usually a bird or snake."

"You mean, like, in the movies?" Noah asked.

"Exactly," Wanda said. "But who the hell knew they were real?"

"If a horzikaan is truly here," Fay said, "his mission's pretty simple: kill me, return back to our own time, and he'll probably take some modern technology with him to make himself more powerful. But he doesn't know where I am or when Shea Karna will happen. I'll also wager he's put some people under his power ta keep his real identity secret. That takes a lot of magic. And even though he's much more powerful than I am, such power isn't limitless. Orrie said he was able to break free from an invisible hold the horzikaan put on him when he refused to answer questions. The result was he got hurt, but he's still alive. That means the horzikaan's power is starting ta wane, and he's got ta preserve it."

"This is a lot of conjecture, Fay," Noah observed.

"Tis the only thing that makes sense," she reasoned. "After weeks of bein' in a coma, Orrie wakes up, and all he wants ta do is tell me about a man in a dark robe with a staff that shoots light. A light that caused his feet ta slide into the path of a swingin' gondola."

"Okay, okay, fine!" Wanda said, both concerned and impatient. "Let's assume Fay's right. What do we gotta do?"

"You shouldn't stay at yer house," Fay advised Wanda. "Not until Shea Karna is over. You shouldn't be alone, either. The more people yer with, the more difficult it would be for the horzikaan to cast a wide net spell. Especially if his power is already weakenin'. Ideally, ya shouldn't be returnin' to New Castle, either. If he's lookin' fer me, sooner or later, he'll find out yer the manager and try ta get information from ya. I mean, if he doesn't know who ya are already."

"I can't abandon my job in the middle of a season," Wanda declared. "I've got responsibilities. Plus, the FBI's pokin' around."

"Yer life's more important than yer job, Wanda," Fay reminded. "It's a life that's very, very dear ta me!"

Wanda smiled, appreciating Fay's feelings, but reiterated her convictions. "I'm not abandoning the festival mid-season! But I *do* have a coworker and friend who'll take Lancelot and me in, and I can make sure I'm not alone on the New Castle grounds."

"Please put these plans in motion quickly," Fay urged. "Meantime, Erin and I can stay with Noah."

"I can go one better than that," Noah's voice said over the phone. "We're going to get the hell out of Dodge."

31

AT THE GALLOWAY'S

"Say that again?" Noah's mother asked, taking a pan full of scrambled eggs, mushrooms, and ham she was making off the stove. Her son's announcement stopped her in the middle of making an omelet. Noah's father, sitting at the kitchen table, likewise lowered his morning newspaper.

"Two years ago, when I shot the Georgia Renaissance Festival as a favor to Cole, I met a young lady who worked there. There was a connection; we had dinner, one thing led to another, and as a result, she had a little baby girl. I didn't know about the child until after she was born, but now I do. The mother and I have reconnected, and we're going to try to share parenting duties."

Ami and Mike Galloway looked at one another for a moment in disbelief; then, a half-smile crept across Ami's face. "Oh my God. I'm a grandmother!"

She was fifty-seven years old and a hopeless romantic. She had dishwater-blonde hair, green eyes, a trim figure, and an endearing smile. It was easy to see where Noah got his good looks. Mike had dark-brown hair and was also fifty-seven with green eyes but a little overweight and much more pragmatic. Noah was standing in his parent's spacious kitchen. They lived in a 3,300-square-foot mission-style home in Decatur, a suburb less than ten miles from downtown Atlanta. Noah's father owned a chain of four lighting stores throughout the Atlanta area. They sold chandeliers, floor lamps, and table lamps and also did custom interior lighting. As a result, they were financially comfortable.

"This baby's two years old, you're just telling us *now?*" Mike asked.

"She's not two; she just turned fifteen months. Look, *I* didn't even know the baby existed until I returned to the festival the following year to track Fay down. Uh, that's the mother's name, Fay."

"You returned the following year to track the mother down?" Mike wondered.

"Yes. I thought the night we shared was pretty special, and I wanted to see her again. But I had no way of contacting her from one year of the festival to the next. Although I did try various things to track her down in the intervening months."

"Aw—that is so romantic," Ami gushed, stepping over from the stove to the kitchen island where Noah stood.

"That is so dumb," Mike countered. "You never heard of a condom?"

"I'm not telling you this to invite a parental review," Noah qualified. "I'm telling you this because it's big news. I'm happy about it, but there are challenges involved."

"What's the baby's name, honey?" Ami asked.

"Erin."

"Erin! Oooo, that's so pretty. Fifteen months old!"

"She never reached out to you during the pregnancy?" Mike queried.

"No."

"Why not?"

"We didn't know each other, and she was probably nervous about telling me. We only spent a little bit of one day and an evening together."

"Not to be indelicate, but are you even sure the baby is yours?" his father asked.

"Yes. I did DNA testing."

"So, you're *sure,*" Mike repeated.

"At least 98.3 percent sure," Noah answered.

"Then, why didn't she tell you about being pregnant?" his dad pressed.

"She went back to Ireland,"

"She's from Ireland?" Ami asked, surprised.

"Yes."

Mike furrowed his brow, still sitting at the kitchen table and not understanding. "She was visiting the country during the Renaissance festival?"

"Not visiting. She works there. She's a fairy."

"She's a fairy?" Mike asked.

"A costumed ambassador. She wanders around, lets

people take selfies with her, does magic tricks, gives directions—stuff like that. She's worked there a while."

"But she lives in Ireland?" his dad queried, wanting verification.

"Yeah. She's only in this country for about eight weeks when the festival happens. That's why I had no way of contacting her. When I returned the following year, Erin was with her and dressed up like a little fairy, too. That's how I found out about her."

"The baby was dressed up like a little fairy?" Ami cooed, putting a hand on Noah's arm affectionately. "That is *so* precious."

"Wait a minute," Mike interjected, rising from the table. "How does this woman who lives in Ireland work at the Renaissance festival? Does, does she have a relative in festival management or something?"

"No," Noah replied.

"Does she have a work visa?"

"I don't know," Noah lied.

"Well, how did she get a job at the Renaissance festival?" his mom wondered.

"I-I think originally she needed the money," Noah said, purposely being vague. "But now, she just likes working there."

"So, she was a traveling student originally?" his mother assumed.

"Something like that."

"Well, *was* she a student or wasn't she?" his father queried, coming over to the island.

"I'm not sure," Noah lied.

"Where in Ireland is she from?" he asked.

"A village at the foot of the Three Sisters," Noah answered, telling the truth but also being vague or out-and-out lying depending on the question.

"The Three Sisters," Ami repeated, picking up her iPhone off the island's granite counter. "Is that on Google Maps?"

"How old is this woman?"

"'This woman' has a name, Dad," Noah said a little defensively. "It's Fay."

"Fine," Mike conceded. "How old is Fay?"

"I don't know."

"What religion is she?"

"I don't know."

"She's probably Catholic," Ami figured, still looking at her phone. "There's more Catholics in Ireland than liberals in Massachusetts. And that's saying something."

"What are her parents' names?" Mike continued.

"I don't know."

"What county are the Three Sisters in, honey?" Ami asked.

"I-I think she said County Sligo," Noah recalled. "But I'm not sure."

"Well, Jesus, Noah—what *can* you tell us about her?" Mike asked impatiently.

"Have you got a picture of her?" Ami wondered.

Noah gently reached over and stopped his mom from hopelessly searching on Google Maps. He took the phone out of her hands and pulled up his website. When

Fay's picture kneeling on the boulder in the middle of a stream came up on his home page, he handed it back to her.

"Oh, my God, she's *gorgeous!*" Ami exclaimed.

"Let me see," Mike said, stepping around to look over her shoulder.

"Red hair," Ami said excitedly. "Does little Erin have red hair? Have you got a picture on your phone?"

"It's more blonde, but that could change at some point," Noah replied. "I do have pictures of her but not on my phone."

"She is very pretty," Mike agreed. "But the fact remains Fay didn't tell you about the pregnancy or the baby until you tracked her down and found out about it yourself. That's odd, don't you think? Last I knew, they had phones in Ireland, internet, mail service."

"I know," Noah admitted. "But now we're trying to work out a, a kind of co-parenting schedule while at the same time trying to figure out how much we, we—y'know—*like* each other."

"So, there are feelings between you two?" Ami assumed.

"Yes," Noah admitted. "There are. I'm sure."

"Is there any possibility that she's married?" Mike continued, leaning intently on the island toward his son like a prosecutor. "Could there be a husband or boyfriend back in Ireland?"

"No."

"Is that what she told you?" Ami asked.

"Yes."

"And you believe her?" she continued.

"Yes."

"Leap of faith. Good boy!" she applauded.

"Sounds fishy," Mike declared.

"Look, guys. I admit there are a lot of unknowns here. Fay and I are attracted to one another, and we're trying to work out some answers. She loves that I want to be a part of Erin's life, but right now at least, she's committed to living in Ireland."

"Are you going to move there?" Mike asked.

"No. My life and business are here, and she knows that. So, it's complicated."

"Could the baby be a ploy for you to marry her so she can gain citizenship?" his father speculated.

"Then she would've told him about Erin much earlier," Ami concluded. "I want to meet Fay and Erin," she said happily. "Can you arrange that?"

"Actually, what I'd like to do is take them to your place in the mountains for a while. Fay's agreed not to work at the festival, and it would give us time to be alone with Erin, focus on each other, and try to find a path on how to proceed with our lives."

"Do you love her, sweetie?" Ami asked. "I mean, it certainly seems like you've got feelings for Fay."

"I do," he smiled. "I've never met anyone like her."

"Eh, maybe your feelings are confined to south of the beltline," Mike suggested, picking up a spare piece of ham off the cutting board on the island and popping it into his mouth. "I mean, she slept with you on your first date."

"I slept with you on our third," Ami reminded.

"Okay, too much info here!" Noah flinched.

"But, clearly, not enough info about Fay," Mike said.

"Hence the request to go to the mountains with her," Noah reminded.

"Of *course* you can take her and Erin to the mountains," Ami decided. "We'll call Jeff and have him get the place ready. This is so exciting!" she said, clasping her hands together.

"It's so 'somethin'," Mike conceded.

"Stop with the judgment, Michael," Ami said sternly. "Our son has something important happening in his life that he's trying to figure out and share with us."

"I'm not being judgmental. I'm being inquisitive like any father would. I'm trying to determine facts and look out for the better interest of our son."

"You've got to start thinking about the better interests of your granddaughter, too," Ami reminded. "Because, no matter what, that's a fact."

Mike paused, looked at his son, and nodded.

"Sure… take Fay and Erin to the mountains if you think it'll help."

"We should have a baby shower!" Ami decided.

"What? No, Mom," Noah hesitantly replied. "We're not there yet."

"Just a little shower," Ami promised. "Nothing big or fancy."

"Oh, my God—here we go," Mike groaned, rolling his eyes and knowing better.

"Or, at some point, after a few days, maybe your dad and I could join you in the mountains."

"Mom, I need time alone with Fay and Erin."

"Does she talk?" Ami went on. "If she's fifteen months old, she should be talking."

"Yes. A little bit. She can put a few words together."

"Does she call you 'Daddy?'" Ami wondered anxiously.

"Uh, no. Fay wants her to call me Da."

"What?" Mike asked.

"Da. It's Irish."

"Oh my God. That is *so* cute!" his mother exclaimed. She looked at her husband. "You've got to get plug protectors from one of your stores. We've got to get gates for the bottom and top of the stairs. And a crib. And a rocking chair. And locks for the kitchen cabinets. And a Diaper Genie!" She looked at Noah. "Best invention ever!" She looked at Mike again. "We'll change your home office into a nursery. Paint it pink!"

"What? *No!*" Mike emphatically responded. "That's my home office. That's where I do work!"

"You have an office at the home store," Ami waved off. "You don't do anything in your home office except check sports scores, the weather, and the occasional lingerie site."

"You're checking my history now?" Mike barked, simultaneously embarrassed and mad.

"I understand it gets you frisky for our date nights," Ami continued, "so it's alright since I'm the beneficiary."

"Oh my God," Noah said, slapping a hand to his forehead.

"And what's wrong with your sewing room becoming a nursery?" Mike countered. "You know, the room you never do any actual sewing in?"

"I use that room all the time," she argued.

"I could write my name in the dust on your sewing box," he claimed. Then he turned to Noah. "She's not kidding about a Diaper Genie, though. You *should* get one."

32

HIGHLANDS

Fay pressed her nose against the passenger side window of Noah's Ram pickup truck and looked up at the blue sky as she, Noah, and Erin—securely strapped into a car seat in the back—drove down Highway 23 toward Highlands, North Carolina on a Friday, May 5.

"Plane," she announced, looking at the vapor trail of a Boeing 737 high above the Great Smoky Mountains. "There are people up there. Dozens and dozens."

"De plane. De plane," Noah cracked, remembering the character of Tattoo from the old TV show *Fantasy Island*.

"What?" she asked, not understanding.

"Nothing," he smiled. "It's just—it's interesting some of the things in this century that grab your attention."

"Ya think things from my time are magical. But, ta turn a knob and have hot or cold runnin' water whenever ya like, ta fly like the noblest of birds above the clouds and take yer entire family along, ta see things occurrin' in different lands but do so from the comfort of yer own home—*that's* magic," she said.

"That's technology," he waved off.

He glanced at her for a moment and smiled at the tips of her pointed ears peeking out from her long red hair. "Sprouting wings and flying is magical. Changing size is magical. Having healing powers is magical."

"Those are the abilities of a different species with different genes. But sure, we do refer ta it as magic."

Fay turned around and looked at a dozing Erin in the backseat. "If I leave her here when I go, and should somethin' happen ta prevent me from comin' back, ya can't let her forget about me or her heritage. Promise."

"You packed the letters you wrote, right?"

"Aye, they're in the back."

"I promise, baby. But, nothing's gonna happen, not with all the weapons you'll be taking back. I just wish you were taking back more decidedly superior weaponry."

"Yer army has sent missile systems and tanks to the Ukraine," she reminded. "But both required education and trainin'. In some cases, months of it. Me people don't have months, Noah. They have ta make a difference every time they encounter Clan Fergus. They need weapons they know."

"Okay, okay," he agreed, wearing out a suggestion he had made several times before.

"So, are yer parents wealthy then?" she wondered, changing subjects. "I mean, havin' a mountain home?"

"They're comfortable. My dad's been lucky with his business."

"And, ya told 'em about me and Erin?"

"Yes. I mean, I had to eventually. But just the bare bones: you're a woman I met who lives in Ireland, works at the Renaissance fair in the spring, and we're trying to map out a plan of how we can co-parent."

"What'd they say when you told 'em about me?"

"My dad had a lot of questions, and my mom wants to throw you a baby shower. Do you know what that is?"

"Aye, it's a party. But it's another term in yer language that makes no sense. Sounds like a group of people that wants ta clean me daughter."

"The idea is to 'shower' you with gifts."

She thought for a moment. "Oh… okay. That one makes a bit more sense."

Highlands, North Carolina was a scenic tourist town and popular destination one hundred twenty-nine miles north of Atlanta, nestled against the Nantahala National Forest. Mike and Ami Galloway's mountain retreat was on Goldmine Road. It started as paved but then turned into a dusty dirt road as it wove its way—sometimes quite sharply—through thick woods up to an area known as California Gap. Along the way, Noah, Fay, and Erin passed other mountain homes, some nice, some humble, and these were little islands of humanity in a wooded world that mainly belonged to deer, bears, coyotes, raccoons, snakes, and the occasional bobcat.

The Galloways had built their getaway home twelve years earlier. It was a tidy one thousand four hundred square feet and took years to build since bulldozers, cement trucks, wood, drywall, shingles, a septic tank, and electric lines had to be brought up the mountain and through the woods to an elevation of forty-five hundred feet. In winter, if there was snow, construction stopped, and since building crews were in high demand in the area, there were long periods of waiting for roofers, plumbers, electricians, painters, and so on. But Mike and Ami always figured the end result and considerable expense would be worth it, and considering the skyrocketing real estate prices in Highlands, they were right.

The view of the surrounding mountains off Goldmine Road was impressive and filled with lush green forests of white pine, oak, hickory, maple, and yellow birch trees that turned into a magnificent palette of colors in mid-October. Like the Galloways', there were other mountain homes in the view, but they were almost impossible to discern unless you were looking for them, and their lights were too far away to be intrusive at night. Mike and Ami's place sat on the edge of a wooded lookout that had to be cleared before any construction began. The house was narrow and had two stories. The front door led into a small mudroom to hang coats and remove boots; then it went into a living room where, on the left-hand wall, there was a wood-burning fireplace and a flatscreen TV mounted over the mantel.

Straight ahead, facing the west, was a wall that consisted nearly entirely of large glass panes, but they were separated by two-by-four framing and interrupted by a sliding glass door that led out to a deck. Occupying the space in between was a nice leather sofa facing the fireplace and TV, a coffee table in front of it, and a leather chair with a reading lamp angled to the side and likewise facing the fireplace. All the furniture in the living room was anchored by a Native American area rug with red, blue, gold, and white.

To the left and behind the back of the living room sofa was a circular iron staircase by the glass wall that led downstairs. Next to that was a small dining table, and next to that was an L-shaped kitchen counter that accommodated three stools. The kitchen was small but had everything you would need. At its end was a full bathroom. Going into the bathroom and turning right, you could go into the master bedroom that featured a queen-size bed, bedside tables, a dresser, and a closet. Going through the bedroom door, you'd find yourself back in the living room and next to the mudroom, having taken a U-shaped route. Beyond the sliding glass doors was a deck that ran the width of the house and overlooked a rocky hillside that consisted of bulldozed rock, green strands of Canadian hemlock, and concrete that helped to keep the beams of the deck in place. Looking straight down off the deck, you really appreciated how much the house sat on the edge of a plateau. The deck also had some nice furniture on it, a covered Char-Broil gas grill and, on a clear day, inspiring mountain sunsets were a guarantee. The iron circular staircase wound down to a second bedroom with another queen-size bed, full bath, and another furnished deck below the first. All in all, the place was cozy, filled with cool lamps that no doubt came from one of Mike's stores, and there were touches of mountain life everywhere. Like comforters with moose images on them and throw pillows shaped like trout. It was a place where a family could escape, commune with nature, play board games, and see some amazing stars around the firepit at night.

After unpacking and setting up a portable crib for Erin in the master bedroom, which made things pretty cramped, Noah, Fay, and Erin relaxed for a few minutes on the deck and took in the view. It was a clear spring day, and the temperature was in the sixties, warm for the mountains in May.

"Cairde!" Erin suddenly announced, standing, pointing, and looking down the mountain between the white spindles of the deck's railing.

"What? What did she say?" Noah asked, sitting in an Adirondack chair.

"It's Gaeilge for 'buddies,'" Fay said, sitting in a matching chair beside him. "She must see a raccoon, a deer, or somethin'."

Noah rose and walked over to the deck. He looked down, then hurried away into the house.

"Oh, hell no," he muttered as he went.

Curious, Fay rose and walked over to the railing next to her daughter. Looking down, she saw four or five rattlesnakes sitting on some stones in the noonday sun. Unconcerned, she picked Erin up to get a better view of the reptiles. Noah returned a few moments later carrying a Glock 9 mm pistol with a fifteen-round magazine.

"Take the baby inside," he instructed.

"What're ya gonna do with that?" she asked.

"Shoot 'em. We can't have our daughter playing outside or enjoy the firepit at night with those things crawling around. This is a battle we fight every year."

"Give a pause there, lad," she said. "Those are cairde—buddies—Erin's bein' taught that everything in the forest are friends. The Tuatha Dé Dannan live in harmony with all creatures of the wood."

"But those creatures can kill," he argued. "Especially a child."

"Aye, if provoked or hungry. Let's just not provoke 'em. And where'd you get a gun anyway?"

"It's my dad's. We're in the mountains. It's isolated. Being able to protect yourself is just plain smart."

"Humans!" Fay groaned, exasperated. She put Erin down and walked toward the sliding glass door. "Put that thing away and watch Erin. I'll just ask 'em to move."

"You speak snake?" he asked, surprised.

"Something like that," she said, going inside.

"You should learn how to use this!" he called after her, gesturing to the Glock.

She ignored him and went through the house and out the front door. He put the gun in an empty hanging basket for flowers high above Erin's reach and picked up his daughter.

"Mommy's crazy!" he said, smiling at his daughter.

"Crazy!" Erin repeated, smiling back.

He carried her over to the railing again to see what Fay was doing.

She walked to the edge of the lookout, then carefully started to step down the steep incline to where the rattlesnakes were. She wore tennis shoes and lightweight slacks that weren't exactly rock climbing friendly.

"You're making me *very* nervous right now, Fay," Noah called. "We don't have a snakebite kit, and I'm not even sure there's a hospital in Highlands."

As Fay approached, the snakes began to coil and rattle.

"Oh, and now they're rattling," Noah said as if doing a play-by-play commentary. "Yeah. That's *so* buddy-like!"

Fay stepped onto a rock that put her ankles within striking distance of one of the snakes. As soon as she did, one of the reptiles sprang at her. But, suddenly moving with a blur-like speed, she grabbed the snake by its neck and firmly held it while its mouth was open and its fangs were bared.

"Holy shit!" Noah said, surprised by the move. "Now she's channeling Barry Allen," he noted, referring to the central character in *The Flash*.

"Tá fabhar agam le fiafrai," Fay calmly said, Gaeilge for, "I have a favor to ask."

The snake looked at Fay, closed its mouth, and she loosened her grip slightly. It flicked its tongue at her, and Fay asked in Gaeilge if the snake and his friends could please move to some other rocks further down the mountain so the humans wouldn't be afraid of them. The snake flicked its tongue at her again, hissed, and moved its head around.

"Fiafróidh mé," she replied, which was Gaeilge for "I'll ask."

"Do ya have whiskey in the house?" she called to Noah.

"Say what?" he asked, surprised.

"Does your father drink whiskey?" she said.

"Yes. But he doesn't tolerate it very well. He likes the idea of it better than the actual drinking. He has a habit of taking a few sips of a whiskey and water—"

"Then tossin' the rest off the deck to the rocks below," she finished. "So I've been told. Could ya bring me down a bottle? I'll take it, go further down the mountain with the snakes, and pour it onto the rocks. They can warm themselves further away from the house, enjoy a drink, and apparently whiskey goes very well with mice."

Noah looked in disbelief at Fay, who was still holding the snake. Finally, he asked. "Do they want anything else? Vodka? Centipede appetizers?"

After moving the snakes without incident and a nice first day, Fay sat in one of the Adirondack chairs on the deck in the evening. She wore a hoodie and sipped on a dark Sam Adams. It was about 9 p.m., Erin had been put down in her crib in the master bedroom, and she was listening to the tree frogs while watching the stars becoming brighter and brighter above the dark silhouette of the mountains. Off the deck and in the woods below, several fireflies were blinking in the woods.

"Fay?" Noah called, opening the sliding glass door and stepping outside with a piece of folded parchment in his hand. "All these letters you wrote—they're in Gaeilge."

"That they are," she confirmed.

"How am I supposed to share 'em with Erin?" he asked.

"Guess you better be learnin' the language," she suggested.

"Guess I better be finding a translator," he corrected.

"Should anything happen ta me, I want our daughter ta know her history and have it be in her own tongue. If you wanna have 'em translated, ya can do that fer sure. But I'm hopin' it'll encourage her and you ta learn the language of her people."

"Okay, he nodded, "I certainly get that. But nothing's going to happen to you." he glanced toward the woods and raised his eyebrows in surprise.

"A-are those *fireflies?*"

"Aye. Aren't they pretty?"

"What are fireflies doing out this early? It's way too chilly for them up here. We never see 'em until July and, even then, rarely."

"I think they know when old-world magic is about,"

she reasoned. "The snakes must've told 'em. Creatures of the wood have an instinct fer it."

"The snakes must've told 'em," he repeated a little sarcastically. "You mean the snakes drunk on Jim Beam? What did they do? Announce it to the dormant firefly eggs, and they just decided to hatch months early?"

"There was a time, y'know, when all creatures lived in a better sense of harmony with each other," she observed. "There was still killin' ta survive and the whole circle of life—but it was more respectful, much less flagrant than today. I think maybe the fireflies are curious about that. Not unlike you being curious about me."

"Oh, so they want to make love to you tonight in about six different positions, too?" he cracked wryly.

"That's desire. Not curiosity," she clarified. "Although I'm not sayin' there's anythin' wrong with that, mind ya."

She rose and walked to one corner of the deck. As she did, the fireflies in the woods followed her to that corner.

"How can you communicate with animals and insects?" he asked.

"I'm not human. I'm Tuatha Dé Dannan. And it's not a fluid word-for-word understandin'. It's more basic. Like, 'Gold water thrown on rocks. Good.' Ya've gotta interpret a bit."

She suddenly looked up and saw the tail end of a shooting star on the other side of the deck.

"Ooo, Noah! Did ya see that?" She hurried to the opposite corner of the deck and pointed upward. "A shootin' star. A bright sparklin' jewel in the sky!"

Instead of looking up, he glanced down into the woods and noticed the fireflies had followed her to the other side of the deck, like Christmas twinkle lights with a moveable will of their own.

"God, I'm lucky you're in my life," he said, smiling. "You make the ordinary events of the day a series of minor miracles."

She smiled at him warmly.

Ninety minutes later, Noah and Fay were making love downstairs in the guest bedroom. They had already discovered that both liked intercourse in multiple positions, so she was on her hands and knees at the edge of the bed while he stood on the floor behind her, thrusting into her. She gasped slightly with each push as his hands firmly held her hips. Her red hair and breasts hung free and loose and moved in a quick, jerky succession of intimacy until Noah came inside her with a loud groan. Then, they both became suddenly still while she slowly moved backward and closer to him as if to extract the last drop of the love he had to offer. After their hearts and breathing had calmed down, he slowly pulled out of her, and she laid down on the bed.

"Get the pillows and put 'em under me feet," she said softly. "I wanna be keepin' ya inside of me."

He did as she requested, realizing she was taking him up on his suggestion of a sibling for Erin and was trying to get pregnant. Watching her lie there with her legs propped up, he sunk to his knees on the floor next to the bed and stroked her forehead gently.

"Tell me about your world," he asked. "I know your family are farmers, you have a brother, and you can spend days without transforming into the smaller versions of yourself. I know you get your magic from the land… but I guess it's not exactly like the mystical, peaceful scenes of small-winged creatures flying through enchanted forests like you see in illustrations or the movies, huh?"

"Oh, there's enchantment in me world fer sure," she corrected. "Ta walk barefoot on a newly plowed field on a spring day with the brown earth so warm and thick beneath yer feet… Ta sit on a large mushroom in the mossy woods when yer wee size and listen ta the sounds of the wind and life around ya… We were speakin' of fireflies earlier—ta stand in a cave and see hundreds of glow worms twinklin' like stars in the night. There's enchantment fer sure. Mine's a world worth keepin'."

"I'm totally in love with you, Fayetta Smith," he confessed.

She smiled. "Smith isn't me real last name, but no matter. I'm totally in love with you, too, Noah Galloway." Then, she frowned a bit. "Though I fear our hearts are gonna be torn ta pieces."

33

THE TWO RUSSES

Russ Hawkins was sixty-two, the chief of police in Fairburn, GA, twice divorced, and had a bit of a crush on Wanda Harrington. He oversaw a department of twenty-nine officers, detectives, and dispatchers, and there hadn't been an officer involved in the fatal shooting of a suspect in six years—something he was quietly proud of. He'd asked Wanda out on a date a couple of times, but she had always let him down gently and said no. This was partly because she hadn't liked cops from the days of her youth and partly because there were rumors about Russ being a chauvinist when it came to the women he was involved with. That said, she understood it was important they have a good rapport and had conscientiously tried to maintain a friendship.

Russ walked into the front door of Judy's Restaurant and saw Wanda sitting with two of her coworkers. It was early Friday morning, just before the sixth of the festival's eight operating weekends. Surprised to see Wanda, he walked over to her table, nodding to a couple of other patrons as he did.

"Hey, Wanda," he greeted, "Charlie… Samantha," acknowledging the others. "Been trying to get ahold of you."

"Hi, Russ," she greeted.

"Can I take you away for a moment?" he asked. "Buy you a cup of coffee? It's official business."

She knew a meeting like this was coming, so she excused herself for a couple of minutes and followed Russ to a more secluded table in the small restaurant. He was tall, fit, and looked younger than he was, something more than one single lady in the community had noticed.

After they sat down, he ordered his usual breakfast, and she just asked for water. Then, he asked her how things were going at the festival, inquired about her injured employee, Orrie, and when all the obvious topics were out of the way, they focused on what the chief really wanted to talk about.

"So, I bet you wanna ask me about Darius and Piper Larkin," she concluded.

"Well, you *do* live next door to them," he reminded.

"Our houses are a quarter mile apart. I didn't know 'em except to maybe wave when he was out on his riding lawn mower."

"But you walk to work sometimes," he reminded.

"Yeah, but when I do, I don't go by their house. I

take a walking trail. My office is offsite from New Castle, remember?"

"So, you haven't noticed anything unusual," he persisted. "No strangers, strange cars, noises, anything like that in the past several days or weeks?"

"No. I'm not even staying at home right now. Lancelot and I are staying at Samantha's," she said, gesturing to one of her coworkers. "I'm helpin' her out with some projects."

"Well, Wanda, what the hell *do* you know?" he asked impatiently.

"Just what the news and everyone else is talking about," she replied. "Darius apparently had some kind of meltdown. He killed Piper, stuck her in the freezer, and at some point, he couldn't live with the grief and guilt anymore and climbed into the freezer with her. A murder/suicide."

"Yeah," he mused, stroking his chin. "But there's just a lot of odd things surrounding it."

"Yeah? Like what?"

He took a drink of his coffee.

"Can't say, it's an ongoing investigation."

"Yeah, but you wanna tell me because I'm cute and adorable," she said, batting her eyes at him and purposely overplaying it.

He smiled at her playfulness and decided to share a little bit. "Okay… Piper's sister, Julie, just wakes up out of the blue one day and decides to file a missing persons report. This is weeks after not having any communication with her sister. Who waits weeks to file a missing persons report when they both work at the *same* Walmart, and she *knows* something is up because her sister had quit? Plus, Piper's not even the one who quit. It was Darius who called the HR manager at Walmart."

Wanda thought for a moment. "I admit, that's weird. But maybe the sisters weren't all that close. Family dynamics can be tricky."

"There are other things, too," Russ admitted quietly. "Darius quit his job as a trucker at exactly the same time he called Walmart for Piper. All the money from the Larkins' checking account was withdrawn. The coroner thinks this happened after Piper's death. Why would Darius withdraw all their money but then commit suicide?"

"He probably originally intended to run," Wanda reasoned, "but the guilt got to him."

"I figured that, too," Russ nodded. "So, what happened to the money? It wasn't in their house, and it was quite a bit."

She just looked at him and shrugged.

"You sure you don't know anything, Wanda? Even a small detail could help."

"I really don't, Russ. But, if you want, send a couple of your boys out to my property and walk the land, be my guest. Maybe there's a clue there."

"I'll take you up on that," he agreed.

She looked at him empathetically. "I *am* heartsick about the Larkins, Russ. We all are. I know you've got your hands full."

"We'll figure it out," he said as the waitress headed toward him with his breakfast.

"Anything else?" she asked. "If not, I should really—"

"Yeah, sure," he said, understanding.

Wanda smiled and rose from the table as Russ was being served.

"There's always a couple of free tickets for you at the festival window if you want," she reminded.

"I appreciate it. But I better stay grounded in the real world until this is solved," he observed.

Four days later, on a Tuesday morning, Noah walked into a conference room at the Hudson Public Library in Highlands. The library reflected the town; it was small but smartly designed with a front brick sidewalk, a beautifully lit A-frame entranceway, and double glass multi-paned doors that looked like you could be walking into a prestigious legal or doctor's office instead of a library. There were gorgeous garden walkways with benches in the back, a fieldstone fireplace inside, and waiting in the library's conference room was a nice-looking man in his early seventies with wavy white hair and a Cary Grant-like cleft in his chin named Russel Burges. He was casually dressed in slacks and a golf shirt.

"Russel?" Noah asked as he stepped inside wearing his usual plain-colored t-shirt—today it was a faded scarlet—with blue jeans and a pair of Hey Dudes. He was also carrying a briefcase for a laptop and had its shoulder strap slung over his shoulder.

"Call me Russ," he said, rising to meet his appointment.

"Hi, Russ," Noah said, shaking hands with him. "Noah Galloway. Cathy, who works here and hooked us up, said you used to teach Irish Language and Literature at Clemson."

"For nearly thirty years, yes. But then, they reorganized the department and focused on only twentieth-century Irish literature. My expertise goes back further, so retirement seemed logical."

"I see," Noah said, setting his briefcase on the conference room table and sitting down. "Do you think you could translate some letters written in Gaeilge and put them into English?"

"Well, I haven't used my Gaeilge in a while," Russ said, sitting down. "But I suppose. What kind of letters?"

Noah dug into his briefcase and pulled out his MacBook. "Letters written by a young mother to an infant daughter. But these are much more than just letters. When looked at in total, other people who read a little Gaeilge have told me what I *really* have seems to be a fictional story about the history and disappearance of the Tuatha Dé Dannan and a several years war they fought with a human Irish clan named Fergus. I suppose the mother wrote these letters by hand, on parchment, and in Gaeilge to be more authentic and put herself in the world she was creating. But in truth, I don't know if the author was young, old, a woman, or even if there *is* a daughter. The writer could have just created the daughter so she could use a first-person narrative. I'm not sure. I-I can't tell you anymore because I don't know anything about the author."

"Fascinating," the older man said. "How did you get these letters?"

"I bought a trunk at an estate sale, and they were inside, tied up with bundles of string. The trunk was locked, and the man running the sale didn't have the key. So, it was a mystery surprise kind of purchase. I haven't had the ink or parchment tested, but they look old."

"Do you have these letters here?" Burges asked.

"Yes," Noah answered, taking a flash drive from his pocket. Then, he took an adapter out of his briefcase and plugged it into his Mac. "Once I jimmied the lock of the trunk and found the letters, I photographed them and put 'em on a flash drive so the originals wouldn't get damaged."

"And, you say you've had other people look at the letters who speak Gaeilge?" Russ asked.

"Friends of friends," Noah replied. "Not a true academic like you. That's how I came up with the theory that the author was actually writing a fictional story through the letters."

Noah was lying through his teeth about the backstory, but he couldn't very well tell the truth. He had anticipated and rehearsed the answers to several questions a potential translator might ask.

"Intriguing," the white-haired man said, folding his hands together while Noah finished hooking up the adapter. "When did you buy this trunk?"

"A year or so ago. I've been toying with the idea of using the letters as the basis for a novel. But to make that determination, I have to have a full and complete translation."

"And how many letters are we talking about?" Russ asked.

"Three hundred twenty-one."

"Oh, wow," the older one said, surprised. "That's a *lot* of translating."

"Not as much as you think," Noah replied. "As I say, they were handwritten on parchment and therefore not that long. I suppose I could do all the translating by computer, but I want someone who truly understands Irish history. That'd be helpful."

He plugged the flash drive into the adapter and called up the first letter. "Just take a look at one, see if you can translate it, and tell me what you think."

The former teacher turned the laptop screen toward him, pulled some glasses out of his pocket, slipped them on, and then read aloud:

"M-my beautiful darling daughter: Know first, that I love thee with all my heart. If ya be knowin' of these writin's, it means either I died early in yer life or we got separated by centuries, and I'm truly sorry I wasn't there for yer learnin' and growin'. But me words are here in these letters, and I need ta be tellin' ya about yer people, the Tuatha Dé Dannan, the greed of humans, and a corridor in time through which ya were able to escape."

Burges looked up from the computer screen at Noah. "A corridor in time?"

"Another person who read this letter referred to it as a doorway," Noah lied. "But either way, pretty interesting, huh?"

Russ rubbed his chin, thinking. "The Tuatha Dé Dannan are as famous in Irish legend as, say, Sasquatch is here in the United States. But like all legends, there are variations. Some say Sasquatch is a product of the Appalachian Mountains. Others say, the Central Rockies. Still others say the Pacific Northwest and into Canada. If you're correct and your author wrote a story through a series of letters, she's got fertile ground to work with because the theories about the Tuatha Dé Dannan are as different as the location of the Sasquatch population."

He turned back to the letter and continued reading. After several seconds, he glanced down at a small drawing at the bottom of the parchment. "These three interconnecting circles at the bottom are pretty interesting," he noted.

"Really?" Noah asked. "Every letter ends with them. What do they mean?"

"In Irish history, there's a symbol called a Triquetra. You've probably seen it on pendants, mugs, even rings. It's a very popular design. Irish Christians adopted its interlocking rings to symbolize the holy trinity: the Father, Son, and Holy Spirit. But its exact origins are unknown. This doesn't look exactly like a Triquetra—the edges of the rings are more rounded than the Triquetra's oblong rings—but that's the first thing that popped into my mind when I saw it. Very curious."

Noah nodded and smiled a little, knowing the former teacher was hooked and would do the translation.

34

GOLDMINE ROAD

Saturday, Noah, Fay, and Erin, being pushed in a stroller, were walking on the dirt road part of Goldmine Road about a half mile from Mike and Ami's. Everyone was dressed for hiking, and Erin sported a white-and-yellow striped hat to keep the sun off her fair face. Fay wore a blue bandana around her head to cover her ears in case they came across other hikers or ATV riders, which were common on this part of the mountain.

Goldmine Road stretched beyond the Galloway place and wove around California Gap for nearly another mile before it ended not far from a waterfall that Noah wanted to share with the girls. "The girls," he said to himself. *"My* girls." He really liked the sound of that and was surprised by how easily it was to go from thinking like a single man to a family man. But he never would've made the mental switch unless he wanted to—

and with every passing day—he wanted to more and more.

"The guy I met with earlier this week asked me about the three rings you drew at the end of your letters. What do they mean?"

"It's a variation of a symbol me people have used fer hundreds of years," she replied. "Legend says they got it from a human tribe from the far north."

"Are you talking about Norsemen? Vikings?" he asked.

"Accordin' to your internet, aye, I believe so. The interlockin' rings mean different things to different people: land, sea, and sky. Or birth, life, and death. But me own design was simply ta represent you, me, and Erin. So, no matter what happens ta me, we're always connected."

"Nothing's going to happen to you," he replied, knowing it was a somewhat silly thing to say considering their circumstances.

"Why are so few birds singin'?" she asked, changing subjects. "A forest this thick should be brimmin' with birds."

"Scientists say that since 1970, we've lost nearly three billion birds in North America alone." Noah replied sadly.

"What?" she asked, surprised, "Why?"

"Loss of forests, wetlands, hunting, birds running into glass windows and towers, plane strikes, and global warming probably hasn't helped either."

"What's that?"

"The view that man's technology has changed the climate and this has had an effect on numerous animals, fish and birds."

"That's tragic," Fay lamented. "Birds are wonderful communicators. Much better than snakes."

"'Eans!" Erin exclaimed, knowing the Gaeilge word for "birds."

"That's right, me darlin'," Fay reinforced. "'Eans ."

"What do you mean the birds are wonderful communicators?" Noah asked.

"They're easy for me people ta understand. They can warn us of danger, announce changes in the weather, they say a lot if ya know how ta listen."

She stopped walking and focused in on a mockingbird. "Hear that mockingbird? He's happy. He's singin' for the sheer joy of it, repeatin' all the songs of the other birds that made *him* happy."

She pointed to a male cardinal. "Hear that one? He's lookin' for a mate. He's lonely and ready ta settle down and start a family."

Noah, who had stopped walking because Fay had, looked around and spotted a little tufted titmouse chirping away on a branch. "What about him?"

"He's a her, actually," Fay corrected, "and she's hungry. She wants her mate ta go huntin' for bugs with her. Probably near water."

"Huh," he said, intrigued, then he started to walk again.

"Wait," Fay said, with an open hand, "give a pause." She cocked her head and listened to one bird's small, continuous chirping.

"That's distress," she recognized. "That's a baby in trouble."

She stepped off the road into the woods near a sheer wall of craggy granite about forty feet high and twenty feet wide. Such outcroppings of rocks weren't as common in the mountains of North Carolina as in California, Montana, or Colorado, but they did jut up from the forest floor now and again.

"Ma?" Erin called, wondering where she was going. Noah watched as she searched around the base of the rock wall.

"Ah, there ya be," she said. "Good thing ya landed on some ferns." She bent down into the brush and gently scooped up a baby sparrow with both hands. "Ya poor little thing," she said, looking up to see where its mother's nest was. "I think I see a bit of twigs stickin' out from the crevice up there," she said, nodding to a crevice about twenty feet off the ground.

Noah lifted Erin out of the stroller and carried her into the woods where Fay was.

"Nobody's here," he said, looking around. "Why don't you just slip off your blouse, unfold your wings, and put it back?"

"That'll actually take more magic than I'd like ta spend," she confessed. "I made a nightlight in the woods for Erin when we first arrived, flew around in yer studio, summoned winged creatures ta help Erin get ta sleep, relieved some of Orrie's pain in the hospital, grabbed a snake in the blink of an eye… I need ta not use so much."

Noah looked up at the rock wall. "Is that where you think the nest is?" he asked, nodding to a crevice with a few bits of twigs and hay peeking over the edge.

"Aye."

He looked carefully at the granite wall, then nodded.

"Okay. Put the bird in my t-shirt breast pocket and take Erin."

She looked at him, surprised. "What? Yer not goin' ta try and climb up there, are ya?"

"If we leave it on the ground, will it die?"

"Probably."

"Then stick it in my pocket and take the baby. The Tuatha Dé Dannan aren't the only ones who care about the creatures of the wood. Besides, I *am* a rock climber, although not a free-form one."

Fay looked at him, concerned. "Noah, if ya get hurt, I don't drive, and I can't spend a lot of me power on healin' ya. I mean, I *will*, but—"

"Put the bird in my pocket and take Erin before I change my mind," he repeated.

She said something in Gaeilge to soothe the little bird, then stepped over and slipped it into Noah's t-shirt pocket.

"Bird," Erin announced in English as Fay took her daughter from Noah.

"Be careful, lad," she said. "This is a kind—but I'm not sure smart—idea."

Noah went over to the granite wall and searched the crags for a natural ladder of protruding ridges to lay a hand and foot. This required a trained and experienced eye, which, fortunately, he had. When he decided upon an ascent path, he put a foot onto a ridge, grabbed another protruding piece of granite with his hand, and began to climb.

"Talk to me," he said as he looked around and found another ridge to step up to. "Me and my climbing buddies do that sometimes, and as weird as it sounds, talking about other things helps to keep us focused on the climb."

"Talk to ya about what?" she asked as she watched him push himself up to about four feet off the ground.

"Anything," he replied, looking around for the next place to put a foot. "If you leave Erin with me when you go back to Ireland, do you care if I take her to church?"

"Ya mean, like, a Christian church?"

"Yeah," he said, taking another step up.

"I didn't figure ya fer the church goin' type," she noted.

"I don't go as often as I should, but if I do sometimes, would you care if I took her? Like, with my parents at Christmas or something? I know that religion can be a sticking point in some relationships."

He took another step upward, then looked around for his next climbing point.

"Christians have the one god, and the Tuatha Dé

Dannan have several," Fay mused. "As long as Erin knows the difference between right and wrong, learns that nature is sacred, and is kind ta others, I don't care what religion ya glue it all together with."

"What about daycare?" he asked. "I mean, she's old enough to be in that now."

"I think bein' around other kids her own age would be healthy fer her," Fay replied. "I'd also like Wanda ta be a regular part of her life."

"Absolutely," he agreed. "She's been your greatest supporter in this time."

As he continued to move upward slowly but steadily, there were a few moments of silence, then Erin started to become anxious and called up to Noah, "Da?"

Now about twelve feet high, Noah stopped and looked down at her.

"Did you hear that?" he asked excitedly. "She called me 'Da'."

"That's lovely," Fay said. "B-but concentrate on what yer doin', will ya?"

"Talk to me about somethin'," he repeated.

"Ya say that ya love me. And I believe ya. But how much of it is love, and how much of it is only because I'm different and our time together is limited?"

"What's it matter?" he replied, taking another step upward. "It's all part of the same package, and that package is you."

"What if it's only about sex? We've got absolutely nothin' in common."

"Not true. We both love Erin. We both love nature.

We both want your people to survive. We both like my pictures. We've got *lots* in common."

"Yeah, but if I were just a normal human girl, would ya be workin' this hard ta save a baby bird?"

He paused and looked down at her. "Maybe not. But I *am* saving a baby bird. Meaning, you make me want to be a better person. That's something to ascend to."

She smiled as he took another couple of steps, peeked his head over the ledge that held the protruding twigs, and saw a nest with two other hungry baby sparrows inside it. Hanging onto a protruding ledge tightly with one hand, he reached into the pocket of his shirt with the other and deposited the fallen bird back into its nest.

"Well done, lad," Fay called.

"Well done," Erin echoed in her small voice.

Noah started to come down as carefully as he went up, trying to retrace his steps.

"Y'know," Fay said, "if I didn't have ta go back ta me century and we had all the time in the world, our relationship would still be a thicket of thorns. I'd eventually run out of magic, and I don't know how I'd be handlin' that."

"Maybe you'd run out of magic," he reminded. "We're not positive. The only way to be sure is to return to Ireland in this time, which we should plan to do next year. Before you go, I'll take a passport photo. Although I don't have the faintest idea of how to get a passport on the black market."

"You'd take me back to Ireland?" she asked, pleased.

"Of course," he said, taking a step down. "We'd have at least a six-week window, right?"

She thought, then nodded. "Wanda might be able ta help with the passport."

"Really?"

"She's quite resourceful. But there are still a thousand things about yer time and culture I know nothin' about."

"Like what?"

She thought for a moment, "Well, I haven't seen any *Star Wars* movies. I only know about 'em because of the festival."

"Easy fix," he said, taking another step.

"I've never ridden a bike. I can't drive a car. I've never played a sport."

"No biggies," he decided, taking another descending step.

"I can make coffee in a microwave, but I've never used an oven, or an iron, or a blender, or a power tool besides Wanda's push mower. I barely know how ta use a cellphone."

"You can learn, and I'm an exceptional ironer."

"I've never seen *"The Real Housewives of Atlanta."*

"That one's actually a plus," he said, looking around and finding another protruding piece of rock to step down on. "I grant you, there are differences. But in the end, honey, it's the basic, instinctive attraction between us that matters, who we are inside, and whether or not we think we're strong enough to take on all the other bullshit."

"Tis a whole big pasture full of bullshit pies, me lad, but I see yer point."

"Bullshit," Erin chirped.

"Your daughter," he joked.

"Your language," she shot back.

As soon as Noah returned to the forest floor, he bent over, took a few deep breaths, and was too absorbed in being on terra firma again to notice much around him. His adrenaline was pumping, and he was thankful that he didn't slip and take a fall, although he'd picked up a few scratches and, no doubt, a bruise along the way. There was a part of him that said what he had just done was probably stupid: risking his life for a baby bird's. On the other hand, he wasn't sorry.

"Listen," Fay said, slowly rubbing a comforting hand up and down his back.

"What?"

He straightened up and looked around. The surrounding woods were now filled with the sound of chirping birds. A lot of them. It was unusual because there were so many singing. It was like their songs were feathered applause. He also saw the mother sparrow return to her nest with a worm in her beak to feed her three babies. He smiled and looked at Fay, then they both looked at Erin.

About forty minutes later, after visiting the waterfall Noah wanted to show his girls, they backtracked up

Goldmine Road. As they neared the house, Noah, Fay, and Erin suddenly stopped as he spotted the familiar Lexus on the gravel driveway parked next to his pickup.

"Oh, Christ," he sighed.

"What?" she asked.

"My parents… they're here."

35

ONE THING AT A TIME

Noah and Fay entered the Galloways' mountain home with trepidation, not knowing what to expect. Fay carried Erin, and Noah carried the folded-up stroller.

"Oh, my God. Here they are!" Noah's mom happily announced. "Helloooo!"

Mike was much more subdued and almost apologetic in his manner about interrupting the younger couple's privacy.

"Surprise," he smiled weakly.

"Hi…" Noah said with uncertainty, looking at one parent, then the other. "W-what're you guys doing here?"

"Well—it's just—" Ami started to say.

"It's just that your mother is channeling a little too much Lucy Ricardo and poking her nose in where it doesn't belong?"

"Who?" Fay whispered to Noah.

"Tell ya later," he said under his breath.

"We're not staying the night," Ami announced. "I mean, I know you two are in the process of figuring things out," she said, using her fingers for quotation marks as she said, "figuring things out." "But we thought Fay getting to know us might be helpful to that process. So we thought we'd come over for a cookout, a little visit, and then we'll head back to Atlanta."

"*You* thought we'd come over for a cookout," Mike corrected.

"You drove three hours to have a cookout, then you're going to drive back?" Noah asked.

"Well, you know your mom," Mike observed, "practicality is her middle name." He looked at Fay and smiled weakly.

There was an awkward silence until Fay smiled, stepped toward Ami while still holding Erin, and extended a hand. "Tis grand ta meet both of you. I'm Fayetta Smith, and this is Erin. Yer granddaughter."

Ami was so happy that her eyes began to fill with tears. She reached over and gently touched an uncertain Erin's hand.

"Hello, sweetheart! I'm your Grandma. I'm so thrilled to meet you. *Both* of you."

"I'm pleased too," Mike added, more quietly but genuinely. "Although I would've had you guys pick the time for Fay and Erin to meet us instead of the other way around."

"It doesn't matter a fig," Fay said, adopting the same attitude she would as if she were working as an ambassador at the festival. "We're glad yer here and so grateful for you lettin' us use yer beautiful home."

"'It doesn't matter a fig,'" Ami repeated, delighted. "Oh, she sounds just like a Lucky Charms commercial."

Noah looked at his mom and widened his eyes, exasperated.

Twenty minutes later, Ami was holding Erin on the deck and talking happily to her while Noah snapped a couple of pictures of them with his Cannon. Google Home was playing Fleetwood Mac in the kitchen, and Mike was putting seasonings on some burgers he and Ami had bought in town before coming to the house. Fay stood by one of the bar stools, chatting with him and sipping on a Sam Adams.

"So, Fay," Mike asked. "I know you're from Ireland, but whereabouts?"

"County Sligo. It's in the northern and western regions in the province of Connacht, which borders the North Atlantic."

"And your people? Your family?" he asked.

"Farmers… I come from several generations of farmers."

"I see," Mike said, still sprinkling seasonings on the patties. "And—how did you wind up working at the Georgia Renaissance Festival?"

"Through school and an international jobs program they offered," she fibbed. "I really had a great experience me first year and have come back in the spring ever since. This is me fifth season."

"But you're not working this year?"

"Uh, no. As I'm sure Noah told ya, we're trying ta figure out how me, Erin, and himself fit together. He's made it clear he wants ta be a part of her life. But me life isn't here, and his life isn't in Ireland. So, we're tryin' ta unravel a few knots."

Mike set the burgers aside, opened a package of hamburger buns, and put them on a plate so he could toast them after the meat was ready.

"If you don't mind me asking, Fay, if Noah hadn't returned to the festival looking for you after you'd given birth, did you intend to tell him about Erin?"

"That's a great question, but I've got a shaky answer. I have responsibilities to me family in Ireland, and bringin' Noah into me life complicates things. On the other hand, he has a right ta know he has a child, and I *did* bring Erin back to the States with me when she was just a wee two months old. So, subconsciously, perhaps yes."

"And now an attraction has developed?" Mike asked, wanting confirmation.

"Yes, sir. Quite an attraction. Yer son's pretty amazin'."

"Well, thanks. We're proud of him."

"So," Fay said, "what specifically would ya like ta know about me? I mean, that's why yer here, right? Education? Religion? Politics?"

"I admire your candor," Mike smiled. "How about education? I mean, if you don't mind. Could you share something about that?"

"Well, I speak several languages," she offered.

"Yeah?"

"English, Gaeilge, Old Norse, Italian, French, Spanish… I'm not that up on pop culture, but I am something of a polyglot." She wasn't lying. Languages were something the Tuatha Dé Dannan picked up very easily.

"Wow, cool," Mike said, impressed, getting a bowl out of a cabinet for potato chips.

"How many languages do *you* speak?" she asked.

"Uh, it's all I can do to communicate clearly in English," Mike admitted with a hint of embarrassment.

Meanwhile, out on the deck, a similar type of Q&A was going on.

"How's it going with you two?" Ami asked her son. "Is love blooming?"

"Love is definitely blooming," he confessed.

"Yes, dat's won-der-full!" Ami said, still holding Erin and speaking to her in baby-speak. "You mentioned you two were talking about co-parenting, honey? How is that going to work? It's not like you can just jet over to Ireland every other week. Or is that what you're thinking?"

"No. I don't have that kind of money, and I know Fay doesn't," he replied. "But it'll be some kind of schedule. Maybe… maybe Erin will stay with me in the States for a while. A few weeks or possibly longer."

"Hhm… it's not likely a mother will leave her fifteen-month-old daughter for an extended period of time with a father she doesn't know all that well who lives in another country," Ami observed. "But, let me put this on the table: Your dad's pretty well off. Would it be helpful if your dad and I sprung for plane tickets to Ireland, say, once every few months, and you could stay for a week or so each visit?"

Noah looked at his mom appreciatively.

"I'm not sure that'll be necessary. But I love you for offering it."

"Of course. You're my baby," Ami smiled. Then, she looked at Erin. "And you're my *grandbaby.*"

The rest of the day went by very socially, with Noah and Fay occasionally shooting each other looks when talking to Ami and Mike to make sure what they were saying was in sync. Being on guard all the time was stressful, but by 6:00 p.m. that evening, Noah's parents were headed back to Atlanta with their goals accomplished: They had met their granddaughter and gotten all the background information out of Fay they could without sounding like a couple of police interrogators. She charmed them with her obvious beauty and smiles, and they seemed to accept her answers to their questions. As for Erin, the love was immediate. They also liked Fay's queries about what Noah was like as a child and whether or not they had any baby pictures of him in their mountain home. By 9:00 p.m., Erin had been bathed and sung to by both of her parents, who offered different tunes. Fay sang a beautiful fairy lullaby in Gaeilge, then Noah sang "My Girl" by The Temptations. When Erin had finally drifted off, Fay removed the blue bandana she'd had on her head and ears for over twelve hours and took a long, hot shower. Noah made a fire in the fireplace, then poured himself a whiskey. He was sitting on the sofa and had his camera bag on the coffee table in front of him while making some notes in his little leather notebook when Fay emerged from the master bedroom wearing his mom's teal terrycloth robe. Her long, red hair was still partially wet after using the hair dryer, and it hung wild and loose. She took Noah's glass off a coaster on the coffee table and took a sip of his drink.

"Quite the day of unexpected events," she observed, running her fingers through her hair. "You rock climbin' and rescuin' a bird. Me givin' a mountain of answers ta yer ma and da, some true, some not."

He closed his notebook and looked at her. "Well, we couldn't very well tell 'em the whole truth. I mean—we *could*—but who knows what problems that would cause."

She glanced out at the fading light and the evening shadows overtaking the mountains beyond. "I've seen some movies on television that warn when a person travels through time, their presence and actions risk changin' the future. Do ya think that's true?"

"I don't know."

"Do ya think me studyin' military tactics and sendin' weapons back can change the past?"

"I don't know, baby," he repeated.

She set his glass down and sunk her hands into the pockets of his mom's robe. "If it *did* make a difference. If me people survived, do ya think we could survive all the way up to today? Or, if we proved the magic was still in the land, maybe I could bring a couple of dozen folks back with me once we know fer sure. Would the humans in this time accept us?"

He looked at her empathetically and wanted to say "yes," but then he thought of Western man's long history of trying to control everything and drive indigenous people and species from their homes.

"I honestly don't know."

She nodded and looked out at the view with a trace of sadness. Noticing this, he leaned forward and took his Cannon out of his camera bag.

"I've got some nice shots of you, Erin, and my folks. Wanna see?"

"Maybe later… I've gotta stretch me wings."

She walked over to the sliding glass doors, opened them, then stepped outside. Noah watched as she untied her robe, slipped it off her shoulders, then let it drop to the wood plank deck. There was still enough light to see the contours of her lily-white legs, rounded bottom, frizzy long hair, and slender arms but enough nighttime to ensure privacy from another mountain homeowner who might be on their balcony. In any event, they would've needed binoculars to see details. Noah watched her beautiful naked figure as the seams on her back opened and her wings slowly appeared, unfolded, then spread out to their six-foot span. He felt a combination of amazement and privilege. He knew he was the only living human on Earth she had chosen to witness this.

He picked up his camera, took off the lens cap,

stood up, rounded the sofa, then clicked off a few shots of Fay's silhouette and extended wings slowly moving back and forth. Slowly lowering the camera, he looked at her lovingly.

"Wow," he whispered.

He set the camera down, noticed the blanket on the back of the sofa, then undressed. Half a minute later, he joined her on the deck with the blanket wrapped around him. The evening was cooler than he expected, and he was surprised by how unaffected Fay seemed by it. He stood beside her as she watched the evening.

"Aren't you cold?" he asked. "Got a nice warm blanket here."

She smiled, turned to him, then retracted her wings. She stepped over to him as he opened the blanket and wrapped her in his arms. When he did, she felt his wet, hard readiness press against her stomach. She closed her eyes and wished they could hold onto each other like this forever.

"Yer folks are good people," she finally said quietly. "They've taken ta Erin like tadpoles to water."

"They're glad they met her," he said. "Glad she's here."

She thought introspectively. "You're here. They're here. Wanda's here. Even Lancelot… I've decided. I'm fer sure gonna leave her with ya when I go."

Her blue eyes began filling with tears.

"Oh, God, Noah, I'm leavin' me baby behind. I-I know we've spoken about it, but now the thing is upon me, and I'm scared. Am I wrong? Abandonin' me child?"

"You're not abandoning her," he said softly. "You're leaving her where she'll be safe, and it's not forever. It's just until the next year's Shea Karna."

"If I can escape the horzikaan. *If* I can survive another year of the war. *If* the corridor's still there."

"One thing at a time," he said, kissing her forehead.

"What're ya gonna tell yer parents about me leavin' Erin for an entire year?"

"One thing at a time," he repeated.

They held each other silently for nearly a minute. Then, he finally asked:

"What do you want to do?"

She sniffled and wiped her tears on the blanket. "Go back to Lilburn. I've got weapons to prepare, and there are only two more weekends of the festival. Shea Karna happens around the final weekend, give or take a week. We've gotta get back, and I've gotta start checkin' the hole in Wanda's oak tree."

"Where the horzikaan will be," he concluded.

"He'll be somewhere around," she verified. "Either himself or his familiar."

He nodded, then made a decision. "We're taking my dad's Glock, and you're *going* to learn how to use it."

36

PACKING

Five days later, on a Thursday at about 6 p.m., Cole Huggins stood behind a tripod holding an Olympus OM-1 camera and shot a four-piece set of Hartmann luggage against an all-white background in his and Noah's studio. Annie, the studio manager, had just left for the day, and surrounding the lighted stage area where Cole was shooting were several long folding tables that held briefcases, shoulder bags, duffels, and other Hartmann products. He was working on the opposite side of the studio from where Noah and Fay had once shared a glass of wine. After Cole was satisfied he had a good final shot for the day, he looked at his wristwatch, then walked over and turned on the overhead studio lights. As he did, Noah came into the studio from the lobby.

"Hey," Noah waved.

Cole nodded at him, then gestured to the other side

of the studio where a dozen long cardboard boxes sat, all addressed to Noah's attention.

"They've been arriving for over a week," Cole said. "A box here, a box there. Annie says they're from different medieval weapons manufacturers."

"Yeah," Noah said. "They're for Fay. She's got a side hustle in Ireland selling these, and she's expanding her suppliers beyond Dale Taylor."

"Uh-huh," Cole mused. "And what about when the FBI came to see Wanda with their claims about modern weapons being buried in an ancient battleground?"

"She doesn't know anything about that," he lied. "I don't doubt what you lip read, but I just haven't got an explanation. I still think the FBI is full of shit."

"It doesn't make any damn sense," Cole responded.

"Nothing does," Noah agreed. "We're living on mud, surrounded by water, on a ball floating in space, surrounded by other uninhabited balls. But we pay tons of money to people who play with balls really well, while the teachers who teach us about those other balls floating in space are grossly underpaid. Go figure."

"Okay… well, thanks for that, Aristotle," Cole observed. "I'm going to go home."

About ten minutes later, there was a knock on the studio door, and Fay, carrying a tote bag, came in, followed by Wanda, who was carrying Erin, followed by Lancelot. After a hug and kiss for Noah from Fay and Erin, Wanda set Erin down and returned to her Honda while Lancelot roamed around and sniffed his new surroundings. She came back inside a minute later with a couple of long boxes and a smaller, square one.

"What've ya got there?" Fay asked, unaware that Wanda had some things in her trunk.

"Two NATO semi-automatic rifles, with two clips for each," she replied, businesslike. "Each clip holds thirty rounds, and there are five hundred rounds in that smaller box."

"Well done," Noah nodded approvingly. *"Finally,* weapons that make sense!"

"Wanda, me people don't know anything about automatic rifles," Fay said. "They're just now getting good with swords."

"They'll learn," she said bluntly. "Instruction books are in the boxes."

"You told me yourself your people are very intelligent," Noah reminded. "I know you were concerned about buying firearms for fear of a background check, but you didn't buy 'em. Wanda did."

"I want my honorary daughter to come back to her child," the older woman said. "I don't give a shit if the FBI finds them tomorrow rusted in some Irish field. I want you and your people to survive."

"The world needs magic, baby," Noah concurred.

Fay looked at the boxes and smiled faintly.

"Well, thank ya… I think I've got the best stockpile of supplies ever, thanks ta both of ya."

Erin suddenly made a face, which was followed moments later by a pungent smell.

"Oh goodness—time for a change," Fay said. Still

with her tote slung around her shoulder, she scooped Erin up and took her into one of the dressing rooms. She'd seen the dressing rooms in previous visits but hadn't actually been in one. As she stepped inside and put her tote bag on a counter in front of the lighted mirror, she turned and noticed some framed candid pictures of personalities that Noah and Cole had worked with on the wall, just inside the doorway. Some of Cole's pictures featured him standing with a well-known NASCAR driver, a CNN reporter, and the king and queen of the royal court from the Renaissance festival. Noah's photos were much more impressive: he stood with the mayor of Atlanta in one shot, a rock & roll hall of famer in another, and a household name movie star in still another. There was also a photo of him and Z-Rae standing next to one another on the yacht during their photo shoot in Greece. The picture was taken by the marketing director of Saint Bart's Swimwear. Noah stood on the flying bridge with a camera in his hand, smiling for the marketing director while Z stood beside him, wearing one of her swimsuits, looking up at Noah. The way she gazed at him caused Fay to have a realization. As a woman, she knew what that look meant. She continued staring at the photo until Erin's fussiness brought her back to the task at hand.

While Fay changed her daughter, Noah got a bowl of water for Lancelot from the closet that had been turned into a kitchenette, then stepped over to Wanda.

"Everything all right? Has anyone approached you, or have you seen any evidence of a powerful wizard?"

"No… I'm still staying with a friend, and I make sure I'm never alone if I go to the office or New Castle. If the horzikaan is attending the festival on the weekends looking for Fay, I haven't seen any evidence of it. But then again, he doesn't need to. He knows the tree on my property is the corridor, and the portal will open sooner or later. All he's got to do is watch that."

"Any new developments with the murder/suicide that happened next door?" he asked, having known about the Larkins from Fay talking to Wanda while she was in Highlands.

"No. The police walked my property and looked around but didn't see anything unusual."

"Do you think what happened next door was really a murder/suicide?"

"Do *you?*" she retorted.

Fay and Erin emerged from the dressing room a moment later. The baby was still fussy, and Fay asked Noah to take her while she turned and looked at the boxes that Cole had referred to. Over two dozen of them were stacked just a few feet from the kitchenette.

"Is this all of it?" she asked.

"Well, there are still the boxes at my place," he replied. "But here, you've got one hundred sixty-eight swords, seventy-two daggers, fifty shields, about sixty helmets, fifty axes, crossbows, arrows, flare guns, flares, smoke bombs, Bic lighters, first aid kits, penicillin—everything you asked for. Then, there's the rifles and ammo that Wanda got, my dad's Glock, and a box of ammo for that."

Wanda surveyed all of the boxes. "It sounds like a lot, but it's not enough for an army."

"It doesn't have ta be," Fay said, stepping over to the stash. "It just has ta be enough for small hit-and-run groups. Besides, we'll pick up weapons along the way." She clasped her hands and rubbed them together. "Right then... let's get these supplies to transportable size. Noah, give Erin to Wanda, and let's set up some boxes on the table. About three boxes at a time." She was referring to the worktable where she and Noah had shared a glass of wine the night she revealed who she really was.

Noah did as she asked, putting three boxes on the worktable, then stepped over to where Wanda was.

"Okay. A little bit of silence, please," Fay requested. "This requires concentration."

She spread her hands toward the boxes on the table, closed her eyes, and mumbled something in Gaeilge. A second later, a golden aura appeared around the boxes, accompanied by what could only be described as a pleasant "om" sound. Another second after that, the three boxes quickly and steadily were reduced to the size of three matchbox cars or a little smaller. As the boxes shrank, there was also the subtle sound of cardboard, tape, and packing materials adjusting to their new dimensions.

"Holy shit!" Wanda muttered under her breath.

"Yeah," Noah agreed, just as quiet and amazed.

"Traic," Erin chirped, forgetting her fussiness. It was Gaeilge for "Trick.""

When the transformation was complete, Fay moved the small boxes to the far side of the worktable and looked at Noah.

"Three more, please."

He got three more boxes, set them on the table, and then stepped over to Wanda and Erin.

They watched again as Fay repeated the reducing process with the "om" sound and golden aura. Lancelot noticed it too and, likewise, stood there watching.

"It's like finding out there really is a Santa Claus," he said, quietly but open-mouthed.

"And he rides a hippogriff," Wanda added.

"And lives in Atlantis," he continued.

"Right next door to a girl with kaleidoscope eyes," she finished.

They looked at each other and chuckled as Fay moved the newly reduced boxes aside and asked for three more.

Meantime, forty-three miles away in Fairburn, Georgia, the horzikaan's raven landed in the branches of Wanda's oak tree and looked around, as it did several times a day. After poking its beak into the hole of the oak tree and seeing nothing unusual, it flew through the woods until it arrived in Wanda's backyard. The bird sat for a moment on the lawn that hadn't been mowed in a while and eyed the dark house, then it squawked and took to the air where it circled both Wanda's place and the Larkins', where there was yellow crime scene tape crossing the door with an X. Next, it started to head back to suite 210 of the Embassy Suites in Fairburn. It was close to a grocery and liquor store and just a seven-minute cab ride to the festival grounds of New Castle. Inside suite 210, the horzikaan sat in an easy chair watching an episode of *MythBusters* and wearing some of Darius Larkin's clothes. He'd rented the suite by temporarily hypnotizing the manager and convincing him he'd received proper ID upon check-in. The wizard even provided the manager with a driver's license taken from a visitor at the festival. Then, after he was safely checked in, he released the manager, who assumed everything was in order due to the spell.

Like Fay, the wizard had concluded that reducing and taking several items of modern technology back would give him an edge in his own time. So, on the dining room table were several items that he'd already shrunk waiting to go into a small satchel also on the table. Some of the items included night vision goggles, tasers, mace dispensers, five-gallon containers of gasoline and, for personal comfort, several packages of toilet paper.

As the horzikaan sat there watching television, he sunk his inch-long fingernails into the fabric armrest and slowly drew his arm back, ripping the chair. It was a subconscious motion he'd already repeated several times, and the armrest was a jumble of torn white stuffing, broken threads, and ripped fabric.

37

CHECKING

On Saturday, the second to the final weekend of the season's renaissance festival, Noah's pickup truck pulled into Wanda's gravel driveway at 6:23 a.m. There were hints in the sky that it was going to be a sunny day. But there were still some evening shadows on the ground and grayish clouds in the sky, so it was hard to be sure. Noah and Fay quietly got out of his pickup and walked around Wanda's house to the backyard. The morning birds chirped as she carried a small Coleman cooler containing all her shrunken weapons and supplies while he held his father's Glock pistol in his left hand. Noah had asked his parents to take Erin Friday night with a Saturday evening pickup, and they were more than happy to do it, although Erin didn't seem pleased with the arrangement when they dropped her off at his folk's place in Decatur. Since Shea Karna could happen almost any time now, and Fay knew from experience that the portal would only be open for about twenty-four hours, the oak tree now had to be checked regularly. At least twice a day. And since a hired gun wizard knew the corridor location, extreme caution had to be used. It was no place for a child.

"Can this horzikaan take on different shapes?" Noah asked quietly as they walked across Wanda's dewy yard. "Be a wolf, or a hawk, or something?"

"I've never heard of them bein' able to change into different creatures," Fay replied, wearing her hair loose to cover her ears, "but we now know that horzikanns change size."

"How did you determine the corridor is only open for about twenty-four hours?"

"Me second year here, I discovered the portal was open one day about noon. When it's open, it's like passin' through liquid, walkin' through a waterfall. But I couldn't leave immediately. I had weapons from Dale Taylor hidden away in Wanda's tool shed, which hadn't been reduced yet. I'd been doin' a lot of things around here to help out—and I would've done 'em anyway—but me doin' the chores kept Wanda out of the shed. It took time to reduce everythin', and then Wanda came home from her office. When I told her I had ta be leavin' soon, she insisted on takin' me out to dinner, and ta make a long story short, it wasn't until about 10:00 the followin' mornin' that I could get back to the tree. The portal was still open, but it was like pushin' things through mud, mud that was gettin' thicker all the time. That's how I established the timeframe."

He nodded and stepped ahead of her as they neared the woods at the edge of Wanda's backyard. He slowed his pace, held the Glock with two hands, and started to look carefully around at the ground level and in the trees.

"Do ya know what yer doin' with that thing?" she asked. "Have ya fired a lot of guns?"

"My dad took my mom and me to a practice range a few times after he got this," he replied. "And I've seen all the John Wick films."

"Well, nothin' ta worry about, then," she teased.

They continued quietly down a woodsy path until they arrived at the oak tree. Having never seen it before, Noah eyed its damaged top from its previous lightning strikes.

"That's it?" he asked. "I thought it would be wider, taller, more majestic."

"That's it," she confirmed.

He spied the hole in the tree some twelve feet off the ground.

"That's your corridor?"

"Aye."

"You ever run into any tenants? Squirrels, owls, doves?" he asked.

"Not yet," she replied, setting the cooler on the ground. "I'll be but a minute."

She suddenly raised her hands above her head and clapped them. The instant she did, she transformed from a five-foot-three slender woman wearing jeans, tennis shoes, and a cotton top into a five-inch-tall fairy wearing her short green dress and fur slippers. Her wings were already out and fluttering. When she clapped her hands, a little cloud of white sparkles burst into the air like someone had just thrown a handful of glitter. Noah jumped back, surprised by the sudden change, and was actually a little frightened until he heard high-pitched laughter and a tiny voice say: "Ya should see yer face? White as flour!"

With a giggle, Fay flew up and into the hole of the oak tree as quickly and nimbly as Tinkerbell introducing an episode of *The Wonderful World of Disney*. Noah swallowed hard, took a deep breath, then clutched the pistol with both hands again and looked around.

"If she ever shrank like that when I was inside of her —she'd explode," he observed. Then, catching himself, he said: "Geez, what a guy thing to say!"

A few seconds later, Fay flew out of the tree, landed on the ground, and clapped her hands above her head again. With another puffy burst of glitter-like sparkles, she transformed back to human size, wearing the street clothes she had been wearing before.

"No, not open yet," she informed in her regular voice.

"That was... intense!" he declared.

"C'mon," she said, looking around. "We shouldn't linger."

She picked up her cooler, and they started to walk back through the woods and toward Wanda's backyard. As they did, Noah suddenly heard a twig snap behind them. He unclicked the safety of the Glock, spun around, and raised it only to find he was pointing it at a doe about fifteen yards away.

"It's okay, Noah," Fay said, stepping over to him and pushing his arm down. "Don't you recognize her? She checked in on our daughter one night."

Noah and the deer looked at one another, then the doe snorted and trotted away.

"What'd she say?" he asked.

"Nothin'… c'mon, let's go."

"No. She said *something*," he argued. "What she'd say?"

"Humans!" Fay replied.

He turned and called out after the animal. "Well, you shouldn't sneak up on us like that!"

"Sshh," his lover urged. "We need to go. Each time we come here, we've got ta be quick and quiet."

They continued through the woods and back into Wanda's yard. As they did, Fay glanced over her shoulder and took one last look around to make sure they were alone.

"When the portal does open, Noah, there won't be much time for goodbyes. If it were open, I'd be pushin' supplies through it right now and followin' after."

"Without saying goodbye to Erin? Wanda?" he asked.

"A final kiss or sweet partin' word isn't goin' ta make things any easier. And a hasty goodbye doesn't mean I love ya any less. It just means this is what I have ta do fer me people."

They walked across the backyard, climbed into Noah's truck, and pulled out of the driveway.

They had been gone less than a minute when the horzikaan's raven appeared in the sky.

As it descended closer to the ground, it eyed the path of fresh footsteps across Wanda's dewy backyard and concluded the tree had recently been checked.

38

PERFECT OPPORTUNITY

The horzikaan stood at the edge of the parking lot of the Embassy Suites in the early morning sun, still wearing Darius Larkin's clothes from the evening before. He had his bejeweled staff in one hand and stroked his beard thoughtfully while his raven familiar sat in a nearby tree branch and clucked at him.

"Could an animal have caused this trail ya saw across the wet grass?" he asked the bird in Gaeilge."

The bird cackled in response.

"And ya saw nothin' unusual inside the tree?" he asked, wanting verification.

The bird cackled again.

The old wizard looked around; his squinting eyes only made his leathery face appear all the more menacing.

"If the fairy bitch is checkin' the tree, that means that Shea Karna can't be far off. I think it's time to put on me robes, call fer transport, and return ta the

Renaissance festival. If she's takin' supplies back with her, they're most likely hidden there. I also think it's time fer a chat with that woman who seems ta be in charge."

He suddenly looked up and noticed a young man in his mid-twenties heading toward his car with an overnight bag, but had stopped to watch a man apparently having a conversation with a bird.

Annoyed, the horzikaan knew he was too far away to hypnotize just by casting his gaze. He illuminated the jewel in his staff, quickly waved it toward the man, and murmured "Forget" in Gaeilge. The man's face went blank for a moment, then he looked around, blinked a couple of times, and proceeded to his car.

"Go back ta the tree. Keep a sharp eye," he ordered in his native tongue. "Give me updates on the half hour. You understand? Every half hour. Go."

The raven cawed and flew away. The wizard watched as the bird became smaller and smaller in the sky.

"The time fer patience is nearly over," he said to himself. "Nearly over."

By 10:30 a.m. this Saturday, three things had happened: The first was that Wanda called Noah shortly before the gates opened and expressed concern about how much longer she could impose on the hospitality of her friend and coworker, Samantha, with whom she and Lancelot had been staying. Noah offered his RV, which was in his studio parking lot in Lilburn, and said he could hook her up with electricity and water from his studio. She was grateful for the offer and happily accepted.

The second thing that happened was that FBI agents Jacobs and Grimble returned to the festival. They wanted to see if they could get some new information out of blacksmith Dale Taylor and talk to employees with distinctive Irish last names. They knew that federal agents interrupting mostly younger employees and stopping them from doing their jobs was intimidating and could likely reveal new insights.

The third thing that happened was the horzikaan arrived at the festival wearing his traditional dark, hooded robe, and his, and the FBI agent's arrivals, were nearly simultaneous. Just past the main three-arch entrance, near the frog pond fountain, Agent Jacobs looked around at the patrons. Some had flintlock pistols tucked into wide black belts, while others wore three-cornered hats with long overcoats and black boots.

"Pirate weekend!" he smiled.

"You bring your kids out here yet?" the blond-haired Jacobs asked, eying the various buccaneer ensembles and Jack Sparrow wannabes.

"Next weekend," the brown-haired agent answered. "You get the best deals the final weekend. Hey, I found out something… I checked with the National Weather Service to see if there were any disturbances connected with Fairburn or the festival."

"What do you mean disturbances?" Jacobs asked.

"Geological tremors, heavy storms, anything like that. The answer is no, but I also found out through

Georgia Power that near the opening and closing of the festival every year, there's a pretty big power outage affecting hundreds of homes."

"Power outage?"

"Yeah. They've had crews out here nearly every opening and closing weekend for the past five years, checking transformers, power stations, the towers. It's pretty weird."

"What?" Jacobs said, taking out his cell phone. "You think the power outages are caused by doors in time that take Irish people and medieval weapons back to the fifteenth century?"

"I think there are too many things going on around here that don't add up. You hear about that murder/suicide? It happened just a mile away from here, y'know."

"Let's not take two and two and come up with eighty-six," Jacobs said, beginning to film the crowd. "Let's just talk to some people, shake some branches, and see what falls out. Especially with the blacksmith."

"What're you doing?" Grimble asked, referring to the camera.

"Trying to convince my wife to wear some skimpy pirate wench outfit. Either here or at home."

"Aargh matey," Jacobs agreed.

Just as Jacobs was starting to film, twenty yards away, there was a family consisting of a mother, father, and three children just starting to walk down the main thoroughfare of costume shops, crystal stores, and stands selling oils, soaps, and the like. One of the children was dressed up as a pirate, complete with a wide red bandana, and was behaving rambunctiously. He wasn't listening to his mother's orders to stay close to the family and was running around in the crowd, circling other visitors while wielding a plastic sword. Unthinkingly, the boy ran smack into the robed leg of the horzikaan.

"Ugh," the wizard grunted. "Out of me way, ya useless little sod," he rebuked in English.

The father came up and scooted the boy back toward his mother. "Tito, get back to your mom," he told the child. "Sorry, man," he muttered at the horzikaan.

"Keep yer little shite out of people's way," the older one barked.

The father had a large tattoo of a cobra on his neck and his veins suddenly bulged, making the snake look bigger.

"What'd you call my son?" he asked challengingly.

"He's a little piglet runnin' wild," the horzikaan growled bluntly. "Take care I don't give him a snout and a curly tail."

"Hey, drop the asshole attitude, old man," the father replied, not backing down. "This whole thing is for kids."

The horzikaan cracked a faint smile at the father, knowing he was aggravating him and not caring.

"If ya can't control your spawn, quit spreadin' yer seed around." He glanced toward his family. "Yer world's got enough garbage in it as it is."

The father took an enraged step toward the

horzikaan. "Did you just call my kids garbage, motherfucker?"

"Javier!" the wife called with a cautionary tone.

The husband paused, looked at his wife, then turned back to the wizard and pointed a finger at him.

"You lucky, old man," he said. "You lucky I'm here with my family." He smiled insincerely and threateningly at the same time. "You have yourself a nice day."

He walked away, returned to his wife and kids, and grumbled angrily in Spanish. Meantime, agent Jacobs, who had filmed the entire exchange, lowered his cell phone, thinking.

"The drug cartel in John's Creek," he said to his partner. "The photos on the whiteboard. Who's the chief enforcer?"

Grimble thought for a second. "Javier Torres."

"Got a cobra tattoo on his neck, right?" Jacobs asked.

"Yeah," Grimble agreed.

Jacobs rewound the video he'd just taken and showed it to his associate while one of the festival's ambassadors started to play a concertina nearby.

"Wouldn't you say that's Javier Torres?"

"Yeah," Grimble said, intrigued. "What's he doing here? Who's he talking to?"

"I don't know."

"You think he's just here socially? Or is it business?"

"Maybe both," Jacobs concluded.

Grimble continued watching the video.

"Looks like a heated exchange. What do you wanna do?"

"We've got to shift gears," Jacobs said, stopping the video. "I'll follow Torres and his family. You see if you can find out who he was talking to."

Grimble nodded and started following the horzikaan while Jacobs followed Javier Torres and his family.

As the horzikaan made his way down one of the thoroughfares of New Castle, he stopped and asked a female ambassador dressed as a pirate and standing on a rain barrel if she knew of a fairy with an Irish accent that might be working. She was a new employee this season and didn't know anyone who fit the description. The old man asked if she knew of an "elderly woman with blondish-white hair that ran the festival." The pirate woman identified Wanda by name but said she hadn't seen her this morning. The horzikaan walked on with his staff. He turned and passed a gourmet popcorn shop, Dale Taylor's shop of broadswords, axes, and daggers, and looked around the area by the Halfwit Harbor Stage. The day was beautifully clear, and the crowd was enjoying the morning, but the wizard with the leathery face, gray beard, and long, pointed fingernails was becoming increasingly perturbed. He was thinking about what other kind of twenty-first-century technology he should take back in time. He'd learned about steel-toed work boots and camouflage clothing and thought both could be valuable. But he was most interested in firearms. He'd seen them on TV as well as in the holsters of police officers working the festival, but he hadn't learned how to use a gun yet. He decided he'd hypnotize a cop for instructions and steal his weapon. He also learned about dynamite from watching *Mythbusters* but didn't know where he could acquire some.

While these thoughts went through his head, he looked around and felt nothing but contempt for the people around him. He acknowledged that humans had evolved technologically, but overall, the people of the twenty-first century were beneath him. He considered them overweight, out of touch with nature, and self-absorbed as they slowly wandered around New Castle like cattle wearing their play clothing while their fat thumbs scrolled on their cell phones.

"Peasants!" he said, spitting the word out of his mouth.

Just past the Halfwit Harbor Stage, he saw a wooden gate that read: "Employees Only."

Making a decision, he walked over to the gate, opened it, and entered the outer wooded perimeter of the village where vendors kept their trucks, vans, campers, and extra containers of merchandise. He'd only taken a few steps when he ran into Cole Huggins, wearing his ID lanyard, toting his camera bag, and heading toward the gate the wizard had just come through.

The old man didn't go through any pleasantries with him and instead gruffly grabbed Cole by the arm.

"Wanda," he demanded in English. "Have ya seen her?"

Cole was surprised by being grabbed but answered.

"Uh, yeah, actually. I-I just saw her. She's headed to the stables behind the joust tournament field."

Cole gestured with his head, and the wizard looked off in that direction. Without saying anything further, the horzikaan released him and walked off.

"Hey—do you work here?" Cole called. "Hey, buddy?"

The robed figure ignored him and continued walking past parked cars and into a stand of tall Georgia pines. A few seconds later, Cole opened the gate and stepped onto the festival grounds. The first person he saw was a uniformed Fairburn police officer on patrol.

"Hey," Cole said, going up to the cop. "There's a guy dressed like a wizard who's in the employees only area, but I don't think he's an employee. He's looking for Wanda, the festival manager, and he seems pretty upset."

The cop, whose nametag read Rosen, told Cole he'd check it out and went over to the gate. About seventy seconds later, Agent Grimble likewise went through the gate.

It didn't take the cop long before he spotted the wizard walking with his staff and called out to him:

"Hey, sir? You, with the walking stick."

The time traveler stopped and turned to see who was calling him. He recognized it was an officer of the law, but his authority meant nothing to him. What he was interested in was his weapon.

"Aa—what a perfect opportunity," he decided.

He held up his staff toward Rosen and said something in Gaeilge. A beam of white light shot out of the jewel at the top of the rod and froze the officer. Then, with a raise of the rod and quickly flicking it, Rosen was lifted about five feet off the ground, then his body flew sideways to the right and slammed straight into a pine tree. The violent impact caused immediate internal injuries and the cop fell to the dirt, both unconscious and critically hurt.

The horzikaan smiled a little and walked over to the motionless body. He bent down, unfastened the clip holding Rosen's sidearm and drew it out of its holster. He looked at the gun, a Glock 22, then put his finger on the trigger and pointed it at the cop's head.

"Now then, how does this expel its projectile?"

He pulled the trigger, but the safety was engaged, and the weapon wasn't cocked. Just as this was happening, Grimble suddenly appeared and saw the horrifying sight of a downed police officer with a man standing over him and pointing the cop's own service revolver at his head. The special agent quickly drew his weapon and took a firing stance.

"FBI!" he yelled. *"Drop the weapon!"*

The horzikaan looked at him and moved his staff in Grimble's direction, but the FBI agent didn't wait. He fired a round that caught the wizard in the right-hand side of his stomach. The bullet went through the older man and exited his back without hitting any vital organs, but it was still very painful. He yelled, dropped his gun and staff, and fell to his knees.

"SHITE!" the horzikaan gasped. He might have

been an all-powerful wizard, but his body was just as fragile as any other man's unless he had cast a protective spell—which he hadn't.

"Down on the ground. Hands behind your back!" Grimble ordered, walking toward him with his weapon poised.

"Look at me!" the wizard yelled. Grimble was now close enough to be caught in the old man's hypnotic gaze, and his face instantly became emotionless while he slowly lowered his weapon.

Grabbing his staff and using it like a crutch to painfully climb back to his feet, the horzikaan thrust the staff toward Grimble, and its white beam shot out again, catching the agent like a fly on flypaper. Next, the wizard quickly raised the staff into the air, and Grimble's body suddenly flew upward like a rocket, brushing by several pine branches along the way. When he was about sixty feet high, the horzikaan turned off the beam, and his victim fell helplessly and silently to the ground. The thud of his body hitting the earth was confirmation of a fatal impact.

Gritting his teeth and painfully grabbing his side, the wizard looked around to see if anyone else was in the area. Not seeing anyone, he then slowly waved a hand over his wound and cast a spell to minimize the pain. Next, he picked up the cop's gun again. He slowly walked over to Grimble's body, saw the pool of expanding blood coming from his head lying face down in the dirt, and picked up his weapon as well.

Just as he was doing so, approximately sixty yards

away, an ambulance was slowly making its way down a dirt service road heading for the back of the First Aid Station. With considerable effort, the horzikaan walked that way and caught the driver with yet another white beam of light from his staff. It happened to be Chris Kramer, the EMT who had questioned Wanda at the impromptu staff meeting just before the festival opened several weekends earlier.

The ambulance came to a stop and Kramer put the vehicle in park while the wizard climbed into the passenger side seat.

"Yer gonna take me ta the Embassy Suites in Fairburn," he instructed Chris. "Yer gonna help me ta me room and tend ta me needs."

The blank-faced EMT put the vehicle into drive and started to turn the vehicle around. At the same time, Agent Jacobs, having heard Grimble's gunshot, followed the sound and headed toward the employees only gate near the Halfwit Harbor Stage. Just as the ambulance had disappeared from view and down the service road toward the festival grounds exit, Jacobs came upon the still unconscious Officer Rosen and the body of his partner.

39

TOTAL SHIT SHOW

It was close to 2 p.m., and Fay and Noah were in his Aspen Trail RV in the parking lot of his Lilburn studio when Noah's cell phone rang. Fay had just finished putting flowers on the table in the dinette area that had been extended, and Noah was wrapping a cord up from a vacuum he'd borrowed from the studio.

"Hello?" he said into the phone. Then, hearing Wanda's voice, he put her on speaker. "It's Wanda," he said to Fay.

"Oh, hey, Wanda," Fay began. "We're gettin' Noah's RV ready fer ya and Lancelot. How's the day goin'?"

"We've got a total shit show here," Wanda's voice replied with weary urgency.

"What's going on?" Noah asked.

"Two cops were killed here this morning."

"What?" Fay cried.

"Two cops," Wanda repeated. "One was a Lilburn police officer, and the other was an FBI agent."

"At, at New Castle? Right in the middle of the festival?" Noah asked, stunned.

"They were killed just outside the village fence. In some trees next to the Halfwit Harbor Stage."

"W-what happened?" Fay wondered, with a hand on her chin and her mouth open.

"They're still piecing everything together," Wanda replied. "But here's what I know: Shortly after we opened, the same two FBI agents that came nosing around weeks ago came back to do some additional investigation about the weapons found on O'Connell's farm. But they got sidetracked. Something else happened that grabbed their attention."

"What?" Fay asked.

"The agent who was killed—a guy by the name of Grimble—was randomly filming the crowd with his phone and happened to catch a heated exchange between two guests: a Hispanic man in his late twenties or early thirties and another older guest maybe in his sixties who was dressed up like a wizard."

"A *wizard?*" Noah said, concerned.

"Yes. I thought about the horzikaan, too," Wanda concurred. "The other FBI agent, a guy named Jacobs, showed me the filmed exchange and kept pressing me to see if I'd seen the Hispanic man at the festival before. I hadn't. But Cole Huggins told the cops that the *other* guy—the wizard—went through a gate to the outer perimeter and was looking for me."

"Cole spoke to the wizard?" Fay noted, surprised.

"Yeah. The old guy grabbed Cole by the arm and was real insistent about finding me. At least, that's what he told the cops."

"Oh, I don't like that sound of that," Fay noted.

She and Noah looked at one another while goosebumps shot across Noah's arms.

"Is Cole okay?" he asked.

"Yes. It was just a brief exchange," Wanda answered.

Fay furrowed her brow, thinking. "Well, I don't know who the wizard was talkin' ta or what their heated exchange was, but I *do* think the older man dressed up like a wizard wasn't playin' dress up. I think it *was* the horzikaan, and he was tryin' ta find ya ta see if ya knew me whereabouts."

"Agreed," Noah said.

"D-did Cole say anthin' about this wizard havin' a staff with a jewel?" Fay asked Wanda.

"Yeah, as a matter of fact, he did," her voice confirmed.

"That's it, then. Orrie said a man dressed up like a wizard and holdin' a staff with a jewel in its top spoke ta him just before he got injured, and it was the *same* staff that he saw the beam of light shoot out of that paralyzed him."

"Jesus," Noah gawked. "He's hunting you."

"We always knew that, darlin'," Fay reminded.

"Shortly after Cole got onto the festival grounds," Wanda continued, "he ran into a Fairburn policeman and told him that this wizard was wandering around in a restricted area. The cop went to investigate, and we think not long after that, Agent Grimble followed and went behind the fence as well. There was a gunshot, then within a couple of minutes, both men were found. Grimble was already dead, and the Fairburn cop was critically wounded. We were supposed to have an ambulance right behind the First Aid Station. But the people directin' traffic out front said they saw the ambulance come onto the property, head into the festival grounds, but then abruptly leave the property again, all within five minutes. Without that ambulance, the Lilburn officer didn't make it."

"My God," Noah moaned.

"Total shit show," Wanda's voice said sadly. "I've been talking to Russ Hawkins, the Fairburn Chief of Police, Agent Jacobs from the FBI, *his* boss, a guy named Meadows, Cole, some of my employees… this is the first opportunity I've had to connect with you two."

"Did you close the festival?" Noah questioned.

"Surprisingly, no. Very few guests and most of the employees don't know anything about it. Although, I suspect most employees will have heard something by the end of the day. The festival's going on as usual, complete with all the performances. I'm calling a cast meeting right after we close, and both the FBI and Fairburn police will be in on it."

"Has anyone tracked down the ambulance that disappeared?" Fay wondered.

"I don't know," Wanda replied.

All three fell silent for several seconds, processing the information, until Fay finally spoke:

"I've heard that horzikaans are very temperamental. If he felt trapped or was even in a bad mood…"

"So, there's no question in your mind he's responsible for the deaths?" Wanda asked.

"None," Fay answered.

"There *is* evidence that the horzikaan was injured," Wanda added. "There was a blood trail leading to a dirt road that the ambulance came down, and the authorities don't think it belonged to either cop."

"The gunshot that was heard," Noah recalled. "Can a horzikaan be shot?"

"I would think so," Fay said. "At least, I've been told they're skin and bone just like the rest of us, only more magically gifted."

"That could explain the ambulance disappearing," Wanda concluded. "Oh my God, the poor driver."

"And you've got no idea about the exchange between the horzikaan and the Hispanic guy?" Noah asked, wanting to double-check.

"No," Wanda's voice replied.

"Like I said, if he was in a bad mood," Fay reminded, "horzikaans are creatures that are used ta bein' feared. But this is a very different world."

"Any chance you can leave the festival and get to us soon?" Noah asked Wanda.

"I've gotta stay until the end of day and the employee meeting," she replied. "But I'll make sure I'm not alone, and I'll even ask Russ Hawkins if one of his officers can follow me to your studio. He likes me a little, so he might say yes."

"I'm so sorry I brought this to your door, Wanda," Fay offered sincerely. "The Renaissance festival should be a world of fun, escape, entertainment, and shoppin'. It should be a reminder of the world of possibilities, not confusion and death."

"You didn't bring this to my door," Wanda's voice clarified. "The asshole who hired the horzikaan did. And history's never been short of assholes."

"Or good people like you," Fay reminded. "Please stay safe; thanks for the call, and we'll speak again soon."

"Erin okay?" Wanda asked.

"Yeah. She's with my folks, but we're gonna pick her up later," Noah answered. "Fay wants to do another check of the oak tree later this afternoon, and we'll get her afterwards."

"Be careful, you two," the older woman warned. "Like you said, Noah. He's hunting Fay."

"Maybe not right now," Fay figured. "Not if he's been shot."

"I'll call you later," Wanda promised. Then, she hung up.

Noah clicked off his phone and looked at Fay soberly.

She nodded knowingly.

"Total shit show," she agreed.

At 4:41 that afternoon, Chris Kramer and the ambulance the horzikaan had commandeered earlier returned to the festival grounds. But the EMT had no memory of where he'd been for the past six hours, which the authorities found very hard to believe. At 6:18 p.m., just about the time the employee meeting was starting in New Castle, Fay and Noah pulled back into Wanda's driveway to check the oak tree for a second time in the day. Before doing so, however, they went into Wanda's house to gather some additional clothing she'd requested via text. Wanda also shared that the ambulance had returned, and the driver was drawing a blank. This reinforced to Fay that her enemy must've been wounded, so his showing up at the oak was a lot less likely. Still, Noah carried his dad's Glock.

After they put Wanda's extra clothing into the back seat of Noah's truck, they started to walk across Wanda's backyard with Fay, once again, carrying her cooler full of shrunken supplies and weapons. They were almost to the edge of the woods when Noah's cell phone rang. He took the phone off the belt of his jeans and looked at the caller ID.

"Hey," he said, pausing and putting the Glock in the back of his belt. "This is Ted Albus, Gino Girard's manager. I need to take this."

"Hurry up," Fay urged. "We shouldn't linger here, and we haven't seen our daughter all day."

Noah held up a finger of patience to her. "Hi, Ted. How are you?" He paused and listened for a moment. "A North American tour?" he asked, his face lighting up. "Uh—yeah—*sure!*"

Fay's eyes widened as well, knowing this was good

news for her lover. She smiled, set her cooler on the ground next to him, and waved him away as if to say: "Take your call. I'll be fine." Then, she turned and continued onto the path and into the woods. As she did, she raised her hands above her head, clapped them, and with a little burst of white sparkles that exploded into the air, she transformed her size and clothing, then flew off toward the oak tree. As Noah watched this, he realized he wasn't paying attention to this important call.

"S-sorry, Ted. What were the dates again?" He turned and looked at his truck, wondering if he should get a pen and paper, but then turned back to the woods to see where Fay was and decided to follow her.

As soon as the small fairy version of Fay flew into the hole in the oak tree, she could tell that something was different. The back of the tree should have been solid, but it had subtle ripples from the wind outside that caused it to look like wooden water.

"Shea Karna!" Fay cried in her tiny voice. "It's already started!"

She turned, crossed the trunk of the tree, and leaned her five-inch body out of its hole. She saw Noah still talking on the phone but walking toward her about thirty yards away.

"Noah! Shea Karna!" she yelled. "Bring the cooler!"

But her calling was in vain. In her miniature form, her voice was too small. While she waited, still leaning out of the tree for him to get closer, she suddenly realized the dappled sunlight that had been dancing on the tree's exterior was now gone, and she was in shadow: a shadow that seemed to be getting wider and darker at an alarming rate. Looking up, she saw the horzikaan's raven diving at her with its beak open.

In the blink of an eye, Fay darted out of the tree and upward into some branches she could weave in and out of that would put some distance between herself and the attacking bird. The raven fluttered its wings to stop, but its extended talons hit the side of the oak tree with enough force to chip several pieces of bark off the edges of the hole Fay had just flown out of.

Squawking, the bird looked up and followed Fay, flapping its wings as it ascended. Simultaneously, Noah saw the raven and instantly realized what was happening.

"Uh—Ted—I'm very sorry, but I'm gonna have to call you back."

He quickly disconnected the call, put his cell in his front pocket, and pulled out the Glock from the back of his belt. Cocking it and clicking off the safety, he aimed upwards toward the bird, but it was already flying over his head and through the woods back toward Wanda's yard. Figuring it was because it was chasing Fay, he ran after it.

The raven was indeed after Fay, who weaved in and out of trees faster than a hummingbird, then flew into the openness of Wanda's backyard. The straightaway gave the wizard's familiar time to nearly catch up to her since it was larger and more muscular, but Fay had a plan. Reaching the house, she zipped into the end of one of Wanda's storm drains, knowing the bird probably didn't know what it was. She flew up the drain attached to the side of the house and came out at the other end in the eavestrough. Pausing for a moment, she leaned over the eaves and looked down. Sure enough, the bird had landed on the ground and had its beak and head stuck into the drain, looking for her. Seeing the bird on the ground and momentarily stationary, Noah, still running across the yard, fired off two quick shots at it. The first round hit the ground about a foot and a half from the bird, causing some grass to fly into the air like a tiny explosion. The second was off by even more and landed in Wanda's gravel driveway, causing a puff of dust.

The raven didn't know what a firearm was exactly, but it knew it was dangerous and suddenly leaped off the ground, flying straight for Noah. Genuinely surprised, he stopped and looked at the oncoming bird, thinking: "Is that thing *attacking* me?" The time it took for him to digest this was time enough for Fay to see another means of escape. A mail carrier truck was passing Wanda's house, and Fay took off for it just as the bird reached Noah.

With loud caws and flapping wings, the raven attached its talons to Noah's long hair on the top of his head, then pecked twice at his skull, immediately drawing blood. A surprised and panicked Noah swatted at the bird with his pistol-toting hand but did little more than strike himself in the back of the head with the barrel of a loaded gun. He waved his arms frantically, and he shook his head violently, screaming: *"Get the fuck off me!"* as the bird pierced his skull a third time.

Then, as if remembering its prey, the raven let go of Noah's hair and flew back toward the house, soaring upward. It climbed above the tree line and saw the mail carrier truck going down the rural road. It also caught a glimpse of Fay hanging onto a rearview mirror attached to the exterior upper back end of the truck on the driver's side. Hearing a third gunshot and feeling something whiz by one of its feathers, the raven veered off and went after the truck.

By this time, Noah had lost sight of Fay but knew the bird was still pursuing her, so he ran to his truck to follow while a trickle of blood started to run down his forehead. "Land somewhere and change!" he said to himself, giving instructions to a lover who couldn't hear him. *"Land somewhere and change!"*

He hopped in his truck, fired it up and, with spinning rear wheels and flying gravel, sped out onto the road in front of Wanda's house. Meanwhile, still holding tight to the rearview mirror, Fay looked behind her and saw the raven had spotted her. *I've gotta land and change back ta human size,* she thought. So, she let go of the mirror, and the wind pushed her away. But she did so without turning around and looking forward. If she had, she would've seen the speeding van approaching in the oncoming lane. Suddenly realizing she was about to smash into a windshield, she veered up quickly. She missed the van, but got caught in the wind turbulence. She violently rolled down the roof of the van, then tried to regain wing control before she crashed into the road. But she was only halfway successful. She fluttered her wings to reduce her speed but still hit the pavement hard and did several somersaults over the blacktop until she stopped on the dusty shoulder of the road.

Her hands and knees were bloody, and she lay there still, momentarily dazed, until her half-closed blue eyes focused on the incoming raven. With a sudden rush of adrenaline, Fay hopped to her feet, checked her wings to make sure they weren't damaged, then took off again.

Less than a hundred yards away, there was a subdivision of about twelve upper-middle-class homes in a single cul-de-sac. This was a beautiful sight to Fay because it meant new places where she could hide from her attacker. She saw a one-hole birdhouse hanging from a tree in someone's front yard and flew past it, touching it as she went by, causing it to swing a little. Diving below the tree line, the raven saw the moving birdhouse and concluded Fay had taken refuge in it. Extending the lower half of its body forward like a fighting eagle, the raven's talons hit the birdhouse so hard that it was yanked off the small chain that connected it to a branch and fell to the ground. Then, the raven angrily pecked at the house until he had split it open.

Realizing it was empty and he had been tricked, the raven looked around and saw Fay fluttering and waving to the bird about three feet off the ground from a side yard that led to the back. The raven cawed angrily and took off after her, flying low. Fay waited for a moment, wanting the bird to catch up, then turned and flew up and over a six-foot-high backyard fence with a gate. The bird was only seconds behind her when it veered up and followed over the fence. When it did, it suddenly realized it was heading straight into an erected badminton net about twelve feet away. It wasn't as nimble as small Fay, and it smashed head-on into the net, pulling the net's poles right out of the ground. The attacker tumbled to the grass, a squawking mess of feathers and netting.

Landing in the backyard, Fay clapped her hands above her head and, with a puff of white sparkles, transformed back into human size and the street clothes she was wearing before.

Looking at the squawking bird, she said: "Serves ya right. Ya filthy bugger!" Then she looked at her hands. They were scraped and bleeding. So was the side of her face from a nasty scratch. So were her knees although jeans now covered them. She looked toward the house. It was a nice four-bedroom, two-story in the half-million-dollar range with a jungle gym on the other side of the backyard, but there didn't seem to be anyone home.

Grateful for this small blessing, she stiffly walked over to a gate that led into the side yard, opened it, and walked through. Then, she rounded the front of the house and walked across the front yard. By this time, Noah was driving down the subdivision's only street and spotted her. Coming to a stop, he hopped out of the truck, clutching his dad's gun, and hurried over. As he did, he had two very noticeable streams of blood rolling down his face.

"You okay?" he called. "Where's the bird that came after you?"

"Am I okay? Are *ya* okay?" she asked, seeing the blood on his face.

"I'm fine… but the fucker pecked at me!"

"Lemme see," she said, reaching for his head.

"Your hands!" he gawked, looking at the bloody scrapes on her palms.

"Aye. We're both a mess because of one attacker. Can ya understand now why I've gotta get back to me people? They're fightin' an army of hundreds of men on horseback wieldin' twelve-pound broadswords. We just took a beatin' from a measly bird." She gestured for him to bend down, then examined his head.

"Ya might need a couple of stitches. Looks like the wounds go deep. I can't heal this, Noah. I can't spare the magic. Do ya understand?"

"Where's that bird?" he asked, hearing the squawks of the raven.

"Tangled up in some nettin' in the backyard 'round there," she gestured. "I don't think the people who live here are home. But I can't say the same fer the neighbors."

Noah determinedly walked across the front yard, heading for the side yard.

"Noah, where are ya goin'?" she asked. "Didn't ya hear me? Shea Karna has started. I've gotta go back. I've gotta go back *now!*"

He ignored her and continued walking across the

yard. As he entered the side yard, he cocked the pistol. Realizing what he wanted to do, Fay ran after him.

"Noah, *no!* Ya can't do what yer thinkin'. Noah!"

He continued to ignore her and opened the gate to the backyard. Going into it, he saw the raven still struggling amidst the netting. He walked over to it and, without any hesitation, shot and killed the bird. Ten seconds after he had, Fay ran up to him, stood beside him, and stared at the lifeless feathered mess.

"Feel better now, do ya?" she asked, crossing her arms. "Now that you've announced ta everyone in the neighborhood: there's a stranger on our neighbor's property with a gun."

He wiped some blood off his forehead, looked at it, then looked at her.

"Yes," he said unapologetically.

"Alrighty then. Can we go now, please? Because it's long been believed that familiars and their masters have a special connection. A spiritual bond that when one dies, the other will know it."

He looked at her. "You mean—"

"Aye. I think ya just told the horzikaan his familiar is dead. Wherever he is, he's goin' ta the tree *now*—if he's able."

"Shit," Noah sighed.

"We've gotta go. Where's me supplies?"

Noah thought.

"Shit!" he repeated, realizing he'd left Fay's cooler in Wanda's backyard.

40

THE OAK TREE

As Noah's RAM pickup raced back to Wanda's, the two lovers were having a hurried conversation while Fay cleaned her hand with some wipes Noah had in his glove box. He was likewise wiping off his face.

"Do you think the neighbors called the police?" she asked.

"I hope so," he replied. "We're heading toward a place where a murderous wizard might be. Backup would be good."

She nodded and wiped some blood off her cheek.

"So—this is it?" he asked. "You're leaving *now?* Don't you want to call Erin? Wanda?"

"Erin won't understand what I'd be tellin' her, and she's at yer folks," Fay reminded. "What am I gonna be sayin' to them? Wanda's in the middle of her employee meetin'. Havin' the time to hug Wanda or kiss me daughter won't make me love 'em any more."

"I get it," he said, tossing a used wipe into a trash bag beside his center console. "You'll want to have your people and weapons in place to deal with the horzikaan when he goes back through the portal and comes through the church archway."

"Uh, aye," she nodded with hesitation.

He shook his head regretfully. "I thought we'd have more time. I mean, I *knew* Shea Karna was coming, but—"

"I know, darlin'," she acknowledged soothingly. "There may be things unsaid or things we haven't learned about each other, but mark me when I say I know enough ta love ya forever. At yer place, be sure ta look in the drawer of the bedside table next ta where I sleep. There's a pouch with coins in there that should cover all the money ya spent several times over."

They pulled back into Wanda's driveway and hopped out of the truck. By this time, Noah had grabbed another wipe and was cleaning some fresh blood dripping down his forehead with one hand while carrying his dad's Glock in the other. Fay's hands were now clean, but the knees of her jeans were becoming spotted with blood from her scraped and cut knees underneath.

"Go ahead and make sure me cooler is still in the yard," she instructed. "Have yer pistol ready and be on the lookout fer company. I need ta fetch a couple of things from Wanda's tool shed."

He nodded and jogged across the yard while she hurried, as best she could, to the tool shed where she once slept. Noah saw that the cooler was right where Fay had left it near the edge of the woods and breathed a sigh of relief. Coming up to it, he cocked his pistol and looked around, trying to remember how many bullets he had left. He figured maybe ten. He wasn't sure. He was very conflicted. He didn't want Fay to go but understood why she had to. She was fighting for her land, her way of life, her family, her people's very existence. He briefly thought of the airport scene from the classic film *Casablanca,* where Rick Blaine says goodbye to Ilsa Lund. He imagined Fay saying something reminiscent of Humphrey Bogart's dialogue: "Where I'm going, you can't follow. What I've got to do you can't be any part of."

He scanned the woods carefully for several moments until he heard Fay approaching behind him. Turning, he saw that she carried a folded three-step footstool in one hand and a sixteen-inch Milwaukee chainsaw with a pair of goggles in the other.

His mouth fell open as he looked at the chainsaw, realizing what she wanted to do. "No," he said as she approached.

"Noah."

"No!" he repeated emphatically.

She set the footstool, chainsaw, and goggles on the grass, stepped over to him, and put her scraped palms on either side of his face.

"This is the *only* way! The horzikaan can't be followin' me back. He's no doubt collected weapons and tools fer himself, and if he goes back in time, he could undo everythin' we've done here."

"No!"

"Even if he didn't take anythin' back," she continued. "He *can't* know about Shea Karna and be usin' the corridor. Otherwise, we'll just be havin' the same fight next year."

"You can't ask me to do this," he protested. "If I cut down the oak tree after you're gone, you can't come back. Erin loses her mother forever! We lose each other *forever!*"

She kissed his hand, then placed it over her heart. "Erin will be safe, and both of ya will *always* be alive right here."

They looked into one another's eyes, then hugged and clung tightly to one another. Both of their eyes were filling with tears, but both knew Fay was right. Finally, she quietly said:

"Ya have yer father's gun. If the horzikaan shows up, use it. I know what I'm askin' might be leavin' ya in harm's way. But I believe in ya, Noah Galloway. Yer a resourceful, strong man. Ya travel the world, climb mountains, and have a daughter dependin' on ya. And if the horzikaan doesn't show up, just go get our daughter and take her home. He doesn't know who or where ya are, and he'll soon be losin' his powers here."

"And what do I tell my folks about you not returning?" he asked, still holding her tightly.

"Tell 'em the truth. Tell 'em I died."

They continued hanging onto each other, trying to

absorb a lifetime of love in just a few precious moments. Eventually, though, Fay let go, wiped her eyes, and picked up the step ladder and small cooler while he picked up the chainsaw and goggles, still holding his gun with the other.

"I thought you said you didn't know about power tools?" he remembered while she led the way into the woods.

"I've seen Wanda use this thing before. Plus, I work in a fictional village in the middle of the woods. I've seen men with chainsaws."

"Okay."

"I need ya ta do something fer me," she requested as she walked toward the oak tree. "Actually, two things."

"Oh, you mean besides me never seeing you again and fighting an evil wizard?" he wondered.

"When she's older and can understand things better, take Erin back ta Ireland. Take her ta County Sligo and the Three Sisters. Let her see where her people came from. Our village is in a clearin' near the base of the smallest hill. I-I don't know what's there in yer time. Maybe the old archway of the church will still be standin' on the highest hill."

"Promise," he agreed with a heavy heart, following behind her. "What's the second thing?"

"I know that ya love me. There's no doubt in me mind. But I don't want ya ta be alone, and Erin's gonna be needin' a good mother." She thought of the photo of Z and Noah back in the studio dressing room. "Find an able woman who can smooth out the rough edges Erin would have bein' brought up by just a da."

"Uh, that one I can't promise," he protested. "D-do *you* intend to find another love? I mean, I remember what you said about fairies being—eh—uninhibited."

"Yer one of a kind," she answered. "But what if I'm carryin' Erin's brother or sister back ta me own time? Should I try ta raise a baby alone and in the middle of a war?" She turned over her shoulder and looked at him. "I'm not sayin' that I would. But if we're lucky, we'll both get ta live long lives. I just want ta make sure you *live* yers, that's all."

"Did you always know you were going to ask me to cut down the tree?" he wondered.

"No. Not until we pulled into the driveway just a couple minutes ago."

They fell silent until they reached the tree. Fay set the cooler down, opened the step ladder, and set it against the trunk.

"I'll change size, fly into the tree, then you open up the cooler, step up the ladder, and hand me one box at a time. This is when you'll be the most vulnerable, so we should do this as quick as jackrabbits."

"Yeah, okay," he replied, unenthused.

They looked at each other, embraced in a soft, lingering kiss. Then, she took two steps back, raised her hands above her head, and clapped. To her surprise, nothing happened.

"Oh, no," she sighed. "Me magic… I fear I used too much ta get away from that raven."

She cleared her throat, straightened her posture, raised her hands above her head, and clapped them again. This time, there was a little puff of smoke, no sparkles, and afterward, Fay now stood about three and a half feet tall and was only wearing her bra and panties with scraped and bloody knees.

Noah looked at her and smiled politely. "Well, Miss Oompa Loompa, third time's a charm."

"I've no idea what that means," she replied.

She raised and clapped her hands a third time, and this time, the transformation worked completely. With a puff of exploding white sparkles, Fay was once again wearing her short green fairy dress and fur-skin slippers. Her wings were fluttering, and she was five inches tall. She flew up and into the hole of the oak tree. Then Noah carefully scanned the woods one more time, slipped the Glock into the back of his pants, picked up the cooler, and climbed up the ladder. The ladder wasn't tall enough for him to see into the hole where the portal to the corridor was, but he could easily raise things up to her.

Fay came to the edge of the hole and looked down. "Ready?" he heard in her tiny voice.

"You sound like a Munchkin," he observed, opening the cooler.

"The Wizard of Oz," she said. "I've seen that one!"

"First box coming up now," he said, reaching inside the cooler.

Meanwhile, at Darius and Piper Larkin's house, a taxi pulled into the driveway carrying the horzikaan wearing his traditional hooded robe. He climbed out of the vehicle, carrying his staff, but he now also carried a black satchel with a strap over his left shoulder that held all of his reduced twenty-first-century tools and police officer weapons that he intended to take back with him.

He rounded the vehicle, then opened the driver's side door.

"Look at me, lad," he ordered.

A blank-faced driver turned to the wizard.

"Forget me and this journey," the old man said. "Go home now."

The wizard closed the driver's side door, and the taxi began to turn around. The horzikaan watched the vehicle until it was back down the driveway and had turned onto the road. Placing a hand with its long, pointed fingernails over the right side of his stomach where he'd been shot, the bearded man felt the gauze pad the spellbound Chris Kramer had securely wrapped around his middle with medical tape, then he turned and started to walk past the Larkin's house paying no attention to the crime scene tape still covering the front door. Instead, he headed toward the back of the house and the clearing about a quarter mile away for the never-ending line of tall silver power poles. This was the only route he knew to get back to the oak tree on Wanda's land.

Back at the tree, Fay stuck her head with its long red hair out the hole and looked down.

"How many more?" she asked.

Noah could see that her hands were getting bloody

again, and there were several streams of blood running down her tiny, pale legs.

"This is the last one," he said, handing a final shrunken box up to her. He lifted the box as if there were nothing in it, but she took and moved each box with its full weight because both she and the boxes were reduced.

"Your hands and legs look pretty bad, honey," he said.

"People will lay hands on me when I get back. It'll be fine," she promised.

She took the last box across to the other side of the tree and pushed it into the rippling wood-like other side. There was a small flash of white light as the box disappeared. There had been small flashes of white light with every box that went into the corridor, but none were as dramatic as when a living being entered it.

After a few seconds, Fay came to the edge of the hole a final time, pulled her hair behind her pointed ears, and looked down at Noah.

"Thank ya fer lovin' me!" she called loudly so he could hear her. "Thank ya fer givin' me Erin and helpin' me people. Thank ya fer understandin' why I have ta do what I'm doin'."

"Fay, if there's another corridor. You *said* there were other corridors…"

"I heard *stories* of corridors. Tales people told around a campfire. We could spend our whole lives seekin' and not find another. And I want you to *live*, darlin'. Go have adventures with our daughter. Take her ta Ireland. Love her well. But cut the tree down first! Do it now!"

"How will I know when you've gone through the portal?" he asked.

"You'll know," she called fondly. "I'd say don't be forgettin' me. But I know you won't."

"Not a chance," he said, looking up at her lovingly.

"Nor will I." she smiled.

As she looked down at him, Noah thought he felt a tiny tear fall from her eyes onto his cheek, but he wasn't sure. Then, Fay disappeared. Two seconds later, a bright light shot out of the oak tree. It was so bright that Noah had to shield his eyes and hop off the step ladder to the ground.

After the light faded, he looked up at the dark hole.

"She's right," he nodded. "I know."

He took a heavy breath and looked up at the empty hole. There was nothing left to do except honor Fay's request. So, he folded up the step ladder and moved it aside, then picked up and put on Wanda's goggles. Lastly, he picked up the chainsaw. After checking it over to see how it worked, he primed it a couple of times, pulled the starter cord, and it came to life. He sized up the tree and decided to make a wedge cut so it would fall just off Wanda's property and onto the service road leading to the power poles. It was an open area, and even though it technically wasn't Wanda's land, the chances of anyone driving on it were next to nothing, and it would be easy to clear away once the tree was down.

The tree trunk was forty-two inches round: medium-sized compared to the other trees on Wanda's land. Noah knew what he was doing with a chainsaw, having cut several trees on his parents' land in Highlands, and clearing trees from behind his studio after storms. As he worked on the tree, he wondered if the gods of the Tuatha Dé Dannan were real and would be angry at him. He wondered if the Christian God he believed in would be angry with him for wondering about pagan gods. As the chainsaw hummed away and shavings of wood flew everywhere, he likened the chips and shavings to pieces of his heart and soul flying away—for no one would ever replace Fay. She was a miracle that came unexpectedly into his life and who, he wondered, gets one miracle in their life, let alone two.

As the horzikaan neared Wanda's land and the sun was slowly turning from daylight to dusk, he stopped to listen to the sound of the chainsaw. He didn't know what it was and couldn't see what was happening yet, but he instinctively knew something was wrong. He picked up his pace until he was jogging. Then his jogging turned into running. He ran until his bullet wound started to bleed again, and his robe showed blotches of blood. As he came closer, now just a little over a hundred yards away, he saw a man was using a device to cut down his only means of passage back to his own time. He instantly knew this man was a companion of the fairy and assumed he knew her true identity. He also assumed that Fay and Erin had already used the corridor, and he was about to be stranded in a place where he'd soon lose his powers.

"No!" he said to himself. *"Nil! NIIIIL!"* he yelled and ordered in Gaeilge

But with the hum of the saw working on the tree, Noah was oblivious to the figure approaching from the direction of the silver towers.

With a desperate primal scream, the wizard thrust his staff toward the ground, and a light emanated from its jewel. But this time, the light was more intense, brighter, like a lightbulb about to burn out. With the staff angled toward the ground, the body of the horzikaan was lifted some six feet off the ground as he outstretched his arms and flew toward Noah. This was an exhausting type of magic that horzikaans used only as a last resort and couldn't maintain for very long.

Noah finished cutting a wedge away that left only two or three inches of undisturbed trunk. He was amazed that the tree was still upright because 98 percent of the trunk had been cut and kicked away. It seemed to defy gravity. He turned the saw off and looked at the tree, wondering if he should drive his pickup down the service drive, tie a rope around the tree, then hook the other end to his truck and maybe pull it down. Just as he considered this, he looked up and saw the frightening sight of the horzikaan soaring at him with clenched teeth like some kind of medieval superhero. The wizard recognized Noah's face and remembered seeing him walking in New Castle with Wanda. But, just in the final ten yards of his flight, the beam from the staff sputtered, stopped, and the wizard fell unceremoniously to the ground on his stomach.

The horzikaan screamed in pain, then rolled over on his back. Suddenly, his body stood straight up without the use of arms or legs. It was like he was a three-dimensional cardboard cutout that some invisible force had just set upright. Seeing his power, Noah wasted no time. He dropped the chainsaw, grabbed the Glock from the back of his pants, cocked it, and unclicked the safety as he rounded the tree toward the old man. The horzikaan looked at him with squinting eyes, trying to hypnotize him, but Noah was still wearing his goggles, so the effort apparently had no effect. Either that or the old man's powers were too weak. Noah spied the bloodstain on the wizard's robe, and that was enough to convince him he could be hurt. He raised the gun and fired once, twice, three times, and all three rounds struck the horzikaan in the chest. He stumbled and fell backward. A second later, the tree behind Noah suddenly gave a loud crack. Realizing what was happening, Noah veered left and dove to the ground as the oak tree fell with another loud crack and landed across the chest of the wide-eyed horzikaan.

A few of the tree's lighter branches also fell on Noah, but he was unharmed. Somewhere in the crashing of leaves and branches, though, he lost his father's gun. It took nearly twenty frantic seconds of Noah getting on his hands and knees, searching through green debris before his fingers finally clutched the warm barrel of the pistol. He didn't know if the horzikaan was dead or merely injured, but he wasn't going to leave anything to chance. His family's safety was at stake. Getting to his feet and taking aim with the gun, he slowly stepped through the leafy tangle to where he thought the wizard should be. Within eight seconds, he spotted the motionless body and discovered that the tree had fallen nearly straight across the horzikaan's chest, pinning and crushing him. His eyes were closed, and blood was trickling from his open mouth and down his white beard.

Noah's shoulders slumped with relief as he lowered the gun. He wiped away more blood on his forehead from the raven's attack and was surprised at himself for how bad he didn't feel, considering he'd just killed a man. Then again, he concluded, this wasn't exactly a man. At least, not a normal one. In any event, if the wizard had never invaded his century or threatened his family, he would've already been dead for hundreds of years. To Noah's way of thinking, there was some odd justification in this.

As these thoughts raced through his mind, Noah noticed the body of the horzikaan was now changing. His white skin was turning brown, the fluids in his body were draining away, and the thickness of his skin and bones were withering. He was watching the wizard's body decay as if it was doing some strange form of time-lapse photography. Within another forty seconds, there was no trace of the horzikaan. It was as if he never existed.

"Whoa!" Noah said to himself. "Th-that's convenient. I don't have to bury your ass."

Just then, his cell phone rang. Taking the phone off his belt, he looked at the caller ID, took a deep breath, and tried to sound normal.

"Hi, Mom... no, everything's fine. But, I—uh—I had a little accident and cut the top of my head. What?... No, it's no big deal, but I need to swing by an urgent care and have it looked at. So—so let me do that, and then I'll pick up Erin afterward."

41

TWELVE DAYS LATER

Twelve days later, things were starting to fall into place. The Georgia Renaissance Festival was over, and despite an employee getting critically injured and the tragic deaths of two law enforcement officers on the festival's outer perimeter, the attendance and vendor sales were the highest they'd ever been, and this fared well for Wanda. The investigation of Darius and Piper Larkin's deaths was concluded to be a murder/suicide, and no connection was ever made between them and any other crimes that happened in Fairburn. FBI Special Agent Charles Grimble and Fairburn Police Officer Kyle Rosen were buried, and the FBI and Lilburn Police Department were both seeking a person of interest who was an elderly robed male. It was thought this person had connections to a drug cartel operating in John's Creek, and the filmed encounter between the robed figure and Javier Torres supported that theory. But what couldn't be explained was how Special Agent Grimble had seventeen broken bones and collapsed lungs like he'd fallen from a great height. Officer Rosen's injuries couldn't be explained, either. So, the investigation was far from over. In the meantime, Orrie Sercombe was making a good recovery from his injuries, and EMT Chris Kramer, who couldn't account for his disappearance from the Renaissance festival for several hours, was questioned by both the police and the FBI. He also underwent a psychological analysis ordered by the ambulance company where he worked. And while he hadn't been charged with anything yet, there were bloodstains found on his clothing and medical supplies that had been used in his ambulance. DNA analysis of the bloodstains turned up no known suspects in the criminal databases, but until more was known, he was suspended from his job without pay.

Twelve days later, at 8:25 p.m., Noah stood in Erin's darkened bedroom, watching his daughter drift off to sleep in her crib. The past several days had been hard on the child. First, she was told that her mother had gone away. Then, she'd gone to a pediatrician and received some immunization shots. Then, she was placed in a daycare routine while Noah went to work. As Noah and Fay had discussed, interfacing with other children would be good for Erin. There were also new people in her life, from the caregivers at daycare to Mike and Ami. Wanda also continued to be in her life too, but

Erin wasn't seeing her or Lancelot as much as she was used to. Things were changing, and although Noah had researched and read online about the surprising resilience of young children, he was still worried about her. He was also worried about himself and his ability to raise a daughter. He wanted her to be an intelligent, compassionate, and truthful young woman. But being truthful wasn't his best quality at the moment. It seemed like every day, he was telling some new kind of lie to either his parents or coworkers about Fay and bringing up a daughter without her mother.

He looked at his wristwatch, then went downstairs to his kitchen table where his MacBook was. He sat down, opened his laptop, and connected to Zoom. Within another minute, he saw the face of Russ Burges, the translator he had hired in Highlands, North Carolina. Russ was sitting at a desk in his home office.

"Hi Russ," he began. "Thanks for taking an evening meeting. My days are kind of crazy right now, and I wanted to give you the time you deserve to talk about your translation. I understand from your email that you're now finished?"

"Hi, Noah. Yes, I finished this morning. Once I got going on 'em, I couldn't stop."

"That's great! Wonderful."

"I have to ask you something, though," the white-haired man said, "and please don't think I'm being rude. But are you *sure* you don't know anything more about the author of these letters?"

"Why do you ask?"

"Because you're mentioned in them by name, Noah Galloway. You're identified as the father of the intended reader, Erin."

Noah's face turned visibly red with embarrassment. He never considered—although he should have—that Fay would've referred to him in her letters by name. He realized he'd have to cover an earlier lie he told Russ with another lie.

"Eh, yes," he replied with a fragile smile. "You're right. I told you I found these letters in a trunk I bought at an estate sale, which wasn't true. The truth is, they were written by a woman I knew who was very imaginative but, frankly, had some mental issues. She imagined a relationship between us that never happened. Unfortunately, she's deceased now and left me these letters, but I wasn't entirely sure of their contents."

"Why didn't you just tell me the truth in the first place?" Russ asked.

"Would you have been interested in translating the letters of a mentally disturbed person?" he answered frankly.

"A translation job is a translation job," the former college professor reasoned. "In any event, it's none of my business. Still, I must ask: disturbed or not, was the author a scholar of Irish history?"

"She did seem to know it pretty well, yes," Noah nodded.

"Because some of the things she wrote about—the daily life of fifteenth-century Irish farmers, the clan wars, the Tuatha Dé Dannan, it all suggests a PhD level of knowledge for both Irish history and mythology. Not to mention her impeccable use of the Gaeilge language."

"She was very gifted in some ways," Noah confirmed.

"Like I say, who the author was, your relationship with her, and how you intend to use these letters is none of my business. But I *will* say these writings are unlike any other papers or books I've read on the Tuatha Dé Dannan. Very, very fascinating. I've emailed you all of the translations, and please don't hesitate to call if you have any questions about anything."

"Thanks, Russ. And again, I apologize for not being honest from the beginning."

"People have their reasons for doing what they do. Just like the author of your letters did."

"That's very gracious of you. You'll have your money in PayPal tonight. And I'm going to have to insist upon your confidentiality in this matter."

"Of course," the older one said.

"Thanks. The next time I'm in Highlands, I owe you a beer."

"I'd like that," the older one smiled. "Take care, Noah."

"Take care."

Noah disconnected the call, closed his laptop, put his elbows on the table, and lowered his head defeatedly. He'd been caught in a lie. How many more lies would he be caught in, he wondered? Two big ones were fake documents Wanda had recently provided him through her underground resources. One was a fake Irish birth certificate for Erin, and the other was a letter from a nonexistent judge declaring that Noah had sole legal custody of his daughter. They were documents he hadn't shared with his parents yet, but sooner or later, they'd figure out that Erin would need paperwork to be in daycare. The lies he was telling people were mounting up. Deceit was quickly becoming part of his new reality. He closed his eyes and took a stressed breath as his cell phone rang. Lifting the phone off his belt, he saw it was his mom calling on Facetime. He paused at first, as if he wasn't going to answer, but then put on a smile and accepted the call.

"Hi, Mom."

"Hi," Ami smiled, sitting on the sofa in her family room. "Where's my little angel?"

"You just missed her. She just went down for the night."

"Oh, darn," Ami sighed, disappointed. "I wanted to blow her some kisses."

"Well, you can blow at her tomorrow," he suggested.

"How's she doing in daycare?"

"The caregivers say she's adjusting well. She was a little shy at first, but now she's making friends."

"Good!"

Mike stuck his head into the frame from the other side of the sofa.

"Have you heard anything from Fay?" he asked.

"Hi, Dad. Uh, no. I haven't heard from her since she went back to Ireland. But she said I wouldn't at first because she had some pressing family business that would require her full attention."

"What kind of pressing business?" Mike asked.

"I'm not sure."

"Yeah, but she's been gone almost two weeks, Noah," his father reminded. His parents had asked if Fay had been in contact at least three times over the past twelve days, and Noah always answered no. "What kind of mother leaves the country and doesn't reach out to her own daughter for two weeks?" Mike continued.

"I don't know, Dad. I can't answer that."

"Well, it *is* odd, honey," Ami agreed.

"Have you called her? Texted her?" Mike pressed.

"Uh… no."

"Why not?" Ami wondered.

"What are you not telling us?" Mike queried.

"Yes, honey. Please fill us in," Ami encouraged.

"Look—Fay left with very little warning. And w-when she did, she didn't leave me any direct way to contact her."

"Well, she's got a cell phone, doesn't she?" his father questioned.

"No, Dad, she doesn't. When she's in the States, she uses Wanda's cell, the manager of the Renaissance festival I told you about who befriended her."

"Well, this manager has to have *some* way of contacting her," Ami concluded. "Fay is her employee, for goodness' sake."

"And her first year at the festival, she came through her school," Mike remembered. "*They'd* have records."

"Actually, Fay working at the festival was kind of an under-the-table thing." Noah replied, actually feeling relieved to finally reveal some level of truth.

"W-wait, wait a minute," Mike stammered. "Are you telling us that Fay just left her daughter in your care, and you have *no way* of contacting her, and she hasn't contacted you in any way, shape, or form?"

"Yes, that's what I'm telling you," he concurred.

"Well, aren't you concerned about this?" Ami said.

"*Of course* I'm concerned. But what am I supposed to do? I may not know Fay's whereabouts, but I *am* sure that Erin's my daughter and needs love."

He saw his parents look at one another, momentarily at a loss. Then, his father spoke up:

"Love… yeah… this must be very hard for you, son," he conceded, almost uncharacteristically. "I know you had true feelings for Fay. I'm really sorry for the way things seem to be going with you two."

"Absolutely," Ami agreed. "But maybe we could call someone? Maybe a detective agency in Ireland to try and locate her."

"Better yet, an attorney to confirm your legal rights concerning Erin," Mike added.

"I don't want to call anybody," Noah announced. "I just want to give my daughter the best, most secure life possible."

"Well, of course, honey. We *all* want that," Ami confirmed. "But—your poor heart!"

"As Gloria Gaynor sang, *I Will Survive,*" he replied, using a song reference from his parent's generation.

"You want us to come over and bring you some of your mother's gummies?" Mike offered.

"No thanks," he replied.

"Some of my Johnnie Walker Black?" his father suggested. "And ribs from Community Q?"

Noah smiled appreciatively.

"Y'know, you guys can be pretty cool sometimes."

42

TWELVE MONTHS LATER

Diary Entry, Monday:

*If a person doesn't believe in magic,
they have no hope in their life.*

Noah's rental car pulled into the gated driveway of a large house in the Hollywood hills of California. After announcing himself at the intercom box on the driver's side of the entranceway, the gate silently slid open, and he pulled up and into the driveway of what could only be described as a luxury home for the uber-rich. It was a modernistic three-story consisting of several square shapes with lots of white exterior walls and lots of glass. The house was seven thousand square feet and sat on the edge of a lush green hill with a breathtaking view of Los Angeles on a clear day. After climbing out of his rental with a small camera bag, Noah saw that the entranceway to the front door was actually a shallow moat where speckled carp leisurely floated just beneath the surface. There were three large square aggregate stepping stones one could easily traverse to cross the water and get to the front door. As he was doing so, he looked to his right and saw an alternative entrance with a sidewalk and handrail for those who might need it.

Z-Rae's manager, Leah Shively, stood in the open front door casually dressed in jeans and a summer blouse to greet him.

"Noah," she smiled. "Long time no see."

"Hi, Leah," he greeted. Since this was a business meeting, he was a little more formally dressed in a red golf shirt and new black slacks. He and Leah hadn't seen each other since Greece when Z-Rae was on tour. They shook hands, and he walked into the house, taking in the spacious and perfectly decorated rooms around him. It was straight out of one of those reality realtor shows on Netflix that had nothing to do with reality.

"Z's new digs, huh?" he said, nodding. "Pretty impressive."

"She's had it for a while, but seven thousand square feet, five bedrooms, a gym, wine cellar, home theater, game room, infinity pool and, of course," she said, walking through the living room toward the ten-foot-high open sliding glass doors, "one of the best views of LA you're likely to find. Cost a cool twenty-five mil."

"She did it," he smiled appreciatively. "The Grammys, millions of followers, a residency at the Sphere in Vegas. She got everything she wanted."

"It's definitely been crazy," Leah agreed. Then she headed toward a coffee table in the living room and picked up an envelope. "You were already sent your first-class airfare, car rental, and booking at the Beverly Hills Hotel, but, as promised, a check for ten grand just to take a meeting."

"Thanks," he said, stepping over and accepting the envelope.

"Can I offer you something?" She gestured to the bar where an assortment of pastries, coffee, and juice was displayed.

"That'd be nice," he agreed. "I didn't have breakfast at the hotel and wouldn't mind some juice and a muffin."

"Please, help yourself," Leah invited.

He set his camera bag down on a long, circular white leather sofa in front of the coffee table, slipped the check inside his bag, and walked over to the glass bar with black leather trim. Leah stuck her hands into the back pockets of her jeans and followed him as he went.

"So, Noah, how're you doing?"

"Alright," he replied. "Is, uh, is Z going to be joining us?"

"Yeah, she'll—she'll be along in a second," Leah replied. "So, you're good?"

"Yeah," he replied, looking over the assortment of pastries. "You?"

"Yeah. We're busier than ever."

"Excellent. Z's going to need to be to pay for this joint."

"I, uh, I heard you turned down going on tour with Gino Girard last year," she said.

"Yeah. I didn't want to be gone from Atlanta that long," he replied, picking up some silver tongs and selecting a blueberry muffin from a platter. "But I shot the cover of his new album."

"That was in Atlanta, right?" Leah wondered.

"Yeah," he said, putting the muffin on a china plate. Next, he retrieved two individually wrapped pads of butter.

"You're staying pretty close to Atlanta these days, huh? I mean, I hear you're shooting bands, personalities, and even the occasional politician. But it's always within a day's flight of home."

"You and Z keeping tabs on me?" he asked, looking over the juice selections. "I'm not sure I like that."

"Don't be offended. You're one of the better photographers in the business. It's just smart for us to know what you're up to and potential availability."

Noah selected some cranberry/pineapple juice and poured himself a small glass.

"No. If you've been checking up on me, what you *really* want to know is: is it true I have a daughter? Yes, I do. She's nearly two-and-a-half, and I don't like to take long assignments and be away from her. Matter of fact, I'm catching a 3 p.m. flight back today. You also want to know about the mother. She left the child with me and is out of both of our lives. Last I knew, she was in Ireland, and we have no contact. Okay?"

Leah's eyes widened at Noah's candor, and she nodded. "Okay."

Just then, they heard some type of sports car pull into the driveway.

"That'll be Z," Leah said. "I'm going to have a word with her outside. Sit down and relax. Good to see you again, Noah."

"You're not staying?" he wondered.

"No, I have an appointment in Century City," she replied, heading for the door. "But, really—it's nice to see you again."

"Good to see you too, Leah," he replied.

Leah went out the front door, and Noah had a few minutes to butter his muffin, return to the sofa with his plate and juice, and eat and drink quietly while he took in the view of the infinity pool and the LA skyline beyond. Being left alone and waiting on celebrities was no big deal to him. He was used to waiting. So, he ate his breakfast and thought to himself how, once upon a time, he aspired to this lifestyle—or at least some version of it—but not anymore. Now, he was more interested in buying a small house in Lilburn with a fenced-in backyard for Erin. He intended to use some of the money he'd recently gotten from selling one of Fay's antique coins as a down payment.

By the time Z-Rae entered the house, his empty plate and glass were on the coffee table, and he was writing something down in his little leather notebook. As she came in, he stood to greet her.

"Hi," she said with a smile. Like her manager, she

was dressed casually in some faded jeans, flat-heeled sandals with turquoise stones, a short-sleeved light-colored blouse, and a long black wig that fell over her shoulders about six inches. Her makeup was, as always, perfect, and her long eyelashes weren't real, but overall, this dressed-down look was out of character for her brand. Still, he liked it.

"Hi," he smiled back. "It's been a minute."

"Yeah," she said, walking over to him. She didn't know whether to extend a hand or kiss him on the mouth. So she settled for a brief hug and he briefly reciprocated.

"Okay—that awkward moment is over," she confessed. "I wasn't quite sure what to do about the greeting."

"I understand," he nodded politely. "So, you've arrived," he said, gesturing to the house. "Honors, legions of fans, a palace on a hill."

"Yeah, the house is what I wanted to see you 'bout. Well, one of two things I wanted to see you 'bout. Thanks for coming, by the way. I wasn't sure if you would."

"Why would you want to talk to me about your house?" he wondered.

Z looked around while stepping outside to the infinity pool. "I've had it for several months but am getting ready to put it back on the market. My realtor says that with my name attached as the owner, plus the current hot market, I can get eight to ten million over what I paid."

Noah followed her outside, looked around at the gorgeous day, patio furniture, flowers, and the outside fireplace, and shrugged. "You've only lived here for months, and you wanna move?"

"I've never lived here," she chuckled, slipping off one of her sandals and sticking a toe into the infinity pool. "I've got a two-bedroom bungalow in Laurel Canyon that used to be owned by one of the members of The Doors. I did buy a new home for my parents, though, and paid the rent on my dad's UPS store for the next year."

"That's really nice," he acknowledged. "Laurel Canyon? That doesn't quite fit your image."

"Exactly. No one will think to look for me there."

He nodded. "So, how do I fit in with this place?"

She put her sandal back on and walked over toward the patio fireplace. Like the house, it was square and modernistic with white painted brick. "I'm gonna throw a party here. Invite all sorts of personalities. I'd like you to photograph it unobtrusively. Y'know, Usher drinkin' at the bar. Ryan Seacrest talkin' to whoever—that kind of thing. It'll add cache to the sale."

"When is the party?" he asked.

"You tell me. I'll work it around your schedule."

"Oh, I don't think Usher and Ryan will wait on little ol' me."

"Those are just examples," she waved off. "You tell me when, and I'll get the people here."

He stuck his hands into the pockets of his black

slacks and looked around for a few more moments, considering.

"I may not be traveling as much as I used to Z, but I haven't stooped to the paparazzi level, either."

"This isn't paparazzi stuff. This is Noah Galloway doing what he does best: capturing candid moments that are actually carefully planned. The star is the house. The space. The celebrity just so happens to be in it. Not center frame, but shot in a way where they won't mind bein' seen, either. Like what you did with the rock climbers or the Native Americans in your landscape book. They're not incidental, but they're not the reason for the photograph, either."

He raised his eyebrows. "You know about the landscape book?"

"Sure. Got a copy of it on the coffee table in my living room. Not this house. My real house. How's it sellin', by the way?"

"Oh—I've sold hundreds, thousands, millions," he joked, "—about two dozen copies, I think."

She smiled. "It's only been out, what? A few months?"

"Yeah. A small independent publisher in Arkansas took a chance on me. But landscape books don't really sell that well unless it's Ansel Adams, Peter Lik, or Ken Duncan."

"I wouldn't have expected that kind of book from you," she observed. "No celebrities. No me."

"Someone I knew took a great interest in my landscapes," he said, referring to Fay. "So, I took a chance."

"I'm glad you did," she affirmed. She looked at the bar through one of the glass windows. "I need a drink."

She turned and headed across the patio toward the house. "So, you gonna take a chance on me and shoot my party? You'll be away from Atlanta maybe two nights, and you don't even have to see me until the jam."

"Now, why would you say that?" he asked, following her.

"I'm not tryin' to sleep with you, Noah. It's a straight-up business proposition."

"We're going to need permission if we're showing famous faces."

"You let me take care of that," she promised.

He thought for a moment. "What's the other thing you want to see me about?" he asked as she went over to the bar.

She poured herself a glass of orange juice and saw that he was surprised by this.

"What?" she asked. "It's 10:10 in the morning. You think I was going for a Dom Perignon?"

"Well, a mimosa, at least," he admitted.

"The party is kinda a warm-up to the second thing," she said, taking a sip of juice. "My fashion line is gonna be coming out pretty soon, and I'd like you to shoot the kick-off campaign. There will be several personalities involved, but different kinds of personalities: Film stars, sports personalities, scientists, even a female astronaut. There's also going to be a lot of locations. But they're all very Americana: Garden City, Kansas, Jackson,

Michigan, Beaufort, South Carolina. Not glam places. Just normal towns. Very accessible. I've got some artist sketches. Not as dictates, but just to give you some inspiration. If you're interested, I can send the sketches to your phone."

"It's a cool idea," he said sincerely. "Low key locations but high-profile personalities from different fields. I like the juxtaposition."

"Thanks. Came up with it myself. Some of the people will be more high profile than others. But all of them are really important. The researcher who helped to develop the shingles vaccine is just as important as the tennis star, who is just as important as the movie star, who is just as important as the music star."

"And you're the music star, of course," he concluded.

"Of course," she smiled, taking another sip of juice. "But none of them are more important than the location or the clothes. It's all in harmony, baby."

"How many shots and cities are we talking about?" he asked.

"Six to eight. Shot maybe over a two-week period."

He furrowed his brow.

"I, uh, I can't be gone from Atlanta for two full weeks."

"How about if I break 'em up?" Z suggested. "A week's shoot doin' locations, take a two-week break, then another week doin' locations."

He was clearly tempted but still hesitant.

"Wow… I don't know, Z… I mean, I'm really very grateful that you thought of me, but—"

"You know the swimsuit shoot we did in Greece? The client was ecstatic."

"That's nice, but—"

"How about sixty grand?" she offered. "That's close to $4,300.00 a day for fourteen days? Not even fourteen because the weekends will be on hold as weather days."

He looked at her. "Why are you being so generous and accommodating to me?"

She took another drink. "Warren Buffet, Rupert Murdock, or one of those old rich guys said it was easy to be generous and philanthropic when you've got money. Well, I've got money now. More than I ever dreamed of. I treated you terribly, Noah, and I'm very sorry. I wanted you as a photographer to advance my career one minute and an accommodating gigolo the next. Then, I fired you and ignored you for months to protect the release of a single. I know the intimate part of our relationship is gone. But that doesn't mean there still can't be a professional part. One that'll benefit you —and your daughter. Look, I'm tryin' to make things right here. What do you say?"

43

THE CASCADES

Jackson, Michigan was a town of thirty-one thousand three hundred people and located along I-94, about forty miles west of Ann Arbor and the University of Michigan, and thirty-five miles south of East Lansing and arch-rival Michigan State University. One of the city's claims to fame was The Cascades: a man-made waterfall and city park situated on a hillside and five hundred feet long. One hundred twenty-six steps on each side of the falls took visitors all the way around the attraction. As they walked up several series of steps, they passed six parallel fountains in the falls that shot water straight up to a height of thirty feet. Five levels of cascading water pumped two thousand gallons of water per minute. Under each level of falls and fountains were colored lights that were synced with music, and the falls were both beautiful to view at night and romantic to walk around. The Cascades were also the centerpiece for the city's firework shows on Memorial Day, Independence Day, and Labor Day. Since its inception in 1932, millions of people had enjoyed the park.

The falls were open seven days a week from Memorial Day to Labor Day, and even though it was now September, the falls were lit and running once again on a Tuesday evening for Z-Rae and her fashion shoot entourage. The crew consisted of a wardrobe person, a makeup artist, Noah, two camera assistants, Leah Shively, a craft services person, a city engineer to run the falls, and two security people. But since the falls had eight-foot-high hurricane fencing outlining its perimeter, security wasn't a big concern. Noah drove his RV up to Michigan to serve as a staging area and dressing room. He didn't charge anything extra for this and—considering what he was being paid—would've felt guilty if he did.

It had been four months since Noah had visited Z's Hollywood Hills house and three months since he'd shot the party they'd spoken about. And even though more personalities balked at their images being used to sell a house than Z anticipated, she nevertheless sold the property for eight million dollars more than she paid for it, proving her financial prowess.

This particular evening at The Cascades, the music was off, and Z stood at the bottom of the falls and off-center to the left with the falls and fountains running full tilt behind her. The top level of the falls was blue, the next level turquoise, the next green, the next pink, and the final level was cherry red. There was still some pale gray natural light in the sky from the fading sun, and there were umbrella lights on either side of Z just out of frame. She wore a casual pinstripe blazer that was open to show a sheer lacy top underneath. Her long, dark-blondish hair fell loose and free, and she had jeans that looked old and were purposely distressed. Noah stood Z on an apple box and told her to give him a minute while he adjusted his lens. But the lens and lights were ready and he was just waiting for the right impromptu moment. When she looked over her shoulder back at the falls with her red lips parted and her right hand touching her hair to push it off her face—he got the shot he wanted. She was slightly miffed because she wasn't ready for a photo yet, but when she saw the picture, she understood. Noah took more formal poses for safety but already knew he had the perfect shot.

Before calling it an official wrap, however, Z asked Noah to take the steps and walk around the falls with her, with no other crew. The city engineer running the falls reminded them they only had fifteen minutes of their contracted time left, but Z was fine with that. She wasn't looking for a photo opportunity as much as she just wanted to talk with Noah. Still, he carried his Nikon in a shoulder bag, just in case a good angle happened.

"So—last night of the shoot," she said as they approached the first set of stairs. "I've enjoyed workin' with you again."

"I've enjoyed working with you, too," he agreed. "You're—I don't know—different these days."

"How so?" she wondered.

"I'm not sure… you're still focused on your career, but calmer."

"What? Was I hyperactive before?"

"No… just… maybe more comfortable with life now."

"Mmm," she mused.

"Your music's different too. Less about partyin', sex, and smackin' authority and more about being positive. Lyrics like: 'If you wanna change their view, show the worth inside of you.'"

"Oh, you've been checkin' out the new album, eh?" she smiled, referring to a song he was quoting.

"The latest single? Sure." he nodded.

"You've changed too," she observed. "You're less about career and more about bein' a dad."

"Yeah, I guess so," he agreed.

They came to the first of the six parallel fountains and had to hurry up the steps. When the wind blew, even slightly, going past the thirty-foot-high fountains could give passersby a good drenching. It was part of the fun of The Cascades.

"Ugh!" she cried. "That water's cold! We could be soaked by the time we go all the way around.

"Do you want to go back?" he offered.

"No… I'm likin' this new level of honesty between us."

They continued walking.

"I don't think we were ever dishonest with each

other," he suggested, "but maybe more guarded. I mean, we never knew how to define our thing."

"Our 'thing?'" she queried with a raised eyebrow.

"You know what I mean."

"Yes… I know what you mean."

They walked on for a few moments in silence, listening to the falls rumble, then he asked:

"I saw a label on one of the garments of your new clothing line that said: 'Partial proceeds benefit Sheri's Garden.' What's that?"

"It's a shelter I founded in Oakland for runaway teens. Named after my mother."

"That's nice," he said, impressed. "Real nice!"

"Thanks."

They walked on a little longer in silence, then Z asked:

"Noah, what happened with Erin's mother?"

"Uh…"

"I don't mean to pry, but I don't understand why a woman would just give up her child and break off contact. Was she ill? Does Erin have special needs that she couldn't cope with? Did you two hate each other?"

Noah searched to find an answer. Z noticed this and waved her hands.

"Y'know what? Never mind. It's none of my business. It's just—y'know—I've seen you naked and was wonderin'."

He chuckled. "Yes, seeing someone naked should *naturally* mean total truth," he punned.

"Of course," she agreed.

He was silent for several more moments, then finally decided to share some details.

"Her name was Fay. We met when I shot the Georgia Renaissance Festival. She worked there… God, that seems like a lifetime ago. We spent an evening together; she got pregnant, and we talked about co-parenting, but ultimately, she wanted to return home to Ireland. That's where she was from. She only came to Georgia once a year to work the festival. When Erin was fifteen months old, she decided the baby would have a better life with me—and she left. That's it. End of story. I haven't heard from her since, and I don't expect to."

Z thought for a moment.

"Will she be coming back to the festival?"

"No. She made it clear she won't be returning."

"Did… did you love her?"

"We were just two strangers at first, but—yes—we spent some time together, and I fell in love with her."

"But she didn't love you," Z assumed.

"No, she did. But she had things she had to do in Ireland," he explained. "Commitments."

"Oh, my God. She was married?" Z asked.

"No."

"She was involved with somebody?"

"No."

"Well, was she in some sort of legal trouble?"

"Her people were. Not legal trouble. But they had serious problems."

"You mean, like, financial problems?"

"I—I—I can't explain anymore without inevitably

telling some sort of untruth," he sighed wearily. And I'm sooo tired of lying."

"Okay. Don't tell me anything more," Z said. "I appreciate what you've already shared, and if that's all you want me to know—okay. But, Noah, you never have to lie to me. You don't have to tell me everything. Knowing everything is overrated. But I don't ever want you to feel you have to lie."

"Thanks," he said. Then, after a pause, he added, "you'd never believe the truth anyway. I lived it, and sometimes I still don't believe it, myself."

They came to the next set of fountains, but the wind had died down, so there was only a light mist they had to climb through.

"Boy, that's a gauntlet if ever I heard one," she observed.

"What do you—"

"First, you tell me you don't want to lie to me," she interrupted, "then you tell me I wouldn't believe you anyway. That sounds like somebody who really *wants* to tell me, but you're not sure if I'll run down your gauntlet and give you the benefit of the doubt."

"If I told you the truth, it would change things between us," he warned. "You might think I'm a crazy person."

"Oh, my God, did you kill Fay?" she asked bluntly.

"What?" No! No-no-no. Nothing like that," he assured.

"Well—then, if you wanna tell me, I'll give you the benefit of the doubt. Promise."

They walked for maybe another thirty seconds in silence while Noah thought it over. Just as they approached the last set of steps that would take them up to the top level of the hill and the third fountain, he asked:

"Can you read in a car? Or, I should say, my pickup?"

"Yeah."

"Could you clear your schedule and ride back to Atlanta with me tomorrow? There's some reading I want you to do in my truck while we travel."

"You want me to read something while we drive back to Atlanta?" she asked, wanting confirmation. "What'd you do? Write a novel? And what's that got to do with Fay?"

"Before you answer," he continued, "there are rules. No Leah or security team following, although it's fine for them to know you're with me, and no using your phone until you've read everything."

"Why can't I use my phone?" she asked indignantly.

"You can't take pictures of the material you're reading, and you can't call anyone and talk to them about it. In fact, you can't talk to anyone about it, ever. And if you're not done reading by the time we get back to Atlanta, you need to promise to take additional time to finish. You need to read everything. Then, we need to talk about it. After that, you can decide whether or not you ever want to see or work with me again."

They reached the top of the falls, went to its center,

and looked down the hill. The sun was now completely gone, and the view was a colorful magnificence.

"You're bein' a little scary here. You know that, right?" Z asked.

"I understand how it must sound. But you're the one with the mace. You'll be reading a series of letters that Fay wrote to Erin in anticipation of her going to Ireland and never returning. It explains her story. I also wrote a few follow-up letters to Erin that fill in some blanks." He looked at her, paused, and smiled. "Look, I understand the strangeness of this request. If you don't want to read the letters, that's fine. But if you do—the rules I'm laying down are more about safeguarding my child than anything else."

She looked into his green eyes for a long moment, then nodded.

"Okay. I'm intrigued. I'll read Fay's letters."

Twenty minutes later, the falls were off, the camera assistants had loaded Noah's equipment into the RV, and now Z was using the RV and changing into street clothes. The camera assistants drove in from Atlanta in their own car and wanted to head back so they could shave time off their twelve-hour ride before they stopped for the night. The craft service person was local and went home. Everyone else would soon be heading to the Jackson County Airport, where a private jet was waiting to take them back to LA. Noah had just finished thanking the city engineer who operated the falls and lights for them when Leah came strolling up.

"I understand Z's going back to Atlanta with you," she began.

"Yeah. Sorry if I'm messing up anything you had scheduled for her."

"Nothing too major. When she's ready, I'll rent a plane for her in Atlanta."

"Cool."

Leah looked him over. "Don't hurt her, Noah," she said. "She's in a good place right now. New album, new clothing line, I don't want her heart broken."

"I wouldn't worry about it," he assured. "I have no intention of breaking her heart. In fact, the chances are pretty good that Z's gonna decide all on her own that she won't want to see me anymore in the not-too-distant future."

"Because you're a father?" she assumed. "Because you've got baggage? Hell, we've all got baggage. Despite hers, though, it's always been you. You know that, right?"

He looked at her. "What are you talking about? We're just two people who worked together then hooked up."

"Maybe at first. But it turned into something more for her. You may have protected her in Greece, but she's protected you, too. *And* she reached out to you in Vegas."

"Oh, I don't know—" he started to say.

"That's right," she cut in. "You *don't* know. You don't know her at all! Have you listened to any of her latest album? Not the single that people dance to, the love songs: "Maybe Tomorrow," "Shutter Speed," "Boys From the South"—you're all over the place. I'm not saying she's been Mother Teresa, but what did you think when you first got together? That you were just one in an endless string of quickies? One of a dozen men? Two dozen? I've been with her night and day for nearly six years, and I'm tellin' you—it's *you.*"

44

BELIEF

Oddly enough, after Z had agreed to ride back with him and read Fay's letters, Noah and his client didn't talk about them. Both figured there would be time for that later. So, they said their goodbyes to Leah and the remaining crew, then found a restaurant to grab dinner. Over their meal, they mostly talked about their families and childhoods, something they really hadn't done before. Noah was surprised to learn that Z began her singing career in a children's Baptist church choir, while she was surprised to learn that in his early twenties, Noah struggled with not following in his father's footsteps and being groomed to take over the family lighting business. Both were surprised by how few people recognized Z while they ate. But then again, her wig was off, and Z-Rae being in Jackson, Michigan, was about as likely as Paul and Linda McCartney staying on a farm for six weeks in

Lebanon, Tennessee, where "Junior's Farm" was written.

Even though they had shared a bed many times, Noah didn't want to put either of them in a compromising situation by sharing the RV and purchased two rooms at the Tru by Hilton hotel just off I-94. He thought a lot that night about what Leah had told him and replayed their conversation in his hotel room when she showed up in Las Vegas. He remembered he was angry with her and concluded that maybe he hadn't really heard what she was trying to say. He also remembered that he took an almost immediate dislike to Bobby Dragon and recalled how Z teasingly accused him of being jealous in Rome. In hindsight, he realized that although he really had no right to be—he was. Then he listened to one of her slower songs called "Boys From the South" from her latest album and was genuinely surprised and moved by lyrics like: "you've gotta be careful with boys from the South. They'll steal your heart while they kiss your mouth."

The following morning, Wednesday, Noah handed a wigless and casually dressed Z a three-ring binder after she strapped herself into the passenger side seat of his Dodge pickup.

"I got this out of a lockbox in a cabinet of the RV. These are Fay's letters. They were originally handwritten in Gaeilge, but I had 'em translated and typed. I also inserted pictures on various pages. At the end, after all of Fay's letters, are my letters to Erin that explain the rest of the story."

She looked at the binder. "You keep this in your RV?"

"I keep a copy in the RV and another on a hard drive. It's Erin's heritage and history. Wanda Harrington also has a copy. You'll find out about her in the letters."

"Okay," she said, taking the binder.

"Thanks for doing this," he said sincerely. "I wondered last night in my room if this was a mistake. But… anyway."

Five minutes later, they were on the road. Nine minutes after that, Z had finished the first letter and looked at Noah with an exasperated half-smile.

"You're kiddin' me, right?" she asked.

"What?"

"Fay was born in 1473?"

"Yes."

"When Edward IV was on the throne."

"You know English history?" he asked.

"I know a lot of stuff," she defended. "And—she found a corridor in time?"

"Told you you wouldn't believe me."

"Oh, I believe *you*—just not *her*. This woman is psycho!"

"Read on."

"And what the hell's a Bo-Diddley-Dannon?"

"That's Tuatha Dé Dannan," he replied. "In Irish mythology, they're a supernatural race. Sometimes referred to as fairies."

"Fairies. You mean, like Tinkerbell?"

"Exactly."

"Oh, c'mon, please!"

"Read on," he urged.

"This is stupid!"

"You promised you would."

Z shifted her weight and huffed disapprovingly but went on to the next letter. Then the next. Then the next. The more she read, the less she rolled her eyes at Noah. After the twelfth letter, she said:

"Well, I'll give her this: she seems to know Irish history and has a detailed imagination when it comes to her family's history."

She rested her eyes for a moment and looked out at the day. Noah glanced over at the trim, brown-eyed woman with short brown hair, no fake eyelashes, and very little makeup, and for the first time, thought of Zeana Ray Colton instead of Z-Rae.

Noticing his glances, she turned to him.

"What?" she asked curiously.

"Nothing," he replied.

Three hours later, when they made their first gas stop, Z climbed out of the pickup and used the bathroom in the RV so as not to draw attention to herself by going inside a Love's Truck Stop. Afterward, she stepped outside and strolled up to Noah, who was still pumping gas.

"How do you pronounce the name of Fay's people?"

"Two-ah-dee-danon," he pronounced phonetically.

"Have Erin's ears become pointed, or has she developed any markings on her back?"

"No, but we're not in Ireland, and Fay always said the land was the source of their magic."

"Very convenient," she mumbled, still not believing what she was reading. Then she looked toward the truck stop. "Get me some trail mix, will ya?"

About an hour later, she turned to Noah after reading a series of letters nonstop.

"I get why she felt she needed to go back. But I don't get why she didn't bring somebody else with her through the corridor to help."

She's getting into the story, he thought. *Maybe she's even believing it.* Then, he replied:

"Her landing in Fairburn, Georgia, being so close to the Renaissance festival, and befriending Wanda was pure chance. Or, maybe not, if you wanna be spiritual about it. But I don't think Fay wanted to explain another wayward soul to Wanda. After all, Wanda had been very kind to her and didn't know who she was for sure until the fifth season."

"I guess not," Z mused. "But it would've doubled her chances of success."

"And doubled her chances of discovery," he added.

"Did y'all ever talk about her presence changing history, timelines, or anything like that?"

"Only in the way that it might benefit her people's chances of survival. Not whether or not reality as we know it would significantly change. I mean, Bobby Dragon would still be a dick."

She looked at him and squinted her eyes.

"So, you're giving me the benefit of the doubt?" he asked.

"I said I would. But it's a big fuckin' dose of benefit."

"I know," he agreed.

It was past midnight when they finally arrived back at Noah's studio. He disconnected the RV at his studio's parking lot, and Z still had a few more of Fay's letters to read as well as Noah's. So, he offered Z the master bedroom at his condo and said he bunk in the RV. She replied that he was being silly and that they could both share the condo if he slept on the sofa in the living room. After a long and stressful day on the road, he didn't argue. He wanted to be in his own home. Even if it was sleeping on the sofa.

Z asked where Erin was staying, and Noah replied at Wanda's. He said if she wanted, he'd take her out to Wanda's in the morning, and she could meet the festival manager and ask anything she wanted about Fay. Z replied that she wasn't sure if she wanted to talk about Fay's letters yet. But she absolutely wanted to meet Erin.

Perhaps not surprisingly, Z was restless after she climbed alone into Noah's bed. She kept thinking about time travel, corridors, beings that could fly and change size, and Noah falling in love with such a creature. She wondered if this was all some sort of elaborate hoax. But if so, to what purpose? If Noah no longer wanted to be in her life, there were a thousand other ways to tell her besides asking her to read a preposterous story and photoshopping some pictures. She found herself compelled to read the rest of Fay's letters, then Noah's. She found herself gasping out loud and saying, "Holy shit! *He* killed the horzikaan?" while reading Noah's final letter.

When she had read everything in the binder, she went through it again, looking at the pictures. They included the first photo Noah ever took of Fay bent over and talking to a little girl dressed as a princess at the festival, the portrait of Fay kneeling on a boulder in the middle of a stream with her wings spread and her hands below her chin as if she were blowing a kiss, the photo of Fay and Erin at Oakland Park Cemetery near downtown Atlanta, the back of a naked Fay standing with her wings spread on Mike and Ami's deck in the mountains of North Carolina, as well as others.

It was 5:51 a.m. when a shirtless Noah turned over on the sofa in his living room and felt as if he weren't alone. Cracking open a tired eye, he saw Z sitting cross-legged on the floor, wearing pajama bottoms and a Black Lives Matter t-shirt, watching him. In her lap was the binder he had given her and a small white leather notebook she'd taken out of her luggage that he'd never seen before. Opening his other eye, for just a moment, it felt like he was a kid having a slumber party.

"Hi," he said. "What's going on? You okay?"

"I believe you," she said. "I believe all of it."

"You do?" he said, sitting up. "I don't know whether

to laugh or cry… but I think I'll settle for a pee. Be right back."

She smiled as he rose and walked to the half bath off the kitchen. She watched him as he went. He was only wearing blue briefs, and she couldn't help but recall the details of his body and all of the passionate moments they had shared. A minute later, he returned and peeked out of the living room. By this time, she had moved from the floor to the sofa holding his binder and her smaller white notebook.

Sun's coming up," he yawned. "Did you stay up all night reading?"

"Yeah. Too many things to process."

He nodded, then went over and sat down next to her.

"I'm really glad you believe me. But why? *Why* do you believe me?"

She handed him her notebook. "I've been keepin' a diary for years. I've got stacks of these under my bed. Open it up to pretty much any page."

He leaned over to a table lamp, turned it on, then opened the notebook. Randomly stopping on a Thursday entry, he read:

Is magic just another name for miracle?
In their purest form, neither magic nor miracles can be explained:
The infant that survived buried in the rubble days after an earthquake. The cancer patient told she has less than a year to live but lives for another ten. The person who

was underwater in a turtled kayak for twelve minutes but was resuscitated without damage.

"I've been writing about magic and the need for it in our lives for years," she said. "I thought maybe you were doing the same. You've been carrying that brown leather notebook around since I've known you. You write in it all the time."

He smiled and rubbed his fingers through his straight brown hair.

"I'm counting calories."

"What?"

"I'm a rock climber. I work out. I keep a log of what I eat and count the calories."

She looked at him and expelled a heavy breath.

"Oh… I thought you were writing deep personal thoughts. Now I feel stupid."

"Oh—and *I* don't?" he asked, gesturing to the binder in her lap.

She shrugged and nodded, and they fell quiet for a few seconds. Then, she asked:

"If you take me out to Wanda's when you pick up Erin, will you show me where the oak tree was?"

"If you like."

"I like… how long has it been since you cut it down?"

"About sixteen months."

"Couldn't she find another corridor?"

"Where would she look?" he answered. "She only found that one by mistake, and from what I know, they only go back and forth from one place to another, the point of origin and a destination. Even if she found another corridor, it could take her somewhere else. A different country, maybe a different time. Besides, she's fighting a war."

"So—she's really, really gone," Z concluded.

He paused, his eyes becoming moist before he continued.

"You know what's the most disturbing thing of all? Not only is she gone, but she and her entire kind have been gone for centuries. I'm taking care of the daughter we made—but her mother's been dead for hundreds of years. Do you have *any* idea how that fucks with your head?"

Her eyes likewise became dewy as she looked at him compassionately. She slowly reached out and put her fingers on his cheek.

"Why did you want me to know all this, Noah?" she asked quietly. "Why did you want me to read these letters?"

"I—I—I'll be telling lies about Erin's mother for the rest of my life. To my parents, her teachers, her friends when she gets older, my co-workers… I just didn't want you to be one of 'em."

A tear ran down Z's cheek. She slowly nodded.

"Okay."

He looked at her with equally wet eyes. Conflicted. Hurt.

"I'm always going to love her," he confessed.

"I know," she answered quietly.

"But, you… you…"

"I'm not the one you wanted," she whispered, understanding. "But in time, I might be the one you need."

They looked at one another as if each was seeing the other's soul, and both knew that something had just changed in their relationship.

45

COMFORTABLE

Three months later, on a Saturday morning in early December, Noah was wearing shorts, running shoes, and a t-shirt as he jogged around the last corner of the quarter-mile walking path that encircled the city park in Old Town Lilburn. He crossed the parking lot he and Fay had once walked across and headed toward his townhouse. Even though it was December, the morning temperature was in the low fifties with a high that day in the sixties. The holidays in Georgia could be cold and frosty, but that was rare.

Erin sat on a pillow at the coffee table in the living room, working on a bowl of cereal while watching *SpongeBob SquarePants,* when Noah came in the door.

"Hi, Da," she greeted.

"Hi, yourself," he said. "Did you have juice with your cereal?"

"It's all gone," she said, pointing to an empty sippy

cup on the island in the kitchen. Z was also in the kitchen and stood at the island next to a mug of coffee. She was blonde today and wore nice fitting brown leather pants that complemented ankle-length, brown suede boots. She also wore a green crew neck sweater with a cream-colored t-shirt underneath. She had her nose in her phone and a rolling overnight bag standing on the floor by her side with its handle extended.

"My Uber will be here in about a minute," she said, barely looking up from her phone. "If the traffic's good, I should have plenty of time to make my plane."

"I wish you'd let us take you," he said, winking at his daughter as he passed through the living room heading for the kitchen.

"What? No. Squidward's got some things to work out with Patrick, and after that, it'll be time for *Bluey* on Disney Junior," she replied, referring to what Erin was watching. "Besides, you're supposed to be at your mom's by noon."

"Right," he said. "I remember. Speaking of remembering—"

"Yes, I took my Adderall," she finished. "Okay," she said, sticking her phone in her purse. "LA for four days, then I'll be back on Thursday."

"And Christmas tree shopping," Erin happily reminded from the living room.

"Yes, ma'am," Z verified. "And what kind are we gonna get?" she asked the child.

"A big one!" Erin smiled.

"You betcha, kiddo!" she smiled back.

He looked at the half-drunk mug of coffee Z had been working on, picked it up, and took a sip.

"You put in some vanilla extract," he nodded approvingly.

"I know how you like to pilfer," she reminded.

Just then, her phone pinged.

"That's my car," she said.

"Be gracious if the driver goes gaga over you," he suggested.

She nodded and walked over to Erin. "Hug, please?"

The toddler hopped up and ran over to meet Z, grabbing her tightly around her legs. Playing along, Z cried, "Oh! Oh! You're such a good hugger, Erin! I can't stay on my feet!"

She fell to her knees, pretending to be overcome, then fell backward onto the floor. Giggling, Erin climbed on top of her and continued hugging.

"C'mon, sweetie," Noah said, bending over to gently remove the clinging child. "You're gonna hug Z's hair right off."

"Then I'll be scalped!" Z said, wide-eyed.

"What's that?" Erin asked.

"Th-that's a discussion for another day and year," Z replied. "Right now, I've gotta go. But I'll see you Thursday."

She climbed to her feet and gave Noah a quick kiss on the mouth. Grabbing the handle of her overnight bag, she went over to the front door.

"Hey," Noah said, just as she opened it.

She paused and turned to him.

"This is getting comfortable, isn't it."

"Yeah," she smiled back. Then she looked at Erin. "See ya Thursday," she grinned excitedly.

"Bye-bye Z," the child waved back warmly.

46

THREE YEARS LATER

During the next three years, the FBI never got a satisfactory explanation about the modern weapons that were dug up on farmer O'Connell's land in Ireland. The case was never closed, but it was never pursued much after the death of Special Agent Grimble. After all, there were actual crimes to solve, like the drug cartel activity in Johns Creek. This was eventually shut down in a major raid where several suspects were arrested, and two more were killed, including Javier Torres. But another hub of drug activity soon sprang up in the Atlanta area shortly thereafter. With the death of Torres, any hope of finding out who he confronted at the Renaissance festival faded, as did the specific causes of the injuries to Special Agent Grimble and Officer Rosen. Their cases remained open as well, but again, there was very little to pursue. Wanda Harrington worked one more season as the festival's manager but then decided to retire. She spent her days working long hours in her garden and, in a change of attitude, sometimes had breakfast at Judy's with Police Chief Russ Hawkins. She also drove to Lilburn to take care of Erin when Noah was on location. He had since purchased and refurbished an older house, and Lancelot, now getting on in years, enjoyed sleeping with Erin. Blacksmith Dale Taylor also quit the Renaissance festival and concentrated more on his insurance business and his children. EMT Chris Kramer, who the horzikaan hypnotized, eventually quit the medical profession and got a realtor's license. He made a good living but continued in therapy for over a year because of his loss of memory.

Now, it was spring, and the Renaissance festival was running again, but Noah and six-year-old Erin were on vacation thousands of miles away in County Sligo, Ireland. With them was Z-Rae, who had been married to Noah for nearly a year and had adopted Erin. She'd recently won an Oscar for "Best Original Song" and had moved from LA to Noah's house in Lilburn. Today, they were traveling in a Range Rover with a guide named Fredrick, who knew the county, and were followed by a second Range Rover with a bodyguard named Sean and a nanny named Brenda.

They rode down a dirt road that was more overgrowth than dirt until Fredrick brought the Rover to a stop. It was a beautiful and mostly cloudless day in late April, and although the foliage was green, things weren't in full bloom yet.

Noah, Z, Erin, and Fredrick climbed out of the first

Rover while Z was talking on her cell. She had grown her natural brown hair out and wore it in a bob just a few inches below her chin. She wore jeans, laced boots over them that nearly went up to her knees, a red turtleneck, and sunglasses. She looked cool and as commanding as ever, but more like a mom on vacation than a pop diva.

"The cell reception here is crap, Leah. But yes, I'd love to do the cover of *Vogue*, talk about the Oscar, and the whole nine yards. But you know who's gotta shoot the cover, right? So please make sure that's part of the deal."

She put a finger in her free ear as if it was hard to hear. "Hey—you're breakin' up. Let's talk when I get back. This is my vacation, bitch."

Erin laughed as Z disconnected the call.

"Mommy, you said 'bitch.'"

Erin was a first grader now and had long reddish hair like Fay. She was average height for her age, had rounded ears, and never developed any seams on her back for wings. By all accounts, she was a normal child whose mother happened to be a Grammy and Oscar-winning superstar. Z slid off her sunglasses, tossed them into the Range Rover, and winced apologetically.

"Yeah, I did. Sorry, baby."

Z looked at the nanny just getting out of the Land Rover behind them. Brenda had a master's degree in childhood development.

"Brenda, please put some bug spray on her," she called. "And sunscreen."

"If you put all that on her and try to hug her, she's gonna slip through your fingers like a greased pig," Noah observed, wearing jeans, hiking boots, and a long-sleeved Columbia shirt. Z put her hands on her hips.

"You callin' my kid a pig?" she asked playfully.

"You just called her honorary aunt a bitch," he retorted.

"C'mon, Erin," Brenda called. "Let's get you ready for the wild."

"Those hills ta the south right behind ya are the Three Sisters," Fredrick said with an Irish brogue. He was in his early forties, lean, and wore a tweed flat-top cap. "Although no one calls 'em that anymore. In fact, no one really comes down this road much."

"Who owns the land?" Noah asked.

"Old man Hillerman," the guide replied. "Been in his family for generations, but his kids are gone, and his wife died years ago. Thirty years ago, it was good farmland, but Hillerman's too old and poor to work it, so here it sits. Hunters come down here sometimes, or kids sometimes use it fer a lover's lane."

"Was there a church up on the highest of those hills?" Z asked, pointing.

"Yes, I believe there was a long time ago," Fredrick answered.

"How about the woods on the other side of the road?" Noah asked. "Could that have been a clearing at one point in time where a village stood? Has anyone done any archeological digging in this area?"

"None that I know of," Fredrick said. "But inquiries can be made."

Noah returned to the Range Rover he'd just gotten out of and grabbed his camera bag.

"We're going to walk up to the highest hill," he said to Fredrick, slinging the bag's strap over his shoulder. "You don't have to trudge up there with us. We just want to see if there's anything left of the old church."

"If you're interested in old churches," the guide suggested, "I can take ya—"

"No, this is good," Z cut in. "We're gonna check this out. Brenda, Erin can explore the hills. Let her run around and wear herself out. Sean," she said to the bodyguard, "hang by the vehicles. You and Fredrick can break into the picnic baskets and help yourselves to sandwiches and beer."

"You sure you don't want me to come with?" Sean asked. He was about twice as big and muscular as Noah.

"No. Stay here. We're going to do this alone. Keep an eye on Erin, though. She's more important than us."

The green overgrowth on the hills was higher than when Fay ran up them at twilight to escape a member of Clan Fergus centuries earlier. There were also a few trees and thickets of bushes that hadn't been there before. Bugs flew up from the grass and scattered as Noah and Z made their way up the first hill.

"You think there's tics?" Z asked, concerned. "I don't want any tics on Erin."

"They'll just slide off," he quipped, referring to all the stuff Brenda was putting on her.

"You think she'll remember this trip?" she asked.

"Probably not. I mean, what do you remember when you were her age? Bits and pieces, maybe. But I'm keeping a promise. Plus, we can always come back."

She nodded.

They were quiet for a while as they descended the first hill and heard the giggles of Erin behind them as she and Brenda began a game of tag on the first hill not too far away.

"I'm really glad you love me," he finally said as they started up the second hill. "Thank you."

"You're welcome. What brought this on?"

"It hasn't been easy for you, has it? I mean, in a way, there's been four of us in the marriage: you, me, Erin, and Fay. You've had to live with a ghost and see evidence of her every day."

"I don't see Fay when I look at Erin," Z said frankly. "I see you. I see *our* daughter. I mean, I respect Erin's heritage and want her to know about her birth mother, but I think about how you two are *my* family, not hers."

They smiled at each other and held hands as they topped the second hill, then descended it and began to go up the third. They talked about laying over in London on their way back so Z could do some shopping and maybe check out Abbey Road Studios. "Maybe I'll wanna record there," she said.

When they got to the top of the third and highest hill, they were disappointed to see no evidence of an archway or walls for a church. The top of the third hill was flat enough to accommodate such a building, but there was no obvious traces of it. They separated and slowly wandered around at the top of the third hill in overgrowth that went well over their ankles.

"Damn," Noah said, looking around. "It's all gone."

"Y'know, Fredrick might be wrong," she suggested. "There are a lot of rolling hills around here. Maybe this isn't the right grouping for the Three Sisters."

"Maybe," he agreed.

They wandered around for at least two minutes before Z noticed something.

"Hey, check this out," she said.

He walked over to where she was.

"There are stones in the ground here," she pointed out. "They're all the same size. Like, maybe two feet by two feet. But I can't say how thick. They're half sunk into the ground. But look—look at the tops. Wouldn't you say each one is cut and rounded slightly?"

"Like, they could've been standing up at one point to make the arched entranceway to a church," he speculated.

"Yeah," she confirmed. "We could dig 'em up, lay 'em next to one another on the ground, and see if they make an arch," she suggested.

Noah got down on his knees beside one of the stones, put his camera bag aside, and brushed the overgrowth away. He put his fingers at the bottom of the stone and tried to budge it.

"We're gonna need shovels," he said, struggling. "But you're right. I think these are definitely cut. Chiseled."

Just then, her cell phone rang, but only once. Z took the phone off her belt.

"It's Brenda," she said.

"What's goin' on? he asked."

"I don't know. The call cut out. Reception is shit around here."

"Okay. Let's go," he said.

"No. You keep checking these out, and I'll go see what Brenda wants."

Z walked to the edge of the third hill and saw Erin on the first hill below, but Brenda waved at her to come down.

"Erin's fine, but Brenda wants me," she called over her shoulder. "I'll be right back."

She descended the highest hill while Noah removed the grass and weeds from another stone.

Because she was standing on the top of the three hills, Z couldn't see a lot of detail other than the two distant figures of Brenda and Erin. It wasn't until she had gone into the valley of the third hill, climbed to the top of the second one, and went down it a little bit that she paused and could see what Brenda was calling her about.

Erin was petting a small spotted baby deer. Standing not too far away was its mother. The breed was known in Ireland as a Fallow Deer, and unlike North American baby deer, this breed never lost its spots. Erin gently stroked the deer's neck while its mother nibbled on some grass about fifteen yards away and seemed unconcerned. Brenda was standing still about twelve yards away from Erin on the opposite side of the hill from where the mother doe stood and was taking pictures with her phone. Leaning forward and squinting from her vantage point, Z also saw three spring butterflies fluttering around Erin's reddish hair, and more were crossing the hillside to be near her. She clasped a hand over her opened mouth, realizing the animals and insects recognized a descendant from the old world and the Tuatha Dé Dannan.

Brenda took her photos, then looked up at Z and shrugged as if to say, "Can you believe this?"

As Z's eyes became wet with pleased emotion, she smiled and made the okay sign with her forefinger and thumb to Brenda. Then she looked to see if Fredrick and Sean had also seen the incredible sight. The men hadn't noticed it. Fredrick was sitting on the back end of the second Range Rover with its rear gate down while Sean talked to him with a beer in his hand. Although she had no way of knowing it, Sean was regaling the guide with stories of other celebrities he had protected. She also had no way of knowing that while Erin stroked the baby deer, she was looking over at its mother and saying: "Cairde," Gaeilge for "buddy."

Even though she wasn't hearing these details, Z, nevertheless, realized what was happening. She turned around and ran back to the top of the second hill, wiping her eyes and nose as she went. She ran down into its valley and then up the third hill to get back to her husband. When she got to the top of the third hill breathless, she saw Noah kneeling on the ground with tears in his eyes and his fingers gently touching a stone. The excited smile on her face quickly faded as she wiped her eyes and nose once again, then went over to him.

"Noah? What is it? What's wrong?"

"This *was* the archway," he said knowingly. "Look."

She walked over to where he was. He'd cleared away four stones, but the fourth stone had a faint carving on it. It was of three interconnecting circles. It resembled an Irish Triquetra, except the edges of the rings were more rounded than the traditional Triquetra's oblong rings. Z recognized the symbol from pictures of some of the original letters that Noah had photographed and put into the three-ring binder. Goosebumps immediately shot over her arms.

"This *was* the other end of the corridor," he said, looking up at her. "She knew I'd come here eventually. This was her final message."

Z sank to her knees next to him and tenderly rubbed his back.

"She wanted you to know she returned safely," she said. "She wanted you to know she tried to make a difference."

He wiped his eyes.

"But, ultimately, she didn't," he said sadly.

"You can't say that. She had guns. They could've extended the lives of her people for years and years."

They looked at the stone in silence for a few moments, then Z asked:

"What do you think happened to the horzikaans?"

"I don't know... they were powerful, but the one I ran into couldn't stop bullets."

He looked around at the top of the hill and gazed up at the blue spring sky. "All that effort... all for nothing," he sighed.

"You don't know that," she reasoned. She lightened her mood and patted his shoulder.

"C'mon. Let's get back to Erin."

"I wanna dig this up," he decided. "Take it back with us."

"If you like. But we'll have to get a shovel and do it later. C'mon," she urged.

He got his camera bag and slowly rose. Before starting back, he took a picture of the stone, then another of the entire top area of the hill where the church once stood.

They didn't talk while they went down the first hill, then climbed up the second. Both were collecting themselves emotionally. He was thinking about the past and Fay, but keeping it in perspective, while she was thinking about the future.

"Thank you again for doing this, baby," he finally said sincerely.

"Of course," she smiled. "You were keeping a promise."

He stopped walking and touched her arm.

"You're not the consolation prize in this," he said sincerely. "It's important you know that."

"I know. After all, I *am* Z-Rae," she observed

jokingly. She looked around. "It's pretty country. Don't you think?"

"Yeah," he agreed. "Beautiful."

"Private… but not isolated. Fredrick said his village was, what, six kilometers away?

"Something like that," he recalled.

"They had a grocery store, gas station and mechanic, pub, a B&B…"

"A thriving metropolis," he quipped.

"I don't know what we'd do about the cell reception, though. Landline, maybe."

"What?" he asked, not understanding.

"We need to talk to the owner of the land. This old man Hillerman Fredrick mentioned," she decided. "See if he wants to sell. We could build a home here. It'd be good for Erin."

He stopped walking and looked at her.

"What're you talking about?"

She smiled and arched an eyebrow.

"Magic, baby. Magic!"

ABOUT THE AUTHOR

Timothy Best is the author of six other novels, all of them award-winning. He's also a Creative Director-Copywriter in the advertising business and has written for Fortune 100 companies like Allstate Insurance, Coca-Cola, GM, Honda, Toyota, Walmart and many others. Readers can connect with him on his Goodreads page at:

https://www.goodreads.com/author/show/6092023.Timothy_Best

When he's not writing, he plays drums in rock & roll and blues bands throughout the Atlanta area.

Thank you so much for reading the Girl at The Renaissance Fair. If you enjoyed it, please leave a review on your bookseller's website.

ABOUT THE PUBLISHER

Harbor Lane Books, LLC is a US-based independent digital publisher of commercial fiction, non-fiction, and poetry.

Connect with Harbor Lane Books on their website www.harborlanebooks.com, TikTok, Instagram, Facebook, X, and Pinterest @harborlanebooks.

Milton Keynes UK
Ingram Content Group UK Ltd.
UKHW042306101024
449571UK00002B/6